*A*

*Other Books in The Vintage Library*
*of Contemporary World Literature*

# CORRECTION

# CORRECTION

# THOMAS BERNHARD

TRANSLATED FROM THE GERMAN
BY SOPHIE WILKINS

**AVENTURA**

The Vintage Library of Contemporary World Literature

VINTAGE BOOKS    A DIVISION OF RANDOM HOUSE    NEW YORK

First Aventura Edition, September 1983

Copyright © 1979 by Alfred A. Knopf

All rights reserved under International and Pan-American
Copyright Conventions. Published in the United States
by Random House, Inc., New York, and simultaneously in
Canada by Random House of Canada Limited, Toronto.
Originally published in Germany as *Korrektur* by
Suhrkamp Verlag, Frankfurt. Copyright © 1975 by
Suhrkamp Verlag. Published in the United States by
Alfred A. Knopf, Inc. in 1979.

Library of Congress Cataloging in Publication Data

Bernhard, Thomas.

Correction.

Translation of: Korrektur.

Reprint. Originally published: 1st American ed. New York:
Knopf, 1979.

I. Title.

PT2662.E7K613 1983   833'.914   83-48034

ISBN 0-394-72210-8

Manufactured in the United States of America

A body needs at least
three points of support,
not in a straight line,
to fix its position,
so Roithamer had written.

# CORRECTION

# Hoeller's Garret

After a mild pulmonary infection, tended too little and too late, had suddenly turned into a severe pneumonia that took its toll of my entire body and laid me up for at least three months at nearby Wels, which has a hospital renowned in the field of so-called internal medicine, I accepted an invitation from Hoeller, a so-called taxidermist in the Aurach valley, not for the *end* of October, as the doctors urged, but for *early* in October, as I insisted, and then went on my own so-called responsibility straight to the Aurach valley and to Hoeller's house, without even a detour to visit my parents in Stocket, *straight* into the so-called Hoeller garret, to begin sifting and perhaps even arranging the literary remains of my friend, who was also a friend of the taxidermist Hoeller, Roithamer, after Roithamer's suicide, I went to work sifting and sorting the papers he had willed to me, consisting of thousands of slips covered with Roithamer's handwriting plus a bulky manuscript entitled "About Altensam and everything connected with Altensam, with special attention to the Cone." The atmosphere in Hoeller's house was still heavy, most of all with the circumstances of Roithamer's suicide, and seemed from the moment of my arrival favorable to my plan of working on Roithamer's papers there, specifically in Hoeller's garret, sifting and sorting Roithamer's papers and even, as I suddenly decided, simultaneously writing my own account of my work on these papers, as I have here begun to do, aided by having been able to move straight into Hoeller's garret without any reservations on Hoeller's part, even though the house had other suitable accommodations, I deliberately moved into that four-by-five-meter garret Roithamer was always so fond of, which was so ideal, especially in his last years, for his purposes, where I could stay as long as I liked, it was all the same

to Hoeller, in this house built by the headstrong Hoeller in
defiance of every rule of reason and architecture right here in
the Aurach gorge, in the garret which Hoeller had designed
and built as if for Roithamer's purposes, where Roithamer,
after sixteen years in England with me, had spent the final
years of his life almost continuously, and even prior to that he
had found it convenient to spend at least his nights in the
garret, especially while he was building the Cone for his sister
in the Kobernausser forest, all the time the Cone was under
construction he no longer slept at home in Altensam but
always and only in Hoeller's garret, it was simply in every
respect the ideal place for him during those last years when he,
Roithamer, never went straight home to Altensam from England, but instead went every time to Hoeller's garret, to fortify
himself in its simplicity (Hoeller house) for the complexity
ahead (Cone), it would not do to go straight to Altensam from
England, where each of us, working separately in his own
scientific field, had been living in Cambridge all those years,
he had to go straight to Hoeller's garret, if he did not follow
this rule which had become a cherished habit, the visit to
Altensam was a disaster from the start, so he simply could not
let himself go directly from England to Altensam and everything connected with Altensam, whenever he had *not* made the
detour via Hoeller's house, to save time, as he himself ad-
mitted, it had been a mistake, so he no longer made the
experiment of going to Altensam without first stopping at
Hoeller's house, in those last years, he never again went home
without first visiting Hoeller and Hoeller's family and
Hoeller's house, without first moving into Hoeller's garret, to
devote himself for two or three days to such reading as he
could do only in Hoeller's garret, of subject matter that was
not harmful but helpful to him, books and articles he could
read neither in Altensam nor in England, and to thinking and
writing what he found possible to think and write neither in
England nor in Altensam, *here I discovered Hegel,* he always said,

over and over again, it was here that I really delved into
Schopenhauer for the first time, here that I could read, for the
first time, Goethe's *Elective Affinities* and *The Sentimental Journey,* without distraction and with a clear head, it was here, in
Hoeller's garret, that I suddenly gained access to ideas to
which my mind had been sealed *for decades before I came to this
garret,* access, he wrote, to the most essential ideas, the most
important for me, the most necessary to my life, here in
Hoeller's garret, he wrote, everything became possible for me,
everything that had always been impossible for me outside
Hoeller's garret, such as letting myself be guided by my intellectual inclinations and to develop my natural aptitudes accordingly, and to get on with my work, everywhere else I had
always been hindered in developing my aptitudes but in
Hoeller's garret I could always develop them most consistently, here everything was congenial to my way of thinking, here
I could always indulge myself in exploring all my intellectual
possibilities, here in Hoeller's garret my head, my mind, my
whole constitution were suddenly relieved from all the outside
world's oppression, the most incredible things were suddenly
no longer incredible, the most impossible (thinking!) no longer
impossible. It was in Hoeller's garret that he found the conditions necessary and most favorable to thought, for getting the
mechanism of his thought going in the most natural, most
undistracted way, all he had to do was to come to Hoeller's
garret from wherever he might be, and the mechanism worked.
Whenever I was in England, he wrote, no matter how I felt, I
was always thinking, if only I could be in Hoeller's garret now,
always when he had reached a dead end in his thinking and in
his feelings, if only I could be in Hoeller's garret now, but on
the other hand he realized that settling for good in Hoeller's
garret was not synonymous with always being able to think
freely and without distraction, and that, if he could stay
forever in Hoeller's garret, it would mean nothing less than his
own total destruction, if I stay in Hoeller's garret longer than

need be, he wrote, I'll be done for in no time at all, that's the end of me, he thought, which is why he had always stayed in Hoeller's garret for *only a definite period of time, how long exactly he could never foresee, but it had to be strictly limited,* he must have considered a stay of fourteen to fifteen days in the Hoeller garret ideal, as his notes imply, always just fourteen or fifteen days, every time, on the fourteenth or fifteenth day, according to Hoeller, Roithamer always packed up in a flash and went off to Altensam, though he did not necessarily stay in Altensam for any length of time very often, but only for the shortest possible time, as little time as he could manage, the absolute, inescapable minimum, no more, he had even been known to take up residence in Hoeller's house with every intention of going on to Altensam after fourteen days or so, but instead of going on to Altensam where he was expected, where his arrival had already been announced, after fourteen or fifteen days, he went from Hoeller's place in the Aurach gorge straight back to England, because his stay at Hoeller's place, in the Hoeller ambience, had not only given him enough, but had actually advanced his thinking so much that he did not need to stop at Altensam but could go straight back to England, specifically Cambridge, where he was *always both studying and teaching* simultaneously and, as he always kept saying, he never exactly knew at any particular moment whether he was studying or teaching because, as he said, *when I was teaching, I was in fact basically studying, and when I was studying, I was basically teaching.* Actually I too found the atmosphere in Hoeller's house ideal, I immediately made myself at home in the garret which had been Roithamer's garret and will always remain Roithamer's garret, from the very start I had always intended to take notes on my work with Roithamer's papers and on the entire process involved, and I soon understood how perfect for Roithamer's purposes Hoeller's garret was, how he had settled into Hoeller's garret with its view to westward, pitch-dark it was over the raging Aurach, and to northward, also pitch-

dark, the water steadily and always noisily slapping and crash-
ing against the wet, glistening rock-face, "rehearsing for Altensam in Hoeller's house" as he called those stays in Hoeller's
house, specifically Hoeller's garret, stays that quickly succeeded one another in those last years, especially *the last three years,*
when he went five or six times, for four or five months at a
time, from England to Altensam, but actually only to Hoeller's
garret, obviously attracted to it by Hoeller's work, those metic-
ulous preservations of animals, and in general by all the cur-
ious conditions of the place, so intimately bound up with the
play of light in the Aurach valley, where every day ran its
course simply enough, but nature was always making itself so
powerfully felt, a nature mostly in pain, and all the people
there, Hoeller's parents and in-laws and his wife and his still
school-age children, for whom everything turned on what
game had been shot and gutted, what wildfowl shot and
gutted, and all the related chores, all the circumstances of life
were bound up with their natural surroundings, it became
clear to me that Roithamer had found here in the Aurach gorge
as he had nowhere else the inspiration for pressing on with his
main task, the building of the Cone, that edifice as a work of
art, which he had designed for his sister in three years of
incessant mental concentration and which he had built in the
following three years with the greatest effort, with what he
called almost inhuman energy, built it in the very center of the
Kobernausser forest. It was in Hoeller's garret, where I had
now moved with Roithamer's papers, most of them relating to
the building of the Cone, and I regard my work on Roithamer's
papers as the ideal occupational therapy for myself after my
long illness and *also feel it is ideal,* it was here that Roithamer
had conceived the idea of the Cone and drawn up the basic
plans for it, and the fact that even now, some months after
Roithamer's death and half a year after his sister's death, his
sister for whom he had built the Cone which is already abandoned to natural decay, Hoeller's garret still contains all the

plans, all the books and articles, most of them never used but all of them collected by Roithamer in his last years with a view to building the Cone, all those books and articles in every possible language, including languages unknown to him but translated for him by his brother Johann who spoke many languages and in fact had a gift for languages like no other man I ever knew, the translations were also here in Hoeller's garret, and I could see at once that there had to be hundreds of them, stacks of translations from Spanish and Portuguese, as I noticed when I entered the garret, hundreds if not thousands of laborious decipherments of probably important considerations for the construction and completion of the Cone by experts unknown to me but probably familiar to him, he hated the word *architect,* or *architecture,* he never said *architect,* or *architecture,* and *when* I or someone else said architect, or architecture, he instantly countered by saying that he could not stand hearing the word architect, or architecture, that these two words were nothing but malformations, verbal monstrosities which no thinking man would stoop to, and I never used the words architect, or architecture, in his presence, nor have I used them since, even Hoeller got accustomed to avoiding the words architect or architecture, like Roithamer we resorted to words such as master builder or building or the art of building; that the word B U I L D is one of the most beautiful in the language, we knew ever since Roithamer had spoken about it, in that same garret where I have now installed myself, one dismal rainy evening when we again, as so often, dreaded the onset of another one of those torrential floods that come tearing down the gorge to devastate the whole area sometimes, though this one receded unexpectedly, those floods in the Aurach gorge would do the most extensive damage but they always spared Hoeller's house, all up and down the Aurach they did the most extensive damage but Hoeller's house, which was built right into the cleft, was spared always, because Hoeller had known exactly what he was doing, everyone was amazed to see the whole Aurach valley buried in mud, ravaged and destroyed while Hoeller's house alone stood unscathed, incredibly, it was on this dismal rainy evening, with all of us living in fear of another such flood about to bemire and ravage everything in its path, though this time it did not happen, when Roithamer revealed to us the beauty of the word *building* and the beauty of the word *build* and the beauty of the phrase *builder's masterwork.* From time to time he would pick out a word like that, a word that had suddenly become luminous with meaning for him, pick out one word from among all those others, any word at all, and elucidate it to anyone, but usually to those of us who often came in the evening to Hoeller's house and always regularly on those weekends when Roithamer returned from England. Once, as I recall, he spent a whole night analyzing for us the word *circumstance,* the word *condition,* and the word *consistent.* It was touching to find all of Roithamer's books and articles and plans and his writing utensils and thinking aids still right there in Hoeller's garret, just as he had left them. Hoeller's garret was where all the ideas and designs for building the Cone had come into being, here all the ideas had *originated,* all the plans were sketched, all the necessary decisions for building the Cone had been made here, it was from here Roithamer had directed everything. Those pinewood shelves, common planks of pinewood, along the whitewashed walls, crammed with hundreds of thousands of books and articles about buildings and the art of building and everything connected with building, about nature and natural history, particularly the nature and natural history of the rock formations involved in the building of the Cone, about statics above all, and about the possible ways of building such a cone-shaped habitation within a natural environment such as the Kobernausser forest, these cheap pinewood boards nailed together with three-inch steel spikes, and instantly, as I entered Hoeller's garret where I had never been alone before, but always in Roithamer's com-

pany or Hoeller's company, or both their company, I suddenly
felt that it was possible for me, from the first moments after I
had stepped inside, to let myself go in Hoeller's garret, to think
freely about Hoeller's garret, to give myself over entirely to all
these suddenly available thoughts, relating of course to my
plans regarding my work on Roithamer's papers and especially
to arriving at an understanding of his chief project, the building of the Cone, to sort it all out, to think it through, possibly
even to pull it together where it did not really belong together,
to reconstitute its original coherence as envisioned by Roithamer, because I had seen clearly from the very first time I
went through Roithamer's basic manuscript that the circumstances that interrupted his work, the death of his sister and
the consequent irregularities in his methodical work-process,
his work interrupted suddenly where it never should have
been interrupted, on his basic manuscript about the Cone and
consequently about Altensam and about Hoeller's garret,
about the course of the Aurach and about the Aurach gorge in
particular, about building materials and, again, everything
connected with the building of the Cone, but as it related to
Hoeller's garret, though basically the building was researched
and planned and put up and actually completed out of venera-
tion for her, his sister, I had seen clearly that because of all
these circumstances the manuscript on which he had been
working most energetically, as I happen to know, for the last
half year of his life in England, in a room he had rented
specifically for that purpose in Cambridge, as he told me, his
purpose being to write at all costs a justification and analysis
of his work on the Cone, even though he basically had no right
to take the time off from his professional scientific work, but
he couldn't be bothered about that because he must have
clearly understood that he simply had to complete his manuscript about the Cone and its attendant circumstances and
everything involved with it, *now,* immediately after his sister's
death, if he was going to complete it at all, he probably felt

that he had no time to spare, that his life was doomed to end soon, that day by day it was increasingly self-doomed, so that he had to proceed with incredible ruthlessness, mostly against himself and his own highly vulnerable mental state, as I happen to know it was, he had to fulfill his intention and complete his manuscript about the building of the Cone, he had in fact begun by making a most energetic effort to plan and construct and put up and complete the Cone, then followed this up by making a similar if not even greater effort to explain the building of the Cone in an even greater, as I now see, a most extensive manuscript, and above all to justify what he had done, because he had been reprimanded on all sides for having had such an idea at all in a time opposed to such ideas, a time predisposed *against* such ideas and their realization, for having realized such an idea, given it embodiment and even brought it to completion, he was reprimanded for being, in a time generally predisposed *against* such men, such heads, such characters, such minds as Roithamer's (and others'!), precisely such a man and head and character and mind, so contradictory a character and mind and man as that, who used his unexpected inheritance in the service of an idea everyone considered crazy, an idea that had suddenly entered his crazy head and never again left it, the idea to use his sudden windfall for building his sister a cone, a cone-shaped habitation, and not only that, but most incredible of all, to erect this giant cone not where such a house might normally be located, but to design it and put it up and complete it way out in the middle of the Kobernausser forest, they had all thought at first that he would never go through with it, but little by little he made it happen, suddenly it was no longer only inside his head or clearly evident only in the intensity of his preparatory studies, but all at once the road through the Kobernausser forest was actually being built, a road that would go to the exact center of the forest at an angle he had calculated for months, working nights, because he meant to build that cone in the exact center of the Kobernausser forest, and he did build it in the exact center of the Kobernausser forest, the calculations all had to be made by him personally because, now I have to come out with it, he hated all architects and he hated all professional builders with the exception of the manual workers, he kept at it relentlessly until he had all his figures as to the exact center of the Kobernausser forest just right so that he could begin with the digging of the foundations, it was a rude shock to all the people who had until this moment refused to believe that Roithamer's crazy scheme would actually be executed, when the road to the center of the Kobernausser forest was *actually built* and he *had* started digging the foundations, he had come back from England, once he had done his calculations, and installed himself in Hoeller's garret and had, by supervising every detail personally, so expedited the building of the road and the digging of the foundations that the experts were mystified that one man could so speed up a project that the road was finished in half the normal time and the foundations dug in a third of the time normally required for such a job. The foundation was the deepest ever dug and the road was the best-laid road, everything had to be the best. Nobody, in fact, had even believed that Roithamer could possibly succeed in acquiring the plot of land for the Cone in the middle of the Kobernausser forest, and certainly not *for such a crazy purpose,* everyone and the experts especially thought it was completely crazy to build such a structure as the Cone and they still do and always will think it completely crazy, anyway the land on which Roithamer built the Cone had become government property after the aristocrat who previously owned it, a Habsburg, had been dispossessed, and the very idea of getting such a piece of state property in the middle of the Kobernausser forest back from the government into private hands, no matter whose, was in itself an absurd and actually an utterly crazy idea, to say nothing of getting back all the land for the road leading to the Cone, buying it all back from the government to be privately held, by whomever, yet Roithamer had managed to reacquire from the government, in the shortest possible time and in absolute, prearranged secrecy, all the land needed for the road he wanted to build and also, immediately thereafter, the large plot of land in the middle of the Kobernausser forest on which he wanted to build the Cone for his sister, then, shortly after acquiring the land and not without having completely settled all the formalities, he began laying out the road and building the road and building the Cone, at which point everyone was horrified, to begin with it was a rude shock especially to Roithamer's brothers who had never dreamt that their brother's crazy scheme could become a reality, made into a reality by the crazy Roithamer, but they had to accept the fact of the valid deeds of purchase, and take note that the road was beginning to be built and, finally, that the Cone was under construction, even at this late date, they had tried to have Roithamer declared incompetent, they instituted a proceeding to have him placed under guardianship, but he was declared *completely sane* by a team of doctors, in any case the experts who testified against Roithamer's mental condition and who had been hired and paid by Roithamer's brothers remained in the minority against the experts who testified that Roithamer was sane. That a man who lets such an idea as that of building the Cone develop in his head, then uses his inherited fortune, for which he had no other use, to turn this idea into a reality, and actually goes ahead, with great energy and enthusiasm, with his project to build the Cone, still does not quite prove, after all, that the man is crazy, even though the majority of bystanders and relatives believe that such a man is crazy, that he simply *must* be crazy, because no sane man could possibly spend such an enormous amount of inherited money, an amount that goes into the millions, the hundreds of millions, on so crazy an idea as the idea of building such a cone, *a cone the likes of which has never been built before,* and Roithamer actually did sink all of his inheritance into the building of that

Cone, except for a sum in seven or eight figures, I don't know exactly how much, which Roithamer had set aside to be at his sister's disposal for the rest of her life, precisely the amount now at issue between the Roithamer brothers living in Altensam, because that amount of money reverted to Roithamer after his sister's death, and to his brothers after Roithamer's own death. At this point let me state that the Cone itself and all the land and property pertaining to it, purchased at such vast expense but in accordance with all due process from the state, has reverted to the state, with the proviso that *the Cone is to be left to decay, never again to be touched by anyone, and is to be abandoned entirely to nature* where Roithamer had placed it. But I won't go into it at this point. Where the pinewood shelves crammed with books and articles ended in the Hoeller garret, the walls were covered with hundreds of thousands of plans, all concerning the building of the Cone, millions of lines and numbers and figures covered these walls, so that at first I thought I'd go mad or at least get sick from looking at all these millions of lines and numbers and figures, but then I got accustomed to the sight of these lines and numbers and figures, and once I had reached a certain degree of equanimity, beyond the point of losing my mind from looking at all those cone calculations, I could begin my study of those notations, beginning with all the calculations and sketches on the walls of Hoeller's garret, then going through the books and articles on the shelves, and finally all the material in the file drawers; I did, after all, have to familiarize myself with the fact that here in Hoeller's garret I was confronted with all the intellectual data, hitherto unknown to me, out of which Roithamer had designed and then built the Cone and everything connected with it. And so it was out of the question to start on my actual studies of all these papers immediately, at least not in the first few hours after my arrival, instead I began by making myself comfortable in Hoeller's garret, unpacked my bag, put away my few indispensable belongings, examined my bed, which had just been made and, like all freshly made beds in the country, smelled deliciously of the surrounding outdoors. It was a good bed, as I could tell by sitting on it; then, I hung my coat in the wardrobe; I am all alone in what I may certainly call Roithamer's garret, Hoeller's garret is Roithamer's garret, even Hoeller referred to this garret as Roithamer's garret, I had the immediate impression of being inside a thought-chamber, everything in this chamber had to do with thought, once a man was inside it he had to think, being in this chamber presupposed incessant thinking, no one could have endured it for a minute without thinking incessantly, whoever enters Hoeller's garret, enters into thinking, specifically into thinking about Hoeller's garret, and at the same time into Roithamer's thinking, and must continue to think these thoughts as long as he remains in the garret, if he breaks off these thoughts he is instantly crazy or dead, I think. Whoever enters here has to give up everything he ever thought prior to entering Hoeller's garret, he must make a clean break with all of his past thinking and start completely afresh, at once, thinking only Hoeller-garret thoughts, to stay alive even for a moment in Hoeller's garret it's not enough merely to keep on thinking, it must be *Hoeller-garret-thoughts,* thinking solely about everything to do with Hoeller's garret and Roithamer and the Cone. As I stood there looking around Hoeller's garret it was instantly clear to me that my thinking would now have to conform to Hoeller's garret, to think other than Hoeller-garret-thoughts in Hoeller's garret was simply impossible, and so I decided to familiarize myself gradually with the prescribed mode of thinking in this place, to study it so as to learn to think along these lines, entering Hoeller's garret unprepared and learning to adjust, to entrust and subject oneself to these mandatory lines of thought and make some progress in them is not easy. Everything inside Hoeller's garret came from Roithamer and I even went so far as to state that this garret *is* Roithamer, even though one's head should beware of such judgments, I yielded up my entire existence to this judgment the moment I set foot in Hoeller's garret. Hoeller himself had not touched a thing in this garret since Roithamer's last visit here, immediately after his sister's funeral in Altensam, as I've since learned from Hoeller, Roithamer had attended the funeral most reluctantly, as I've also learned, not of course on account of his sister but because of his brothers, Roithamer wore black, Hoeller said, which he'd never worn before, no matter who was being buried, Roithamer wore black only this one time in his life, it was only for his sister's funeral that he dressed in black, he looked extremely well dressed in those black clothes, Hoeller says, and so there he was in his elegant black clothes in Hoeller's parlor and sat there in silence, in *total* silence, as Hoeller says, without eating or drinking anything, Hoeller had the impression that Roithamer, with his sister now dead and buried, had come to an end himself, except that he was still alive, but though he was still alive he actually felt that he was already dead, because his sister, for whom he had built the Cone, had meant everything to him, next to his work, his natural science, which he taught at Cambridge, as I have said, he simultaneously taught and studied at Cambridge, but now, Hoeller said, you know how an educated man can suddenly look as though he had been mortally wounded, and Hoeller described Roithamer as looking not only completely exhausted after his sister's funeral, but looking as if he were already dead, Roithamer had entered Hoeller's house a dead man, not merely an exhausted or totally exhausted man, and there he sat in Hoeller's family room for two hours, and would not let Hoeller's wife give him anything to eat or drink, though he had never refused her before, except that after three hours he took a glass of water which he drank down in one long gulp, and nothing else, then he kept on sitting there in the downstairs family room deep into the night, in silence, Hoeller himself didn't dare to say anything, not in this situation, said Hoeller, who could describe the situation very well, though he couldn't explain it, in fact every time Hoeller talked about Roithamer he could describe everything very well though he couldn't explain it, but Hoeller didn't need words to make himself understood and to explain whatever and wherever something needed explaining, Hoeller's method of elucidation always worked best when he operated in silence, and so Roithamer sat in the parlor all night long and did not wish to retire to the garret, Hoeller said, he probably didn't want to return ever again to the world of the garret, which stood for *everything*. Around midnight Hoeller's wife wrapped a coverlet around Roithamer's legs because of the sudden cold, and Roithamer had let her do so without offering any resistance, Hoeller said, then, at about four in the morning, Roithamer stood up and went upstairs without a word, to the garret, where he stood stock-still for a few moments. He made no changes at all in the garret, Hoeller said, never again touched anything in it. The garret is still exactly as it was when he left it. Nor have I changed anything in the garret, Hoeller said. Then Roithamer went away and they never heard from him again. The news of Roithamer's death came as no surprise, so Hoeller said, everything about Roithamer on that last evening and that last night had pointed to his death, Hoeller could see clearly during that night, during all of that last encounter with Roithamer that he, Roithamer, didn't have much longer to live. I no longer exist, was the last thing Roithamer is supposed to have said to Hoeller. I personally saw Roithamer one last time in London, after he'd sent me a telegram and I'd gone to meet him at Victoria Station and had accompanied him to his apartment, where he told me about his sister's funeral, in those brief sentences of his that brooked no contradiction. Now in the garret Roithamer was present to my mind's eye, because he had in fact been present here, I saw him distinctly and I heard what he said when I saw him, even though he was not present in reality, so conscious was I of his presence as I gazed at his things, breathed the air he had breathed those last years in the garret, thought the thoughts he had always thought here, sensed the Hoeller atmosphere which had become second nature to him in the years when he'd been disengaging himself from Altensam and had, gradually at first and then altogether, given himself up to his project, the Cone, for Roithamer had often told me that the Hoeller atmosphere and the circumstances of the Hoeller atmosphere, the line of thought directly bound up with the Hoeller atmosphere and the circumstances bound up with the Hoeller atmosphere had become his one necessity, the only compelling necessity of his life, no matter where he happened to be in those final years, whether in England, where he had to teach at the university in Cambridge, or in the Kobernausser forest, where he had decided to build the Cone, wherever he had stayed in those final years, whether in England or in Austria, whether in the English place, which called for great decisiveness and presence of mind, or in the Austrian place, with great attachment and love, though also with equally great contempt and dislike, with a mixture of distrust and disappointment felt so keenly as to border on hatred for his homeland, a borderline he was often sharply aware of crossing, in fact, because he realized that while on the one hand he loved Austria as the land of his origin, he also hated it because it had rudely affronted him all his life long, it had always repulsed him when he needed it, it had never let a man like Roithamer come close, basically men, people, characters like Roithamer have no business in a country like his homeland and mine, where they have *no chance* of developing and are continually aware of their inability to develop, such a country needs people who are not angered to the point of rebellion against the insolence of such a country, against the irresponsibility of such a country and such a state, such a totally decrepit, public menace of a state, as Roithamer said again and again, a state in which only chaotic conditions, if not the most chaotic conditions, prevailed; this state has countless men like Roithamer on its conscience, it has a most sordid and

shabby history on its conscience, it is no better than a *perma-
nent condition of perversity and prostitution in the form of a state,* as
Roithamer said again and again, quite impassively, with his
innate firmness of judgment based on solid experience, indeed
Roithamer had never accepted any criterion other than that of
experience, as he said again and again, when his limit of
tolerance toward this country and this state had been reached,
and he said that he could not give a full account of this state's
sordidness and shabbiness and dangerousness in just a few
quick words, nor could he take the time for a full analysis in a
scholarly work on the subject, intent as he was on his professional duties and on his building of the Cone, nor did he have
the head for exhausting himself in political argument, he had
never been able to pour himself out in political—the common
kind of political argument—he had to leave this sort of thing
to *other kinds of heads, foreheads, occiputs, more suited to it than his
own,* he merely felt driven now and then to bring his judgment
to bear on the country of his origin, the country where he
belonged, Austria, this most misunderstood country in the
world, this country more problematical than any other in all
world history, so from time to time he had to risk expressing
himself on the subject of Austria and the Austrians, this state
that was economically more decrepit than any other, which
had nothing left, apart from its congenital imbecility, but its
hypocrisy, hypocrisy in every conceivable area of administration and policy, this country, once the very center of Europe,
was, according to Roithamer, no longer anything more than a
rummage sale of intellectual and cultural history, an unsold
remainder of government merchandise, on which the citizen is
granted only a second or a third or a fourth but in any case
only the last bid, only the leftovers, Roithamer had known
from the beginning, as I did too, how impossible it was to
grow up and develop in this country, under this government,
no matter what the auspices, as Roithamer said, this country
and this government do not favor the development of a man of

intellect, here every sign of intellectual energy becomes immediately transformed into a sign of intellectual weakness, every
effort to get ahead, to move up, to move on, is made in vain,
wherever you turn your eyes, your mind, your efforts, you see
nothing but the failure of all efforts to make one's way, to rise,
to get on, to develop, every Austrian is born to failure and has
to realize that he must give up the struggle if he is to remain in
this country and in this state, under whatever auspices, he has
to decide whether to stay and go under, to grow old in misery
and without ever achieving anything in his own country and
his own state, watching his own mind and body die a horrible
slow death, whether to accept this lifelong process of decline
while remaining in this country, under this government, or
else whether to get up and out as soon as possible, and by so
doing save himself, save his mind, save his personality, his
nature, because if he doesn't get out, Roithamer's words, then
he is sure to be destroyed in this country, if he isn't yet
contemptible, he is sure to become contemptible in this country, and under this system, and if he's not a vicious or an
infamous type, he's sure to become a vicious or an infamous
character, and a vicious and infamous creature in this country
and under this system, so a man has to save himself from the
first, from the very first moments he begins to think, by
escaping from this country and this system and the sooner a
man of intellect turns his back on this country and this system
the better, he has to make up his mind to leave behind everything that constitutes this state and this country, to go no
matter where, to the ends of the earth if necessary, but not to
stay where there is nothing for him, or else if there is something, it's sure to be only the most miserable, the most mind-
destroying, the most head-wrecking kind of thing, sure to
drive him to every kind of pettiness and meanness, here everything exists only to crush him, to vilify and disown him at all
times, he must realize that here in his Austrian homeland he is
chronically exposed to vulgar misunderstanding and vulgar

vilification, sure to drive him to his destruction and to his death and to the annihilation of his existence. Surely it is clear that Roithamer had no alternative but to leave his homeland, which doesn't even deserve that honorable title, since it still is an honorable title, because his so-called homeland is actually, for him as for so many others, nothing but a horrible lifelong punishment for existing, for the blameless act of having been born in the first place, a man like Roithamer never ceases to feel punished by his homeland for what is not his fault, because no man can be blamed for his birth, but Roithamer had to understand very early in his life, in his earliest child-hood, in fact, which he spent with his three siblings in Alten-sam, that he would have to get away, as fast as possible and without any ifs or buts, if he was not to go under, as his siblings have gone under, in the last analysis, because there is not the slightest doubt that Austria has been the ruin of his siblings, his older brother certainly went downhill in Alten-sam, because of the circumstances characteristic of Altensam, the conditions that prevail in Altensam and always did prevail in Altensam, Roithamer's older brother never once made any attempt to leave Altensam, his development took the course characteristic for Altensam, from the first he had given himself up without a murmur to that process of dying a slow death in Altensam, the place is nothing but a process of slow death, he never tried to break away from Altensam, to give up Altensam, he simply could not muster the minimum of necessary energy, qualities such as courage, decisiveness, adding up to a spiritual power of decision, were altogether lacking in this elder broth-er, whom I knew from early childhood, as I knew Roithamer's younger brother, he simply accepted this order-in-the-guise-of-disorder which always prevailed in Altensam, quietly put up with the inexorable processes of the dying-off of a huge country estate, because this was what his parents expected of him, and he grew up in Altensam as they all grew up in Altensam, and what became of him is what became of them all, a typical Altensamer is what he became, a man who basically knows nothing else and also accepts nothing else than Altensam, who has awakened with Altensam and who, having lived through Altensam, is going to die with Altensam. And Roithamer's younger brother was always the older brother's willing slave, he was even weaker and feebler than the older brother and both of them together actually formed a lifelong death club in Altensam, nothing else, even though they did outlive Roithamer, their middle brother, and their sister too, who died in the Cone, of course, they did out-exist, out-vegetate their sister and their middle brother, Roithamer; if I were to go to Altensam, which I have no desire to do, I could see for myself how they keep on vegetating there, I could see them, the two remaining Altensamers, being exactly what they have always been and nothing else, being Altensam through-and-through, and it was precisely this *Altensam through-and-through* that Roithamer always resisted, as he said, his whole life, his whole existence, his whole effort to survive had basically been nothing more than resistance to Altensam, anything but surrender to Altensam, anything but getting stuck in Altensam is what he must have been thinking always and in every way, I think that this reflection must have been part of every slightest thought, every least idea in his head: anything but becoming Altensam, *becoming Altensam through-and-through* like my brothers, because actually Roithamer would never have been capable of accomplishing his intellectually demanding work otherwise, work such as he has left us as his legacy, all these papers of his, even the least significant of them, testify to Roithamer's lifelong concern with not getting stuck in Altensam, throughout all of his life, all of his difficult existence, there was nothing of greater urgency in his head than the need to loosen his ties to Altensam, because to disengage himself from Altensam, consciously and radically, meant the freedom to think, to be freed of Altensam to do his own thinking, because he had finally freed his thinking from

Altensam even though it would not have been possible without Altensam, because actually Altensam and his coming from
Altensam and the constant connection between his person and
his personality and his scientific work and Altensam were
necessary, to enable him to think as he had thought and
worked, away from Altensam, beyond Altensam, never again
back to Altensam. His brothers had been destined from the
first to remain in Altensam, to accommodate themselves in
Altensam to their fated decline in Altensam, no one expected
anything else from them, in fact, and no one noticed that these
two men, by staying in Altensam, were gradually and with
increasing intensity being annihilated by Altensam, even
though they still exist, they have long since been annihilated
by Altensam as Roithamer was never annihilated by Altensam,
although he was always debilitated by Altensam, by all but his
sister, who was an exception. To her Roithamer clung with all
the love of which such a man is capable and as the highest
expression of this love he had envisioned and undertaken and
accomplished and completed the building of the Cone. But
that a person like Roithamer's sister cannot endure so climactic
a condition has proved true, in that she is no longer alive
today. But more of this later. That he must get out of Altensam, Roithamer had understood even as a child, clearly understood as though he had an adult's head on his shoulders, and
he had always kept apart from the others in Altensam as if in
preparation for his removal from Altensam, from earliest
childhood on everything about him had pointed to his eventu-
al departure from Altensam, to his actually leaving Altensam
completely behind him, because his kind of thinking was
incompatible with Altensam and impossible without a separation from Altensam. It will have to be a radical separation, he
had decided quite early in his life, and when he decided
subsequently to give up not only Altensam but Austria, he
actually achieved the most radical separation possible from
Altensam and Austria. Because if I ever do go back again—and

the temptation to go back again could not be greater—I shall
be destroying everything I have achieved, he noted, it would
mean yielding to a weakness, nothing less than a deadly
weakness, it would mean succumbing in a moment to the
imbecility which I have so far managed to escape. He had
always perceived Altensam as a state of imbecility, and those
who lived in Altensam, his relatives, as the imbeciles in this
imbecility, and there was nothing he feared more than a return
to this imbecility and to these imbeciles. Even if the torment of
absence and of pursuing, of advancing one's objective, one's
intended continuous improvement of one's intellectual condition, is the greatest torment, and even if the hardship of taking
root so far from home, in a so-called foreign country, is the
greatest and most depressing of hardships, I shall not return to
this state of imbecility and to the imbeciles of Altensam and
Austria, he noted. Many of his notes of that period had
attracted my attention during the first hours after my arrival at
Hoeller's garret, but I deliberately avoided concentrating on
Roithamer's mental state just yet. To penetrate Roithamer's
mental state prematurely was dangerous, it had to be done
warily, with great care, and above all while keeping watch
over my own mental state, which is, after all, also and always a
precarious state of debility, as I was thinking during those first
moments and hours of contact. And so I approached that mass
of papers from Roithamer's hand and mind, and which I had
brought with me to Hoeller's garret, timidly and with restraint,
because I fully realized the dangers of a possibly precipitate
and careless involvement with Roithamer's papers, with his
entire literary estate that had fallen to me by a court decision,
fully aware that I had to guard myself against this involvement, because it was clear to me that my mental state and my
entire constitution were extremely vulnerable to every kind of
injury from Roithamer's papers. But I had seized the opportunity of my pulmonary infection, meaning simply these months
of *reflective illness,* to concern myself at once, without post-

ponement, with this legacy of Roithamer's, *afraid as I was
originally to plunge* into Roithamer's papers, because I knew
how vulnerable I was, in my uncertain state of health involv-
ing not only my body, I was too weak to confront Roithamer's
mental world head on, knowing that I had never been a match
for Roithamer's ideas and what he did with them, but had, in
fact, sometimes succumbed entirely to these ideas and actions
of Roithamer's, whatever Roithamer thought I also thought,
whatever he practiced, I believed I also had to practice, at times
I had been wholly preoccupied with his ideas and all his
thinking and had given up my own thinking even though it
had been, after all, like every line of thought, an independent,
autonomous, self-propelled line of thought, I had become
quite incapable of thinking my own thoughts for long periods
of my life, especially in England where I had probably gone
only because Roithamer was there, all I could think was Roithamer's thoughts, as Roithamer himself had frequently noticed
and found inexplicable, and consequently also unbearable, he
said, to have to see me so subjected to his thinking, if not
entirely at the mercy of his thinking, that I tended to follow
his every thought wherever it might lead, that I was always to
be found in my thinking wherever he was in his thinking, and
he warned me to take care, not to give in to this tendency,
because a man who no longer thinks his own thoughts but
instead finds himself dominated by the thoughts of another
man whom he admires or even if he doesn't admire him but is
only dominated by his thoughts, compulsively, such a man is
in constant danger of doing himself in by his continual thinking of the other man's thoughts, in danger of deadening himself out of existence. For the longest time I could not manage
to think my own thoughts in England, all I could do was to
think Roithamer's thoughts, so that during all that long time in
England I had, in effect, given myself up. Since my thinking
had actually been Roithamer's thinking, during all that time I
simply had not been in existence, I'd been nothing, extin-

guished by Roithamer's thinking into which I'd suddenly been
absorbed for such a long time that Roithamer himself lost
track. My extinction by Roithamer's thinking probably lasted
until Roithamer's death, I am only just now beginning to
perceive that I am once more capable of doing my own thinking, owing to my having come into Hoeller's garret, I think.
Now, after such a long time, I think that I am once more in a
position to form my own image of the meaning of the objects I
look at, instead of Roithamer's image of the scenes at which he
and I were looking. I think that when I stepped into Hoeller's
garret, I suddenly stepped out of my long years of captivity, if
not incarceration, within Roithamer's thought-prison—or
Roithamer's thought-dungeon. For the first time in years I am
now looking at Roithamer with my own eyes, and at the same
time I have to think that I have probably never seen Roithamer
with my own eyes until now. Such a man, such a character,
such an existential genius as Roithamer was bound to end, I
think, at a certain point in his development, at its extreme
point, in fact, where he would end explosively, be torn apart.
When I concern myself with Roithamer, with what order of
magnitude am I dealing? I ask myself, clearly I am dealing with
a head that is willing and compelled to go to extremes in
everything he does and capable, in this reciprocity of intellectual interaction, of peak record performances, a man who takes
his own development, the development of his character and of
his inborn intellectual gifts to its utmost peak, its utmost
limits, its highest degree of realization, and also takes his
science to its utmost limits and to its utmost peak and its
highest degree, and in addition also takes his idea of building
the Cone for his sister equally to its highest point and its
highest measure and to its utmost limit, and is even willing to
provide an explanation of all this in the most concentrated
form and in the greatest measure and to the utmost limit of his
intellectual capacity, a man who must force everything he is,
in the final analysis, to coalesce in one extreme point, force it

all to the utmost limits of his intellectual capacity and his nervous tension until, at the highest degree of such expansion and contraction and the total concentration he has repeatedly achieved, he must actually be torn apart. He had freed himself and his head from Altensam and Austria so that he could achieve this highest degree of concentration, and he had always had the will to achieve this height of concentration, in every aspect of his being, he had this will to concentration, the will to reach the absolute limit which was his most salient characteristic, he had given up practically everything he had ever been in order to achieve what he had not been and what he ultimately became by dint of superhuman excessive effort. We rarely meet a man like Roithamer, I must admit, and probably never again in our lifetime, a man who, having recognized his capacity for it, does all he can to achieve the record performance of his being and who, once he has embarked on his scientific discipline, intensifies this discipline every day and every moment until he brings it to the utmost point of concentration within himself and *must* go on concentrating it to the utmost possible intensity, having suddenly no longer any alternative to perfecting his possibilities, anything else has become impossible for him, he must keep his eye fixed undeviatingly on his highest possibilities, unable to see anything apart from these, where such an extraordinary talent for life and therefore for science as Roithamer's is involved, such an enduring and lifelong concentration means an enduring and lifelong incarceration within that extraordinary talent for life and for science, because from a certain moment onward, such a man can no longer live for anything other than his genius for reaching his aim which, once he has clearly perceived it, suddenly outweighs everything else and becomes his only motive, all at once such a man's entire being is concentrated in his resistance to everything that might stand in the way or even merely distract him from the gradual achievement and ultimate fulfillment of his aim; resisting everything, concerning himself with nothing except whatever will advance his aim, such a man goes his increasingly lonely and painful way, a way such a man must invariably go alone and without help from anyone, as Roithamer realized quite early in life, suddenly he had left behind everything, especially everything to do with Altensam and its surroundings, consequently all his relatives, physical and spiritual, in whom he had suddenly recognized the greatest impediment to his aim, he had given up what the others, siblings and other relatives, either were not ready to give up or incapable of giving up, the habit of the habit of Altensam, the habit of the Austrian habit-mechanism, the habit of the familiar, of all one is born to, he gave it all up, everything the others did not give up, all he had to do was to think of giving up, leaving behind, everything the others did not give up and leave behind, all he had to do was to observe what the others did or did not do in order to do it or not do it himself, their omissions were his activities, his activities were their omissions, a simple trick in which he had been able to achieve great facility from earliest childhood, by constantly observing everything around him, by a persistent testing and receiving and rejecting of everything other than himself, his character, his mind, because he had always been different from everything else and everybody else and so, by his constant observation of everything else and everyone else he had arrived at an even higher degree of lucidity, he could see that he had to take a different direction from all the others, travel a different road, lead a different life, a different existence from theirs and all others, as a result of which, in fact, quite different possibilities had opened up for him from those of the others and from those otherwise constituted, under whose dominance he had come with time, more and more, in a very special quite idiosyncratic innate rhythm of his own in which he had schooled himself, Roithamer had understood early in life what the others had not understood until much later or had never understood at all, the most salient feature of his

relationship to the others is always their total failure to understand and the resulting non-stop incomprehension on their
part, they always understood each other among themselves,
but they never had understood him, and they still do not
understand him even now, after his death. Basically they had
never really noticed his development at all, for what they had
perceived as his development was something other than his
actual development, he had always gone some different way,
just as he had always pursued other ideas than they had
assumed, they had never had any insight into Roithamer's
nature, which differed fundamentally from the nature of all
the others, their view of him was conditioned by their heads,
their feelings, their limited perceptions, but Roithamer's development was something else, they saw their brother (or son)
only as they were able to see him but not as he was, since they
saw him as they wanted, not as he truly was, and even his
sister, whom he loved as he loved no other human being, did
not face the truth and the reality of this extraordinary man,
whenever she was involved or in touch with him. Their vision
was beclouded when they should have been looking at Roithamer with unprejudiced eyes able to perceive the truth and
the reality and so, all his life, they confronted a man other
than he was, they saw him as they wanted to see him, as
someone they could control, even if he sometimes seemed
weird to them, or not weird but basically not in the least like
one of themselves, had they seen him as one of themselves,
they would have felt they were seeing *clearly.* They would
have liked nothing better than to eliminate him altogether
from their world, but now he has become the chief heir of his
parents, the others being paid off, because his father chose him
to be the heir of Altensam instead of his elder brother, whom
the father perversely wished to humiliate, as I now know, the
father had quite deliberately wanted to involve his middle son
in a catastrophe called Altensam, such was the father's idea, to
choose as his heir the son who was absolutely wrong for

Altensam, as the father knew he was, the son who not only was all wrong for Altensam but who quite simply hated Altensam with all the fervor of his head, about Roithamer's being chosen to take over Altensam and pay off his siblings a special dissertation could be written, but it is not for me to do this, the father's stipulation that Roithamer was to take over Altensam and pay off the others, who were attached to Altensam with every fiber of their being, their father had not even reserved to them the right to be domiciled in Altensam, they were to be paid off, nothing else, the chances are, it seems to me, that Roithamer's father intended solely to destroy Roithamer by leaving Altensam to him and not to the others who loved the place, by leaving it to the one who hated it and so to destroy Altensam as well, such an idea and so destructive a decision is just what you would expect of Roithamer's father, it perfectly suited his character, his life, his circumstances, by leaving Altensam to my middle son after my death, the old man might have thought, I shall destroy not only my middle son, whose destruction I have had in mind all my life, but destroy Altensam as well, which is after all what I mean to do, and in addition I shall destroy the lives of my other children, nothing could have been more in character for this man than to destroy his progeny and his origins at the same time, his children and Altensam together, an effect guaranteed by his stipulation that Altensam was to be inherited by his middle son, and sure enough Roithamer's brothers had used up the moneys paid out to them in the shortest possible time and were now quite destitute, dependent on the magnanimity and the unscrupulousness of their brother, whose own sense of truth, justice, and consistency was supposed to have led him to destroy them by driving them out of Altensam, to which they were attached with every fiber of their being, yet he let them go on taking refuge and shelter at Altensam, he made it possible for them to live there, to have their existence there, all the income from the Altensam agricultural enterprises went into their pockets, a not inconsiderable income in view of the vastness of the estate and its high productivity, there was no equally profitable agricultural property to be found within a large radius from Altensam, not for hundreds of miles, Roithamer waived his claims to the income and even put up with a cousin as manager whom Roithamer knew to be in league *with his brothers, not with him,* though wondering himself whether such generosity did not border on stupidity, as I see by a note he made, but Roithamer's conduct and decisions were always in character. The brothers had nothing of their own, they were using their brother's land, and his sister reported from time to time on their activities, which were always directed against their brother who was busy teaching or studying or obsessed with some idea in England. While the Cone was under construction, the brothers are supposed to have done their brother out of several million, but Roithamer would not admit that he knew what they were doing, he just let things take their course without lifting a finger, Altensam and the fate of his brothers in Altensam had long ago ceased to matter to him. Between my brothers and me, he wrote, there's always been a total lack of sympathy, nothing but mutual dislike, I have left Altensam and my origins behind me like a foul smell. Here, in Hoeller's garret, Roithamer realized even during the most strenuous periods of preparation for building the Cone for his sister, which had long since become identical with his purely scientific pursuits, that just a few miles away his own brothers, occupied with nothing but squandering moneys which in fact belonged to their middle brother, brothers who hated everything intellectual, automatically despised everything that had to do with thought, and far from making a secret of their attitude took every occasion to make it public, these handsome, as Roithamer writes, but thoroughly degenerate men who are my brothers, with nothing in their heads but the exploitation of my land and everything else they can get their hands on, who lead a life of nothing but stupid externals, as

mindlessly as life has always been led at Altensam, *while I,
buried here in my scientific studies, don't even indulge myself in the
barest necessities, a new pair of pants, for instance,* because I simply
cannot take the time for shopping, Roithamer wrote, my
brothers keep piling up heaps of new, fashionable clothes,
ordering a new car every minute, and in every way doing
absurd things that run entirely counter to my views, but I have
given up making them see their conduct in the right light,
much less reproaching them with it, while it is true that I
indulge myself only in the barest necessities, I don't, after all,
need anything but the barest necessities, all my happiness rests
precisely on making do with the strictly necessary, all I do, I do
in the interests of my studies, which happen to be my deepest
concern, all I do, all my plans and finished projects, whatever I
may consider and propose and carry out, serves only my
research, which is my happiness, so Roithamer wrote, so I have
no right whatsoever to judge my brothers, to judge them is to
inject myself into their being, which I have no business doing,
I must remind myself again and again that their nature is quite
different from mine, when I do, it always cuts off thinking
about my brothers or anybody else and resolves the momentary problem as it arises. While it is a fact that Roithamer had
millions and a vast fortune at his disposal, yet was content
with the barest necessities for his own person, the absurdity of
this naturally caused a persistent misunderstanding, but
Roithamer knew why he was content with the barest necessities, even though he was possessed of a so-called vast fortune,
the sudden windfall of which he was using for his own aims,
for his research, which happened to be in natural science, and
which had come to a climax with the building of the Cone.
Nothing could make him happier than to have at his disposal
precisely the amount of money necessary to realize his plan of
building the Cone in the Kobernausser forest, it was for this he
needed those millions which came to be at his disposal after
his father's death, once he had paid off his siblings. He used

his inheritance, which came to a so-called enormous figure, for his experiment, ultimately his cone-building, never before possible, because no one who might possibly have had such an idea before him, to build a cone as a human habitation, such a cone, that is, as *he* had planned, no one had ever had at his disposal the necessary enormous sums for executing such a plan, his conscience was clear, considering the billions being squandered daily by politicians in this world in the course of their totally useless machinations, the vast national resources being destroyed day after day by the politicians for their useless and senseless purposes, he could certainly claim no less than this: that it isn't often, and probably only this once that the chance comes along to use such a sum, so suddenly made available, for actually constructing such an edifice *as I have done, the only one of its kind in the world and in any case the only one in the so-called world of architecture,* and he could say to himself: I have built the Cone, I was the first to build the Cone, no one did it before me, I alone took all the steps and subordinated my entire existence and all my other possibilities single-mindedly to designing, building, and completing the Cone. Not only did I design this Cone, he could say to himself, a thought which enabled him time and again to surmount the many setbacks, the sheer impossibilities that rose every year to obstruct his work, his research on the Cone, not only did I design the Cone, and I know that no one else in the world has to this day even designed such a cone, such a cone has never yet existed even in the form of a sketch, so enormous a cone, a cone of such monstrous size and so habitable, in so unique a natural setting as this natural setting in the midst of the Kobernausser forest; not only did I design such a cone, *I've actually built this Cone and everyone can see that I've built this Cone,* so Roithamer wrote. Yet he didn't care in the least whether anyone else saw his Cone, his masterwork, especially not the so-called professionals, the professional building experts, from the so-called world of architecture, who had naturally turned up soon after the Cone was finished and even before its completion, he did not feel the need to prove to anyone that such a cone could be designed *and* built, specifically even in the midst of the Kobernausser forest, not to anyone but himself, that is, and he had certainly proved it to himself once the Cone was completed, for six years he'd thought of nothing else than proving to himself that such a cone could be built, built specifically in the Kobernausser forest, and in accordance with all the specifications he, Roithamer, had set down for himself in regard to this Cone, and the Cone met his conditions in every respect, it had turned out exactly in accordance with all his specifications and was completely functional, the highest accolade a building could be awarded. Before supper, which I was to take with the Hoellers, I'd been busy putting my things in order, I'd unpacked them and laid them on the table and the two chairs and the bed and I'd hung my jacket and coat in the wardrobe, the process of unpacking and sorting my few things, I'd taken along only what seemed absolutely necessary for a five- to six-day stay in the Hoeller house, I'd taken over two hours, all the time thinking about Roithamer, of how *he* had lived, under such constant great difficulty, leading a life of such great self-discipline for such long periods of time, always with a view to his scientific work; and under what conditions he did it while also subject to such chance occurrences, and how he lived in England and in Altensam, and *how* he finally ended up. These thoughts were constantly stimulated by the presence of Roithamer's belongings in Hoeller's garret which, from the first moment I had set foot in it, held the same incomprehensible and really indescribable fascination for me as it had for Roithamer, judging from his description of the place, and Roithamer had described Hoeller's garret very often, as the germ cell of his scientific work, as the wellspring for the last third of his life, once he actually told me that without Hoeller's garret, without the possibility of going there at any time to live, to use it, even to exploit it, he could not have gone

on living from a certain moment on, from that moment when
he had devoted himself exclusively to his scientific work, that
moment had come as a sudden turning point, one day when
Roithamer had just returned from Altensam to England and
had spoken to me about the Hoeller garret's fascination for
him, we'd met in Roithamer's lodgings in Cambridge, probably
to discuss some scientific or philosophical or scientific-philo-
sophical topic with which he was then preoccupied, some
problem that had most likely just arisen as it so often did in
the course of a confrontation with his students or his profes-
sors, and Roithamer was not the man to take up a topic that
has suddenly arisen, in whatever way it has arisen, only to
drop it again at a certain point, as is usual in conversation; a
topic he took up had to be *thought through to the end,* everything
involved in it had to be gone over point for point before he
could be satisfied, to take up a topic means to think it through
to the end, no aspect of it must be left unclarified or at least
unclarified to the highest degree possible, but in this instance,
I now recall, he was suddenly speaking not of our topic but
about Hoeller's garret, for the first time with such an intensity,
I was quite taken aback to hear Roithamer, who never spoke of
such things as lodgings beyond what was absolutely necessary,
go on for over an hour about Roithamer's garret, trying to
describe Hoeller's garret to me in every detail, making me
visualize it little by little, not all at once, which could only
result in something hazy, unclear, not graspable in its entirety,
but little by little, with a scientist's carefulness, object by
object, peculiarity by peculiarity, until the entire Hoeller garret
with all its objects and peculiarities stood clearly before my
eyes, fascinated by his description and explanation of Hoeller's
garret, as an entity I could understand exactly as he understood it, I could see it distinctly, and could see how its significance and importance for his scientific work and for his future
existence *was suddenly to be understood as an unconditional signifi-*
*cance and importance.* As I now stood looking at the inside walls

of Hoeller's garret, I compared what I now saw with Roithamer's description of many years ago, to see whether what I
was looking at and noticing coincided with what Roithamer
had described to me, whether the concepts I had formed on the
basis of Roithamer's description coincided with the reality,
which *I* now had the opportunity to check out point by point,
and with Roithamer's descriptions, I was listening to Roithamer's voice in my ear, on the one hand, while at the same
time looking around and noticing and checking out Roithamer's description of Hoeller's garret, all the walls and finally
the ceiling of Hoeller's garret and the floor made of irregular,
rather wide planks of larch wood, their grain forming the
strangest patterns that instantly brought to mind earth formations as seen from the air, surface formations in some non-
European regions, in Asia or South America, I heard what
Roithamer said at the time as though he were saying it now,
his voice exactly, with its rising and falling inflections, his
characteristic pauses, the way he would slow down as he
spoke and then speed up again, and in addition there was, that
time in England, the impact of his discovery of Hoeller's garret
as the ideal place for him, everything about Hoeller's garret
was new to him then, and so Roithamer described Hoeller's
garret to me in that tone of voice in which one imparts an
incredible piece of news, as incredible as it is staggering,
stressing again and again that Hoeller's garret was perhaps,
and probably, his greatest and most important find, probably
the most *important for his survival,* as he insisted, in the second
half of his life, his existence, which he had basically been done
with long since, he kept on and on about nothing but Hoeller's
garret which we both knew about, of course, because we had
often watched Hoeller's house going up in the Aurach gorge
while it was still under construction, but at the time it was
being built in the Aurach gorge we could not possibly have
had any inkling of its now suddenly manifest significance, a
significance and importance Hoeller's garret could only have

achieved through Roithamer, for whom it suddenly became,
during his first stay in it, that first night, when he frequently
got up from his bed to walk over to the desk which then as
now stood by the window, that writing table which had never
been intended as a desk in the first place, not even as a
student's desk, it was an heirloom that somehow came into
Hoeller's possession from the Gmunden widow of an engineer
involved in the damming up of the mountain stream, Hoeller
didn't know what to do with it and so he put it in the garret
after it had simply been in the way for a long time inside the
house, as is so often the case with so many heirlooms that fall
into one's hands, it was always in the way, so Hoeller suddenly hit upon the idea of putting the desk, a simple desk with a
maple top, into Hoeller's garret, the desk was of absolutely no
significance until the moment Roithamer got up out of bed
that first night he spent in Hoeller's garret and walked over
and sat down at it, and Roithamer had told me that the idea of
building the Cone had come to him at this desk, *at the moment
when he first sat down at this desk,* suddenly, as I sat down at the
desk, I had the idea of building my sister the Cone, to give her
the greatest happiness, as he immediately felt it would, and
from that moment on the idea of making his sister supremely
happy, by building her a cone to live in, had given him no
peace and right there, sitting at that desk where I had never sat
before, so said Roithamer, I made a vow to carry out this idea
of building the Cone, to build it entirely on my own, out of my
own head, to make it into an actuality, and that same night I
started to make notes and draw sketches, on that very desk,
sketches of the Cone and even the idea for *the site of the Cone,
namely, the dead center of the Kobernausser forest, came to me in
those first moments* while I was making notes and drawing
sketches, the Cone must be situated in the dead center of the
Kobernausser forest, I said to myself over and over, while I
was already at work on the first sketches, the first notes,
concerning the size and the height and the depth and the

width of the Cone, the statics involved, since the building of
the Cone is primarily a problem of statics, I thought, and I then
spent all night sitting at that desk drafting sketches and notes,
it was four in the morning before it dawned on me that I was
actually exhausted, those sketches and notes, he told me that
time in England, while he was describing Hoeller's garret, were
the basic sketches and notes for the Cone which I subsequently drew on repeatedly during the six years I worked on the
Cone, those first sketches and notes were the most important,
during all the time spent on planning and building they turned
out to be the *most important of all,* time and again, upon the
foundation of these sketches and notes, and their spontaneity,
I then built the Cone during those long six years, years intensified by being aimed at this single objective, so Roithamer. And
now here I was myself, settled in Hoeller's garret just as
Roithamer had described it, trying to get a clear idea of its
interior, and as I sat on the bed or at the table or at the desk or
on the corner chair, or paced back and forth, I had been pacing
back and forth almost the entire time, because I believed I
could gain an even greater intensity of concentration on everything I was considering, looking at, observing, and checking
out as well, and I was not disappointed in my aim of gaining
such great concentration on Hoeller's garret, the object of my
observation and examination, as I suddenly found myself pacing back and forth quite rapidly, I could hear even better, more
intently, what Roithamer had said that time in England, and so
I could understand it better and more intently, while at the
same time my observation of the Hoeller garret's interior had
become even keener, little by little and under the spell of
Roithamer's characteristic cadences, I finally caught all the
meanings in everything Roithamer had said, I remembered, as I
heard him again in Hoeller's garret saying all he had said that
time in England, suddenly it all came back to me with all its
full significance, and so I had the ideal opportunity for making
comparisons and was more and more struck by how exact

Roithamer's description had been, while describing Hoeller's
garret to me in England as if he were inside it, he must have
been seeing it in his mind, otherwise so precise a description
would have been impossible, but I know how precise Roithamer's descriptions always were, without being in the least
distracted by any sound, the incessant rushing of the Aurach
had never distracted me or Roithamer during his sojourns in
Hoeller's garret, a place so totally noiseless apart from the
deafening noise of the torrential river, especially torrential at
the Aurach gorge, so that it was possible for me to concentrate
entirely on Roithamer's original description then, and on my
own present observations of Hoeller's garret now, I had concentrated totally upon that description and this observation,
no noises would have disturbed me in this effort, but luckily
the whole Hoeller house suddenly went completely quiet just
at this moment of concentration, which was odd because the
Hoeller children had just come home from school and I'd just
seen a number of the local foresters entering the house to see
the taxidermist, I'd seen them from my attic window at the
moment I began to concentrate on listening to Roithamer, on
his description, my observations, on my own looking and
noticing and reexamining of the garret with reference to his
description of it, yet at that moment and in fact the whole time
I was concentrating on this subject there was perfect quiet. So
it was possible for me to check on all the objects in Hoeller's
garret one by one, as one systematically goes over a scientific
experiment which must suddenly be checked out for one
reason or another, there is always a reason for such testing.
Because he was so self-absorbed, always intent upon his scientific work, and because his preoccupation and concentration
made him appear to be totally wrapped up in himself and his
scientific work to the exclusion of everything else, it was
always amazing to find him so well informed, every time, in all
fields other than his own, he was, for example, exceptionally
knowledgeable about everything that seemed to be of no

concern to him at all and need not concern him, such as, for instance, the world of politics, which he must have been following with the utmost attention since he could not, otherwise, have acquired so sophisticated a knowledge of politics and everything connected with politics as he had, the result of regular observations made, again and again I saw with what thoroughness he had kept himself briefed on the latest political events and was prepared to bring into the discussion at any moment such current political events, many of them not those everyone was talking about but those *operating under the surface of the world political scene continually and decisively to determine the political realities* and to relate them to his own current interests even if these happened to be at the furthest possible remove from the political events, he was always making remarks which gave evidence that he let nothing escape him which brought life or, on the contrary, stagnation into the political world, he was, as an intelligent man of course must be, a *daily* attentive and critical reader of every newspaper and periodical within reach and in every possible way kept himself informed about the political scene which, as he said, held the greatest fascination for him, once he even said that the art of politics was the highest-ranking of all the arts, a remark indicating that he regarded politics not as a science but an art, were he not, he said, who he was, he would have devoted himself always and with the greatest possible energy to the political art, but he did after all regard natural science and the study of its foundations as the primary task of his life, which is why he had not taken up politics or rather, as he always expressly phrased it, the *political* art, as I now can see, he was always most excited by politics, especially the always monstrous, even if in so-called peaceful periods quiet politics, he was always excited about the actually always world-shaking and world-changing and consequently world-destroying political events and was generally in a chronic state of excitement about the political factor as such, perhaps to an even greater degree than

one might expect of him, occupied as he was with his own
scientific work, in natural science; because he was a man who
was interested in everything, politics was bound to interest
him more than anything, even though his actual intellectual
life was entirely concentrated on natural science and on nature,
*natural science as my actual science,* as he once said, he was
always at a peak of excitement and readiness-to-explain resulting from his observations of primarily all the political
events in the world, observations that sustain me, as he said, in
my isolation which enables me to get on with my scientific
work. And so it is self-evident that he would be tempted to
elucidate his subject when he spoke about it and while he
spoke about it, in clear language, in short sentences, using all
his skill of phrasing while constantly intent upon simultaneously elucidating and reexamining his theme, always while
conquering and reconquering his primary subject matter, natural science, during every moment of his preoccupation with
this subject matter, since to think is to regain and recover,
moment by moment, everything previously thought, to make
it new, and so it is self-evident that he always had to consider
politics, always specifically the actual political events of the
time together with their political history and at least relate all
that to his own thinking, since the thinker must think not only
his own special discipline but everything else which is, after
all, logically related to his own subject, as conversely everything else is related to his own subject, that is, all his own
possibilities or impossibilities and probabilities and *im*probabilities are always interrelated with all the others. And so it is
not at all strange that I have found many notes of a political
nature in Hoeller's garret, I had noticed immediately that many
of the notes tacked or pasted on the wall were political notes,
just as he had loved covering the walls of his rooms in England, also, with political notes primarily, he felt in his element
in this on the one hand scientific, on the other hand decidedly
political, interest in the inconspicuous as well as the conspicu-

ous relationship of his thought and his intellectual labors and always, when he spoke of science, he was also speaking of politics and everything else, and when he spoke of politics he was also speaking of science and everything else, because the scientist, or the man we regard as a scientist, or the so-called scientist, who has given himself up to a science because he had to give himself up to a science, has to think not only about his own scientific subject, if he is to be taken seriously as a scientist, but must continually think about all the other fields as well, and then again in the light of all the other fields about his own field and the other way around, and his entire existence is nothing but such incessant testing in which he, the scientist, must incessantly examine what he is thinking at the moment, which should be everything, because unless one is thinking of *everything at each moment* one is not thinking at all, according to him. Everything that is thought, all thought resulting in action, he said, is political, and we are involved in a totally political world and a totally political society which keeps this world in constant motion. The truth is that a human being is a political creature in every fiber of his being, do what he will, think what he will, deny it if he will, whenever he will. There were also indications of his love for the arts, music most of all, second only to politics as the art to which he was most receptive, as he said, and which he had eventually made his favorite art, indications of which I instantly noticed in Hoeller's garret, the many notebooks, excerpts of piano scores, etcetera, also musical notations written in his own hand, musical motifs which he, who had perfect pitch, expected to be helpful to him in advancing his scientific work because, as he always used to say, music is the art closest to natural science and the nature of man; music, he said, was basically mathematics made audible, a fact enough in itself to make music indispensable to the scientist as an instrument toward all his objectives and discoveries and the achievement of ever-new knowledge and discoveries, which is why he, Roithamer, concerned himself, in addition to his specialty and natural science in general and all the related disciplines, above all with music as the art medium most useful to him, and I know that he often left Cambridge to spend several days in London in order to hear a particular composition by Purcell or Handel, because he regarded hearing such music as absolutely indispensable to making progress in his own field, what I think about and what I am working on I could never think about and work on without music, as he said, it is always music which enables me to take the next step in my scientific growth, by listening to Purcell or by listening to Handel, as he said, it becomes possible for me to progress more quickly than if I were *not* listening to Purcell or to Handel, he loved Handel and Purcell more than any other composer, he esteemed these two above Bach, and next to them it was Mozart and, probably because of his Austrian origins, Bruckner, for whom he felt special preference, on one occasion when we were joined by a third man, a musicologist from Oxford, I suddenly had the confirmation that Roithamer's knowledge of music, which must unhesitatingly be termed a *scholarly* knowledge of music, was indeed knowledge on the highest level, I still remember the Oxford musicologist's recurrent outcries of amazement—he had been booted out of Vienna by the Nazis just before the war broke out, a man whose *intellectual incorruptibility* (an expression of Roithamer's) instantly convinced me of his superior competence, the most distinguished musicologist in all England at the time—his amazement every time Roithamer made a remark on musical scholarship and art, and the chances are that Roithamer went to England also to research Purcell's and Handel's art of composition, since he'd loved Purcell and Handel and studied them even before he went to England, he had even written a short paper, a so-called comparative study entitled *Handel and Purcell,* but it is lost, one of many gems Roithamer wrote in his mid-twenties which are lost, probably because he was really unaware of their value and because he was the kind of man who in any case did not appreciate his own written works of art once they were finished, no matter how successfully, and paid no further attention to them, like that essay of his on Anton von Webern which I also remember, which had outlined a quite original theory of music, also lost like the paper on Handel and Purcell mentioned earlier, his studies of Hauer's and Schönberg's theories would keep him immured in his turret room in Altensam for weeks at a time, and everyone around him was always amazed at how he had managed to master the art of playing the piano, which had been indispensable to his studies, since the music lessons he and his siblings took in Altensam, from a former professor of the Schottengymnasium in Vienna, the capital's foremost humanistic school, who had left Vienna because of a serious lung disease and had come to Altensam with the help of a friend of Roithamer's father, where he also gave lessons in Latin to children and adolescents, his music lessons were nothing beyond the usual, since Roithamer's parents, and the professor as well, did not attach the greatest importance, in the education of the Roithamer children, to the so-called *aesthetic subjects* such as music, but rather to mathematics and foreign languages, but Roithamer had always been different, and while his siblings shone in foreign languages, even in the ancient, the so-called *dead languages,* all of which simply did not interest him, he was the keenest of music students who from the first regarded the indifferent teaching of the Viennese professor, who continued to be sick in Altensam but without infecting the Altensamers with his disease, as basically instruction in the most important, to him, of all the arts, music as a means to making greater strides in the natural sciences which the growing boy had already fastened upon, for even at the age of eleven or twelve Roithamer had instinctively perceived that music and the knowledge of music was a necessary condition for his ability to enter into the natural sciences, and so he had even then seized upon every opportunity to improve his knowledge of music and, with only that basic instruction in musical theory and practice and in piano playing, he had achieved a mastery of his subject all on his own, and had not only retained that mastery all his life but had even managed to expand and intensify it. Listening to music had always meant the same to him as studying music, so listening to music was for him not only a way of raising his spirits but, by the way he combined hearing and studying the music, he became *plunged in thought.* While others listen to music and, *when* they hear, they feel, it was possible for Roithamer to hear music *and* to feel *and* to think *and* to study his science. His chief musical interest had been, on the one hand, Purcell and Handel and Mozart and Bruckner, and on the other hand, the newer and newest music such as Hauer, Webern, Schönberg and their successors. The opening bars of the Webern string quartets which he'd hand-copied on the back of a bill, he'd tacked on the wall above his desk in Hoeller's garret. He loved this opening, it had always meant much to him. The books that mattered the most to him don't take long to list, I knew them from his constantly reiterated remarks in which he established a connection with these books, they were always basically the same: Montaigne, Novalis, Hegel, Schopenhauer, Ernst Bloch, and, because he thought that he recognized himself in them, the writings of Wittgenstein, a native of the same region as Roithamer and always a keen observer of Roithamer's regional landscape, they were always just the same few books of philosophy and poetry which, with his name inscribed on the flyleaf, he always carried about with him no matter where he had been staying or working, so few that he had always been able to slip them into his traveling bag and take them along, they always had to be within reach. Here in Hoeller's garret they had been left, after his death, where he himself had placed them, on the shelf above his desk, so now they belonged there forever, in this place that had been Roithamer's actual study, his idea- and thought-chamber, where in his lifetime no one but myself and Hoeller had ever been permitted to set foot, Roithamer had made sure, in a secret understanding with Hoeller, that no one but himself ever set foot in this room, and in Roithamer's absence only Hoeller, not even me, no one except for Hoeller, who had to enter the garret if only to air it out regularly, but under strict orders to change nothing in the garret, to leave everything as Roithamer had seen fit to leave it, and always in the best possible order, everything in Hoeller's garret had its own fixed place, closely corresponding to Roithamer's character, his peculiarities, and clearly explicable out of his own special view of the world, Roithamer would instantly have noticed the slightest change in Hoeller's garret the moment he set foot in it after his return from England, or from South Tyrol, where he had often gone directly from England to visit a close friend, a musicologist who was also, as Roithamer always emphasized, a theoretical mathematician at the University of Trent who, when he was not teaching at Trent, had lived and worked on an isolated family estate, over a thousand meters above sea level, near Rovereto, where for many years he had devoted himself entirely to his work, so Roithamer said, having made himself the object of his extremely interesting investigations, or when Roithamer returned from Carinthia, another occasional refuge of his, because he had a beloved cousin there, the daughter of a Klagenfurt lumber merchant, he liked to spend a day or two with her every two or three years, but most times Roithamer came straight back from England to Hoeller's garret, it would have been unthinkable to let anything be changed in Hoeller's garret during Roithamer's absence, Hoeller had always made absolutely certain that nothing was ever changed in Hoeller's garret and he insured himself against such changes by simply never letting anyone set foot in Hoeller's garret in Roithamer's absence, Roithamer had offered Hoeller a regularly payable rental for the use of his garret, but Hoeller had firmly refused to accept anything of the kind, he considered it an honor that

Roithamer could use this garret, otherwise completely unused and used by no one, for his own purposes, it was enough for Hoeller that the garret would be used, lived in, by Roithamer, a man known for many years before he ever moved into Hoeller's garret to be quite extraordinary, a man of rare worth who was superior to at least all *known* men and, as Hoeller said, a *brilliant phenomenon,* it was enough for him, Hoeller, that this extraordinary and invaluable man, Hoeller said, this brilliant man, with regard to whom one could safely assume that he would come to be known even more widely as the extraordinary and rare and brilliant man he was, would be using Hoeller's vacant garret, which otherwise was likely to decay quickly from lack of use, for his scientific purposes, and besides, he, Hoeller, considered it only natural to put this garret at the disposal of a friend, a childhood friend, a school friend, a friend of his youth, for that friend's scientific and artistic pursuits which he, Hoeller, did not pretend to under- stand, but which he certainly admired as the continual mani- festations of Roithamer's extraordinariness; as Roithamer always waved away his friend Hoeller's expressions of admiration, in fact he always was quick to rebuff his admiring friend whenever this friend showed his admiration too explic- itly for the sensitive Roithamer's comfort, he always did all he could to get Hoeller to understand that he, Roithamer, did not deserve admiration of any kind, although he did lay claim, like any man doing his job, to respect, an attitude of mutual respect was the most helpful attitude between friends, the most suit- able and appropriate to them and especially to their friendship, people were always admiring where they should simply re- spect something or someone, the trouble with admiration was, it ought to be nothing but respect for the other person, some- thing of which most people were incapable, apparently re- specting the other person was the hardest stance to maintain between individuals, most people are simply incapable of re- specting others, but respecting others is most important, people prefer admiring to respecting even though they only irritate the other person with their admiration and destroy with their admiration what is valuable in the other person instead of preserving it by duly respecting it, but that man Hoeller was virtually addicted to admiring Roithamer, and as time went on Roithamer tired of fending off Hoeller's admiration by rebuffing it. But perhaps Hoeller's admiration for Roithamer had been nothing more than just his respect, they esteemed each other, in fact, as I know, they held each other in the highest esteem, each in his own way and in accordance with his own capacities. In opening the chest of drawers, which simply does not match the rest of the Hoeller furnishings, it's a rare eighteenth-century period piece of nutwood, with three drawers, simple ornamentation, so I suppose that it was brought over from Altensam to Hoeller's garret at Roithamer's request and perhaps even from among his own personal possessions, it could be one of Roithamer's favorite pieces, I thought, the aroma also, when I opened the top drawer to put in my toilet articles, this exceptionally well-made chest, not veneered but carpentered out of the whole, evenly grained nutwood, instantly reminded me of Altensam, Altensam where I had gone so often, even in earliest childhood, with my grandfather, who had been a friend of old Roithamer's, and afterward by myself, almost every day, I must say that when I was at home I was always and constantly drawn to Altensam, that unfailingly mysterious and vast, inexhaustible Altensam with its innumerable, infinitely ancient walls, its hundreds of rooms with their thousands upon thousands of furnishings and pictures that are bound to attract, even to fascinate a young man, especially a child, raised in diametrically opposite, rather restricted circumstances, not to mention the people of Altensam, the most mysterious people in the world to the child I was; in opening that drawer—the chest, I suddenly thought, undoubtedly came from that vast collection of furniture in Altensam—I discovered the yellow paper rose Roithamer won that time at the shooting gallery, the story is as follows: on Roithamer's twenty-third birthday which he had decided, on an impulse in his rooms at Cambridge, to spend with me in Altensam, and which we actually did spend together in Altensam, after a journey made adventurous by vast inundations of the Dutch coast, from Altensam Roithamer and I went to the annual music festival in Stocket, in early May, we spent the whole evening of his birthday and the night until dawn at this open-air music festival, eating and drinking without restraint, both of us in a mood to let go completely, to go wild, because we'd spent the previous four or five months totally immersed in our studies, he, Roithamer, in his scientific research and I in my mathematical studies, both of us quite consciously and completely isolated within the scientific world of Cambridge. As may be expected this music festival was just the thing to bring us release from our scientific obsession, and we'd instantly and most eagerly seized upon this chance to relax completely at this music festival, to take our minds completely off the subjects of our intellectual obsessiveness upon which we had naturally been concentrating to a really dangerous degree. In itself that music festival was nothing special, these music festivals in our country are all alike, performing a most useful function especially for all those people who are chained to their labors, year in and year out, so naturally everybody comes flocking to the two or three music festivals per year, with their actual and their so-called amusements and distractions, these affairs are called music festivals because unlike the usual so-called country fairs they feature a band, an enormous attraction to the populace, that's all it is, but the organizers know that they can draw a much larger crowd by calling it a *music festival* rather than a *country fair,* so it has become the custom to call these events music festivals even if they are nothing more than country fairs, everybody attends these music festivals which usually begin early on Saturday night and end late on Sunday morning. In Altensam, where nobody had remembered even Roithamer's birthday and none of Roithamer's siblings were home, we soon turned the possibility of going to the music festival into an actuality, after dressing suitably for the occasion. We immediately got into the swing of it, drinking several glasses of beer and schnapps in quick succession, we quickly got ourselves into the necessary high spirits for such an occasion, both of us naturally meeting lots of familiar faces of schoolmates and their sisters and wives, with whom we soon got involved in all sorts of conversations, but these conversations mostly consisted of our, Roithamer and me, having to explain why we had gone off to England and what we were doing there and what had become of us in England, and why we hadn't stayed at home and made something of ourselves here, at home, as they had. At first these conversations, consisting basically of questions addressed to us both, had not bothered us and we readily answered all these questions put to us, such as whether we were now English, no longer Austrians, whether we were living in London or if not, where, whether we had become scientists, known experts, whether we were thinking of returning home and most of all, again and again, how much we were making, in Austrian schillings not in English pounds, it was evidently too much trouble for them to convert English pounds into Austrian schillings, and was it true that it was always raining in England and that everything was always shrouded in fog there, had we ever seen the Queen, had we met her personally, had we ever spoken with her, the questions came at us in an endless stream and a constantly growing number of people had so questioned us and we had to keep on answering more and more, they kept asking and we kept answering questions until we could no longer stand it and finally made our way through these hundreds of people, drunk as they'd been for some time, to a shooting gallery. Both of us were astonished at finding ourselves, suddenly, standing *in front of a shooting gallery,* since neither I nor Roithamer had ever been to a shooting gallery for any reason whatsoever, we had apparently never in our lives had any business at a shooting gallery, in contrast to Roit- hamer's brothers, who did not merely claim to be but actually were excellent proven marksmen who had of course always taken part in all the shooting matches and hunting shoots, and had on display in their rooms hundreds upon hundreds of trophies attesting to their prowess, they were known and respected far and wide as brilliant marksmen, in fact as fanati- cal hunters and great shots, in contrast to me and my friend Roithamer, who not only couldn't shoot and had never in- dulged in any illusions about being able to shoot, and who basically despised hunting and everything related to hunting, in fact, deep down, we hated it, I know that Roithamer hated it as I did, he understood hunting but he hated it, he had often talked to me about his brothers' passion for hunting and, again and again, talked about how he loathed this passion of theirs, but he knew that it was a Roithamer family passion for hunting, even his father had been a great hunter and marks- man, he had been Chief Game Warden and Hunting Commis- sioner for years, indeed for decades, that to be born in Alten- sam was synonymous with being born to hunt and to shoot, it was probably the first time in Altensam's history that someone had actually turned up who not only did not like hunting but in fact despised hunting and most decidedly hated it, so it was quite understandable that the Roithamers regarded their devi- ant brother, for no reason except that they simply couldn't understand him, if not with hatred, then with a certain reserve, though they naturally had not dared to show him either contempt or hatred on this point for a long time, since they were dependent on their brother, who suddenly was the sole owner of Altensam, actually they felt they were at his mercy and that he might one day drive them, in all their degenerate state, out of Altensam, something he'd never do, however; but to get back to hunting, what a peculiar situation, that a Roit- hamer who defied all the rules of Altensam's history by being

absolutely no hunter and absolutely no marksman, had nevertheless turned out to be the man, he and no other, I thought, as
we found ourselves, out of the blue and only because we'd
been forced to escape from those hundreds, even thousands, of
crazy questions which were getting on our nerves and driving
us out of our heads, standing in front of that shooting gallery,
he and no other is standing here in front of this shooting
gallery. To shoot? I asked myself and at the very same moment
Roithamer paid for two dozen shells and started to shoot, he
was shooting at those paper roses lined up in quite disorderly
fashion in their holders opposite him, he was shooting them
down one after the other, to the momentary stupefaction of all
the bystanders, including even the owner of the shooting
gallery, whom I recognized as a woman from the village and
who had also recognized us, since of course none of the
onlookers had believed that Roithamer would hit even a single
one of the roses, yet he had shot down *every last one* of the
roses in the shortest possible time. As the shooting gallery
owner bent over to pick up the paper roses in order to place
them, all tied up in a bunch, in Roithamer's hand, I was
observing the onlookers who now, like it or not, agreed that
Roithamer was the best shot of paper roses they had ever
encountered at one of their music festivals. Roithamer himself
looked as though he were asking himself how it could have
been possible for him, untrained as he was, in fact he had
never held a gun in his hand but once in his life when he was
nine years old and with his father's help had tried shooting at
paper roses and had of course made a sad mess of it, how could
he possibly have brought down twenty-four roses with twenty-
four shots? The onlookers of course challenged Roithamer
at once to shoot down another series of paper roses, but of
course he did not yield to such a provocation. He just waved
his bunch of roses in the air above his head and made his way
through the crowd, away from the shooting gallery and toward a table with some seating room left. I followed him there

and saw him suddenly presenting all the paper roses he had
won which, tied together as they were and held high in the air,
looked more beautiful than fresh roses, to some unknown girl
passing by who reminded him of his sister. All the paper roses
but one, that is, all except this yellow paper rose I had just
rediscovered in the top drawer of the chest when I opened it to
put my toilet things inside. So all these years, I thought,
Roithamer has kept this yellow paper rose here, it probably
reminded him of that music festival on his twenty-third birthday and everything connected with that music festival. I had
taken the paper rose out of the drawer and held it against the
light, it was unquestionably the paper rose he shot down at the
Stocket music festival along with twenty-three others. That
music festival where we stayed till dawn at one of those large
plank tables, in company with several of the country boys and
coal miners we had known from childhood, has remained a
pleasant memory, how Roithamer suddenly told them all
about his childhood in Altensam, in that intense way he had,
the characteristic narrative style of the country folk around
Altensam, actually Roithamer had much in common with the
countrymen around Altensam, while he had almost nothing in
common with his own Altensam family; how very familiar he
was with the ways of the country folk around Altensam, and
how very much he loved their ways, I thought, as I stood by
the window, with the paper rose in my hand, contemplating
Hoeller's attic from my vantage point at the window, looking
toward the door, it was after all among them, these country
folk, that he had grown up, as he would say, not in Altensam
but among the country people and their families, and it is true
that as a child Roithamer had spent more time among the
country people in the villages around Altensam than he had in
Altensam itself, his own home, he took advantage of every
free minute he had to get away from the drill in Altensam,
which was little more than a cruel and incomprehensible parental fortress to him, and escape to where he might find *actual*

*kinship,* in the villages around Altensam, with the people of
these villages, the farmers and young fellows and men working in the coal mines of Altensam, he would simply leave
Altensam right after supper, without permission and go down
to the villages below Altensam, to the people there who understood him, away from those who lived in Altensam and
never understood him nor wanted to understand him, because
down there, below Altensam, in the farmhouses and in the
homes and hovels and huts of the miners down there he was
always a welcome sight, and he could always count on having
the attention of these simple people whose minds were as clear
as they were incorruptible, *they listened to me,* Roithamer's
words, *whenever I said something, and they tried to understand me
and they did understand me,* and I could count on them to help
me whenever I came to them, often in sharp distress, my
conscience deeply troubled, they were friendly in their crude
manner, always offered me food and drink, I could have
stayed with them as long as I wanted and actually I would
have preferred to stay with them always, even as a child, but
the mere thought was out of the question. While I felt cold in
Altensam, within the walls of Altensam, even among my
parents and my siblings, going down to the villages always
warmed me up, as a child I was always strictly forbidden to go
down to the villages, even when they gave permission they
didn't like my going down there because they sensed that I felt
good in the villages, that Altensam was a prison to me I had
often told them, even as a child I had this idea that Altensam
was nothing more than a prison, a prison from which I would
one day have to escape, is what I always thought, even if I
have been sentenced to life imprisonment in this dungeon of
an Altensam, I must get out, get away from Altensam, where
even my parents seemed always to have been there to guard or
punish me, never to protect me, which is what parents are for,
to take care of their children, what they should have been in
Altensam is the preservers and protectors of their son and their

other children, which is what my parents never were, instead
they were inordinately strict and relentless in turning us children, without exception, into people according to their concep-
tions, their own absolutely and completely horrible concep-
tions, trying to turn us into physical and mental manikins in
their own image, so that their chronic dishonesty and incessant
cruelty shadowed, really darkened, all of our childhood and
made my brothers what they are today, physical and mental
effigies of their parents, and made my sister the unhappiest
person I ever knew, everything in Altensam was most hateful
to me, so I broke out of Altensam every chance I got, to go
down to the villages and visit the farmers and their families
and the coal miners and their families, with whom I could be
happy as I never was in Altensam, Altensam was to me one
continuous darkening of the spirit, Roithamer's words. But
just as Roithamer took every opportunity to get out of Altensam, so I seized every opportunity to get into Altensam, every
welcome possibility of going to Altensam and being allowed
inside, inside the Absolutely Other, where I could come to life
again, for Roithamer it was the other way around, he had to
get out of Altensam and down to the villages, where he came
to life, most often in our house, my parents' house; it is here,
in your house, he always said, that I come to life again,
everything inside me gets choked almost to death in Altensam,
but here, near your (my) father and your (my) mother, I can
breathe again and think again, the kind of thinking that always helps me to survive, Roithamer's words, if I had to stay
in Altensam all the time I'd be done for in no time at all,
Roithamer's words, while I for my part would tell him from
time to time that the chance to go to Altensam, to walk those
four miles through the forest that I had walked with my
grandfather as soon as I could walk at all, each walking at his
own pace, we had an unspoken agreement, he and I, beginning
in my fourth or fifth year, each of us deeply absorbed in his
own thoughts, wholly lost in his own thoughts, nothing in all

my life was dearer and more important to me, as I now realize, nothing was ever of greater consequence for my life than these walks to Altensam with my grandfather, and so, while I staked everything and every day, whenever possible, on getting to Altensam, Roithamer had staked everything on getting out of Altensam, he loved my father and the special ambience of a village doctor's household, the supreme orderliness of everything, the neatness, on the one hand, and its free-and-easy air on the other, so entirely and benignly different in every degree from the disorder in Altensam, the general negligence in Altensam, and from what Roithamer felt to be the spiritual confinement of Altensam, all the advantages held for me by Altensam were for him to be found in Stocket and in our house, he always used to tell me that he could never find in Altensam the happiness he found in Stocket and in our house, while I for my part told him that Altensam was to me what Stocket and my home were to him, drawing new breath, making progress, firing the imagination, productivity, joy in living, and so both of us strained eagerly, Roithamer in his way from Altensam to Stocket, to our home, our village, landscape, our world of nature, while I conversely was drawn away from our village life, from Stocket, from our home, up to Altensam, inside those walls, the enormousness of those walls which fortified everything inside me, I felt drawn upward to Altensam where everything unattainable to me in Stocket suddenly became attainable because once I was up there in Altensam my mind and my emotions actually opened up in the same way that Roithamer's did in Stocket, in our home and in its environs, where he found what he never could find in Altensam, refuge and liberation in every way. While Roithamer loved my father, with whom he always spent all the time he could, always interested in my father's medical work, he was, as I have always known but now can prove, now that I have dipped into the contents of his posthumous papers, Roithamer was always interested in everything relating to

diseases, in the constant mutual interrelations of physical and
mental diseases, he was most interested in this from childhood
on when, at our house, he might encounter the strangest cases
of disease every day and he, Roithamer, had always demanded
that my father tell him everything about every disease, in fact
he was never interested so much in anything, other than his
scientific work, all his life, than in *human diseases,* of which he
had come to know and explore, here in his closeness to my
father, the greatest variety of the most widespread diseases,
especially those of our own region, the diseases native to our
province. In Cambridge he had often spent half the night,
when he had tired of his own work but wasn't yet ready to go
to bed, not yet relaxed enough to sleep after the mental strain
of his day's work, when he asked me to stay with him, stay the
night if necessary, as he frequently did when I had come over
just for a minute after I had stopped work myself, to take
refuge in his company from going crazy, as soon as we were in
England and in Cambridge we had made a habit of breaking
off our concentrated mental work and dropping in on each
other for a chat because we were afraid of going crazy, even
though we only talked about some other mentally demanding
subject, but that no longer mattered because once we were
together, in each other's company, we felt safe from going
crazy, and so, when we were together in his rooms or in mine,
the distance between our digs was only about eight or nine
hundred yards, we each had two rooms and a kitchenette, one
room was the study and the other the so-called leisure room,
then Roithamer used to talk half the night, in Cambridge, of
his observations, and the experiences resting on such observations, of the diseases he learned about quite early in life in the
company of my father, a respected and probably quite capable
general practitioner, since a scientist, no matter what his specialty in science, should begin to concern himself early in life,
long before he gives himself up to his (to a) special field, with
disease, especially the mental diseases, which arise from the

physical diseases. While I myself had hardly any rapport with my father, and my father, conversely, had really never sought any rapport with me, Roithamer had the best rapport with my father, and it was the same with the Roithamers, Roithamer himself had never entered into any rapport with his father and his father, conversely, had never sought any rapport with his son, yet I had an excellent rapport with Roithamer's father, as Roithamer had with my father, and also with my mother, though I found it very hard to communicate with my own mother, yet I always communicated very well with Roithamer's mother. What I had never found at home, meaning in our house and in our village down here, I found up there at Altensam, while Roithamer, conversely, never found in Altensam what he had always hoped for, and so we were drawn away from home even as children, I felt drawn up to Altensam, while he felt drawn away from Altensam down to us in Stocket. This tendency for me to feel drawn to them up there while he felt drawn to us down here, which we never understood clearly then, I now understand perfectly as a perfectly natural tendency. Just as I felt attracted, in Altensam, to the outlook of Roithamer's father, so Roithamer for his part felt attracted by my father's way of life and his profession, up there in Altensam I heard things I never heard at home, Roithamer heard things at our house he never heard in Altensam, all the time, hence our restlessness based on our dissatisfaction with our own home life, at home we had been seeking and hoping for what could never be found at home because it simply wasn't there in our own homes, he, Roithamer, had never been able to find in Altensam what he sought there and had a right to expect, though it could never come to pass there, while I, on the other hand, had always sought in Stocket and in my home what simply wasn't there, I had hoped for the impossible, and so we both always lived in hopes directed toward the other's home, where we had actually found what we were looking for, consequently we were always the most

miserable creatures at home where we could never understand
or express what ailed us, all we could do was suffer our
condition and be driven by it to nearly total despair in those
most difficult years, between nine and eleven and beyond, but
we had never gotten over it to this day. We loved everything
in the other's home and really hated everything in our own
home from the earliest years in our lives, we liked everything
in the other's home while disliking everything in our own, we
felt that our talents and their development were most wonder-
fully appreciated in the other's home while they were never
appreciated in our own home and as a result never developed,
either, because everything in us and about us had met with
nothing but rejection in our own home. The lack of sympathy
which was always to be expected at our own home gave way,
once we had gone to the other's home, to a sympathetic
understanding supportive to us in every respect, here at last we
could relax and breathe and think freely. The prey of misun-
derstandings at home, we were always in a state of extreme
irritability, Roithamer in Altensam and I in Stocket, we had to
give all our attention to escaping from this state or easing it
down to something bearable, and we did find life bearable at
home when we were not left entirely to ourselves and our
families, when Roithamer had come to me or when I had gone
up to Altensam to see him. When we were together we managed to find something, perceive something and make use of it
for our own satisfaction, even when we had thought there was
nothing, nothing at all, for us; this Roithamer did for me in
Stocket and I for him in Altensam. It often happened that our
paths crossed, his downward path toward Stocket, my upward
path toward Altensam, crossing at the same midpoint, the
clearing in the forest. About this clearing, where we had often
met and always stopped at once to talk about the coincidence
of our meeting and all sorts of things besides, Roithamer had
once written a short essay, which he in fact later published in a
local periodical, he was moved to write it by his interest in

Adalbert Stifter, the writer, and especially in the local lime-stone, about which Stifter had written, both only in relation to the clearing which had meant a great deal in our lives and still means much in my life, this piece of prose had been a good example of Roithamer's logical cast of mind, everything he later became, all he came to be, was already prefigured in this short piece, a description, in measured, clearly articulated terms, of a segment of nature familiar to us in the smallest detail. I'd have been glad to reread this piece about the clearing between our village and Altensam, but I'm afraid that this piece of prose, superscribed with the title *The Clearing,* is lost, though it ought to be easy to determine in which number of the local periodical it appeared originally, it would be most important to know this now, after Roithamer's suicide in the clearing. A description of the road from Altensam to us in Stocket and a description of the road from Stocket to Alten-sam, naturally two entirely different descriptions, was once done by Roithamer in England, during his first stay in London, he was deep in his studies of Purcell and Handel at the time, but these descriptions too, I believe, are lost. He used to go in for writing short prose pieces from time to time, descriptions of nature, as an aid to perfecting his scientific method of thinking, to dwell constantly in thought on nature, its inner workings and outer appearances, and to capture these thoughts by writing them down now and then, had become a lifelong exercise of his, his last exercise of the kind had been a descrip-tion of Hoeller's garret, which I suspected I might find in the desk here and which I actually did find in this desk in Hoeller's garret. The very first lines of this effort, when I reread it, gave me the idea of editing a book-length collection of Roithamer's short descriptive pieces, in a time such as ours when everything *but* what is noteworthy, everything *but* what is truly original as well as most brilliantly scientific is edited and published, when every year hundreds and thousands of tons of imbecility-on-paper are tossed on the market, all the decrepit garbage of this totally decrepit European civilization, or rather, to hold nothing back, this totally decrepit modern world of ours, this era that keeps grinding out nothing but intellectual muck and all this stinking constipating clogging intellectual vomit is constantly being hawked in the most repulsive way as our intellectual products though it is in fact nothing but intellectual *waste* products, at such a time it is simply one's duty to bring out a work of art as unassuming and unadorned as the art of Roithamer's prose, to publish it, even though it would not be likely to make any kind of a stir, I think, but just to make sure that it would never be lost again, once it is printed and preserved forever, because these prose pieces of Roithamer's are indubitably precious gems and the greatest of rarities anywhere, including our country. As to the difficulties of bringing out especially such exquisite prose, I am aware of them, just as I am fully aware of the difficulties involved in publishing Roithamer's posthumous papers, especially his longer study on Altensam, which he began at the instigation of a publisher friend of his, in Cambridge, he'd tackled and finished it in a great burst of energy just after his sister's fatal illness had manifested itself, but soon afterward, when he was already on his way to his sister's funeral, crossing the Channel from Dover to the Continent, he destroyed it again by starting to make corrections in it and correcting it over and over again until in the end he destroyed it entirely by his incessant corrections during his stay in Hoeller's garret after his sister's death, he felt he had corrected it to death and so destroyed it, but as I know now, as I have ascertained in the shortest possible time of my stay here in Hoeller's garret, he did not really destroy it by his utterly ruthless, hence utterly perfect corrections, but turned it into an entirely new work, because the destruction of his work by his own hand, by his keen mind which dealt most ruthlessly with his work was, after all, merely synonymous with the creation of an entirely new piece of work, he had gone on correcting his work until his work was not, as he thought, destroyed but rather a wholly new piece of work had been created. This work of his, seen as a description and accordingly a justification of everything in Altensam and everything connected with Altensam meant to him, with special attention to the planning and execution and completion of the Cone for his sister, was not destroyed by him but perfected by him, as I now see clearly, especially by his corrections, he, Roithamer believed that he had destroyed, by totally correcting, this work which I have brought with me and temporarily stowed away in this desk drawer, this work about Altensam and everything connected with Altensam, with special attention to the planning and execution and completion of the Cone for his sister, and it is certain that he intended to burn this work after correcting it out of existence, because I have a note of his stating that he would burn the essay after he had destroyed it by totally correcting it into the exact opposite of what he had started out to say. But he never got around to burning it, probably the essay had suddenly ceased to matter all that much to him, since it is not likely that he had, in the end, forgotten the essay altogether, when he killed himself, because *in the end nothing matters all that much,* as he also wrote on another slip, and on his last slip he'd written, *it's all the same.* His essay on Altensam and everything connected with Altensam, on what Altensam had meant to him, with special attention to the planning and execution and completion of the Cone for his sister, he had completed by totally correcting it, these are his own words, until it meant the opposite of its original meaning. The essay actually became a completed essay only after Roithamer had turned it around to mean the exact opposite, by a monstrous process of total correction, but more of that later. Slowly adjusting to the mood prevailing in Hoeller's garret, at first the mood of the late afternoon, later the mood of the evening, I had intended to get to work on the Roithamer papers starting early in the morning, the *earliest* possible time in the morning if I could, not

even to go near them before that, but only to get used to
Hoeller's garret, to get everything in readiness for the morning,
for the earliest morning, the twilight before dawn, I thought,
when I would get going on my task, but first I had to create the
right conditions for such an undertaking, far from easy to get
going, and so I had to begin with my preparations at once,
though moving slowly, considering the nature of my undertaking, and because after my illness I was in just the right
condition for working on Roithamer's literary remains, I had to
begin by thoroughly preparing myself for this task, which
meant straightening out my place of work, the desk unquestionably in front of the window, I had to find a way to control,
if possible to change the light to suit my needs, whether to
draw the curtains or not to draw them? I kept wondering, as I
stood at the door considering the desk, should I draw the
curtains or should I not draw the curtains, and I went to the
window and drew them closed and moved back again to
consider and stepped forward to open them again, I opened
them several times and closed them again several times and so
on. First of all I must have everything in order for beginning
work tomorrow, everything must be ready, I thought, before I
can start to work. But before I did anything at all, I had to let
the character of the Hoeller garret, as it was and without
changing anything in it, I had to let its ambience have its full
effect on me. Time was no problem. This must be done systematically and most resolutely, yet slowly, too, I thought,
standing near the door, nothing, absolutely nothing, must be
done in haste, I had plenty of time, besides I was not quite
over my illness, it was still manifest in every breath I took, the
air along the Aurach river was the best, this was the most
richly wooded region anywhere and the air here was the best
medicine for bronchi affected like mine, considering that I
might have spent several more weeks in the hospital if I had
listened to the doctors and stayed, but I suddenly stopped
paying any attention to the doctors, often enough in my life I

suddenly stopped paying any attention to the doctors and this was my salvation every time, I probably wouldn't be alive this minute had I not always stopped, from one minute to the next, listening to the doctors, at the right moment, the doctors may count at the beginning, when it turns out that medical help is essential right away, when only the application of medical skill can save you, when it happens, as it did in my case, suddenly and to my absolute horror, when I was right in the middle of an unfinished piece of work, a dangerous disease broke out, a really deadly, threatening, so-called fatal disease, since a severe pneumonia is still considered a deadly disease even today, suddenly waking up at night with a high fever and lying there alone, unconscious, for days, could easily lead to a quick death, but they found me and took me to the hospital and the doctors got the fever under control in record time, but even so it was a painful business for weeks, with no cure in sight, at first, all they could do was relieve the pain, help me to endure this dangerous illness, not cure me, there was at first the relief of finding myself safe in such an excellent hospital, then suddenly the need to get out of there, while I was still pinned down and leaving the hospital was out of the question, the disease had been checked but it was not even under control, as yet, it took five or six weeks to get it under control, with infusions, injections, every conceivable natural and chemical antidote applied against the disease, every possible self-applied medication against it, then, while I was still sick, I decided out of the blue to leave the hospital, on my own responsibility because the doctors would accept no responsibility, I decided to defy the doctors, simply to clear out, and I remembered Hoeller's invitation to me and left the hospital as quickly as possible though actually still a sick man, I went to the Aurach valley, into Hoeller's house, into Hoeller's garret, my mind set on putting Roithamer's literary remains in order, now, as a form of convalescence, to do again what I had always done when in the grip of a fatal illness, to leave the

hospital against doctors' orders and repossess my life by taking
up my occupation, and I thought, standing beside the door,
that my decision to leave had been equally correct in the case
of this pneumonia. It had always been the right moment to
leave the hospital against doctors' orders and cope with such a
fatal illness myself. There had been no indication at all, when
he left England, that he would never come back to England, I
thought, as I brushed my jacket and hung it in the closet, of
course I had expected him back shortly after his sister's funeral
for which he had gone to Altensam, I can still hear him saying,
I shall stay only the shortest possible time, what is there now
to keep me there, in Altensam, in Upper Austria, in Austria,
beyond the necessary minimum, the shortest possible time,
one or two days in his opinion, which he did not even intend
to spend in Altensam but in Hoeller's house on the Aurach, he
had gone to Austria already intending to spend only the
inescapable minimum of time in Altensam, to stay the night in
Hoeller's house and in Hoeller's garret, there being now, after
his sister's death, no further reason to stay in Altensam,
though there is no way to avoid talking over the problems
inescapably arising from the death and the funeral of my
sister, so I must go to Altensam, but again and again: *only the
absolute minimum of time necessary,* for now, after the death of
his beloved sister, there was virtually nothing left to tie him to
Altensam, with the death of my sister, he said, my relationship
to Altensam has come to an end. Altensam is nothing more
than past history, now, in future there will be no reason for me
to set foot in the place, and he was thinking of selling Altensam, an extremely valuable property because of its fertile
meadow- and farmlands in particular, and because of its easy
access, Altensam, isolated as it was, did have the advantage of
good roads, and this combination of remoteness and privacy
on the one hand, with easy access on the other hand, guaranteed a high price for it, and now after his sister's death Roithamer was thinking of selling Altensam, he even had an idea

of what he wanted to do with the money realized from the sale, an idea characteristic of him, which was to hand over the entire sum to his ex-convicts, without bothering at first to go into details, at one point he had even thought of giving them Altensam as a refuge after their release from prison, he had always wanted to help ex-convicts, those poorest of the poor, men totally excluded from society, with whom actually no one wanted to have anything to do no matter what their hypocritical pretenses, Roithamer had frequently donated sums of money for the benefit of prisoners released from penal institutions, but in the end he dropped the idea of opening Altensam to ex-convicts, it seemed a better idea to sell Altensam and assign the proceeds to the ex-convicts, though he did not quite know how to go about this, *there is in fact already some talk* that he made provision for the sale of Altensam and assignment of the proceeds to former prisoners of the penitentiaries at Garsten, Stein, and Stuben, entrusting the execution of this plan to his Schwanenstadt notary Süssner, the same notary who had been taking care of all the Altensam affairs for many years, in his will. But of the actual contents of Roithamer's will I had no knowledge up to this point in time, even though Hoeller told me immediately upon my arrival at his house that Roithamer had, 1) left a will and 2) ordered Altensam sold, the proceeds to go to the ex-convicts of Garsten, Stein, and Stuben, he would not have been Hoeller had he not understood our friend's last will and testament as I did, as characteristic of Roithamer's whole being. It had always been the outsiders, especially those pushed to the outermost fringes of society, for whom Roithamer felt sympathies, the criminal elements, with whom no one wanted to have anything to do, were always secure in his affection, for this tendency Roithamer had always been under attack or at least regarded with suspicion, most of all these sympathies of his for the most miserable members of society, the most helpless in the world, had soon earned him the radical dislike of his family and they, his family or what

was left of them, whichever, must have been horrified at the
reading of his will, suddenly hearing all those provisions in
favor of the poorest, the most unwanted, society's pariahs,
openly set forth, now they had suddenly to face it that he not
only had what they considered these eccentric ideas about
leaving his inheritance to criminals, murderers, no matter what
kind of criminals, but that he had actually carried these ideas
out in good earnest, this shock suffered by his family and all
those involved in a widely ramified conspiracy with his family
must have been an experience of *primal* horror, for while I
know that Roithamer was always in earnest about everything
in his mind, though the people around him could never quite
believe it, his ideas as also his feelings were always most
earnest and most serious, his ideas and feelings always had to
be in full accord with his existence, otherwise it would have
been simply impossible for him to go on, to keep going, they,
beginning with his closest kin who, in Altensam, probably
never could think or would think so, namely that he would
actually carry out his ideas, yet he had carried them out in his
will just as in his life, all his life had been a carrying out of his
ideas in reality. The sale of Altensam, I thought, would be no
easy task for the notary from Schwanenstadt, who could not
sell for less than a certain minimum, while being an open
target for all sorts of harassment from, first and foremost,
Roithamer's brothers. What would Roithamer's parents, especially his father, have said of their middle son selling Altensam
through a notary, I wondered, looking out the window down
at the raging Aurach, and then: but the father in particular
must surely have taken into account that to leave Altensam to
his middle son meant the end of Altensam, for old Roithamer
of course knew full well what manner of man his middle son
was, and I firmly believe, I thought, that when old Roithamer
left Altensam to his middle son, he knew that he had thereby
legalized the end of Altensam, for old Roithamer probably
knew or at least felt or must have seen or felt or known that

Altensam's time had come, that these times are no longer right
for the likes of Altensam, and he may have thought, I'm
leaving Altensam to my middle son, who has the least use of
anybody for Altensam, and so I can be sure that he, my middle
son, will make an end of Altensam and that, in whatever way
he does it, it will be over with. On the other hand, no one can
expect a man who inherits something he doesn't want to
inherit, doesn't want to own, to preserve this inheritance he
didn't want in the first place, the logical thing is for him to get
rid of this inheritance and Roithamer did get rid of his Altensam inheritance, he got rid of it in his own characteristic way,
namely by ordering that the proceeds from the sale of Altensam should go to aid ex-convicts on their release from prison.
Quite possibly, I suddenly thought as I stood at the attic
window, he had gone to Austria and to Altensam already
determined to kill himself, but there is no evidence for such an
assumption, none, the fact is that he meant to go straight back
to England immediately after his sister's funeral, without any
detours whatsoever, not by way of South Tyrol, nor France
nor Belgium, but straight back to Cambridge, I can still hear
him saying *by plunging at once back into work I shall save myself
from this worst of misfortunes,* this is word for word what he said,
I believe it was his last spoken statement to me, I'd accompanied him to the station, he traveled as always by rail and ship
because he shrank from setting foot in an airplane, loathed it,
in fact, for myself I'd intended to spend the brief interval, so I
thought, of his absence, on correcting a paper of my own, but
was distracted by a peculiar uneasiness which I could find no
way of understanding, from doing this, and went instead to
Reading to visit a mutual friend, a teacher, who was busy with
the construction of some machine, what kind of a machine it
was I don't know to this day, even though I had been briefed
on this construction by its constructor for years now, nor did
Roithamer know what kind of machine this Reading machine,
as we called it, was, anyway I spent two days in Reading

waiting for news from Roithamer, we had agreed that he would send me word every second day, what I mainly wanted to hear was when he would be coming back, but there was no word at all for fourteen days, then suddenly there was a message, not from Altensam but from Hoeller, that Roithamer was dead, I left for Austria that same day, at home they told me all about Roithamer's suicide, he had hanged himself in the aforementioned clearing between my father's house and Altensam. Meanwhile Roithamer, who had wished to be buried in the village graveyard, not up in Altensam, that is, but in our village graveyard in Stocket, had been buried. My parents gave me a full account of the funeral, and later on I heard about it from Hoeller too. I made a brief visit to Altensam to see Roithamer's brothers but there was no one in Altensam, at least I thought there was no one home since all the window shutters were closed and nothing stirred, which incidentally suited me very well, because now I would be able to say that I had been to Altensam after my friend's death to look up his brothers, but nobody was home. Actually Roithamer's death, his suicide so soon after the death of his and their sister, must have come as a severe shock to those left in Altensam, and I supposed that they had all left Altensam for once, for a long time, at least until things settled down and the problems arising first from the sister's and then the brother's death would be solved. When I got there, Altensam actually looked extinct to me, as if everything in Altensam were dead. I had also gone to the cemetery in Stocket, it was a simple grave, a few wreaths, a few flowers. Roithamer had once told me that he wanted only a simple wooden cross. Several days went by as I grew more and more depressed, with absolutely nothing to do, I wandered forlornly about the landscape that suddenly looked all empty and drained of any meaning to me. I had visited various people whom I usually visited every time I came home from England, but none of these people meant anything to me any longer. The nights I spent lying awake in

bed without even any need to go back to England, what was I
to do in England with Roithamer no longer there. The nights
were absolutely horrible. There were times when I got up and
went to the window when I came close to doing away with
myself. But in the morning my head was always clear again.
Toward noon I'd be depressed again, locked into my mood of
growing despair. I didn't know whether to go back to England
or not, suppose I look for something to do here in Austria,
perhaps a lectureship at nearby Salzburg University. Just a lot
of crazy notions. Whenever I tried to read the books from my
father's library, I soon broke off reading every time. They said
that Roithamer had willed me his papers. Everything seemed
to me intent upon my destruction. I escaped to my father's
shack in the mountains. There I suddenly fell sick. Pure
chance, I thought, still staring down into the Aurach from my
window, that they found me up there. Most likely, I thought,
suddenly conscious again that I was here in Hoeller's garret,
most likely I shall go back to England. Then I paced back and
forth in Hoeller's garret. Suddenly the mere idea of going back
to England alone and without Roithamer felt horrible. I sat
down at first on the chair beside the door, then got up and sat
down at the desk. I took the yellow paper rose out of the top
drawer and held it up to the light that had ceased to be a light,
the twilight had already darkened everything, soon it will be
pitch-dark, I thought, and laid the yellow paper rose back in
the drawer. Was I right in going from the hospital, not to my
parents' house, but to Hoeller's garret, I thought, and I kept
going over it in my mind how deeply my parents' feelings
would be hurt when they found that I left the hospital and
went directly to the Aurach and into Hoeller's house. Even
though they like Hoeller, I thought, they probably still won't
understand my going to Hoeller instead of to them. My father
visits the Hoellers often, as a child I used to go along when he
visited the Hoellers in their old house, the one on the lower
Aurach which Hoeller suddenly sold in order to build the new

house with the proceeds, plus a hefty bank loan. He had sold
the old house on condition that, though the new owners had
moved in long since, he and his family could stay in it another
two years, or only as long as he needed to build the new house
he had designed. The whole thing had been Roithamer's inspiration for his Cone, Roithamer had quite unconsciously, as I
now know, modeled his own plans and their execution for his
Cone on Hoeller's plans for Hoeller's house and the building
and finishing of Hoeller's house. Hoeller, given his circumstances, had needed four years to plan and build and finish his
house, while Roithamer had needed six years to plan and build
and finish the Cone for his sister. If Hoeller had not built his
house, the idea of building would probably never have entered
Roithamer's head and so today there would be no Cone, that
unique instance in Europe of a cone built as a habitation, in the
middle of the Kobernausser forest. But Hoeller's procedure
had been the same as Roithamer's, I thought, the one built
himself a house ideal for his purposes, the other an ideal cone,
as he believed, for his sister. On the one hand I thought: what
audacity for Roithamer to build that Cone, on the other hand:
what audacity for Hoeller to build his house in the Aurach
gorge. After all, I thought, it is right here in Hoeller's garret
that the idea of building the Cone was worked out, so the
Cone unquestionably comes from Hoeller's house, from
Hoeller's garret. I had never yet been more conscious of this
fact than at this moment, when I was summoned to come
down to supper with the Hoeller family, by three brief knocks
on the ceiling, that is, the attic floor, from below, with a hazel
stick. I put on my jacket and went down at once. Hoeller and
the children were already seated at the table, on which a large
stoneware bowl full of dumplings was steaming, I could sit on
the window side of the table, where I had a comfortable view
of everything in the room which happened to be directly
under the garret, conversely I was being most attentively
watched by the Hoeller children and by Hoeller and his wife,

each and every one had a stoneware plate and a fork in front of him, Hoeller's wife had served a boiled smoked ham and put a pitcher of cider on the table. She sat down opposite me. She was the daughter of a roadworker from Steinbach on the Atterlake, raised, accordingly, in the humblest circumstances, dressed according to the Aurach valley custom, about thirty-six or thirty-eight years old, no more, and quietly took care of her family along fixed guidelines that had been in effect here for hundreds of years. Who, I'd wondered, will be the first to start eating, and it was Hoeller who started and invited me to start eating, then the children helped themselves and lastly Hoeller's wife whom I have never yet heard speaking a single word in all this time I have now been in Hoeller's house, she was the most self-effacing woman, self-effacing like all these women rescued from the worst poverty by the men who married them, always the daughters of roadmenders and woodcutters, sawmill workers or dirt farmers, taciturn women always absorbed in caring for their own families in a daily round of always the same chores, bed-making, cooking, farm-yard chores and so on, women who never argued and whose matter-of-course attachment to their husbands and children was such as has already become unimaginable in a major part of our world today, but here along the Aurach we still had the same conditions and therefore the same relationships and therefore the same circumstances as existed two hundred or four hundred years ago, nature hadn't changed and so the people in their natural setting were still the same, with all their malevolence and frightful fecundity, we have here a breed of men, I thought, actually the same breed we had at the dawn of history, progress has passed them by, they're bone ignorant, with only a dim intuitive sense of everything which keeps them bound in trust to nature, a bond that, dangerous and painful as it may be, nevertheless guarantees their survival, and to which they have totally surrendered themselves, like their parents and grandparents and great-grandparents, because they never had an alternative, once born they had to cope with their native situation, circumstances, conditions, which are already unimaginable to the modern mind, and they did cope; if ever they bucked against it, if ever the discrepancy between their world and today's world flashed on their minds, it was only for the briefest moment, after which they submitted again to the rules that have remained the same as they were half a millennium ago, and whatever they found incomprehensible when they thought about it, the Church made comprehensible to them, as it does wherever it is still influential. This woman had always been reserve personified, never a loud word, never the first to speak, everything in and about her was oriented toward taking care of things around her, she took care of her children, her husband, and her and her husband's and her children's house and the garden and the riverbank and everything under her care was always in order and, depending on the season, always kept in yellow or blue or red or white colors by her special love for flowers and plants, probably always her secret and surest refuge. All of Hoeller's house was kept clean, though not oppressively clean, by this woman who scrubbed the floor boards regularly once a week with cold water, no spiderwebs on the walls, everything white, the few sticks of furniture, part of Hoeller's inheritance from his parents, not hers, who'd had nothing, the whole house filled with an aroma characteristic of Hoeller's house from the foods stored here and there, apples and pears atop the wardrobe or under the beds, it was an aroma I'd suddenly find myself breathing in often, sometimes on a street in the middle of London, and identifying as the Hoeller house aroma, all of a sudden there was this aroma, no matter where I happened to be, but at such moments I was always very far away from Hoeller's house, abroad mostly, and it would start me off thinking about my so-called homeland and the things of home, so-called, seeing the images of home, for a longer or shorter time, depending on my state of mind or emotional state or both together, which these memories made bearable again. Roithamer too once told me that the aroma of Hoeller's house would suddenly remind him of the Aurach and Hoeller's house and Hoeller's family and consequently of Altensam, and that this aroma had very often brought him back to life. Hoeller's wife looked older than her years, what with taking a major part in building their house while at the same time taking care of the children born not long before they began building, all the worry about *whether the house would be any good,* as Hoeller once said, plus the worries about financing the house, all these inroads on her health had caused Hoeller's wife to age rapidly, though in an incredibly attractive way. Watching this woman I could see how very comfortable Roithamer must have felt here in Hoeller's rooms and up there in the garret, whenever he arrived from somewhere, anywhere, even from England, here at the Aurach and in Hoeller's house and in Hoeller's garret, coming out of the cold into a haven where there was someone who actually had so soothing an effect on a man as Hoeller's wife did, under such conditions he could soon recover what he had lost, his love of life and, consequently, his love of work. The Hoeller children were well brought up by their parents, they were as unspoiled and open to everything as one might wish, incidentally I had noticed immediately that the girl took more after her father, the son more after his mother, what it was I didn't know, they just reached up to their parents' shoulders in height, they were full of curiosity and watching me all the time, they seemed wholly intent upon the new man so suddenly among them, they ate and drank exactly like their parents and were, while they ate, just as silent as their parents. They too would never have said a word to me unless I encouraged them, just like their mother, and for the longest time I found it impossible, for whatever reason, to say anything to the children, or to Hoeller's wife, I probably wanted the experience of this meal taken in absolute silence to have its effect on me, I should have said something to Hoeller's wife or to the children right at the start, I thought, but I said nothing and they did not dare to say anything, because Hoeller had not encouraged them to speak, Hoeller had come in from his workshop, had washed his hands and had sat down at the table, as I saw him doing when I walked in, the children were already seated at the table when I came in and was invited by Hoeller, not by his wife, to take the window seat from which I had the best view of the whole room and everything going on in it, this seat was probably Roithamer's seat too, I thought, knowing Roithamer as I do, this very seat where I have just sat down must have been his seat, how often he had told me about the meals in Hoeller's family room, *suddenly not reported but told,* it was the sort of thing that made a story, not a report, he told me how these meals were conducted, always the same way, always in silence, just as it was now in my experience, again I compared Roithamer's story with my own observations made just now, and again Roithamer's stories (about mealtime in Hoeller's family room) and my observations coincided, and I thought that Roithamer always sat like this with his back to the wall in every room, it was characteristic of him, the moment he entered a room he looked for a seat where his back would be to the wall and never sat anywhere but where he could have his back to the wall and keep his eye on the whole room, I also had the same habit, I had not picked it up from Roithamer, this tendency always to sit back-to-the-wall especially in restaurants or coffee shops had been characteristic of me always and long before I noticed it in Roithamer, so I was now thinking that this window seat facing the door, opposite Hoeller's wife, would have been the appropriate choice for Roithamer and I wanted to ask whether Roithamer had also sat where I had sat down, but I didn't ask, the time for such a question had not yet come, everything in the room was already, at this time, against such a question and so I did not pose that question, nor any of the other questions that had suddenly arisen in my mind, I ate and drank and watched and was watched and I mean I was watched even if not openly watched, the children for example were watching me every minute even when they did not look at me directly, just as Hoeller's wife was watching me every minute even though she did not look at me, she looked down at the table and watched me and Hoeller did exactly the same. Conversation at meal-times is unknown in these homes, I thought, though just now it was probably my doing that no one said anything, all I had to do was to say something and they would speak up too, but the fact that they were all eating and drinking in silence and that this eating and drinking in silence could be prolonged by my own silence made me go on eating and drinking as silently as they, they were all waiting for a word from me, I thought, but I said not a word. One by one I rediscovered all the things I had seen the last time I was in Hoeller's family room, years ago, with Roithamer. Suddenly I heard the Aurach and I thought how all this time I'd believed there was a perfect silence in Hoeller's family room, while in fact one always hears the roaring Aurach here, even I had grown so accustomed to the incessant noise, especially loud at this particular spot in the Aurach gorge, that after a certain point I had ceased to notice it, so that I believed, while actually surrounded by the thunderous roar of the Aurach in the Aurach gorge, that here was perfect quiet, because I no longer heard the incessant roar of the Aurach, just as the Hoellers no longer hear it, except once in a while, when they suddenly become aware of it again, they hear it all the time without a break and because of that they no longer hear it, only for moments, when they think of it, just as I had ceased to hear it, although the most striking feature of the Hoeller house is undoubtedly the roaring of the Aurach, the arriving and the arrived are totally enclosed in this roar, actually it is always hard to communicate with those who live there, one has to scream to be heard, yet everyone gets used to it very quickly, probably because the Aurach roar is so deafening, and then it may be quite soon that one perceives as perfect stillness what is actually in uproar, as I have just experienced it myself. People passing by Hoeller's house wonder how anyone can stand the uproar of the Aurach torrent, sure that no one can, they don't realize that the hearing and then the whole being of anyone living in the midst of such an uproar gets used to the fact of living in such an uproar. Hoeller didn't mind building his house in the midst of this uproar, he did it deliberately in fact, *I am building my house right into the Aurach uproar*, he once said to Roithamer, who couldn't see how he could do such a thing, yet Hoeller could have done no better thing, I can see that the building of Hoeller's house and everything involved turned out successfully. It is precisely the roaring of the Aurach which attracts me, or at least the roaring of the Aurach *also* attracts me, Roithamer once said, this roaring of the Aurach torrent, when I am in Hoeller's garret, absolutely fascinates me. So it hadn't been perfectly quiet in the room, as I had been thinking all this time, but actually very noisy because of the roaring of the Aurach, to which I had, however, already become accustomed during my several hours' stay in Hoeller's house. How else could the Hoellers sleep at night, hearing that uproar, they get used to the uproar and fall asleep and wake up and no longer hear the uproar of the Aurach at all. Houses on the banks of torrential rivers are absolutely fascinating, Roithamer had once said, of course the people in them live in constant anxiety of being wiped out by such a flood, from one minute to the next, everyone knows that even the smallest mountain streams may, under the right circumstances, especially when the high snow melts in spring or during those long-lasting storms in the fall, turn into enormous floods sweeping with them everything in their path. Every year we read or hear about rampaging rivers that have swept away many houses with their inhabitants. But Hoeller had so constructed his house, Roithamer said, that it could not be swept away, it is so situated that under no circumstances can it even be affected by the Aurach, he, Hoeller, had constructed his house at the Aurach gorge so that it was *immune* to all the violence of nature, the very idea of building a house at the most dangerous place on the Aurach, at the Aurach gorge, where no one would ever have built a house for himself, that idea had given Hoeller no peace, he kept thinking that's where I must build my house, where no one else would build himself a house, right there, in the Aurach gorge, which everyone fears, that's where I'll build my house, I'll build it right in there, and he naturally opened himself up to the greatest opposition, his persistence and intransigence in pursuing his plan, setting his house in the Aurach gorge just where the roar of the torrent is at its loudest and where the danger of being swept away and totally wiped out one day, lock, stock, and barrel, by the floods, is the greatest, Roithamer said, made Hoeller a laughingstock everywhere he went, but he didn't give up his plan and he went on with his building and finished it. Today anyone can see and say that Hoeller's house, built the way it is and placed where it is, can't be swept away by the Aurach, Hoeller says. Yet the general mistrustfulness still lingers. Anyway Hoeller believes that his house can't be swept away and can't be destroyed by a mud slide (Roithamer). That it's the first house on the Aurach that can never be swept away by the Aurach and be destroyed by a mud slide brought on by catastrophic weather because, Roithamer said, all the houses hitherto built on the Aurach ended up being swept away by the Aurach or destroyed by a mud slide coming down the Aurach valley, again and again the Aurach valley people have built their houses by the Aurach and again and again these houses have been swept away by the rampaging Aurach, an Aurach gone suddenly crazy, usually in the night, and they've been destroyed in mud slides, but none of this ever prevented these Aurach valley people from building their houses by the Aurach again and again, however it's a fact that Hoeller's house is really the first, Roithamer once said, that can never be swept away by the rampaging Aurach and destroyed by a mud slide, because it was conceived and designed and built in full awareness of everything involved in the rising and the turbulence of the Aurach and all the destructive possibilities of the mud slides, and by a man like Hoeller at that, a man who built his house by the Aurach only because he is certain that this house of his cannot be swept away or destroyed and who took four years in all to design and build his house with all these destructive possibilities well in mind. Though Roithamer was still far from having conceived even the idea of building his Cone, he was already fascinated by the building of Hoeller's house and by the manner in which Hoeller had personally designed and created the house, unbeknownst to him as yet the idea of building the Cone for his sister had already been born inside him, even before the actual building of the Cone for his sister, and in the middle of the Kobernausser forest at that, existed even as a gleam in his conscious mind, his witnessing of Hoeller's art in building, and Hoeller's work on his house in the Aurach gorge must certainly be rated as an art, Roithamer said, had long since started him thinking about the Cone, sparked the idea of building the Cone, and this idea, to build the Cone and to build it, actualize it, in the Kobernausser forest, came to him in Hoeller's house, it was in Hoeller's house that Roithamer had decided, unconsciously at first, but then suddenly inspired by the idea of building the Cone, he reached the fully conscious decision of building the Cone, after watching Hoeller building his house, seeing the progressive stages of that project, in the Aurach gorge, Roithamer decided to confront such a project himself and to build something that so far, as Hoeller had also felt, no one before him had ever built (Roithamer), Roithamer's constant watching of Hoeller's building project had effected the creation of the Cone in Roithamer, at first in his head, then on paper, on hundreds, on thousands of papers, then at last in reality, because he, Roithamer, was the kind of man who had to create a reality, always a reality, out of what he had at first only imagined, to make it a fact, just as Hoeller had to turn into a fact the habitation he had at first only imagined for himself in the Aurach gorge, all that preparatory work for Roithamer's Cone had in reality been done, as I now saw clearly, by Hoeller when he decided to build himself a house in the Aurach gorge, suddenly to sell the old house he had inherited from his parents and build himself the new one in the Aurach gorge with the proceeds plus some bank loans and the strength of his determination and his actual force of mind, he himself, Hoeller, had been hesitant at first in *daring* to tackle his project, but then he'd hastened with all the more energy to get it *done*. Like all country folk he, Hoeller, had acquired the basics of building by constantly watching building operations from childhood on, but had expanded his knowledge, once he had decided to build on his own, by private studies and reading of the technical literature, and had managed to perfect himself, up to a point, in the art of building himself a house to live in, basically it was the same process as the one followed later on by Roithamer, that sudden concentration of all his forces in Roithamer, the same Hoeller had been the first to experience, on the building of his work of art, with all the possibilities of expanding his knowledge of the art of building, of steadily developing and perfecting it, this total concentration on building in Hoeller had probably fascinated Roithamer years before his own decision to build the Cone, just as he'd always been highly interested, even absorbed, as I know, in building, the art of building, especially the art of building homes. But whether Roithamer knew that Hoeller had been both cause and model for his own building art, I don't know, even though Roithamer was always talking about Hoeller's building activity, meaning he always talked of it with the greatest respect, he was quite possibly not at all aware that Hoeller and Hoeller's building activity was the cause of his own building activity, that he, Roithamer, might never have thought of building anything without Hoeller and Hoeller's decision to build himself a house in the Aurach gorge. But just as Hoeller had wanted to build something special, a home, the contrary of what everybody else did, something contrary to all the precepts and all the concepts of the others, contrary to their reason, and in the most dangerous spot besides, something to make their eyes pop, Roithamer also wanted to build something special, something different from all the others, a cone, meaning a cone-to-live-in for his sister, and to top it off, as they said, inhuman in scale, in inhuman surroundings, at an inhuman location, namely in the middle of the Kobernausser forest. They both proceeded in the same way, each seeking to realize himself by means of what they both believed to be, Roithamer as well as Hoeller, and both achieved, an unusual deed in building a unique work of art, each in his own style. It was a good half hour before I broke the silence in which the Hoeller family had been sitting at table watching me without letup, to say that I thought Roithamer had hit on the idea of building the Cone while watching the Hoellers' house being built. Since neither Hoeller nor his wife had anything to say to my remark, I fell silent again thinking that I was right, that everything in Hoeller's house proved to me that Roithamer had been motivated to build his Cone by the building of Hoeller's house, the briefest stay in Hoeller's house was enough to confirm this supposition of mine, but this supposition had never yet been so clearly confirmed as it was while I had been sitting at table with the Hoellers considering the circumstances that had led to the building of Roithamer's Cone, as they had led to the building of Hoeller's house. Hoeller had to build his house in the Aurach gorge, considering all (his) circumstances, Roithamer had to build his Cone in the middle of the Kobernausser forest, all (his) circumstances considered. And in fact everything in Hoeller's house, I thought, twist and turn it how you will, is original, just as everything in and about Roithamer's Cone is original, the more closely you study it, consider it, observe, check and recheck every detail, the more absolutely original it must be called. And so, I thought, Roithamer had always sat here at this table, as I was sitting here now, in Hoeller's family room with Hoeller's family in the evening, at noon Roithamer was on his own, as I happen to know, he ate hardly anything at noon, a mouthful of clear cold water, a piece of bread at the most, were enough for him, but in the evening, exhausted from his work, he could indulge himself in a little contact with the Hoellers, in their company, he could go down to their family room to share their meal with them, it isn't every day that a man like Roithamer, incessantly preoccupied with his kind of work, can afford to have such contact with people like the Hoellers, not just any time, but only at quite definite times and at quite regular intervals, such as in the evenings, after he had quite exhausted himself up in Hoeller's garret, and couldn't have gone on, not one moment longer, in Hoeller's garret, Mrs. Hoeller's three or four knocks on the ceiling, viz. the attic floor, with the hazel stick, were actually always his signal for dropping his work and getting to his feet and going down to the Hoeller family room, I know about this routine and I can imagine that Roithamer greatly valued their adherence to this routine as a ritual, Hoeller's wife knocking three or four times on the ceiling, viz. the attic floor, which Roithamer had often told me about in England, had been his signal for dropping his work, and Hoeller's wife, Roithamer said, always timed these knocks exactly right, not a moment too soon and not a moment too late. He, Roithamer, had never told Hoeller's wife that she always knocked at the right moment, but she must have assumed that it always was the right moment because it was never followed by any kind of protest on Roithamer's part. Not that Hoeller's wife and I had ever come to any special understanding about it, but I had instantly grasped that her knocks on the ceiling, viz. the attic floor, meant that supper was ready and that she expected me to come down and join them at the table. In Hoeller's workshop the noise made by the chamfer bit Hoeller was probably using also stopped immediately after the knocking, a sign that Hoeller too was stopping work and coming in to supper from his workshop. But even had I not been noticing and observing all this for myself, Roithamer had described it all to me, the whole process, how pleased he had been at her punctuality every time Hoeller's wife knocked with her hazel stick, which meant that he had apparently never considered her knocking a disturbance, it often came as a liberation from some blind alley he had constructed, speculated, thought himself into, andsoforth. The Hoellers, I thought, were probably behaving toward me now as they had behaved toward Roithamer, the moment I had moved into Hoeller's garret I had become locked into the mechanism of their behavior with Roithamer, everyone who now lives in Hoeller's garret after Roithamer is probably locked into the same behavior mechanism that functioned for Roithamer, and now it is I who live in Hoeller's garret, though there would probably be others living there after me, even if Hoeller denies it, I thought, the sort of people suitable for Hoeller's garret, and it seemed to me that the Hoellers regarded me as nothing else than the man who had taken Roithamer's place. Most of all it was from the behavior of Hoeller's children at table that I immediately deduced that they thought they had to behave toward me as they had behaved toward Roithamer. Suddenly I'd discovered on the wall opposite, near the door, a death notice on which I could read Roithamer's name, all the way across the room, it was a big room, I could read Roithamer's name. Everything in this room and in this house, I thought, still shows the impact of Roithamer's suicide, which was of course classified by everyone, Hoeller included, as the result of *mental confusion,* so-called, and I thought that everyone in Hoeller's house still behaves, such a long time after Roithamer's death, as if Roithamer were still among them. To the left of the door in the wall opposite the window is where they, the Hoellers, had pinned Roithamer's death notice, and to the right of the door, the death notice of Roithamer's sister. For a long time to come the mood throughout the whole valley will probably be determined by these two dead people, I thought, and most noticeably in Hoeller's house with which these two, each in his or her own way, had such strong ties, the one by actually having lived here, in fact until his own violent death, the other as his sister, because she was always welcome in Hoeller's house and especially popular with Hoeller's children, with whom she had made friends. While Roithamer had been drawn to Hoeller, originally, by Hoeller having been his schoolmate, and subsequently by Hoeller's idea of building his house in the Aurach gorge and Roithamer's sudden clear perception, derived from this building plan, of the kinship between himself and Hoeller, whose inward and outward simplicity had always been attractive to Roithamer, *Hoeller's house as a building, in itself,* which had interested Roithamer so much that he often took part all day long, for weeks on end, in the building of Hoeller's house, it was not in Altensam he spent his vacations from England but taking part in the building of Hoeller's house, then it was, for Roithamer's sister, Hoeller's children for whose sake she often visited the Hoellers, at Christmas or Easter, Roithamer's sister always brought Hoeller's children presents particularly suited to these children, from time to time she would buy them completely new outfits and take them on trips to the lakes or even into town. The Aurach gorge with Hoeller's house, so perfectly, because so functionally, adapted to the Aurach gorge, had always been the destination, in their last years, of these two people whose faces I now saw pictured on those death notices on the wall opposite me, I thought, and I couldn't take it in that the deaths of those two should have come so quickly and, after all, so unexpectedly, plunging everything in the Aurach valley into such gloom as had certainly been prevalent here for some time now, ever since the

death of those two. The Hoellers had always had a tender spot
in their hearts, as I know, for the two Roithamers, as they most
affectionately referred to the now dead brother and sister, who
were so different from their brothers and parents, they had
never looked down on the simple inhabitants of the valley and
the villages below Altensam, as their birth might have entitled
them to do, as the people hereabouts put it, but had rather,
from earliest childhood on, felt more kinship with them than
with their own family, the two Roithamers had felt closer to
the Hoellers than to their own brothers, their own parents, and
they had never made a mystery of it. Whenever they had a
moment they'd used it, as I've said, to escape from Altensam
and go down to the valley, to go down there was all they ever
wanted, and always preferably to the Hoellers. It was owing to
those two that in earlier days, when they were still children,
Hoeller's house was always filled with life, first the old house
and then the new-built Hoeller house, the two young Roithamers had always seen to it that the rather overburdened and
drab life of the Hoellers in the Aurach valley, which tended by
nature to a certain even, depressing grayness, was brightened
up and so made bearable again, every time. By their mere
presence, being basically amusing people, Roithamer and his
sister had often rescued the Hoellers from one of their usual
states of despair, as young people almost always will. They
owed much to the two Roithamers just as, conversely, the two
Roithamers owed much to the Hoellers. This catastrophe, I
suddenly said when we had all finished eating, need not have
happened, meaning the death of the sister and the suicide of
the brother, though what I had been thinking just then was
that everything had led directly to this catastrophe and that
actually it had to happen. Because my remark that Roithamer
had probably got the idea of building the Cone from Hoeller's
building his home in the Aurach gorge had brought no reply,
whether in agreement or disagreement, for such a long time,
from the Hoellers, I felt blocked about saying anything else,

yet it was after all impossible to keep sitting in silence at table
with the Hoellers, merely eyeing the family room, and anyway
I felt that the Hoellers were waiting for me to come up with
something, something to say, but I, looking at those death
notices on the wall opposite, was not about to come up with
another remark for them, it was still possible, I thought, that
even after so long a pause Hoeller might have something to say
in response to my previous remark or even that Hoeller's wife,
who'd been most attentive toward me, might say something,
but what really puzzled me was that the children, who were
probably not always so quiet and whom I knew to be not at all
tongue-tied, hadn't a word to say, though they had long since
finished eating and drinking and were now sitting there, el-
bows on the table, poised as if only waiting for their father to
give the signal to rise, so they could jump up and run out of
the room. The darkness outside was now total, suddenly I
heard the roaring of the Aurach again, fatigue couldn't have
been the only reason for Hoeller's not talking, so I tried again
to get a conversation going by making a second remark. Everything's so very quiet now in Altensam, I said, after the death of
our friend Roithamer's sister and after his own death, nothing
but closed blinds, I said, locked gates, everything makes it look
like a house of death, the whole valley has been darkened even
more under the impact of the two Roithamers' deaths, wherever you go, that pervasive silence, this speechless wait-and-
see attitude of all the people, which simply must be linked
with the deaths of the two Roithamers, it was foreseeable,
meaning from a certain point in time onward, I said, whereupon they suddenly all listened to me even more attentively
than before, and I said that Roithamer's sister had been
doomed, that splendid creature, who simply couldn't bear the
fact of the Cone, that her brother had made his idea come true,
to build the Cone for her, meaning *for her alone and particularly
in the middle of the Kobernausser forest,* Roithamer himself had
fully realized, when he came back to England after the Cone

was finished and presented to his sister, that the perfected Cone could not actually be the greatest, in fact the supreme happiness for her, as he had believed, could have believed, but that it actually meant her death, because there can be no doubt whatsoever that Roithamer's sister was destroyed by the creation of the perfect Cone, from the moment the Cone was finished, when it was presented to her, as I recapitulated the story for the Hoellers, she was suddenly a different person, at that moment she fell prey to a terminal disease, to this day no one knows what this terminal disease was, people like Roithamer's sister tend to go suddenly into a decline, all at once at a certain moment in their lives, a moment naturally favorable to such a terminal disease, and they can then be seen slowly *sinking deeper into sickness,* developing a pathological eccentricity, little by little falling victim to this disease quite in accordance with their nature, because in reality, so I said to the Hoellers, Roithamer's sister never believed that her brother could make his idea of building the Cone for her come true, she had always considered it a crazy, an unrealizable idea, but then she had underestimated her brother's abilities and his toughness and his unyielding nature, though she loved her brother above all others, and so she had deceived herself about her own brother, who was closer to her than anybody. Roithamer, I told the Hoellers, was a man who wouldn't let anything in the world deter him from whatever aim he had once set his mind on, nor was he a dreamer, because he was every inch a scientist, as well as being consistent and incorruptible in every way, he was a *natural scientist* and the very fact that he taught at an English university made him every inch a realist, I myself, I told the Hoellers, had never in my life met a man with a more down-to-earth head on his shoulders, no character more precise in his thinking and in making his will prevail. Furthermore, Roithamer so deeply knew his sister, and never ceased from deeply understanding her *anew,* that it was unimaginable that he should not have foreseen the effect upon her of his finishing the Cone and presenting the Cone to her. A man of such equally far-ranging and deep vision should not have overlooked this, that perfecting and presenting the Cone to his sister must result in her death. The fact is that Roithamer's sister had consistently refused to believe *even in the planning of the idea of the Cone, not to mention the actual realization and completion of it,* had in fact, as the Hoellers knew, always refused to visit the site of the Cone while building was in progress, although her brother had kept inviting her to visit the site, to *habituate* herself to it, as it were; he had tried to visit the site in the middle of the Kobernausser forest with her several times a year, but he never prevailed upon his sister to come because, I now told the Hoellers, she was afraid, afraid in all kinds of ways, not only with respect to the Cone but afraid for her brother, meaning that she felt a growing fear that was becoming nearly unbearable for her, as I know, the ways in which building the Cone was affecting her brother, inwardly and outwardly, caused her increasing anguish through a growing suspicion that the project would undermine his health and could, in the end, because of everything involved with the Cone, *kill* him, and now I see, as I said to the Hoellers, that the Cone has in fact destroyed them both, first the sister and shortly thereafter the brother. All this I said while staring fixedly at the two death notices on the wall opposite, and my listeners at the still uncleared table in the Hoeller family room were most attentive. From a certain unforeseeable moment on, young men, mostly those getting on toward thirty-five, tend to push an idea, and they push that idea so far until they have made it a reality and they themselves have been killed by this idea-turned-reality, I said. I see now, I said, that Roithamer's life, his entire existence, had aimed at nothing but this creation of the Cone, everyone has an idea that kills him in the end, an idea that surfaces inside him and haunts him and that sooner or later—always under extreme tension—wipes him out, destroys him. *Natural science or so-called natural science* (Roithamer's words), I told the Hoellers, had served as a preparation for this idea, everything in his life had served only as a preparation for the idea of building the Cone, and then the outward spur for building and realizing the Cone had been Hoeller's building of his house, on the one hand, I said, looking at those death notices on the wall opposite me, the idea of building deliberately in the Aurach gorge, while on the other hand the idea of building right in the middle of the Kobernausser forest, in the one case to assert oneself at last in the teeth of all reason and all accepted usage here in the Aurach gorge, in the other case the same process by other means, but from the same motive, in the middle of the Kobernausser forest. A man has an idea and then, at the critical point sometime in his life, finds another man who, because of his character and because his state of mind answers to that critical turning point in the other man's life, brings that idea to fulfillment, finally perfects it in reality. Such a man with such an idea Roithamer undoubtedly was and he, Roithamer, just as undoubtedly found Hoeller at the critical point in his life, who made the fulfillment of his idea in reality possible, I said. And in the last analysis Roithamer's Cone exhibited some striking characteristics of Hoeller's house, as conversely Hoeller's house did, of Roithamer's Cone. The nature of the case was the same in both. But while Roithamer's Cone had been his destruction, after his idea and his fulfillment of his idea had first, for good measure, killed his sister, Hoeller was still alive, he lived on not only in his idea, as people say about a dead man, a man killed and destroyed like Roithamer by his idea, which he had realized and fulfilled, but Hoeller was living on as an actual living man in his idea and in the realization and the fulfillment of his idea, namely the Hoeller house in the Aurach gorge, and there could be no doubt that Hoeller would go on living for a long time yet because he, Hoeller, unlike Roithamer, was not the kind of man to be killed off and destroyed by his idea andsoforth, no, Hoeller would ultimately be destroyed, like every man, by something else, not by an idea. While I was looking at the death notices, also at Hoeller's wife, who was listening to me, and at the death notices above her head, I was thinking that they were expecting me to tell them, even though they were not asking, they were not saying a word, still not saying a word to ask how this disaster could have come about, but they were expecting from me, as one always expects from a person who is believed to have inside knowledge of something as yet unclear to oneself, believed to know the underlying and deepest reasons for it, an explanation of what they don't know, *cannot* know, waiting for me now to tell them what I know because they believe that I know something, at least much more than they know, because I'd been with Roithamer longer than anybody and on such an intimate footing, as they know, meaning an intense closeness such as is very often regarded by outsiders as a kind of total absorption in the other man, they were waiting for me to explain to them here and now, sitting with them at their table, what was as yet unclear to them, even if it was not at all clear to them what it was that was unclear to them, waiting for me to solve for them a riddle or various riddles concerning Roithamer which they could not solve, because I was equipped like no one else to judge the worth or worthlessness of the various assumptions or suppositions, *because I was,* so they thought, even if they did not say so because they clung stubbornly to their silence, while ever more intently staring at me, believing that they had got me not only into their charge but under their control, *Roithamer's best friend who had the key information,* so they felt it was time to learn from me more about my friend, who had also been Hoeller's friend, more than they knew themselves, that is, but for me it was the other way around, after all, I was hoping to find out more about Roithamer *from them,* especially from Hoeller himself, who must, as I thought, know more than I did at least about Roithamer's final days, about the last fourteen days in his life, since Hoeller had after all spent those last days, if not always in his company, still always in Roithamer's vicinity, perhaps Hoeller even was, in the last analysis, *Roithamer's closest confidant,* I felt that Hoeller must know crucial things about Roithamer which I did not know, and so we were probably each waiting for the other to say something about Roithamer which he himself hadn't known, Hoeller waiting to learn something from me which I didn't know, couldn't know, while I was waiting for Hoeller to tell me something he didn't know, couldn't know, because Hoeller's friendship, his ties with Roithamer were quite as close as mine, the friendship was probably equally intense in both cases, though the friendship was in each case entirely different in kind, because I'm not Hoeller and Hoeller, conversely, isn't me. But in the expectation that we, Hoeller and I, would find out something we didn't know about Roithamer from each other, time passed and soon a whole hour had gone by and Hoeller's wife had meanwhile risen from the table and taken the empty plates out to the kitchen, the children had followed her out, through the kitchen door we were aware of the dishwashing and the children's footbaths, while Hoeller and I remained seated at the table treating each other to a copious silence. The thing was, I didn't want to broach the subject of Hoeller's having been the one who *discovered Roithamer hanging from a tree in the clearing,* not yet, the time to speak of it hadn't quite come, nor did I have any intention to be the first to speak of it, before Hoeller saw fit to broach this delicate and in fact terrible topic. I'd known for a long time, had in fact heard it from one of my hospital visitors, the farmer Pfuster, that Hoeller had found Roithamer in the clearing and *had personally cut him down from the tree with his own hands.* Roithamer had been missing for some time, he could not be found either at Altensam or at Hoeller's house for eight days after his sister's funeral, but both families, the Altensamers and the Hoellers, had assumed that he'd gone back to England without telling anyone, which would have been entirely unlike him, though of course I too was waiting for him there all that time, and without a word from him, despite the fact that we had agreed he would send me word to my Cambridge address every second day, besides, Hoeller should have noticed that Roithamer's things, the clothes he was wearing on his back, that is, were not in the garret and where could he have gone without his clothes, anyway, it ought to have occurred to Hoeller soon enough that Roithamer must have had some mishap, because it certainly was most peculiar that he had gone away without saying good-bye, to anyone, and then those missing clothes, it's true the Altensamers for their part had inquired after Roithamer at Hoeller's but nobody *did* anything, probably because both families, the Hoellers at the Aurach and the Roithamers up at Altensam, had assumed, after all, that Roithamer had long since gone off to England, until Hoeller went once more to Altensam to ask if they knew anything of Roithamer's whereabouts, and this time he, Hoeller, had found Roithamer in the clearing between Stocket and Altensam. Not a word from Hoeller about the fact that he personally had found him, nor did I bring it up, since my arrival that afternoon I had several times avoided pronouncing the word *clearing,* in fact, even though I needed the word *clearing* several times if I was to make myself understood in a matter I had mentioned. But everyone knows of course that it's a shock to come upon a hanged man, and in this case it was, naturally, a terrible shock. While I felt I had a right to find out more about our friend's last days from Hoeller, Hoeller expected to find out more about Roithamer from me, and since both of us kept waiting the whole time for the other to say something, naturally something about our friend Roithamer, we said nothing at all the whole time. I only kept wondering what Hoeller could be thinking about, while Hoeller probably was wondering what I could be thinking about, but in each case it had to be something to do with Roithamer, what else. That this was where he had spent his evenings and, as Hoeller told me, often the whole night, in this room, which was built by Hoeller quite in the style of the old traditional Aurach valley rooms, the floors were made of well-seasoned larch wood planks, so that it was always a pleasure to look at the floor, and Roithamer had often sat here alone till dawn, only listening to the torrential roar of the Aurach, withholding himself from *scientific paperwork*, so as not to slip into taking notes here as well, where the atmosphere was just as favorable to his ideas and his scientific work as it was upstairs in Hoeller's garret, and possibly go on to doing more than taking notes, so that he would succumb to his scientific, his intellectual pursuits even down here in Hoeller's family room which, unlike Hoeller's garret which served Roithamer's intellectual purposes, was meant to serve only eating and drinking purposes, it was enough that he let his intellectual work consume him utterly up in the garret, that he daily exhausted himself mentally up there, down here he had been able to relax, sharing food and drink with the Hoellers, and the children were always sure to divert him, everyone knows that he got along well with the Hoeller children, he knew all their ways, unlike other brain workers who have no idea how to behave with children, Roithamer had excellent rapport with children, as befitted his character, he had been able to spend hours with the Hoeller children in the Hoeller family room, playing with them, telling them stories, fairy tales he'd made up himself, that came to him in the telling, so that their spontaneity made them extraordinarily effective, when the children had to go wash up in the kitchen, or to bed, they always begged and pleaded to be allowed to stay, as all children do, though they could not prevail against the Hoeller child-raising routine, so then Roithamer was left alone with Hoeller at the table and they either fell into conversation or else they did not fall into conversation, it was only when such talk, very often of the simplest descriptive kind, or else of a philosophical kind, came about in the most spontaneous way

that the two men left alone in the room, Hoeller and Roithamer, continued it. Roithamer had often told me about these
conversations. All our talks were always *such as would come
naturally to us,* Roithamer said, and so they thoroughly suited
both him, Roithamer, and Hoeller too. Roithamer spoke mostly of England and of his studies and about the things he knew
of Altensam, and most recently, of course, he spoke of his
preoccupation with the Cone, Hoeller spoke of his work as a
taxidermist, he was the only one for hundreds of kilometers
around, and about all the noteworthy occurrences in the villages as well as, of course, about the building of his house. He,
Roithamer, had kept asking Hoeller, as I know, Why in the
Aurach gorge, of all places? and he, Hoeller, as I also know, to
Roithamer: Why in the middle of the Kobernausser forest, of
all places? These questions *never were answered.* All that Hoeller
had to go on with respect to the middle of the Kobernausser
forest was his intuition, it seems to me, just as Roithamer had
only his intuition with respect to the Aurach gorge question,
just as I have my intuition about it. But Hoeller's building of
his house was not, according to Hoeller himself, comparable to
Roithamer's building of the Cone, to build such a house as his
in the Aurach gorge was simple compared with building such a
cone in the middle of the Kobernausser forest, which was
extremely difficult, a simple head like his own (Hoeller's)
would do for building the house in the Aurach gorge while for
building the Cone a scientific head like Roithamer's was needed. He, Hoeller, had seen the Cone only once after it was
ready, he didn't say, as I and Roithamer did, *finished* (in the
sense of *perfected*), Hoeller always spoke of it as being *done.*
While the Cone was under construction, Hoeller had often
driven with Roithamer into the Kobernausser forest to see
how the construction was progressing, to give his expert opinion as well, for after Hoeller's achievement of his own building
project Roithamer naturally regarded him as an expert, the
only building expert for him, since basically Roithamer had

not engaged anyone else but Hoeller as expert toward the realization of his, Roithamer's, building plans, considering as he did the so-called building experts to be no better than charlatans, incompetents one and all, and perverse exploiters of their helpless clients. He accused all the professional build- ers of messing up and destroying the surface of the earth. Those so-called architects (how he hated the term! as I have mentioned) and all the builders and their minions nowadays do nothing but wreck and ruin the face of the earth, every new building they put up is another crime they commit, a building crime against humanity, he once cried out with much feeling: *every building put up by builders these days is a crime!* And all these crimes can be committed with ease, in fact these criminal builders are actually being encouraged and challenged espe- cially by the governments and their administrators to cover the earth with their perverse cultural filth and to do it in a manner and with a speed that will have the whole surface of the globe choked with these building abominations and building crimes. *Then, when the whole world has been most horribly and tastelessly and criminally cluttered up by them, it will be too late, the face of the earth will be dead. We are helpless against the destruction of our global surface by the architects!* he once exclaimed. If I had assumed that Hoeller and I, once we were alone, left to our- selves, that is, after Hoeller's wife had left the room and taken the children into the kitchen, would soon fall to talking, the continuing silence now that Hoeller's wife had left the room with the children and gone into the kitchen gradually in- creased my uneasiness, suddenly it was no longer enough to just sit and contemplate the room, to keep me there, yet I couldn't go back up to the garret so soon after supper, it was barely half-past five, of course I could have gone up to the garret, no one would have interfered, but I really couldn't on my first evening in the house. The silence between Hoeller and me was probably owing to Hoeller's expectation that I would ask him about his finding Roithamer in the clearing and cutting him down from the tree, because he probably had nothing else in his head, he'd been haunted by it for weeks now, mostly while finding refuge in his work, in his workshop, or busy with his chores behind the house, the kind we see done all the time behind the houses of the Aurach valley, sawing wood, chopping wood, piling logs andsoforth, all of which probably enabled him to bear up better than the inactivity to which the fact of Roithamer's suicide had undoubtedly driven him, but he had been countering this inactivity resulting from the fact of Roithamer's suicide and Hoeller's finding the body in the clearing by keeping himself occupied with constant work, so that he could bear it more easily, as anyone can bear a catastrophe, once it has occurred, by at least seeming to avoid it through keeping busy, no matter which work routine he forces himself into, Hoeller had more ways of finding work in his house than anyone, which is why he got out of bed very early every day, mostly around four in the morning, after this gruesome and truly shattering experience, because he could not shake it off even at night, those endless sleepless nights afterward had weakened him, as anyone could see at once, Hoeller had told me on my arrival that he never spent a peaceful night in his bed, not for a minute, most of the time he paced the floor in the bedroom they all shared, so that the children's sleep was also disturbed by his restless pacing, he would spend half the night staring through the window, down at the raging Aurach, probably harboring terrible thoughts, his wife said, a man like Hoeller, his wife said, could get over such an experience, survive its aftermath, only with the utmost effort, she felt free to express herself like this only because I understood her husband better than anyone. But left to himself and with time on his hands he was the image of despair even when she and the children were present, she felt justified in hoping, she said, that my visit would help her husband to recover gradually from the shock of Roithamer's suicide, especially the fact that her husband had found Roithamer in the clearing and had to cut him down from the tree, she hoped my presence would have a *healing* effect on his depression caused by that shock. I must say that he gave me the impression of a broken man, as he sat at the table with me, staring down at it. It is my duty, I thought, to speak to him now, to say something, anything, to take his mind off Roithamer's suicide and everything involved with that suicide. But what I suddenly came up with was how we, Hoeller, Roithamer and I, used to go to school together, first Roithamer, coming down from Altensam, picked up Hoeller, then me, and the three of us walked together to our grade school in Stocket, in winter with a piece of firewood tied to our leather satchels, every pupil had to bring a piece of firewood to school every day, the children of affluent or rich parents, like Roithamer of Altensam, a piece of hardwood, the poorer and poorest a piece of pine or softwood each, with these pieces of wood brought to school by every pupil the old tile stoves kept the school warm, I said. I looked down at the table, then up at the door opposite me, alternately at the two death notices and then again at Hoeller, and I was determined to continue with what I was saying even though I instantly felt and therefore knew that I should have stopped this recital, that I must not go on with it, but I couldn't stop, it all seemed too significant for me to stop now that I had begun to speak at last, besides I was suddenly aware of the impact on Hoeller of what I was saying, he looked as if he already knew where my reminiscence, this story of our childhood, was going to take us, it was too late for me to stop, and so I said, quite calmly outwardly but inwardly in the greatest excitement, that *the most conspicuous thing about the three of us walking to school together was our taciturnity,* and again I spoke of the firewood we always brought to school in winter, so that the school could be heated with our firewood, the memory of this firewood brought to school by the pupils seemed to me most significant for what I had to say, and I asked several times whether he, Hoeller, also remembered how each of us had always had to bring a piece of firewood to school in the wintertime, and how we always used to make a fire in the old tile stoves of the old grade school with our wood, the rich kids, I reiterated, had to bring *hard*wood, the poorer ones and the poorest could bring softwood, and did he remember that I and he both had always brought softwood, because it was all we were supposed to bring, while Roithamer, as I recall, had to bring not one but actually two pieces of hardwood. Where this order came from, I couldn't remember, probably from the principal's office, but it could have come from the city administration of schools, in any case it was based upon absolutely correct information. You and me one piece of pine or softwood each, I said, Roithamer *two* pieces of hardwood. And I continued my description of our way to school, going to school together had of course been the basis for our friendship, I said, which had become a friendship for life, even though we had often lived for a long time very far apart, our friendship had never been affected by that, regardless of all the ups and downs of history we had already lived through, for example all through the war; on the contrary, the friendship that bound the three of us had deepened from year to year and was, I actually said this too, because I suddenly felt that I must get it all said after that long and finally tormenting silence, I had to get everything said all at once, it was the most beautiful of friendships. And I let myself go so far as to state that such friendships as ours had been, for the three of us, endured beyond death itself. The minute I made this statement I felt embarrassed by it, and Hoeller noticed how painfully embarrassed I *was* to have come out with such a statement even though it was probably quite a natural thought in itself, and so, to put this embarrassment behind me as quickly as possible, I tried to say a great deal quickly, moving purposefully toward my point, suddenly I'd found a way to make up for that overlong silence between us earlier on. It was as though that unbroken silence at table, in

the presence of Hoeller's wife and Hoeller's children, had been
necessary for what I could now say with all the more vehe-
mence and yet vividly as well. Suddenly I no longer had to
hold back anything. I said, putting off a little what I'd primarily meant to say, that my finest memory, and probably
Hoeller's as well, and Roithamer's too, was my memory of our
walks to school together, it was on our way to school that we
had our most intense experiences, I said, when we think of
everything on that way to school over the rocks and through
the woods, along the Aurach, past the mine workers' cottages
and on past Stocket, that is, right through the village, where
we noticed all sorts of things, *things that would determine our
lives,* rich in meanings, already determining the whole shape of
our future and in fact already controlling it, since actually
everything we are today, everything we see and observe and
encounter on its way toward us, is influenced by what we saw
and observed on our way to school then, if it isn't altogether
made up of it, as I actually asserted to Hoeller, after all our
way to school was not simply a way to school, I said, since, to
begin with, we were scared on our way to school, it was an
extremely dangerous way to school, dangerous because it led
only over rocks and through dense woods, along the Aurach
which was dangerous all along the way, and most of the time
on our way to school we were frightened, too, I identified *our
way to school as my way through life,* because our way to school
was from beginning to end comparable, with all its peculiarities, occurrences, possibilities and impossibilities, to the course
of my own life and probably also the course of Hoeller's life,
since the course of our life was after all also always a dangerous course, on which we are bound to be frightened always,
with all its occurrences, peculiarities, possibilities and impossibilities to be faced by us day after day as we go over rocks and
through woods, I said, my childhood is always connected for
me with this walk to school and nothing in my childhood
exists apart from it, there we had all our experiences, the kind

we'd have later on again and again, everything that happened later had in some way already happened on this walk of ours to school, this fear that we often feel today we already felt on our walk to school, these thoughts, closely attached to that fear, they keep coming today, though differently, yet always referring back to the thoughts we had on our walk to school, our way to school, just like our way through life, has always been a *Via Dolorosa* to us, a way of suffering, yet it was always also a *way to every possible discovery and to utmost happiness,* indescribable happiness, I said, did he, Hoeller, also remember our way to school so well, did he remember many thousands and hundreds of thousands of details, sensations, perceptions, feelings, intimations of feelings, those earliest important beginnings of thought on our way to school, for it was then we began to think as we still think today, the kind of precise thinking which has since then become the mechanism of our adult intelligence, I could remember those thousands, hundreds of thousands of weather conditions on our walk to school, abrupt shifts in the weather, I felt them suddenly take place, transforming our way to school from one minute to the next and thereby transforming us inside from one minute to the next, and the incessant changing of colors in the woods and in the Aurach as it tumbled headlong from the woods down to the plain, everything on our way to school had always been changes of color and of temperatures and of our moods, that muggy atmosphere in the summertime that sickened us on our way to school so that we came to be horribly sick later in school; or the cold in winter that we could cope with only by attacking it all along the way to school, we had to counterattack the cold, *stomping* all bundled up and scared through the deep, the deepest snow, *running* through the Aurach gorge where the snow was not quite so high, from one clump of ice to the next, and in school we felt as though we had lost our minds through the effort of making our way to school so that we no longer had the strength to keep up with the lessons. Did he, Hoeller, remember the young teacher who always appeared in a black dress buttoned high to the neck, whom we liked to listen to and whom we loved because she behaved considerately toward us, she was always considerate of us and therefore of our conditions and circumstances, when as a rule people and especially teachers are never considerate, I never again had a teacher who was in the least considerate of me, I said, but this teacher was considerate in every way, took everything about us into consideration, all my life long I never forgot this considerateness in the midst of so much ruthlessness, at the mercy of which life or anyway existence, all human existence, finds itself. Our way to school took its course just as our subsequent life did, I said, with all its passages through darkness, back to light, with all its habits and unexpected coincidences, our way through life like our way to school kept being subjected to abrupt changes of weather, kept following the course of a torrential river always to be feared, for as we always lived in fear on our way to school, fear of falling into the raging Aurach among others, so on our way through life we always lived in extreme fear of falling into this river where we lived, always terrified of this river which is invisible but always torrential and always deadly. However, I said to Hoeller, while we were always suitably dressed for our way to school, we weren't always suitably dressed for our way through life, and I said that, of the three of us, Roithamer had the longest way to go, that he, Hoeller, had the second longest way to go, and I had the shortest way to school, Roithamer had had to clamber down those rock-faces from Altensam all alone on his way to Hoeller, the two of you, I said, Roithamer and you then came to me in Stocket and from Stocket all three of us then went on together to school. So by the time Roithamer met you, I said to Hoeller, he'd already experienced quite a lot, and the two of you had been through quite a lot together by the time you picked me up, all things considered, Roithamer always had the longest way to school, seven kilo-

meters, Hoeller had five kilometers to go, I had three, of course
the Altensamers up there could have put some sort of vehicle
at Roithamer's disposal to take him to school, but it was never
customary for the Altensamers to put a vehicle at the disposal
of their school-age children, and I said that the three other
Roithamer children were at boarding school, our Roithamer
had not been sent to boarding school, by their deliberate
choice Roithamer was the only one not to be sent to boarding
school, the others had spent their entire childhood and adoles-
cence in the cities, in the city boarding schools, while Roithamer attended the village school in Stocket, at his own request, as I know *and* in accordance with his father's wish. This
fact was crucial for Roithamer's life, I said. Then, later on, I
said to Hoeller, the others returned from the cities and stayed
in Altensam, where they are still today, while Roithamer left
home just when they returned, and this departure at the right
moment was decisive for Roithamer's whole development, he
even attended preparatory school in this area, in Gmunden,
the county seat, but never went to a boarding school, nor was
he forcibly sent to a boarding school, Roithamer's wishes with
regard to his so-called schooling were all granted by his parents, and especially by his father, he was not required to enter
a boarding school, in contrast to his siblings, all of whom,
including his sister, were eager from the first to go to boarding
school, they had left Altensam prematurely, I said to Hoeller,
only to return, to return, that is, as complete failures, while
Roithamer, our friend, left Altensam only at the right moment,
the moment of their return, that is, and then went directly to
England, which had always fascinated him, and where he
gradually, but with the greatest assurance, became the man we
knew, I am not classifying Roithamer at this point, because no
classification would hold one hundred percent for him in any
case, but my remark about Roithamer's personality certainly
showed that I hold him in the highest esteem, as Hoeller's
reaction proved. In England Roithamer became the man we

admired, I said, the man whom, as his friends, we still admire today, as a scientist, I said, and as a personality, I had managed at the last possible moment to switch from the word "man" which I already had in mind to the less embarrassing word "personality." It was amazing, every time, how many people go to England early in life, and very often at exactly the right moment, for a chance to develop, and almost all of those who went to England made something of themselves, they became distinguished personalities, at this point I used the expression *distinguished personalities* deliberately, to convince Hoeller, just as Roithamer himself in England became a really distinguished personality, a *so-called distinguished personality*, because every personality is distinguished, I said, but what the world means by a distinguished personality is something else, which is why I now speak of a so-called distinguished personality. Because he went to England at the right moment, in the right, the ideal circumstances, I said. Had the idea of building the Cone not surfaced, he would still be in England today, but his life had to turn out as it has, in fact, turned out, the idea of the Cone brought his life to a new high-point, the highest possible in fact, I now said, the six years he spent on the Cone were undoubtedly the high-point of Roithamer's life, certainly the perfecting of the Cone was. At the moment he had finished, perfected, the Cone, he had to put a period to his own life, with the Cone perfected, Roithamer's existence had come to a close, that's what he felt and that's why he put an end to his life, with the perfecting of the Cone two lives had lost their justification, they had to cease, I said to Hoeller and looked again at the two death notices on the opposite wall to the left and right of the door, the life of Roithamer himself and that of his sister, which he had uncompromisingly bound up with his own life. The time had possibly come now, I thought, to say what I had actually wanted to say before, but had put off saying because it had seemed premature, reverting to our walks to school I tried to test Hoeller's memory, I imagined that Hoeller's memory was as good and as clear as my own, but after all Hoeller is an entirely different kind of man and no two people are the same in any respect, on that assumption I began to remind him of details along our common path to school, beginning with certain characteristic, striking rock formations jutting out into the road, then the less striking, less characteristic ones, then I recalled the odors at certain points along the way, plant odors, earth odors, our path was characterized by constant changes in earth odors and rock odors and plant odors, certain birds' nests, bird swarms, bird species, I kept testing Hoeller's memory in general using objects such as, for example, had been tossed into the Aurach and left lying there by all sorts of passersby, old bicycle parts, cans, boxes, mill wheels, all of which I remembered vividly, I questioned him about remarks I had made frequently and others I'd made less frequently on the way to school, about all sorts of things, about remarks made by Roithamer, too, about encounters along the way, for example in the Aurach gorge where formerly, during our grade school days, the gypsies often made camp, we were afraid of them because we had been told that gypsies kidnapped children, the more the better, about reflections in the air, on the grass, and most of all on the riverbank, about peculiarities in the bark of the trees, about certain oddities in the behavior of the animals particularly along this stretch of our way to school along the Aurach, did he remember how I, together with him and Roithamer, had once discovered twelve frozen deer among the trees and pulled them together in a heap, how we suddenly, yielding to an impulse when halfway between my home and our school, decided to cut school and went instead to the abandoned mill standing where today there is nothing but an overgrown hole in the ground, like a bomb-crater, and anyway, did he remember certain things along the way that had to do with the war and how we lived in fear all that time, and I found that Hoeller remembered everything or almost everything that I still remembered. My mind

keeps coming back to that schoolway, I said to Hoeller, and
then: One day we came to school in winter, I said, and we had
to face the fact that the teacher had hanged himself in our
schoolroom during the night. Because he had been accused by
a schoolmate of ours, we both knew his name, of having
molested him, the pupil, down by the Aurach under a rock
ledge. This accusation, though never proven to this day, I said,
led to the suicide of the teacher, whose name I have forgotten,
Hoeller also had forgotten his name. I can see us now, the first
to arrive as always, opening the classroom door and putting
down the pieces of wood we had brought beside the tile stove,
intending to start the fire with them, for as he, Hoeller, knew,
we had never waited for the school janitor, whose job it was,
to do it, but had always started the fire ourselves right away, it
was no trouble because there were still glowing embers in the
stove, so we'd never needed any kindling, all we had to do was
put the fresh logs inside and the schoolroom was soon warm
enough for us, I can see myself bending down to put a log on
the fire, I said, and it was then I noticed that the teacher had
hanged himself above the tile stove, from the hook where
usually only the saw hung which the teacher took down spring
and fall to trim the apple and pear trees in the schoolhouse
garden. There was no need to remind Hoeller of this incident
which had probably influenced Hoeller all his life as it had
influenced me all my life as a primal experience, and yet it was
in order suddenly to bring up the teacher's suicide again, and
the slandering of him by our schoolmate, whose name we had
now forgotten, which led to the teacher's suicide by hanging, I
was impressed by how calmly I could now speak of the
teacher's suicide and of how I had discovered his hanged body,
it was the first time after so many years, after two decades in
fact, that I was able to speak calmly about this experience,
Hoeller was also impressed by my calm in speaking of all this,
anyway I could have made these remarks about the teacher's
suicide only in this calm way, because I had been moved to

make these remarks by the two death notices opposite me, which is why I had begun to speak, by way of preparation, of our walking to school together and all the circumstances of our walking to school together that have remained as present to our minds as they were in the earliest school days of our childhood, circumstances which are different today, and so I had brought up our schoolway and perceptions related to our schoolway then as perceptions of today, in preparation, so to speak, for what I basically wanted to say, all that description of our way to school, my own recollection of it, as well as Hoeller's recollection of it by way of first testing my own memory and then Hoeller's memory, all used in order to arrive at the fact that our teacher hanged himself because of a vulgar slander against him by a schoolmate of ours. Probably there is some connection between our teacher's suicide such a long time ago and Roithamer's suicide, naturally, I said to Hoeller, there's a connection, Roithamer's suicide and the teacher's suicide so many years ago, since, as I know, Roithamer's life too had been crucially affected by the teacher's suicide. Anyway, like all children in such so-called remote places, we were no strangers to suicide quite early in our lives, such country places always have their share of chronically unhappy people and the resulting general unhappiness leads to dozens of suicides annually within the smallest circumference, with the help of the oppressive weather conditions in these foothills, here everybody is *always* inclined to suicide, everyone feels he is suffocating because he can't change his situation in any way, in this landscape they all have a keen sense of being handicapped by their birth, nor was it any use, evidently, for one of the most vulnerable, like Roithamer, a man whose actions were determined by his head and not, as with all the others, by his feelings, to leave the country, as Roithamer quite simply left it, because he had the opportunity to leave, but everywhere he went, no matter where he sought refuge, he could not escape this handicap of his birthplace, the landscape of his

birth and the depressive constitutional tendencies so characteristic of his fellow countrymen, and of course, I said to
Hoeller, Roithamer finally did kill himself anyway, he'd tried
to escape his fate by running off to England, hoping to get
away, he'd soon settled in England because he had the (financial) means to do so, but it was no use, he was doomed just like
the others who have no chance of leaving the country, I said.
Even a man like him, who seems to have every chance of
escaping, I said, can't overcome the fact of having been born
into a chronically depressed state of mind and body, it is
precisely that kind of a man in whom the general unhappiness
reaches its most tragically concentrated form, yet it would be
wrong to regard a man like Roithamer as someone who is
always unhappy, no man is always unhappy, especially not a
man like Roithamer, so variously gifted and certainly capable
of always keeping himself in trim mentally and physically,
there's no limit to such a man's possibilities, the utmost unhappiness, for one, but of course also the utmost happiness,
naturally a constant intense alternation of happiness and unhappiness will eventually make an end of any man's life, it
will lead to a death according to his nature, whether he comes
to a quiet end or to a troubled end, it is always an end
consistent with his nature, clearly a man like Roithamer, with
his capabilities, always straining toward some ultimate experience, or achievement, could not endure life as long as lesser
men might. In our country suicide is commonplace, nothing
unusual at all, I said, quite a natural subject of conversation.
Anyone who pays attention can see for himself that everyone
in our region and in fact all Austrians everywhere talk about
suicide all the time, quite openly, even habitually, they would
all have to admit that the thought of suicide is never far from
their minds, at the very least, though of course they don't all
kill themselves, but the idea of killing oneself, of doing away
with oneself in the quickest possible way, of obliterating
oneself as best one can, is an idea shared by all of them, no

matter what anyone thinks, it's actually their only idea. Basically we have here a people given to constant discussion of its own suicide, while at the same time constantly having to prevent itself from committing suicide, this is as true of each individual as of the population as a whole, they're always at it, singly and collectively, and what it actually amounts to is a state of incessant suffering made bearable, however, by the high intelligence applied to it by each individual and therefore by the people as a whole. It's a folk art of sorts, I said to Hoeller, always longing to kill oneself but being kept by one's watchful intelligence from killing oneself, so that the condition is stabilized in the form of lifelong controlled suffering, it's an art possessed only by this people and those belonging to it. We're a nation of suicides, I said, but only a small percentage actually kill themselves, even though ours is the highest percentage of suicides in the world, even though we in this country hold the world's record for suicide, I said. What mainly goes on in this country and among these people is thinking about suicide, everywhere, in the big cities, in the towns, in the country, a basic trait of this country's population is the constant thought of suicide, they might be said to take pleasure in thinking constantly, steadily, without allowing anything to distract them, about how to do away with themselves at any time. It is their way of keeping their balance, I said, to think constantly about killing themselves without actually killing themselves. But of course the rest of the world doesn't understand, and so whatever they think about us and regardless of what they say about us and of how they always and invariably treat us, every single one of us, they are all wrong. It's a simple fact, I said, that our country is misunderstood, no matter how well intentioned the rest of the world may appear, what it sees when it looks at Austria and its people is total madness as a stable state of mind, a constant. I'm going to start, I said to Hoeller, by putting all of Roithamer's books and papers in order, even though I've no idea

how to do it, since the chances are that the disorder among
Roithamer's books and papers *is* their order, no matter, I
would try first of all to get myself *acclimated* to the garret up
there, to make myself at home first, and only then organize
myself with respect to my work on Roithamer's literary legacy.
That he, Hoeller, had put the garret at my disposal for this
purpose, was the greatest help to me, just as my recent sickness, from which I have just recovered, even though not quite
recovered, is an equally opportune circumstance for my work
on Roithamer's legacy. A stay of four or five days, I said,
would give me time to look everything over, and I'd need
another four or five days for a more intensive study. More I
could not say as yet. Hoeller then gave me his account of
finding Roithamer in the clearing and how he had cut him
down from the tree, the big linden tree out there. Suddenly
there was no problem about getting him to talk, he told me
everything, in his own orderly fashion showing signs of Roithamer's influence, he restricted himself to what was important
and necessary, told in proper sequence. His account took a
quarter of an hour and as I listened to him I felt that everything was exactly as he said, Hoeller was a so-called truth
fanatic, his voice and its rhythms were familiar to me. There
was no further sound coming from the kitchen, the children
had gone to bed, their mother was still at her sewing machine,
audible on the floor above, though it was already nine-thirty,
a late hour for the Hoeller house. The rattle of the sewing
machine above and the roar of the Aurach below combined in
a quite definite musical rhythm. It would be a pleasure for me
to take my meals together with the family, I said to Hoeller,
then I got up, said good night, and went up the the garret. But
I was far from ready for sleep, just like Hoeller who did not go
to bed either as I soon noticed, probably because of his insomnia, but went instead to his workshop, his preservatory as
Roithamer always called Hoeller's workshop. I'd expected that
if I sat still long enough on the old chair by the door, fighting

off the new thoughts that kept coming after I'd forced myself to think through all the old thoughts, to cut them off if necessary or else spin them out to a conclusion if possible, I'd get sufficiently tired out for bed, but it didn't work and I finally had to get up from the old chair to pace the floor. Suddenly I was full of doubts, had I done the right thing in moving into Hoeller's garret, in accepting Hoeller's offer so precipitately, without considering what it would do to me and to my immediate future and in general, all of a sudden I asked myself, what am I doing here anyway? Should I have taken on Roithamer's papers so soon, perhaps it would be better to go up to the mountains, into a shepherd's hut up there, far better, probably, for my still convalescent body, the doctors had in fact recommended such a stay in the mountains, for the mountain air, the absolute quiet up there, the doctors would probably have been totally against my staying down here in the damp, the cold, the darkness of the Aurach valley, especially the Aurach gorge, after my premature release from the hospital which was nobody's idea but mine, I should have aimed to avoid stress of any kind, instead of which I'd moved into Hoeller's garret, which would be in itself a strain on any organism and any mind, and in addition I'd taken on the burden of working on Roithamer's legacy, I wondered whether I should not postpone this, leave tomorrow, end my stay in Hoeller's house early tomorrow morning, I could easily make up some excuse for breaking off my stay, and go up to the mountains. Caught up in this question, whether to break off my stay in Hoeller's house the next morning or not, always coming back to the decision to leave, then again the decision not to leave, not to start working on Roithamer's legacy, not *now* in any case, then again, working on it now is sure to do me good, especially now, I kept pacing the floor in Hoeller's garret, considering all the advantages of a stay in the mountains and all the disadvantages of staying at Hoeller's house this time of year and in the Aurach gorge in my present

condition, then again I could see only disadvantages in a stay
in the mountains this time of year and in my present condition, while seeing only the advantages of staying at Hoeller's
house, swinging like a pendulum between preferring the
mountains and downgrading the Hoeller house, and vice versa
was rapidly driving me crazy, walking to the window I
thought, for instance, that I must have the strength and the
guts to pack my things in the morning and leave, no need to lie
to Hoeller, I'd tell him the truth, get out of his house and up
into the mountains, up to an elevation that would be better for
my health than Hoeller's house, with its atmosphere which,
taken all in all, could only make my condition worse, I
thought, and then again, turning back from the window toward the door, where I stopped, thinking that it was wrong to
move out of the garret again tomorrow, an affront to the
Hoellers, only to go up to the mountains, any mountains,
which deep down I hated, I've simply always hated high
altitude mountain landscapes with their distant views, their
so-called infinite horizons, I'd be making a mistake to leave
the Hoellers' house for some furnished mountain hut or even a
mountain hotel, the mere idea of having to live in such a
mountain hut for even the shortest time imaginable, or in one
of those horrible mountain hotels, I'd always regarded those
mountain huts and mountain hotels as nothing but horrible,
and soon I found myself thinking how well off I was here in
the company of Hoeller and his wife, together with the Hoeller
children, and after all I could stay here without working on
Roithamer's legacy, since I was under absolutely no obligation
to work on it, simply to stay here in Hoeller's garret and in the
Hoeller ambience and simply let this atmosphere have its
effect on me and to simply let myself go in this atmosphere
would at the moment probably be the best thing for me, I
thought, the chances were I'd probably be feeling much easier
the very next day, it was too much to expect that easing of
tension which I had hoped for, expected, on my very first day

in Hoeller's house, such relief, though in fact I needed it immediately, could not come at once, it could come only gradually, perhaps only after a few days, I could find other reading matter than these papers which had to do exclusively with Roithamer and would be constantly reminding me of Roithamer, virtually chaining me to Roithamer, after all there were plenty of other books in Hoeller's garret, books which need not remind me of Roithamer, as I had noticed as soon as I got here, a few walks along the Aurach, maybe even longer walks out onto the plain, toward Pinsdorf, would help to calm me down, maybe it was simply *idleness, perfect idleness* that I needed, to put myself into a state in which I could gradually become more and more relaxed, I thought, while hearing Hoeller down there in his workroom, his preservatory, busily filing and honing and sawing away, I had become so accustomed to the roaring of the Aurach that I could hear Hoeller at work all the way up here in my garret, from the various sounds coming up from Hoeller's workroom I was able to *imagine* the tasks he had just finished, I felt that Hoeller was a man who, just like myself at this moment, was wholly under the spell of Roithamer's suicide, he too was trying to distract himself by means of activity or inactivity from the fact that Roithamer, our friend, had killed himself, perhaps it would have been better had I not reminded Hoeller, and thereby myself, in such exact detail of our old teacher's suicide, of the horrible discovery of his corpse in our classroom, anyway it was all wrong to have brought up our walks to school together and everything connected with those walks, to have spoken in my insistent way only of miseries and horrors which after all precipitated Hoeller as well as myself into disastrously sickening recollections from which we now both found it hard to escape, Hoeller is going through the same thing as I am, I thought, as I stood by the window, he's also trying, so late at night, to cope with his problems and simply can't cope with his problems, instead of making it easier for him, all I have

done with my appearance and my subsequent by-no-means
cheering presence is to have disturbed him as I should never
have done, just as I have disturbed myself in the same inad-
missible fashion, instead of easing my mind, there's a great
deal I should never have done or said, *never have suggested,* it is
my suggestions above all, my habit of suggesting everything
without explicit statement, which tends to disturb my inter-
locutor, or at least my listener, instantly makes him uneasy, as
I'd made Hoeller instantly uneasy with my tactic of suggestion, possibly made all the Hoellers uneasy during our meal
together, although I was as silent as they were, whether I was
silent because of them or they because of me I don't know,
that it may have been wrong, I thought, possibly, for me to
have stayed on after Hoeller's wife and the children left the
room, to keep sitting there and do my worst in irritating
Hoeller. Most of all, to be quite honest with myself, I could
have spared myself *forcing* Hoeller to give his description, his
account of how *he discovered Roithamer in the clearing,* because
Hoeller wouldn't have said anything about it of his own
accord so soon, but I'd wanted to hear his story *now* and I
forced it out of him without saying a word, by my silence, it's
a way I have which I myself find distasteful, of forcing people
who are with me, now and then, to statements or accounts or
even more descriptions which at the very least create an uneasiness, yet I drive them to make statements and give accounts which cause the speakers to become extremely upset
mentally and emotionally, hard to calm down afterward, just
as I tend to drive myself into an upset mental and emotional
state. This characteristic relentlessness of mine is rooted in my
extremely complicated nature which is always striving toward
simplicity but by that very effort keeps moving more and
more and further and further away from simplicity, dealing
with others as it does with myself, capable only of relentlessness and thereby driven very quickly to exhaustion. It may be
possible to transform by sheer willpower everything which is

at the moment undoubtedly harmful to me in Hoeller's garret—and I suddenly felt almost everything here to be harmful
to me, everything in Hoeller's garret suddenly had a destructive effect on me, not to say a deadly effect—possible to
transform all these harmful and destructive, not to say deadly,
influences into something useful, useful to me. The willpower
to turn a dangerous situation, a situation of absolute danger,
which is how I suddenly had to regard the garret, into a
situation that might be useful at least for my constitution, the
willpower, meaning the intellectual power and the physical
power as well. Suppose I asked Hoeller to let me work in his
workroom, to give me something to do, no matter what,
because I believe that at the moment any physical activity
would be better for me than mental activity, just now I dread
mental activity more than anything, yet what was I intending
to do in Hoeller's garret if it wasn't mental activity, working
on Roithamer's legacy was naturally a mental activity, one
which in fact is likely to tax me beyond my mental and
physical capacities, to let me bevel or saw or cut or pack or
unpack things or paste them on or carry them in or out of the
workroom or let me chop wood or saw wood or pile up wood
behind the house or plant or dig or improve something in the
garden. In my present vulnerable physical and therefore mental condition I cannot allow myself, permit myself, a mental
activity, especially not the infinitely exacerbated kind of mental activity I can expect in occupying myself with Roithamer's
legacy now, leading to cerebral exhaustion and so also to
physical exhaustion. But then again I thought that it might be
precisely such mental work as my work with Roithamer's
legacy which could restore me, regenerate, normalize, my head
and my body. Absorbed in these considerations I'd slowed
down my pacing the floor in Hoeller's garret. Then, standing
by the window and looking down at the river as the light from
Hoeller's workroom windows fell brightly on the water, I was
thinking that the greatest effort of all would probably be

required for working on that part of Roithamer's legacy which
dealt primarily with Altensam and with everything connected
with Altensam, with special emphasis on the building of the
Cone for his sister, a radical statement from beginning to end,
which never for a moment neglected the philosophical aspects
involved, it described Altensam as the making of Roithamer,
the source of all he ever was and still is in what remains of
him, his legacy, a most extraordinary personality entirely devoted to his scientific work, yet on the other hand it also
described Altensam as the cause of his destruction, how Altensam simultaneously and with equal force destroyed him, how
it killed and annihilated him. This manuscript of Roithamer's
which, with its corrected version, makes up Roithamer's testament, as aforesaid, gives a full account of Roithamer's conscious existence as well as a full account of the destruction of
Roithamer's conscious existence, and so it represents Roithamer's entire life in the form of this verifiable manuscript,
which I placed at once, before I did anything else, in the desk
drawer, when I entered Hoeller's garret, for fear that I might
otherwise go *immediately to work on it, a self-destructive thing to
do, sure to have a devastating effect on me or at least on my mental
state,* as shown by this manuscript which is simultaneously, in
consequence of his total correction of it, a destroyed manuscript, it is his own destruction of his manuscript which makes
it the only authentic manuscript. While still at the hospital I'd
started, timidly at first but soon driven by mounting curiosity
and uncontrollable interest, to glance over this manuscript and
its corrected version, quite superficially, in full and clear
awareness that I must first concern myself with the *original*
and only thereafter with the *corrected* version and only then
with the *original and corrected* version, this idea as my basic
condition for working on his manuscript at all I'd had at my
first contact with the manuscript, from the first it seemed a
death-defying undertaking to let myself in for Roithamer's
manuscript at all, and thinking about it, as I again paced the

floor of Hoeller's garret, one moment I'd feel capable of working on it, then again I'd feel incapable, optimistic one minute, apprehensive the next, alternating between feeling fully capable of working on the manuscript not to mention Roithamer's other posthumous papers, and feeling definitely not up to such work, especially after so grave an illness by no means overcome as yet, how could I let myself in for such a backbreaking task, besides, what if I wasn't the right person for it? Roithamer's show of confidence in me by leaving me his papers moved me deeply, of course, but I also knew full well what a terrible business this was. More than anything else Roithamer needed freedom of thought, but while he had to be free to think anything whatever, he had to speak only the truth, something he, like any other thinking man, found most difficult to do, but his life had actually been based on this tacit understanding with everyone else, how easy it is to say of one man or another that he's been a man of intelligence or even of intellect, but actually to be such a man of intelligence or intellect is the hardest thing in the world, and to be a man of intelligence or intellect all the time is impossible, Roithamer said. Just a few cursory inspections of Roithamer's papers had given me a clear idea what sort of task I was taking on in accepting Roithamer's literary legacy, yet I still had the courage to address myself to it again, time after time, in giving me this task he may well have meant to destroy me, which is why I lived in constant fear, actually, of getting involved with this legacy of his, I fully expected to be annihilated or at least destroyed or at the very least to become permanently disturbed by it, irreparably chronically disturbed. On the other hand I could understand Roithamer's line of thought, first making an end of himself and his sister, then of me, by leaving me his papers, what else could he have meant by making me his literary executor than to destroy me, because I was so entirely part of his development, as he felt. Such thoughts, which I had as I continued pacing the floor this way and that, hither and yon, in the garret, thoughts suddenly in my mind, even against everything in my mind, actually did have a devastating and destructive effect on me, all these thoughts connected with Roithamer, and I was suddenly made up of nothing but such thoughts, I'd already spoken of this downstairs at Hoeller's table to Hoeller, of my fear that working on our friend's literary remains would disturb me for a long time, and that it would get in the way of my own work which I had totally neglected all this while, though during my hospitalization I had always thought that, once I was released and had recovered or at least halfway recovered, I would immediately resume my work which I had abandoned months ago, before Christmas in Cambridge, yet suddenly the fact that Roithamer had willed me his papers, incidentally by an unequivocal proviso tacked on at the end of the slip of paper which he designated as his will and which he had probably written just before his suicide, probably when he was already in the clearing, this fact that Roithamer's will ended with the proviso that his literary remains were to go to me, because by means of this unequivocal proviso, presented in a fashion as if to say that this was the most important concern in his head at the last moment, he had taken complete possession of me, so that it had now become my foremost duty. But what if this is my chance to free myself of this legacy? I thought, having meanwhile taken my jacket out of the closet and put it on, why don't I just leave this whole mass of papers I've brought with me, the whole legacy, right here in Hoeller's garret, *leave it here, leave it here,* I kept thinking while pacing the floor and wondering whether I was disturbing the Hoeller family with my endless pacing back and forth, disturbing the children in their sleep, who would know that I'd quite simply left the Roithamer legacy here and gone away again, perhaps up into the mountains after all, I could take refuge somewhere as high up as it was possible to go, I thought, I could leave everything behind me for once and think of nothing but my own health, all I had to do was stack up the papers neatly and leave them here and work on them later, at the right time, suddenly I felt that the moment for working on Roithamer's papers hadn't come yet, I've been too hasty, I kept thinking, I've acted overhastily, too precipitately, this needs time, preparation, it can't be done in such a rush, so thoughtlessly as I've gone about it, better put it off for a year or two, or at least a few months or a few weeks, after I've had a chance to pull myself together and only then, when I'm really fit for the job, I can try to come to terms with Roithamer's legacy. I've always had this unfortunate tendency to rush things, Roithamer hated rushing things and the tendency to rush things more than anything, everything in the world is done in a great rush nowadays, he'd say, everything is rushed, too rushed, every time, nothing is allowed to develop at its own natural pace, it's all done in a mad precipitate brainless rush wherever you look, people simply rush into action and the results are sheerest chaos. The universal chaos in the world today, especially in recent times, is chiefly the result of every kind of *precipitate action* taken without first carefully *considering* what should be done, precipitateness and rushing things are the most terrible characteristics of our world today, Roithamer said, and this is why everything is so chaotic. In every area of life there's nothing but chaos. Wherever we turn there's chaos, in the sciences there's chaos, in politics, it's chaos, whatever we do, it's all chaotic, wherever we look, purely chaotic conditions, chaotic conditions are all we ever have to deal with. Because everything is being done precipitately, in a rush. In such a time of precipitateness and overhastiness and the consequent chaotic conditions a thinking man should *never act precipitately or overhastily* in anything that concerns him, but every single one of us constantly acts precipitately, overhastily, in every way. What a terrible situation I've let myself in for by accepting Hoeller's invitation and moving into Hoeller's garret, I thought. I looked down at Hoeller's workshop windows and I

thought, there he is working away on and on because he can't
sleep, and then I thought that he must be thinking that I can't
sleep either, which is why I keep pacing the floor of the garret.
People are always having to face things that upset and disturb
them, mostly it's at the very moment when they suppose
themselves to be at peace, that they're catapulted into turmoil,
when they feel well balanced, they're thrown out of balance.
All we ever have is an illusion of peace, because at the very
moment at which peace could enter into us, *could could could,* I
say, we're right back in the worst turmoil. So Hoeller down
there in his workshop, his preservatory, may well be thinking
that I'm in the greatest turmoil up here in the garret, because
all the indications down in the workshop must be pointing
that way, just as I was bound to think of Hoeller down there
being in the greatest turmoil, because up here in the garret all
the indications pointed to it. Of course I could leave the attic
and go down and walk into the workshop and ask Hoeller why
he was still working at an hour when nobody was up and at
work any longer, I could probe into the reasons for his present
condition, his work obsession, and I could in turn let Hoeller
probe into my reasons for pacing the floor of the garret,
marching up and down and back and forth as I was doing
instead of going to bed. But I controlled myself and sat down
on the old chair beside the door and stared at the floor. One
lamp is enough, I thought, and I got up and turned off the
ceiling light, with only the desk lamp on, I thought, the garret
won't be so brightly lit, and that may help to calm me down, I
tried everything I could think of to calm myself down, but
because I was so intent, working so hard without a letup at
considering what to do in order to be able to sleep, to be able
to go to bed in hopes of getting to sleep, I was undermining my
own effort to relax, on the contrary, these efforts of mine kept
driving me deeper into sleeplessness. Still there's nothing so
extraordinary for me, I thought, in not being able to sleep, I've
had to struggle with insomnia all my life, let's face it, from the

beginning of a certain stage of mental development, a certain age, that is, I never again had a real, satisfying, deep sleep in the natural way, in a fully relaxed state of my brain and my body. From a certain point in time onward, probably from the beginning of my present state of mind which has now been going on for two decades and which I call, as Roithamer did, *my English state of mind,* I haven't even been able to imagine myself in a fully relaxed sleep, I see it as a privilege reserved for others, I said to myself, for a quite different breed of men, quite a different sort. Some people are so constituted that they can sleep well all their lives, or during the best part of their lives, or at least a tolerably good part of their lives, I thought, while some others, those like me, can't sleep, they never sleep, they are condemned never to be able to sleep, for even when they are sleeping they are never really relaxed by nature and what they do can't be called sleeping, these people never sleep as long as they live because all their lives, no matter how long they live, they have never had the advantage of a perfect relaxation of their head and their body. This entire valley is now at this hour filled with people who're asleep, probably even deeply asleep, in all these houses and huts they are sleeping, and there isn't a light anywhere, but here in Hoeller's house there is lots of light and they're not asleep, I'm sure that even the kids aren't sleeping now, I thought, even Hoeller's wife isn't sleeping, because they're all disturbed by the light from Hoeller's workshop and from Hoeller's garret. They've gotten used to the roaring of the Aurach, I thought, but not to the light from the workshop and from Hoeller's garret. In this unusually disturbing condition they quite naturally can't sleep, I thought. And for how many more nights will they be unable to sleep, because this unusual situation connected with Roithamer's death will certainly continue for a time, I thought, Hoeller is likely to be in his workshop and not in bed for days to come and I, unless I've picked myself up and gone off altogether, and as I thought this, everything in me was against getting out and away, suddenly I was all for staying put again, I too would be unable to sleep in the nights ahead and I'd be leaving the lights on in Hoeller's garret, after all I really couldn't stand it in the pitch-dark in Hoeller's garret, I thought. And I doubted that Roithamer had ever succeeded in falling asleep in Hoeller's garret, because Roithamer was another one of those who can never sleep, who can't ever relax by any means whatever, a man condemned to lifelong sleeplessness despite all those much-discussed and propagated relaxation gospels of our time. Even as a child Roithamer, as he often told me, couldn't sleep, he fell asleep in the evening and woke up in the morning but to call it sleep, whatever it was between his nodding off and waking up, would be a lie. People made like Roithamer (and me), really *always defenseless characters, beings,* whatever, had no sleep capability, they may fall asleep and wake up again, but they never sleep. They've got something forever in their heads and their nerves that won't let them sleep. All their lives they keep looking for a cure for this unbearable condition and they never find one because there is no cure for this disease, which really is nothing but a mental disease. All those insomniacs are born with this mental disease, they already have this mental disease in childhood and whether they are of the Roithamer type or the Hoeller type, they are incurable. The nights, Roithamer said, are always the worst. Everything is blown up out of all proportion at night, no matter how insignificant, at night it becomes monstrous, the most insignificant, the most harmless thing there is grows monstrous at night and won't let a man like me or Roithamer or Hoeller sleep. And this persistent thought that one can't sleep, under any circumstances, makes it worse. Sitting on the old chair by the door I was thinking with what a difference, and yet with what *in*difference, we went our ways, he coming from up in Altensam, me from down in Stocket, Hoeller, whose father had already been a zoological taxidermist in the old Hoeller house, the one Hoeller sold, which has since been torn down by its subsequent owner. How we moved from our different points of departure, our positions, toward one single point, the single acceptable point, death. Now Roithamer was dead, after first catapulting his sister to her death by his idea, and I lived, and Hoeller lived, and how he lived and how I lived. But it is already clear that I too must now be going quickly toward my death, even though I am differently constituted from Roithamer, not with the same bent toward suicide, probably somewhat more of a survivor than Roithamer, for I always seem to find a way out, while Roithamer could no longer find a way out, but one day I too shall no longer find a way out, everyone is destined, one day at some moment which is the crucial moment, to find no further way out, that's how a man is made. Thinking it over, one's life is both the longest possible and the shortest possible, simultaneously, because it can be rethought and reexperienced in a moment, always in that moment in which such a (bold) thought occurs to one. Always wanting the impossible and left with the possible in his minimal existence, the individual always finds himself in the lowest depths of dissatisfaction. Nevertheless he always manages to create another life situation for himself, probably because he really loves life, just as it is. We always crave something other than we can have, than we have, other than what is suitable for us, and so we're unhappy. When we're happy we immediately analyze this happiness to death, if we're like Roithamer andsoforth, and are right back in misery. As I'd heard something that was different from what I'd been hearing till then, I'd gotten up and gone to post myself at the window, to look outside. The darkness was kept at bay by the workshop lights, Hoeller was busy stuffing a huge bird, I couldn't tell what kind of bird. It was a huge black bird which Hoeller held on his knees, cramming polyurethane into it with a stick. It was eleven o'clock, and inasmuch as Hoeller always got up at four in the morning, all his life, even as a child, he'd always gotten up at four in the morning, because his father also had always been up by four in the morning, everybody in the Aurach valley got up between four and five o'clock in the morning, and so because Hoeller is always up at four in the morning, keeping such late hours, such very long late hours as these in these circumstances, will undermine his health, I thought. From my window up in the garret I kept watching Hoeller down there in his workshop stuffing that huge black bird, how he kept cramming it with more and more stuffing, I thought I'll watch him from this excellent vantage point until he's finished stuffing that bird, and so I stood there motionless for a good half hour until I saw that Hoeller had finished stuffing the bird. Suddenly Hoeller had thrown the stuffed bird down to the floor, he'd jumped up and run off into the back room where I couldn't see him anymore, but I waited, looking into the workshop, until I could see Hoeller again, he came back and sat down on his chair again and went back to stuffing the bird, now I noticed a huge heap of polyurethane on the floor beside Hoeller's chair and I thought this huge heap of polyurethane is now going to be crammed into this bird which I'd supposed had already been crammed full long since. By stuffing this bird he is making the night bearable for himself, I thought. At twelve he was still busy stuffing that bird. Off and on I kept wondering what kind of a bird this was, I'd never seen so large and so black a bird before, probably a species never seen in our country at all, and I toyed with the idea of going down to the workshop to ask Hoeller what species of bird this was. It's certainly possible that this bird is of a so-called exotic species, that one of the hunters living out there on the plain, living in affluence in that fertile country out there, men who take frequent hunting trips to foreign countries and overseas, brought the bird back from South America or Africa, with what incredible energy Hoeller was now stuffing that bird with polyurethane, I couldn't imagine that so much polyurethane could be crammed inside that bird, yet Hoeller kept stuffing some more of the polyurethane into the bird, suddenly I felt repelled by the process of stuffing polyurethane into the huge black bird, I turned around, looked at the door, but found it impossible to look at the door for more than a second or so because even looking at the door I kept seeing the huge bird Hoeller was stuffing with polyurethane, so I turned back again and looked out the window and into Hoeller's workshop, if I must see Hoeller stuffing this huge, black, really horrible bird, then I might as well see it in reality and not in my imagination, clearly I could not possibly expect to get any sleep now, full as I was of my impression of Hoeller stuffing that huge black bird with polyurethane, constantly accelerating the speed with which he was doing this job, it was nauseating, still I had to keep looking out the window and into the workshop as if hypnotized. I could no longer turn away, compelled to surrender myself entirely to watching this procedure of Hoeller's cramming that bird with polyurethane, I was about to vomit when Hoeller suddenly stopped his horrible activity and set the bird down, with its huge claws and long heavy legs, on his worktable. Now he's going to sew the stuffed bird together, I thought, and sure enough Hoeller had gotten up and disappeared into the back room of the workshop to bring in whatever he needed for sewing the bird up. Or else he's stopping work now and is leaving the workshop to go to his room and lie down, I thought, but Hoeller was already back with various balls of thread and needles and had sat down at his worktable to continue his work. Why am I watching Hoeller at his work, I thought, why don't I do something myself, start something that I can keep on doing all night if I like, I thought, no matter what I do, as long as it gets me through the night. But what could I do? There was no manual work of any kind I could have done in Hoeller's garret, it wasn't set up for anything like that, and my head was no longer clear enough for any kind of mental work. On the other hand I didn't permit myself to go down to Hoeller's workshop, in case I could be of some help there. I certainly could have found something to do in Hoeller's workshop, even if it was only to sweep up. It took all of my willpower to get myself away from the window and I turned around and took a few steps toward the door, thinking as I did so that my situation was really desperate, that I was possibly already quite seriously insane. Had I gone crazy as a result of moving *precipitately* into Hoeller's garret? I wondered, but then I immediately thought, what an idea, *that's* what's crazy, *such* an idea as that, and I walked over to the desk and took the yellow paper rose out of the top drawer. Something happened to Roithamer at that music festival, I thought, as I held the yellow paper rose up to the light, a change had come upon him during that music festival, even if I don't know, or can't know what kind of a change it was. But don't we always immediately see and seek a meaning in everything we see and think? How could a man who never fired a shot in his life, suddenly, at a music festival, pick off twenty-four paper roses with twenty-four shots? And then hand twenty-three of these paper roses over, in passing, to an unknown girl, or an unknown young woman, keeping only one yellow rose for himself. And then keep this one yellow paper rose for so many years, taking it along wherever he goes, apparently unable to live without it ever again. By taking the paper rose out of the drawer I'd calmed myself down. I sat down with the paper rose in my hand on the old chair and held the paper rose up to the light. We mustn't let ourselves go so far as to suspect something remarkable, something mysterious, or significant, in everything and behind everything, this is a yellow paper rose, *the* yellow paper rose, to be precise, which Roithamer shot down at the music festival in Stocket that one time, together with twenty-three others in different colors, that's all. Everything is what it is, that's all. If we keep attaching meanings and mysteries to everything we perceive, everything we see that is, and to everything that goes on inside us, we are bound to go crazy sooner or later, I thought. We may see only what we do see which is nothing else but that which we see. Again I watched Hoeller from my window in Hoeller's garret, as he sewed together the huge black bird which he had stuffed to bursting. Suddenly I saw, perhaps my eyes had become adjusted to the lighting down there in Hoeller's workshop, or else the lighting had suddenly changed, anyway I saw several such huge birds, the back of Hoeller's workshop was filled with such birds, not all of these great, indeed huge birds were equally large, not all of them were black, but these were absolutely *no local birds*, probably, I thought, these are birds from the collection of some bird fancier, one of those rich bird freaks who can afford to travel to America, to South America or to India, in order to shoot such huge birds and add them to his collection. A huge bird collection, I kept thinking, a huge bird collection, and I slapped my forehead as I thought again and again, a huge bird collection, a huge bird collection! Roithamer had always spoken at length about Hoeller's work, his procedures in preserving, stuffing andsoforth all kinds of animals, every possible kind of fowl, Roithamer had always profited, so he himself said, from watching Hoeller at work, seeing how those dead creatures were dissected and stuffed and sewed up. For Roithamer, I now thought, these products of nature, stuffed and turned into artifacts, always provided an occasion for various reflections on nature and art and art and nature, to him they were almost the most mysterious products of art because they were only just barely works of art andsoforth, mysterious by virtue of the fact that they had been made into artifacts here in the midst of a natural world still abounding with hundreds and thousands of creatures still purely natural andsoforth, that they had been turned into artifacts by Hoeller, products of nature turned by Hoeller's hands into products of art here in nature's own bosom andsoforth. Hoeller turns nature's products into art products and these artificial creatures seem always more mysterious than the purely natural creatures they once were. Hoeller's work of turning purely natural creatures into

purely art(ificial) creatures had often served Roithamer as a
basis for ideas on art vs. nature, and all these ideas, which
Roithamer naturally always linked immediately with everything else, everything other than these ideas, that is, were all
coming back to me now. However, I was no longer up to
formulating a definition. But I did muse about how it could be
possible for so many generations, at least four or five forebears
of Hoeller can be documented, to give their lives to the stuffing and preservation of animals and to keep on for centuries,
consciously or unconsciously, turning purely natural creatures
into purely art(ificial) creatures. This meditation lasted an
hour. Pacing the floor in Hoeller's garret I thought that I need
only *approach* Roithamer's legacy, *approach* it to begin with, if I
tackle Roithamer's papers now it is in order to sift them and
then possibly edit them, which I have no right to do, neither
the right nor the necessary ruthlessness, for editing involves a
certain ruthlessness toward the subject, but I can never muster
the requisite ruthlessness in the face of Roithamer's legacy. For
me to bring together all these bits and pieces, perhaps to put
them in the right relation to each other so as to make a whole
out of all these bits and pieces of his thought, something to be
published, was out of the question, for I'd had to consider,
from my first contact with Roithamer's papers, that they consist for the most part of mere fragments which he had intended to combine into a whole himself, after completing or perfecting (Roithamer), finishing (Hoeller) the Cone, first he had
devoted all his powers to the completion of the Cone, once I
have completed the Cone (Roithamer), once he had finished
the Cone (Hoeller), he would immediately set to work with all
the intensity of which he was capable and after the completion
of the Cone with a fresh, even more intensive intensity, with a
fresh afflatus, as Roithamer said just a few months ago in
England, to work on completing (Roithamer) or finishing
(Hoeller) his writing, for all these years, Roithamer said, while
I was busy with the Cone, I've been able to put together only

fragments of my scientific writings, and such mere fragments by themselves aren't enough, such fragments must be combined into a whole when, and only when, I've got my head in shape for it, *when my head's really set up for it, you understand,* Roithamer said to me. So what we have here are in fact hundreds, or thousands, of fragments which Roithamer left to me, but which I shall not edit, because I have no right to edit them, anyway no one has a right, no matter who is editing what, he never has a right to do it, even though everywhere in the whole world so-called unfinished works, the labors of heads which suddenly could not continue their undertakings for whatever reasons, though mostly because of sickness or despair or self-criticism, Roithamer said, because they had rejected their ideas and simply abandoned everything they had thought all their lives, and then other people come along and proceed to edit such fragments, shreds of ideas that have been abandoned and left lying around, thinking they must edit and publish them, no matter where, publicize them, all these publications are criminal acts every single time, perhaps the greatest crime there is, because what's involved is a product of an intellect, or many such intellectual products that have been abandoned, lying around, for some sufficient reason, by their begetter, pacing the floor heatedly in Hoeller's garret I said to myself what I had already thought many times, thought it already at the hospital, I shall never edit Roithamer's legacy, I shall not commit this editorial crime, I shall never be a so-called editor, the most detestable kind of criminal there is, I shall put Roithamer's papers in *order, sift* them, then possibly pass them on to his publisher, only because he has expressed an interest and not only to Roithamer but also to me, he expressed his interest in a letter to me at the hospital, though he did so in a way that has greatly aroused my suspicions, I shall let this publisher have a look at Roithamer's legacy, I thought, pacing the floor and possibly disturbing the Hoellers in their bedroom as I did so, I didn't really believe that the

Hoellers, I mean the mother and her children, were actually asleep anyway, I simply couldn't imagine that they could sleep, everything was against it, even the sudden change in the atmosphere and wind direction militated against it, suddenly I'd understood the real reason for my sleeplessness and still growing unrest, it was a change in the weather this evening which was making everyone terribly restless and which is probably also the reason that Hoeller stayed up and took refuge in his workshop, a quick glance down at the workshop window was enough to ascertain that Hoeller was still busying himself with that huge black gigantic bird, there was no sign whatsoever that he would stop now or shortly, not even in a foreseeable time would Hoeller stop his work on that bird, I thought, and right away it struck me that here at the Aurach gorge they're exposed, always, to these sudden, these lightning changes of weather, in many cases lethal changes of weather, that people are driven to the very edge of their existence by these abrupt turns in the weather and can work their way out of this despair, this total desperation, only by some form of activity, like Hoeller busying himself with that bird, like Hoeller's wife who sat down at her sewing machine again after supper and who is probably not in bed yet, I thought, but still at her sewing, though not at the sewing machine, she's probably sitting at the little table in her room and sewing by hand, or mending, or knitting, whichever, she has to get through this night that has brought such a change in the weather somehow, they all have to get through this night somehow, all of them, all of them, everything, I thought and while I was thinking this and again walking to the door and then again back to the window I was feeling a little easier in my mind, because thinking about other people like this always brings a little relief. I would sort and sift Roithamer's legacy, I now concentrated on these two concepts of sorting and sifting and said it aloud several times, *sort and sift,* and then again several times more, *sort and sift,* but I will not edit it  I won't change a line, I won't move a comma, I shall sort and sift it, I just kept saying *sort* and *sift* over and over again and in saying *sort* and *sift* out loud I gradually succeeded in calming myself after all, I felt myself calming down while I was saying *sort* and *sift,* which is why I repeated it so often and then again, sort and sift, I said to myself, but no editing, absolutely none. As to Roithamer's major work, the paper entitled "About Altensam and Every- thing Connected with Altensam, with Special Attention to the Cone," which after all contains everything Roithamer ever thought in the most concentrated form and in his most charac- teristic style, as I perceived at once when it first came into my hands at the hospital, and which is more publishable than anything else he ever wrote, I shall pass it on to his publisher untouched, just as I found it, the first eight-hundred-page draft, and the second three-hundred-page revision of this first draft, and the third version, boiled down to only eighty pages, of the second version, *all three of these versions of Roithamer's handwritten manuscript,* for all three versions belong together, each deriving from the previous one, they compose a whole, an integral whole of over a thousand pages in which everything is equally significant so that even the most minor deletion would reduce it all to nothing, and now I thought, again pacing the floor of Hoeller's garret, that Roithamer, after completing the first version after many years of working on it and then being of two minds about it and then substituting a second version for this first version and then being of two minds about the second version and writing a third version, each a revision of the previous version about which he could not help being of two minds, and when he finally, just before his death, already on his way from London to Altensam, in fact, had started on the train revising even his final eighty-page version, correcting it and taking it apart and thereby, as he believed, starting to destroy it and by proceeding to shorten even that latest short- est version, as he believed, to arrive at an even shorter one, imagine! boiling down the material contained in over eight hundred pages of manuscript to a mere twenty or thirty pages, as I know he did, anyway this whole piece of work, to which he always referred as his major, his most important work or brainchild, though he would later find fault with it and destroy it, as he believed, yet it was precisely through this process of always overturning every earlier conclusion throughout the whole work and correcting it and ultimately, as he believed, totally destroying it on his journey to his sister's funeral, when he had passed beyond London, through Dover, Brussels, etcetera, as I can see by his corrections, that it was nevertheless by this process of boiling down a work of over eight hundred pages to one of only four hundred pages and then a mere one hundred fifty pages and then no more than eighty pages and then finally one of not even twenty pages and in fact, ultimately leaving absolutely nothing of the entire work behind, that all of it together *came into being, all this taken together is the complete work,* I said to myself, as I stood looking down at Hoeller's workshop, watching Hoeller and thinking at the same time that I had dragged this whole thing in my knapsack from the hospital into Hoeller's garret, this so-called major work of Roithamer's together with the rest of Roithamer's legacy, in the knapsack my mother brought to me at the hospital and how grotesque it is that I dragged Roithamer's legacy out of the hospital in this knapsack, of all things, which ordinarily contains only our family's provisions when we move up to the mountains, only such things as woollen socks and sausages, goose fat and foot warmers, earmuffs and shoelaces, sugar and bread, all scrambled together, to think that I dragged Roithamer's legacy into Hoeller's garret in this mountain climber's backpack, of all things, and I have to say *dragged* it, because it's a matter of thousands of pages, however, as I know, it's a case of hundreds of thousands of fragments, interrelated ones on the one hand, but completely unrelated ones on the other hand, and then again, standing by the window and considering whether to go sit down on the old chair or not, I thought: I won't edit these fragments, I absolutely will not edit this legacy, I shall sort it or at least try to put this huge heap of writings into some kind of order, but I shall edit nothing, the mere word *edit* or *edition* was always enough to nauseate me. On my arrival here I actually put only Roithamer's so-called major work, the manuscript on Altensam and everything connected with Altensam with special attention to the Cone, into the desk drawer, while the rest of the papers were still in the knapsack, because I was uncertain how to get them all out of the knapsack without mixing them up even more, I had extracted the so-called major work and put it in the drawer and put the knapsack on the sofa beside the desk, there on the sofa it was still, the knapsack which, as I now saw, was stained with dried rabbit blood, probably my father's doing, and I was now considering whether to unpack the knapsack, to remove its contents carefully, all those hundreds of thousands of pages, and put them all away in the desk, whether this might not be the right occasion, while I was in this well-nigh alarming condition, totally undecided and in a steadily increasing state of tension over the actual abrupt change in the weather, to remove the contents of the knapsack from the knapsack, little by little, with great care and using my head and keeping my hands as steady as possible, so as not to turn what seemed to me to be the great disorder of those papers into an even greater disorder, this dilemma, whether to unpack the knapsack or not, drove me to the edge of despair, I kept changing my mind, now I'd think I'll unpack the knapsack, then again, I won't unpack the knapsack, finally I walked over to the knapsack and grabbed the knapsack and emptied its contents on the sofa, I had suddenly grabbed the knapsack and turned it over and dumped its contents on the sofa. This was not the time to do it, I said to myself, and took a step backward, and then another step and then still another step and watched from the window, with my back to the window, that is, how some of the pages slid down from the top of that heap of papers, which was still in motion as I watched it from the window, where there were still some air spaces left in the heap of papers, these air spaces caved in and more papers slid to the floor. I clapped my hand to my mouth to hold back an outcry and I turned around as if in fear of being seen in this horrible, this farcically horrible situation. But in fact, and of course, nobody had seen me. Hoeller had that huge black bird on his lap and was sewing it up. I went over to the sofa and grabbed handful after handful of the Roithamer legacy and crammed the desk drawers full of it. Again and again I grabbed a handful of papers and crammed it into a drawer, until the last sheet of paper was inside, in the end I had to use my knee to force the drawer shut which, being the last drawer, I had crammed full to bursting. Then I grabbed the knapsack and threw it on top of the wardrobe. With my back to the window I now said to myself that I had done a terrible thing. But what matters, I thought, is that those remains are now out of sight, that I don't have to see those papers anymore. But of course the fact that the papers were now inside the desk and no longer inside the knapsack hadn't in the least changed the situation in which I now found myself, it was an atrocious situation. If anything, my conscience was hurting even worse because in unpacking the knapsack, by abruptly turning the knapsack over on the sofa, I had probably, I thought, mixed the papers up even more hopelessly than before. And since Roithamer's papers are hardly ever dated or numbered or anything, as I know for a fact, there was no hope at all that I could ever put them in order again, even to try to put them in order would drive me crazy, I thought, over and over, putting them in order would drive me crazy, so there I stood and said over and over that such a hopeless effort to put them in order would actually drive me crazy, and I kept thinking what a mess I'd made, I know what a mess I've made even if nobody else knows what a mess I've made. I sat down on the old chair by the door, in a state of exhaustion, of total exhaustion, it was suddenly clear to me what a hopeless fix I was in, I had apparently in a moment of total confusion lost my mind altogether and grabbed the knapsack and dumped its contents on the sofa and got all the papers so thoroughly mixed up they could never be straightened out again. So there I sat on that old chair and again said sort and sift, sift and sort, several times, until I had said it so often that I burst out laughing, suddenly I was laughing out loud, very loud. Afterward it was quiet as never before. Hoeller had turned out his light and I stood up and looked down and saw that it was dark in Hoeller's workshop. Now I didn't know why Hoeller had turned out the light just then, had he turned out the light because I had burst out into a laugh, or had he turned out the light without hearing me at all, simply because he had finished working on that huge black bird, actually Hoeller must have stopped working on the bird and left the workshop, unless he was still inside the workshop and had, for whatever reason, turned out the light, to stay in the workshop in the dark? I moved quite close to the window and listened, but I heard nothing, except suddenly the roaring of the Aurach again, but nothing else, as if all at once everything were asleep, as it seemed to me, on what basis I made this assumption I don't know, but all at once it seemed to me that the whole house was asleep, but why had Hoeller turned out the light at the very moment I burst out laughing, just after my laugh the light in Hoeller's workshop had been extinguished. But what would Hoeller be doing in the dark of the workshop, where he can't see anything, or is it possible that the light from my window, from the attic window, falling on the Aurach, is enough light for the workshop as well, could Hoeller have thought that if he turned out his light he'd have enough light coming from the attic window, I thought as I stood at the window, and then I thought but why should Hoeller suddenly stop working now, at half-past twelve in the morning when he seemed to have been all set for work all through the night, it wasn't at all an uncommon thing for him

to do to stay at work in his workshop all night long, while his
wife sits up in her bedroom all night long sewing or mending
or knitting, with only the Hoeller children able to sleep, it was
possible, I thought, that Hoeller was still there in his workshop, with his ears pricked up, watching me because, so I
thought, once he had turned out the light in his workshop and
could no longer be seen by me from the attic window, it was
easy for Hoeller to watch me, that's the kind of man he is, I
thought, to watch me up here at the attic window where I am
looking down at his workshop, while he's hidden in the dark,
watching me from where he sits, protected by the darkness at
his workshop window, possibly observing the state I'm in and
possibly drawing conclusions based on his observations with
regard to my constitution, my mental and physical constitution, so that in the morning he may treat me quite differently,
because of these nighttime observations, than he would have,
had he not observed me, after all it was I who attracted his
attention to myself by bursting into a loud laugh after all that
brooding over sorting and sifting the Roithamer legacy, I
thought, he can hardly do otherwise than keep me under
observation now, turning out the light gave him the opportunity to observe me. He didn't even have to get up and come to
the window, he can keep an eye on me from his workbench
where he might even yet be working at sewing up his bird,
from where Hoeller is now sitting, as I suppose, watching me,
he can observe me very well when I show myself at the attic
window, I thought, if I show myself at the window I can be
seen by Hoeller, in that case why am I showing myself? I
thought, after all I don't have to show myself at the window, I
can step back, I can step back so far that Hoeller can no longer
see me, can't possibly see me, and so I stepped back and I
thought, now that I've stepped back Hoeller might turn the
light on again in his workshop, because he'll assume that I'm
no longer interested in him now that I've stepped back from
the window, he can feel free to turn on the light, as I'm no

longer looking down there, I thought, he may well think, now I can turn on the light again here in the workshop, because he (me) is no longer looking down, quite possibly Hoeller was annoyed to see me constantly watching him, nobody likes to have someone constantly watching him, especially when he is absorbed in his work as Hoeller was absorbed just now in stuffing and sewing up that huge black bird. Now he has no reason not to turn up the light in his workshop again, I thought, as I was no longer watching him, Hoeller, I had sat down again on the old chair, though as I sat down I did slap my forehead with the flat of my hand several times, as though slapping my forehead was any use, I'd slipped into a state of excitement I couldn't get out of, here I've tried every trick in the book already, I thought, pacing the floor, walking to the window, walking away from the window, walking to the sofa and away from the sofa, to the door and back again, then staring at the floor, studying my own hands, my own feet, for I'd taken my shoes off as soon as I'd come back from supper downstairs, then later on I took off my socks too and I'd been barefoot the whole time I was up in the garret, barefoot if only to avoid disturbing the Hoellers by my constant pacing the floor, I had this habit of rapidly pacing the floor, when I pace the floor barefoot, I don't disturb anyone, so I'd always thought, and I'd always taken off my shoes, and naturally also my socks, even in England, anywhere at all, when I succumbed to my habit of pacing the floor, but studying my hands and feet and finally every object in Hoeller's garret, including a black rubber sausage hanging on the wall of Hoeller's garret which the Hoellers formerly used for driving cattle and which had attracted my special attention, what was this rubber sausage doing in Hoeller's garret of all places, I thought, probably Hoeller himself one day cut this piece off a black rubber cable and converted it to a truncheon with a steel-band grip, back in the days when he still had cows and goats, he had to have this kind of rubber sausage, everybody around here has such rubber sausages made out of pieces of old cable, you can see them all over the Aurach valley, driving their cattle with these black cable sausages, out of their farmyards and into their farm-yards, but what was this rubber sausage doing in Hoeller's garret? I asked myself, could it have meant something in particular to Roithamer, and if so, what? but I couldn't waste any more time on this rubber sausage, so I simply broke off thinking about this rubber cable sausage and took up another idea: namely, that thinking always came easier to me when I was barefoot than when I wasn't barefoot, and why should it be that I can think not only more easily but more thoroughly about everything when barefoot, so that by now it's an almost lifelong habit of mine to take off my shoes at once indoors wherever it's permissible, and to run about barefoot, in Hoeller's house I hadn't taken off my shoes at first, I'd realized on entering that here I couldn't take off my shoes, not right away, but upstairs in Hoeller's garret I'd immediately taken my shoes off and walked around in my socks, going back and forth in my socks, unpacking and sitting down and inspecting Hoeller's garret for the first time, until I put on my shoes again to go down to supper because it seemed impossible to me to go down to supper in Hoeller's family room in my socks, because the Hoellers all wore shoes too, they didn't go barefoot, prob-ably it was *on my account they didn't go barefoot, just as it was on their account that I didn't go barefoot,* so none of us went barefoot, even though it would have suited all of us, the Hoellers as well as myself, to go barefoot, but right after supper, once I was back in the garret, I took off my shoes and my socks too and went barefoot. Going barefoot dates from my childhood, when I always went barefoot too, I even went barefoot to school, throughout the year, except only in the coldest months, we all went to school barefoot, all but Roithamer who wasn't allowed to go barefoot because no child had ever come down from Altensam barefoot, how he'd longed to go barefoot with us, but it was never allowed, so he was always the one in school who never went barefoot, as even I had always been allowed to go barefoot, a rarity for the son of a doctor. If I walk barefoot they won't hear me, I'd thought, and so as soon as I'd entered Hoeller's garret I walked around and back and forth a lot in my bare feet in order to practice this barefoot walking in Hoeller's garret, but once I'm aware how walking barefoot cuts down on the noise, even the barefoot walking becomes louder, I thought, so I mustn't be aware that I am walking barefoot and therefore walking quietly. Actually, Roithamer had always gone barefoot in Hoeller's garret, as I know for a fact, but he never went barefoot down to meals with the Hoellers, not even in summer, when it was quite normal and natural for all the Hoellers to go barefoot. Somehow that rubber cable sausage on the wall annoyed me and I took the rubber cable sausage off the wall, it was black and heavy and I cut the air with it a few times, then I repeated this cutting-the-air several times while looking out the window, in case I might be observed doing it. And suppose, I thought briefly, suppose I hit the desk with this rubber sausage? but I didn't hit the desk with the rubber sausage, for fear of doing something with this rubber sausage that I'd better leave undone, I hung the rubber sausage back on the wall. But I couldn't get my mind off the rubber sausage so I took it down again, opened the door, and hung it on a hook, out in the corridor, which had a straw hat hanging on it, probably Mrs. Hoeller's straw hat, I thought. Back inside Hoeller's garret I thought, all right, so now the rubber sausage is no longer inside Hoeller's garret, and I wonder if I'm not being watched after all, it seemed to me that I was being watched but I couldn't say for sure. People always do whatever they do for themselves alone, only for themselves and never, in no instance, is it done for someone else's sake. If Hoeller is still in his workshop, I thought, then why hasn't he turned on the light again, it seemed to me that I'd heard a sound from Hoeller's workshop, a sound connected with Hoeller's work, as I thought, so Hoeller must still be down there in his preservatory, but if so why was he hiding from me, at half-past one in the morning? I thought. Just then some metal object must actually have dropped from Hoeller's hand, for I heard something metallic fall in the workshop. But then again: why isn't he turning the light on again? So it suddenly occurred to me to turn out my light, to cast Hoeller's garret into total darkness, to make Hoeller think I'd gone to bed now, finally gone to bed, so that he could keep on working undisturbed in his workshop, unobserved by me, working on his huge black bird, with all his lights on. I'd turned out my light and posted myself at the window in the expectation that Hoeller would now soon turn on the light in his workshop again, I was convinced that Hoeller was still in his workshop, after all I'd never heard him leave his workshop and go to his room, so he had to be in his workshop still, now that I'd completely darkened Hoeller's garret, actually it was now pitch-dark in Hoeller's garret, and when I looked outside I could also see nothing but total darkness, I might have suddenly heard the roaring of the Aurach again but I couldn't see the Aurach, couldn't see a thing, for it is well known that the darkness here along the Aurach, in the Aurach valley and most of all in the Aurach gorge, is the most impenetrable and so the darkest possible, that Hoeller chose the darkest point of this darkness, the Aurach gorge, to build his house in, and that Roithamer felt most comfortable here in this darkest darkness or, more precisely, that he found in the darkest place of all the ideal conditions for his purposes, is just what you'd expect. As for me, I never felt anything but frightened by the Aurach gorge, every minute I was there, at least that evening after my arrival and the subsequent night I have just described. From one moment to the next I expected Hoeller to turn on his light, but he didn't turn it on, possibly, I thought, because he'd caught on that I'd turned out the light in the garret only so he'd turn on the light in his workshop again, because he knows that I haven't gone to bed as I've tried to make him think but that I'm still at the window only waiting for him to turn on his light in the workshop again so that I can see him and watch him again. Better be on my guard against such people (like me) he'd probably thought and kept putting off turning on the light in his workshop, he'd sooner sit there in the pitch-darkness without turning on the light, I thought, ruining his eyes because he's probably continuing to work on his huge black bird in total darkness, but as for turning on the light and letting himself be watched again by me, never. So I simply couldn't stand it anymore and suddenly turned my light on again in Hoeller's garret and I rushed to the window to see Hoeller's reaction to my turning the light on again in the garret. I actually saw Hoeller sitting there at work with that huge black bird on his lap. He, Hoeller, is looking up at me, he's working on the bird and looking up at me too, I thought. But then I stepped back from the window, because I didn't want him to see me, and in stepping backward I overturned the big clothes tree that was standing beside the window, in my haste I'd stumbled over it. Almost immediately my door flew open and there stood Hoeller, at the door, in his night-shirt. What happened, he said, and I pointed to the fallen clothes tree. He helped me to pick up the clothes tree. He expressed surprise that I hadn't gone to bed yet but was still up and dressed. Once he had helped me to set up the clothes tree again, he left the garret without saying a word. So he hadn't been in his workshop, in his preservatory, at all, I thought. I took off my clothes, turned out the light, and went to bed. It was half-past two and I thought, just before falling asleep, how utterly exhausted I felt. In the morning I'll sneak up on Roithamer's legacy, I'll just sort of *sneak up* on it first, then I'll *sift* it and *sort* it.

# Sifting and Sorting

He, Roithamer, had never had to get away from Altensam, he had, in fact, struggled all his life only to draw closer to Altensam, to make himself understood where it had always been impossible, a crazy dream, where it always would be impossible for him to be understood, Roithamer had written, nor had he ever achieved the slightest rapprochement with Altensam, for he had always been a foreign element in Altensam. He simply wasn't the man to adapt himself, against his grain, against the dictates of his character, the word *opportune* was totally alien, totally inapplicable to anything he could ever think or do, but as for me and my outlook and my ideas and everything, I'd always been an opportunist, Roithamer wrote. Everything in Altensam had always been impossibly hard for him, so he couldn't stand Altensam from the beginning, he couldn't give in to Altensam and its rules, he took the first opportunity to get clear of Altensam. Just as Altensam was alien to him, so he must have seemed a foreign element to his family, they had in the end worn each other out and used each other up in chronic mutual recriminations, primordial recriminations, Roithamer wrote, that is, he, Roithamer, on the one side and Roithamer's family on the other side, were wearing each other out all the time in Altensam in the most inhuman way, a way least worthy of human beings, in this process of sheer mutual exhaustion. His natural bent for studying, i.e., for studying everything, however, had enabled him quite early in life, by studying Altensam, to see through Altensam and thereby to see through himself and to achieve insight and to take action, and thanks to these constant ongoing lifelong studies he'd always had to do as he ended up doing; all his life, though he'd rather call it his existence, or better still, his deathward existence, everything he'd ever done had been based on nothing but this habit of studying which he'd never been able to shake off, where other people get ahead easily and often quite rapidly, he'd never gotten ahead easily or rapidly, obsessed as he was with the habit of always studying, all of him, his organism, his mind, and everything he did, determined by this habit of studying. Everything had always come to him the hard way, the hardest possible. Yet it was evident almost from the beginning that such constant, above-normal efforts paid off, Roithamer's words, because of them everything I did went deeper, no step was taken without a thorough grounding in what preceded it, Roithamer wrote, nothing without completing all prior studies or at least trying to complete them, without trying to have first a clear understanding of everything that went before, although I knew, of course, that no clear understanding of anything is possible, only an approach to an understanding, an approximate though not an actual understanding, nevertheless an approximation. And so, while I loved Altensam more than anything in the world, because Altensam has always been closer to me than anything in the world, I also hated it more than anything in the world, because I've always been a foreign element there from the outset, and all my life, my whole existence, my deathward existence, had always been determined by that circumstance, causing a monstrous waste of all my energies. The question has always been only, *how can I go on at all, not in what respect and in what condition,* so Roithamer. But no one in my vicinity had even the merest inkling of what was going on inside the young man I was, they were never capable of conceiving the possibility of so devastating a state of mind that could determine and devastate and ruin an entire life like this, because they simply did not want to think about it, everything in Altensam always opposed thinking as such, it must be said categorically once and for all, to the discredit of Altensam, that Altensam was opposed to any kind of thought. Altensam was always a place disposed to take action, there one

took action without stopping to think, there action always
excluded thought, and it still is like that, except that nowadays
there's not even any action left in Altensam, the Altensamers
today are incapable of taking action, they are condemned to
impotence, for lo these many years, they've been condemned
to inaction, because their time is up, it's all up with them. But
what was Altensam like only thirty or thirty-five years ago?
It's a question I must face again and again, it's the most
important question of all, I must ask myself, What was Altensam, where I come from, thirty or thirty-five years ago, when I
was beginning to think for myself? A composite of masonry
and men where action was taken without prior thought, for
centuries on end. At the outset, in earliest childhood, he, Roithamer, had not yet revealed himself as the person he manifest-
ly came to be later on, not for a long time, not until he was
well into grade school, had he himself understood who he
really was, that basically, even though he was from Altensam
or because he was from Altensam, he had always been against
Altensam, as a child he had not yet been recognizably against
Altensam though he'd turned against Altensam long since, but
outwardly his childhood, at least his earliest childhood, had
seemed to be a normal Altensam childhood, *not yet an anti-
Altensam childhood,* although even then, as soon as I began to
think at all, as I've said, everything inside me turned against
Altensam, against everything connected with Altensam, connected with Altensam to this day, anyway there have always
been two Altensams, so Roithamer, the one that I loved because it was not against me and the other one, the second one,
which I've always hated because it was absolutely against me,
from the start and with the utmost ruthlessness. The Altensam
that I always loved, however, is not the Altensam that has
nothing to do with the people in Altensam, Roithamer wrote,
it is the one in which my nature always found sanctuary, while
the other one, the one I hated, was always the one in which I
never found sanctuary, the one that always rubbed me the

wrong way. So when I say that I hate Altensam I always mean the Altensam in which I never found sanctuary, the one that always rubbed me the wrong way, rejected me, which is why I had to reject it in turn, and not the other one in which my nature always found refuge and where I was at least left in peace. Of course I tend to be preoccupied with the Altensam that refused me and rejected me and rubbed me the wrong way, not with the other one, as I am always preoccupied with everything that gives me no peace, repels me, rubs me the wrong way. There's always the kind that leaves us in peace and lets us be ourselves and lets us develop in so many, sometimes quite wonderful ways, and then there's the other kind that rubs us the wrong way and gives us no peace, no peace all our lives long, and so we are preoccupied with it all our lives long, it makes us fidgety, we become more fidgety day by day, there is no escaping it for the rest of our lives, and so we become angry with everything for the rest of our lives. All the stuff that's constantly on my mind comes from this, this turmoil, and not from the other, the one that leaves me in peace, Roithamer wrote. From my earliest childhood, in Altensam, it was always the one that gave me no peace that I kept thinking about, not the other one, naturally. We speak, when we speak with all our being, only as we are driven by that unrest, not the other, Roithamer wrote. I have always spoken only out of that unrest, I was never driven to speak by the other one, which after all leaves me in peace, and *so enables me* to speak of my unrest. It is not only a need we have to speak constantly, and to complain, and at least keep our attention on whatever is born of our unrest, since only these thoughts and feelings and thought-feelings and vice versa of course have the greater significance. Peace is not life, Roithamer wrote, perfect peace is death, as Pascal said, wrote Roithamer. But such phrases will get me nowhere, I must get away from these phrases, so Roithamer, I shouldn't waste my time on truisms already demonstrated by history. My awakening in Altensam

was the simultaneous decision to get away from Altensam, to
get away from everything, to push off from everything that is
Altensam, and this process of pushing off is all I have accomplished so far, no matter where I did it, or under what circumstances, and even when on the face of it there seemed to be no
connection with Altensam whatsoever. An awakening in my
room in Altensam, perhaps, in my turret room, an awakening
at the south wall or the east wall, I loved the south wall and
the east wall equally, an awakening perhaps under the linden
tree or in the kitchen or in the entrance hall where I often sat
for hours on end, waiting for my parents, in the icy cold,
studying the floor planks in the hall and then, beginning with
the floor planks, studying everything, the staircase, the lamps
on the staircase, the chapel door, the kitchen door, the objects
in the hall, or else an awakening in one of the cellars where I
used to hide so often, sometimes in the wine cellar, sometimes
in the beer cellar, sometimes in the apple cellar, so many cellars
in Altensam, in one of those cellars came that awakening
against Altensam, against everything connected with Altensam, or perhaps on that cliff in the woods where I went so
often, or in the clearing where they put up the iron-cross
memorial for an ancestor who was killed by a falling tree hit
by lightning, or in my brothers' room or in my sister's room,
the music room perhaps, or possibly the farm buildings, wherever the woodcutters, the farmhands, the maids are put up, I
don't know, Roithamer's words. It might have been during one
of those walks I took with my father, those silent walks,
always in the same direction, year in, year out, the same way
down from Altensam into that vast primeval forest, that forest
which my father always referred to as the *natural forest,* since it
hadn't been planted in accordance with the rules of forestry
but had simply grown, without human intervention, a forest
that simply *blew in by the most natural route,* as my father
always said, my father loved this forest, Roithamer wrote, his
walks took him only into this forest, and I could come along,

but I had to keep quiet. Quite possibly it happened on one of those walks that lasted six or seven hours during which the silence must never be broken. Deep down my father had loved only this natural forest, with its seeds blown in from anywhere, its random mixture of trees, Roithamer wrote, and nothing else. My father's life was unimaginable without this natural, wind-seeded, mixed forest, Roithamer wrote. On one of those walks my sudden awakening against Altensam and against everything connected with Altensam, Roithamer wrote, "everything connected with Altensam" is underlined. Or else it happened the time I was with my mother in the so-called pine woods, or with my sister in her room which was next to my room, I don't know. But it was an awakening, a sudden awakening of my opposition against Altensam and against everything connected with Altensam, which determined the entire rest of my life. From that moment on I wanted to get away, to get out, but I had many more years to wait. Light broke with my school years, with the opportunity to get away from Altensam on the way down to school, to make contact by myself with other people on this road, with the kind of people who at least had nothing directly to do with Altensam, a wholly different sort of people. For I'd had no opportunity to make contact with other people, in full critical awareness, before my school days, for I'd always been prevented from making such contacts as I could have had in Altensam, in preparation for later contacts as it were, from making contacts up in Altensam to prepare for making contacts down below. If I visited the woodcutters, I was immediately called back home, the same for our own farmhands, but of course I'd always felt attracted to these people, probably from my earliest days and to a great degree, *because* such contacts were forbidden. And it was precisely their keeping me away from all others than those born at Altensam which caused me to hate them, later on, to hate all of them and everything connected with them. It was hatred, nothing but hatred, Roithamer wrote. The word "hatred" is underlined. But the people with whom I was denied and forbidden to make and keep contact, I loved, so Roithamer. The word "loved" is underlined. My childhood was nothing but wanting to get away from what I'd been forced into from the beginning, in Altensam, that is, and wanting to get into that other world which I was refused and denied and forbidden, wanting this with a perverse determination, as I now see. They must have sensed that I was different even from my own siblings, who had unquestioningly obeyed all the rules at Altensam, who had never rebelled, in contrast to myself who had rebelled from earliest childhood, three or four years old, as I know, against the regulations and against the brutality of those regulations enforced by my parents or the other so-called authorities in Altensam, they had sensed that from my earliest childhood I had felt absolutely independent, and later on had thought along absolutely independent lines, never willing to submit to their ideas and their orders. It was their misfortune to have brought me into the world, this could not be undone, though they probably often wished they could falsify history to this extent, so Roithamer. Neither my parents nor my siblings nor any of the others who came from Altensam or were connected with Altensam, the whole family in all its distant branches, could ever understand that they were confronted with someone who was always against them and their circumstances and conditions with all his mind and feeling, someone they themselves had brought into the world and who bore their name. And so the fact that my father left Altensam to me, so Roithamer, thinking that his other two sons and his only daughter, my sister, could be satisfied with a financial settlement by me, is nothing but an expression of my father's intention to destroy Altensam by making such a will, giving a rude shock to all and sundry, a will which incidentally was contested in vain, by my brothers, father meant to destroy Altensam by such a will because he knew and above all consciously felt that he was destroying Altensam by leaving it to me, so Roithamer. No mad caprice on his part, he knew what he was doing, so Roithamer had added. For my father knew (seismographically) that Altensam's time had come. But he preferred, so Roithamer, to destroy Altensam totally by willing it to me, thereby to destroy it totally in the shortest possible time, because he always fully understood that I hate Altensam, rather than let it gradually sink further into decline as would undoubtedly have been the case had he left Altensam not to me but to my oldest brother or to the younger one, or to both of them together, for there was never any question but that he'd have my sister's share paid out to her. When I sell Altensam, as I now intend to do, so Roithamer, and use the proceeds, and that *must be a very high sum,* I'd rather drag out the sale a little longer than rush it, Altensam must bring a very high price indeed, and when, using these high proceeds, I do all I possibly can for the ex-convicts after their release from the penitentiaries, then my father's wish to destroy Altensam totally will have been fulfilled. Ads, possibly contact real estate agents, but cautiously, so Roithamer. By selling Altensam I'll fulfill my dream of doing all I can for the outcasts of society, for the most outcast of all, whom society itself has always most complacently driven into crime, and by that I mean always most complacently without giving it much thought, let alone paid any attention specifically to what it was doing to them, I shall be helping those people whom society has made into, as it pleases to call them, criminals, because society doesn't *think*, because it hates thinking, which is alien to its nature, more than anything. For me nothing can be more important than helping those released prisoners, using the proceeds from the sale of Altensam, but also to do something for those still imprisoned, as much as possible. And to smash, to destroy such a property as Altensam, which has simply outlasted its time, for the sake of such an undertaking, is at the moment more important to me than anything else.

First, I must put the finishing touches on the Cone, the end is in sight there, secondly, I must sell Altensam for the sake of the convicts. Human society is absolutely shameless vis-à-vis its criminals, whom it locks up in its penitentiaries, so Roithamer, in full consciousness and with all the˙ brutality and meanness and inhumanity which are its distinguishing characteristics, society catapults these people into their so-called crimes which are simply nothing but traps, death traps, set up for them by this inhuman society, and then turns away from them. If I have a mission at all, it is surely this, to help the convicts, those so-called criminals, who are actually our sick people, so Roithamer, those whom society has catapulted into their sickness. No man has the right ever to speak of criminals, no one and never, so Roithamer, it's always, as with the others, a case of sickness, of those sickened by society, and all of society is nothing but hundreds and many hundreds of millions of people fallen sick of themselves, except that some of them, the unlucky and the most unlucky of them, the most slandered and betrayed, the victims of all the ridicule and mockery and meanness and all that human filth, are locked up and the others aren't. The purchase price must be the highest possible, so Roithamer. Get various assessments etcetera, so Roithamer. Use the money to do everything possible for those people, so Roithamer, build homes, buildings for them, taking into account my experiences with the Cone project, so Roithamer, always near the centers, population centers, avoid anything contributing to isolation, disregarding the fact that *everything is isolation,* opportunities for work, opportunities to find occupations, optimal freedom of the individual. *Intellectual freedom, physical freedom,* so Roithamer. Create new provisions for these people. Provision for their entertainment. *Growth,* so Roithamer. When we are obsessed with an idea and suddenly have an opportunity to realize this idea, because we have been constantly and incessantly preoccupied with this idea and always to the highest degree, always concentrated upon this idea (see Cone), until we became nothing but a mind concentrated only on this idea, when we can make our prediction come true, no matter how crazy we've been thought to be and even considered ourselves to be on account of such an idea. When despite everything we've succeeded in the realization of this idea. When for years, for decades, we've paid attention to nothing but this idea, with which we are identical. We achieve only that aim upon which we concentrate one hundred percent, including our so-called subconscious, when we pay heed to nothing but this one aim for the longest time until the moment when we have fulfilled this aim. When we are always aware of the fact that everything unites in conspiring against our aim, that everything outside ourselves and very often too a great deal within ourselves is nothing but a conspiracy against our plan, against our aim. When we ruthlessly take a stand, and most ruthlessly of all against everything that obstructs our work toward our aim, everything that torpedoes our aim, until we finally take a stand against ourselves, because we also can no longer believe that we can achieve our aim despite this whole comprehensive, all-comprehending resistance and therefore revulsion against our aim, because we are constantly attacked by doubts of ourselves and thereby of our aim and become weakened by these doubts, which makes it seem impossible that we will achieve our aim, but we must allow nothing, "nothing" is underlined, to deter us from our aim, as I have never let myself be deterred from an aim of mine, so Roithamer, for, so Roithamer, everything is always against every aim. Even the smallest objective must be achieved despite total opposition, how much more so the great objective, so Roithamer. Suddenly there's an idea and it demands realization, our entire life, our entire existence consists only of such ideas demanding realization, once this process breaks off, our life breaks off, we're dead. We consist of nothing but ideas that surface inside us and that we want to realize, that we must realize, or else we're dead, so Roithamer. Every idea and every pursuit of an idea inside us is life, so Roithamer, the lack of ideas is death. And the person under consideration may appear as simple as we choose to think, which he never really is, however, or else as complicated as we like to think, which he never is either, so Roithamer. A man's lack of ideas is his death, so Roithamer, just think how many there are quite without ideas, entirely lacking any idea, they don't exist. Ads to begin with, then real estate agents, so Roithamer, but the utmost caution is called for with those real estate agents, it's the same as with everything else, the utmost mistrust is in order, the more mistrust the better, but then, once a certain point of understanding has been reached, action must be taken. We always need to compare the various possibilities, without a chance to compare, we can't think, we can't act, we're stymied, so Roithamer. Compare properties and prices, so Roithamer. Find out about the actual situation in real estate, the market situation. Understand that sellers and buyers always play the same roles, always liable to be conned by the other fellow. What a sensation when I sell Altensam, so Roithamer, so it must all be kept in the background, handled as inconspicuously as possible. No talk about it, not even when it's done, no talk whatsoever about it. And take care beforehand that, first of all, my sister's interests are safeguarded, that no one is unfairly implicated in that sale, not even my brothers, although to spare my brothers verges on idiocy, when did they ever spare me? *they* are not sparing me even now, but I won't throw them out without compensation, though they have no right whatever to compensation, *neither legally nor morally,* they've always been against me, their aberrant brother, they made no bones about their contempt and their hatred for me, they really worked at becoming adepts in the art of tormenting me, not to forget their inventiveness in torturing me, their finesse in humiliating me was always extraordinary, not to forget that they never had any use for me whatsoever, still, that's no reason to treat them without any consideration

at all, anyway I'll spare them, not because they deserve it, they
*don't* deserve it, but only because I want them out of the way,
out of my way. And I want my sister inside the Cone I've built
for her, once the Cone is all furnished she'll move in, it's the
perfect work of art, building art, for her to live in, which I was
actually capable of though it runs counter to my mind and
counter to all, even my, reason. The Cone's placement in the
center of the Kobernausser forest is exactly right for her.
Supreme happiness? Then we wake up and see that we've
achieved what we wanted to achieve by being relentless and
most of all relentless toward ourselves, by not deluding ourselves and by paying no attention to what other people say, for
if we'd paid attention to other people, so Roithamer, we
wouldn't have achieved anything, because the others are always against us, that's the only truth. Sell Altensam and use
the proceeds to put the released convicts back on their feet.
Offend against so-called good taste, against which I've always
offended, all my life I've always offended against so-called
good taste. Once we fail to offend against so-called good taste
by doing something tasteful, we can say good-bye to our
character, our reason, our self. Anyway it wouldn't make sense
to remodel Altensam for the convicts, the place wouldn't suit
them. It would make Altensam nothing more than one of
many such places, in our country so many penitentiaries are
located in the most beautiful landscapes, oh no, that's out,
why, that would be crazy! "that would be crazy" is crossed
out, then stetted. The thing is to sell Altensam with everything
in it, sell it at a good price, not at a loss, without squandering
it, to sell it, using my head and perfect timing. Keep a sharp
eye on the notary and pay him only for work actually done,
not by the official legal tariff (or his own inflated expectations). His fee must reflect *his actual success* with the sale. But
the question is whether I can't sell Altensam myself, on my
own, by some lucky chance perhaps, in which case I'll save the
middleman's fee. They've always let themselves be taken by

the notaries and the lawyers, all of them, that hasn't changed. "Buy a smaller property for my brothers" is crossed out. Take care of all my sister's needs for life. "Contractual basis" is underlined. We reject everything having to do with contracts, because we reject bureaucracy *in toto,* but in fact the world is only held together by a patchwork of contracts, as we soon perceive, and in this network of hundreds and thousands and hundreds of thousands and millions and billions of contracts the trapped human beings are squirming. There's no way to get around contracts except by suicide. Contracts everywhere, they've already choked everything to death, a whole world choking to death on its contracts, so Roithamer. To suppose that it is possible to exist without contracts or other written agreements and run away, anywhere at all, is to find ourselves soon caught again in contracts and written agreements, anyone who thinks otherwise is a madman, a malicious falsifier of the nature of things. It's only in childhood that we don't know what kind of a trap it is in which we squirm and despair and keep on despairing as we go on squirming in it, ignorant that these are the nets of contracts and other written agreements made by the grown-ups, by history. If anyone were to succeed in doing away with all these contracts and other written agreements, all he'd have accomplished would be the end of the whole world. In the future, where everything is possible, this too is possible. But so far it hasn't been possible, nor is it possible in the immediate future, so Roithamer, the foreseeable future is all contracts, written agreements, and the resulting fits of despair, impediments, sicknesses, causes of death, that's all. Our entire being is tied to contracts, written agreements, assessments, we're trapped in them for life, no matter what we do, no matter who we are. Still we keep trying all our lives to escape from these contracts and other written agreements, efforts as painful as they are senseless, so Roithamer. Look up lawyers, notaries, find out just how sharp they are, conversely, how defenseless I am, compare the ignorance of the lawyers, the notaries, with my own defenselessness. Remember that everything that was sold hitherto was sold too cheaply, everything bought hitherto, bought too dear. Commercial instincts, perceptions, money, usury, swindle, forgery, sharp practice, so Roithamer. Ours are the finest forests in the world, as well as the most productive, a hundred years' growth. Quality of the soil A-1. And all those rights belonging to Altensam, fishing rights, lumbering rights, hunting rights etcetera. Bound to fetch a record price, anything else unthinkable. All living and dead inventory included. Make a study of traditional and untraditional agreements-to-purchase, financial regulations, buying-out nonsense, so Roithamer. Get the Cone finished, forget work on Cone, resume my scientific work while also getting on with selling off Altensam, so Roithamer. Working out of England at first, because I must get back into my Cambridge routine, where I hardly feel at home anymore, using Hoeller's insights in Hoeller's garret everything's to be considered toward securing my career, my future, then operate from Hoeller's garret. Observe my sister as she enters the finished Cone, show her the Cone's interior from top to bottom, not from the ground up, may have to blindfold her when we enter the Cone, lead her up to the inside tip of the Cone, then open her eyes and bit by bit familiarize her with the entire interior of the Cone. Clear my head of everything connected with Richter's Fundamentals of Statics and stress analysis, forget Chmelka, Melan, forget everything I was absorbed in during the building of the Cone, *first during three years of planning, then during the three years it took to build the Cone,* try to clear my head of everything connected with the Cone, try especially to get rid of the word "statics" that keeps turning up through the night, makes it impossible for me even to think of falling asleep, the moment I drop off, the word "statics" comes into my head and actually stops me from falling asleep, for years now. Terminate everything connected with the Cone and with finishing the Cone before I liquidate

Altensam. Sister provided for by being stuck away in the Cone by her brother, as I hear it, that crazy eccentric brother, so Roithamer, that crazy, mad, eccentric, blasphemous, insane construction. Just the same I shan't let any so-called architects come near the Cone even in the future, I must secure the Cone against all building professionals. These so-called architects and building professionals only show up in order to kill off the work of art, which it is, by setting foot in it, they destroy it, merely by looking it over. It's the work of a madman, a violent intellectual, a crazy obsessed with a senseless idea, so said my brother, so Roithamer, the word "crazy" underlined. But I've never in my life cared what people said, not even what they always thought (about me), so I'm sure that I won't bother about them in the future either. Professional riffraff, so-called architects, intellectual charlatans, so Roithamer, exploiters of their clients, knuckleheads, brains of cement. Never answered a single inquiry, its origin suspect, some architect or building professional might be behind it. They never heard of James Gandon, for example, Sir John Soane, John Nash etcetera. When we act, we know the source of our action, when we think, the source of our thinking. Boulle, Hamilton, Vignon, conceptual change etcetera, so Roithamer, we mention in vain. I'd merely make a suggestion, and they go to pieces. Nothing from Neutra's publications, everything from Mies van der Rohe's, "nothing" and "everything" underlined. No dealings with the professionals because they destroy our ideas, they are single-mindedly intent upon undermining our idea, upon destroying it. Never advance an idea to a professional because if you do it won't be long before that idea will be shaky, the image dubious, impossible to realize, leave the idea in its hiding place until it's realized, fulfilled. Leave the thought and the idea in its isolation cell until the utmost degree of realization, substantiation, perfection has been reached. Think how many will then be living off our idea, the idea we had, "we" underlined, our idea gets picked up and shamelessly exploited, we see it happening time and again, how an idea is picked up and shamelessly exploited by hundreds of imitators, which is a way of destroying the idea, but if it's a good idea it can't be destroyed. An idea, always an extraordinary idea, attracts hundreds of parasites who hook onto it and suck it dry and ruthlessly capitalize on it, always to the loss of the person who had the idea in the first place. Keep thought and idea immured as long as possible. Yield it up when perfected, pay the price of absolute misery for it. Most people, the highest percentage of people, live off ideas not their own, which they exploit to the utter limit without shame, but they're never called to account for this, on the contrary, they're praised for it everywhere. Wherever we turn we see exploiters of (other people's) ideas, making good money off them. So, I won't let the so-called professionals come near my Cone, but the time must come when I can no longer hide the Cone, whereupon the so-called professional world will pounce on the Cone and exploit the idea, there's no point in holding back the inevitable, sooner or later the Cone will be discovered, they'll all pounce on the idea and on the hundreds and thousands of ideas connected with it, and the Cone will be exploited, ruthlessly. But no one can say the idea is mine, mine for life, "for life" underlined. We draw attention to something new and they all hurl themselves into this new thing even though this new thing was pointed out by *us,* but that's never mentioned anymore. We're the ones who make a discovery but we don't exploit this discovery, it's the people who exploit it who make a splash with it. First I must finish the Cone, then concentrate on the sale of Altensam, then resume my scientific work, Cambridge, London, London, Cambridge alternately, because that's always done me good, if this leave of absence is to have served its purpose, in that the Cone will have been built and finished, Altensam will have been sold off. Although we hate everything at times, we find it possible, or even because we at times hate everything, it is at times possible to move onward, propelled by nothing but hatred, to move ahead. Because we are weak, infirm, we must tolerate no weakness whatever. And if it isn't life and if it isn't nature then it's what we read, it's the life and the nature of what we read, for long stretches there's only the nature we get out of our reading, life out of books, periodicals, all kinds of writings, we bridge the gaps between our contact with nature itself by reading that represents nature, represents life. Because we can't always, no organism is capable of it, absorb nature into ourselves, absorb life-as-nature into ourselves, we go for long stretches, for *years on end absorbing it only through reading matter,* from the newspapers, from written stuff. In several languages, for variety's sake. At certain points in our existence we break off the nature of our existence and proceed to exist only in books, in written stuff, until we again have the opportunity to exist in nature and continue to exist in nature, very often as another person, always as another person, "always as another person" underlined. We couldn't endure a life in nature, necessarily always a free nature, without respite, so we always step outside nature, for no reason but survival, and take refuge in our reading, and live for a long time in our books, a more undisturbed life. I've lived half my life not in nature but in my books as a nature-substitute, and the one half was made possible only by the other half. Or else we exist in both simultaneously, in nature and in reading-as-nature, in this extreme nervous tension which as a form of consciousness is endurable only for the shortest possible time span. The question can't be whether I live in nature as nature, or in reading-as-nature, or in nature-as-reading, in the nature of nature-as-reading andsoforth, so Roithamer. To everything that we think and fill our own life and that we hear and see, perceive, we always have to add: the truth, however, is . . . as a result, uncertainty has become a chronic condition with us. Those abrupt transitions from one nature into the other, from one form of awareness into the other, so Roithamer. When we think, we *know* nothing, everything is open, nothing, so Roithamer. The nature of the case is always something else, so Roithamer. First, the Cone offers views in all directions, then, the Cone offers views only southward and northward, then, only to the west and to the east, finally, only to the north. The spaces, not rooms, the spaces are such as to correspond perfectly to my sister's nature, they are designed to adapt themselves to whatever state of mind my sister finds herself in as she enters these spaces, and to do so immediately. To achieve this it was naturally necessary to have kept my sister under constant observation, continuous observation of my sister from earliest childhood on, it's been most helpful that I've always kept her under the most intensive observation, and always quite objectively, trying to understand her nature through all the years of her life, even before it ever occurred to me to build the Cone for her. My observation of my sister turned into an art and into a science of observation. And I naturally also observed everything connected with my sister, above all her habits, her possibilities, "possibilities" underlined, her impossibilities, what she was born with, what was bred into her, what she displays openly. Constant study of her inner life, insofar as this was possible by means of constant, continual observation and the constant and continuous study of her appearance, the inside and the outside are the same, everything depends on the observer's judgment. Knowing that I must never relax this observation of my sister, must never relinquish this observation, mustn't allow my judgment to be swayed, to become imprecise. First I had to concentrate my entire being, meaning all my mind and feeling, on my sister, then I had to do the same for the construction of the Cone, finally I *applied* my observations as insights to the construction of the Cone, so that I must assume that the Cone is ideal for my sister. The Cone's interior corresponding to my sister's inner being, the Cone's exterior to her outward being, and together her whole being expressed as the *Cone's character,* the inside and outside of the Cone are as inseparable as the inside and outside of my sister, but the *incessant observation of my sister and the incessant observation of the construction of the Cone* have led to the result which now stands in the center of the Kobernausser forest. Therefore, if my observation of my sister is correct, then the construction of the Cone is correct, so Roithamer. The consistent study of one object (of my sister), the consistent mode of construction of the other object (the Cone). The construction of such a Cone for such a person as my sister is feasible only after the study of the person (my sister) for whom such an edifice (the Cone) is being erected, has been completed. First I study the person for whom I am building such an edifice, then I build the edifice on the basis of my study, and such a study must be ultraconsistent. And only after I have truly studied that person's nature and gone far enough in my study to have grasped that person's nature, or at least grasped it insofar as it is humanly possible to grasp it, can I be sufficiently clear in my own mind as to what I am building and what materials I must use to build with. This is an edifice of stone and brick. The problem of the statics of the one (the Cone) is the problem of the nature of the other (my sister). And to build *against that person's will,* because one can build only against the will of a person like my sister. Not because of this person for whom I am building, but because of the person's character, and in that character the one, if not *emotionally* sensitive, perhaps the one *intellectually* sensitive point. We decide to build though we don't know what it means to build, as everyone knows, especially not what it means to build such an unheard-of edifice as the Cone for a person like my sister, we don't realize that it is basically a lethal process. Insofar as we have taken into consideration everything that must be taken into consideration we have to say that the art of building is a philosophical art in the highest degree, but the building professionals or the so-called building professionals have never understood, they shy away from this realization and refuse to enter into the problematics of it, and so we almost never get

an *art* of building, all we see is the *vulgarity* of building. We
must know the person and have seen through the person, or at
least know the person up to the crucial point, and be familiar
with him to the crucial, necessary degree, before we can build
for him, for even after we have passed our tests on this score it
remains questionable whether our edifice truly suits the person for whom we have built it, we assume that it suits him,
just as I only assume that it suits my sister one hundred
percent, because I must make this assumption, had to make
this assumption all the time I was building, otherwise I'd have
gone crazy and could never have finished the Cone at all, the
completion of the Cone would have remained a utopian
dream. Our buildings, no matter which, those intended as
habitations as well as the non-habitations, would look rather
different if those who built them had been in the least concerned about the people for whom they were building them,
all of these buildings were built without asking those who
would be affected, not to mention studying them. Just as we
investigate the causes of disease nowadays, knowing they
must be investigated, as the doctors can no longer evade this
necessity of investigation, those who build should investigate
those for whom they are building, they must investigate them,
the investigation of the man for whom a building is being put
up should be the duty of the man who is doing the building,
the builder should be forbidden to build for someone he has
not thoroughly investigated or at least understood to the necessary or the minimal necessary degree. The builders build
without having concerned themselves with the nature of those
for whom they are building, though the builders of course
deny this when confronted with it. With nothing in their
heads but their fees and their careers, those professional builders or whatever they may choose to call themselves put up
their buildings without any idea of the people for whom they
have built them, thereby committing one of the greatest
crimes, "greatest crimes" underlined. After all it took me six

years to build the Cone, a long time when subtracted from my
life, and yet a short time when I consider that first I solidly
prepared for it and then did a solid job of building. And I
actually worked with a clear head the whole time, no building
sickness, no building psychosis, so Roithamer. Then, after I
had thoroughly studied my sister, above all her mental and
emotional condition, it was clear that the edifice to build for
her was the Cone. No other form. And I knew that no cone
had ever been built before by any man, not even a Frenchman,
not even a Russian, my Cone will be the first cone ever built to
be lived in, I told myself, and I decided to build the Cone.
When we set out to do something we're constantly being
sidetracked, we're thought to be crazy, our refusal to yield and
to compromise makes many enemies for us (enemies we've
always had), but that's just what impels us onward, those
constantly mounting accusations against us, slanders against
us, ruthlessness against us which is far greater than our own
ruthlessness, all of it ultimately makes it possible for us to
make our way through this human filth to which we're continually exposed, through the filth of their slander, their false
accusations. The world around us is constantly balking and
hindering us and it is precisely by this constant inhibiting and
hindering action that it enables us to approach our aim and
finally even reach it. We're told and we're made to feel that we
have neither the right nor the nerve nor the brutality to
achieve our aim, but we do have the right and the nerve and
the brutality and because we are what we are, our nerve and
our brutality and our right keeps increasing. We're constantly
badgered with insinuations by those who don't want us to
accomplish our aim because they begrudge us our achievement, so we're constantly subjected to their meanness, their
spying presence which only fills us with disgust, they never
cease their vulgar spying. Most of the time we have to deal
with human filth, so Roithamer, we're forced to wade through
it, and when we've made our way through one heap of filth we

must get through the next, on and on, each time faster, more radically than the last, because we've caught on that there's nothing but this human filth, which we have to get through. To reach our aim we must traverse this human filth, human filth in the form of common filth in the head, the sole purpose of which is to do us in. Whoever says otherwise commits the violent crime of hypocrisy, "violent crime of hypocrisy" underlined, the words human filth always first underlined, then crossed out, then stetted. At first we hope for support from the person closest to us, but to cling to our "neighbor" would mean, as we soon find out, the suicide of the (of our) spirit, suicide of our being, our soul, "soul" underlined. Then we think that we must turn to the professionals (of the mind, the soul, the world of things), because we're constantly looking for help, but there we keep meeting only with deepest disappointment, "deepest" underlined, we encounter only disappointments. We're up to something, as we know, it's invariably something stupendous, even our most insignificant, unimpressive brainchild is always the most stupendous thing, and we feel we must speak of it, go into it, and we're disappointed, either we're not understood, no matter how clearly and forcefully we put our case, or else we don't want to be understood. We're always left without an answer, and of course in a more debilitated state than before, because no one, no expert or person, whichever, wants to help us. And so we naturally have to depend entirely on ourselves all our lives and we go our way alone, depending on ourselves only, working to earn everything ourselves, with no outside help. And so we're always full up and never come to rest, so Roithamer, "never come to rest" underlined. We're surrounded by malice, so Roithamer. First twenty-one chambers in the Cone, then eighteen, then seventeen chambers. A single chamber under the Cone's tip, with a view in every direction, but in every direction the same vista into the forest, nothing else. Three-storied, because a three-storied edifice accords with my sister's character, "my sister's character" underlined. Of the seventeen chambers, nine are without a view, among them the meditation chamber on the second floor, beneath the chamber in the tip. The meditation chamber is so constructed as to make it possible to meditate there for several days in a row, and it's intended for no other use but meditation, it's totally devoid of any objects, there's not to be a single object in the meditation chamber, nor any light either. A red dot in the center of the meditation chamber indicates the actual center of the meditation chamber, which is also the true center of the Cone. The radius from this center in every direction is fourteen meters long. Spring water on tap in the meditation chamber. Underneath the meditation chamber, areas for diversions. Above the meditation chamber, the circular chamber inside the tip of the Cone, affording views in all directions, but in every direction nothing but forest is to be seen, the Kobernausser forest, under this rotunda the meditation chamber, under the meditation chamber the diversions areas and under the diversions areas what I call the antechambers into which whoever enters the Cone, enters to prepare himself for the Cone, on the ground floor, in fact. On the ground floor there are five chambers, all without any designation in particular. These chambers must be left without the specific designation, like all the chambers in the Cone, always, without designation, except for the meditation chamber. If the person domiciled in the Cone, my sister, in fact, should be tempted to assign specific functions to the individual chambers, for she is sure to be suddenly *inclined* and then impelled to designate the individual chambers as, say, a bedroom here and a workroom there and thirdly a kitchen andsoforth, she must remind herself, if necessary tell herself aloud, that the individual chambers in the Cone are not to be specifically designated, it must be possible to live in a building in which the individual chambers are undesignated, though it is only natural for the chamber constructed as a meditation chamber to be designated as a meditation chamber. The chambers are all

whitewashed. No windows but look-outs that are neither to
be opened nor shut, natural airing of the inner-spaces always
without having to open or shut the look-outs. Solar energy for
heating. Stone, bricks, glass, iron, nothing else. The Cone is
whitewashed outside as well as inside. The Cone's height is
the same as the height of the forest so that it's impossible to
see the Cone unless one is standing directly in front of it, the
road leading to the Cone doesn't lead directly to it through the
Kobernausser forest but winds toward it six times in a north-
easterly and six times in a northwesterly direction, so that the
Cone can be seen only at the moment when the new arrival
finds himself directly in front of it. Eight thousand loads of
coarse gravel, two thousand loads of a finer grade, so Roithamer. At first I was going to let my sister in on my plans from
the beginning, but I dropped the idea when she showed her
aversion to my plan, I'll build about a third of the Cone first, I
thought, then *I'll show her the Cone, a third of it already done,* but
I dropped that idea too, because I suddenly realized that I must
finish the Cone before I show it to my sister, there's the risk in
showing my sister the Cone before it's finished, that I may
(owing to her reaction) lose the strength to finish the Cone, the
Cone must be finished, perfect, when I show it to her, it was
built to be perfection for her. If anything happens to my sister
during my lifetime, I'll let nature take its course with the Cone,
so Roithamer, after my sister no one is to set foot in the Cone,
this stipulation to be included in my will to be drawn up
eventually, so Roithamer, this will musn't be put off too long.
(Roithamer did in fact stipulate in his will, viz. the slip of
paper he had on him when Hoeller found his body, that no
one should be allowed to set foot inside the Cone now, after
his sister's death and after his own death, and that the Cone
must be entirely *abandoned to nature.* There's no telling how far
Roithamer's heirs will go along with that stipulation.) Once
she sees the Cone, she's bound to be happy, "bound to be
happy" underlined. A perfect construction is bound to make

the person for whom it was constructed happy, "must make her happy" again underlined. The idea was to make my sister perfectly happy by means of a construction perfectly adapted to her person, so Roithamer. Perfect to the degree to which perfection is possible, anyway, let's say nearly perfect, "nearly" as with anything else. To materialize the idea to the point of securing my sister's perfect happiness. But what if she doesn't understand any of it? I ask myself. We'll see. The idea was to prove that such a construction, bound to bring perfect happiness, is possible, so Roithamer. Then, when my sister has moved into the Cone, so Roithamer, when she has entered the Kobernausser forest, I shall have no more fears for my sister. For the time has come when my sister also must leave Altensam behind, must above all leave my brothers, who are as alien to us (my sister and me) as we (my sister and I) are alien to them. Once a year, at most twice a year, I shall visit my sister and shall observe and study her and the Cone and both of them together in their mutual relationship, so Roithamer. And then I'll retreat to Hoeller's garret to work up my notes. I shall personally bury all the cost accounts regarding the Cone on the ground floor, so Roithamer, the day the Cone was finished. The Cone was meant to be a surprise, it is no longer a surprise because my sister knows of my plan and also knows how far I have progressed in my plan. Nevertheless she will be surprised when she actually sees the Cone, when she sees how it expresses her one hundred percent, or let's say nearly one hundred percent, because a one hundred percent expression is impossible. Then everything within me will be resolved, as it will be resolved in my sister, at the moment when I show her the Cone. We have to go along with a crazy idea, our own, even when we don't remember how we got it, we must go along with this crazy idea all the way, bring it to realization in the teeth of all the doubts and all the rules and all the recriminations, despite *everything*. We bring this idea to realization in order to bring ourselves to realization for a loved person, "loved person" underlined. It was always obvious that no help was to be expected from anywhere at all, and under no circumstances from Altensam. To finish the Cone means to destroy Altensam, once the Cone is finished, Altensam is destroyed. It's all directed against my brothers, everything I've ever done in my life perhaps. Everything always for my sister, but against my brothers. These proceedings, *against my brothers, for my sister,* I have made into a personal art. Instinctively I have always acted against my brothers and for my sister. And now, by realizing my idea of building the Cone, I am proceeding most radically against my brothers and for my sister. The Cone, my proof, "my proof" underlined. I kept telling them I can do what I like with my money. And because the time has come. The Cone is the logical consequence of (my) nature. But I won't satisfy the curiosity of the professionals or those who call themselves professionals though they're not. None of them shall get near my Cone. So far I've managed to keep the site fenced off. By deploying my lookouts everywhere, who report anyone they see approaching the site, people are turned away, pushed back, before they have had even a glimpse of the Cone. But there's no preventing people from coming one day, at a certain point when I have lost all influence over this situation, and from taking possession (mentally) of the Cone, or from thinking they have taken (mental) possession of it, and from exploiting my idea. "Exploiters of ideas" underlined. At first I kept my idea of building the Cone under scrutiny for a long time, while engaged in my scientific pursuits, I kept mulling over this one idea, scrutinizing it, then I tested it, and then I proceeded to work on its realization. I never asked anybody, one never should ask anybody, when one has this kind of an idea, whether it's a good idea and whether the idea should be put into practice or not, because the reply is sure to be deadly. I turned to no one, no other head, and started to put my idea into practice without knowing what the realization of my idea means. The question of the meaning of the realization of this idea arises only after the Cone is finished. It's because I got away from Altensam so early in life, and went to Cambridge, because I got away from the actual scene of my thoughts, which has always been, and still is Altensam and its environs, whatever I'm thinking about, having to think about, that I had the opportunity to concern myself with problems and ideas which, had I remained in Altensam and its environs, let's say within a radius of two or three hundred kilometers, I never could have concerned myself with, I could not have thought the thoughts I could think in Cambridge, I'd never have had the ideas I've had in Cambridge. To do one's thinking on a scene, though actually far away from the actual scene, one's best thinking by virtue of being at the farthest possible remove from the scene of everything relating to that scene. Everything about Altensam, for instance, is always best considered at the farthest remove from Altensam, not in Altensam itself, everything concerning the Cone, for instance, is best considered in Cambridge. It was not on the Kobernausser forest site itself that I supervised the building of the Cone, but from Hoeller's garret. We must be removed as far as possible from the scene of our thoughts if we're to think properly, with the greatest intensity, the greatest clarity, always only at the greatest distance from the scene of our thoughts, in Cambridge my thoughts about Altensam became the clearest possible thoughts about Altensam, conversely in Altensam the clearest possible thoughts about Cambridge. Always the problem of how to get to the farthest point away from the subject I must consider or think through, in order to consider or think through this subject the best possible way. Approaching the subject makes it increasingly impossible to think through the subject we are approaching. We become absorbed in the subject and can no longer think it through, we can't even grasp it. And so I, wanting basically only to think about, to think thoroughly about my native scene, Altensam, Austria, etcetera, had to go to Cambridge. In that sense my scientific pursuits in

Cambridge were always nothing but an opportunity to think hard, in Cambridge, about the scene of greatest interest to me, Altensam and everything connected with Altensam, to go over it in my head. To think a subject through, one has to assume a position at the farthest possible remove from this subject. First, approach the subject as an idea, then, take the most distant position possible from this subject which at first we'd approached as an idea, to enable us to evaluate it and think it through, a process leading logically to its resolution. A thorough, logical analysis of a subject, whichever subject, means the resolution of the subject, an analysis of Altensam, for instance, means the resolution, dissolution, of Altensam and-soforth. But we don't, we never think with the utmost analytical rigor, because if we did we'd solve, dissolve, everything. In that case I'd never have been able to get the Cone ready, as Hoeller puts it, so Roithamer, "get ready" underlined. Hoeller has made no changes in the garret since I last stayed in it, so Roithamer, and none of the Hoellers was allowed to set foot in the garret, because I asked Hoeller to let no one, not even his own wife and his own children, into the garret in my absence; now that I've entered Hoeller's garret I have the proof that Hoeller hasn't changed a thing in the garret in my absence, that I'd only imagined that Hoeller had changed something in the garret, so Roithamer, but now I have proof that he changed nothing in the garret, everything in the garret is in the same place where it was when I left the garret, he, Hoeller, enters the garret once or twice a week only to air it, so that there's absolutely no musty smell in Hoeller's garret, my thought-chamber at the Aurach gorge, so Roithamer, "thought-chamber at the Aurach gorge" underlined. At the very instant I entered Hoeller's garret for the first time together with Hoeller who wanted to show me his garret because he thought it might be a suitable place for me to think especially about building the Cone, it had always occurred to him, every time he stepped into the garret, to wonder whether his garret wasn't the most suitable place for me and my purposes, I'd known at that earliest instant that Hoeller's garret could enable me, as no other retreat so far had enabled me, to get on with my thinking, especially in regard to the Cone, and so I told him immediately, while we still stood in the doorway to the garret, that this was the most suitable place for my purposes and that I wished to rent it, *rent* is what I said to Hoeller, but Hoeller said that I could move into the garret as often and whenever I wanted, stay there whenever and for however long I wanted, he wouldn't rent it to me, he was of course putting it at my disposal gratis, this offer I immediately accepted and I moved into Hoeller's garret that same day and was confirmed in my assumption that I could advance in my thinking in Hoeller's garret, from that point where I had gotten stuck in Cambridge. Here in Hoeller's garret I'd been able to make my most important calculations, those referring to the statics of the Cone, in a short time. If I'd become blocked in thinking about the Cone at Cambridge, I enjoyed a fresh start in Hoeller's garret. I lost my fear of having to give up the idea of building the Cone, of realizing it, perfecting it. When it comes to finishing the Cone, I owe everything to Hoeller's garret, so Roithamer. Suddenly it was possible to "go on living, go on working," underlined. The problem of everything coming at once, so Roithamer, beginning with early childhood (three years old, four years?) having to cope with myself, with those around me, with the past on the one hand and with future prospects, so Roithamer, and with a constantly rising degree of responsibility, irresponsibility. Because we were born into Altensam, without preparation, as we're all born unprepared into some environment unknown to us, a world that does its utmost to destroy the newborn, born into it, just as Altensam has always tried to destroy me, the concept Altensam, destruction of my person, of a being at its mercy, defenseless, totally unprotected. Suddenly facing Altensam without knowing what it is, and everything beyond and around Altensam, without knowing what that is. Our

parents were not the right teachers for us, our rightful educators as it's called, but they had no right to educate us, they
merely brought us up for their own purposes, always only for
their own purposes, with the result that my brothers were
always ready to serve their purposes, but I was always against
their purposes. By bringing me up for their purposes my
parents succeeded in setting me against their purposes, my
brothers for their purposes, me against their purposes, education for a purpose, "education for a purpose" underlined. The
restlessness of my parents, everything in and about my parents
was unrest, but unrest against everything, not *for* everything,
the way they'd move from one bedroom to another every
week, for instance, use a different room as a dining room every
week, constantly change their preferences, now they'd opt for
one thing and then again for quite another, now for one set of
characters and then for the opposite kind of characters, for one
kind of landscape, for the opposite kind of landscape, in reality
they lived in a constant state of unrest because they were
incapable of deciding in favor of a definite person, a definite
landscape, anything definite for the long run, because they
always believed they had to think, have, reject, attract, everything at the same time, so they were basically the unhappiest
people imaginable. They'd punish us constantly, thinking it
was a way to draw us closer to them, but they always repelled
me with their strategy of punishment, parents taking possession of their children by means of punishments, so Roithamer,
"taking possession of their children" underlined. How my
father always referred to the *tragedy,* my mother always to the
*drama of their shared life.* Weeks of silence between them, not a
word spoken, openly parading their shutting each other out,
weeks at a time of never opening the one (father's) being to
the other (mother's), and the chaotic conditions that always
reigned at Altensam because of this situation between my
parents. They made children together, but were basically quite
unsuited to having children and never really wanted children,

my father only wanted heirs, not children, not descendants, just heirs. I remember my parents only as old people, "old people" underlined, who couldn't stand each other and who could stand their children even less, miserable to have brought into the world these basically alien, strange creatures, to have them on their conscience, to be guilty of the crime of giving life, actually more than once, though without knowing toward whom, with respect to whom, they were guilty. Misfortune comes overnight, my father always said, so Roithamer, "overnight" underlined. My mother lived in a state of chronic anxiety, with frequent fainting spells that came on the heels of my fainting spells or vice versa. We children weren't allowed to ask questions, so that our parents wouldn't have to find answers. We were kept, as they say, on a tight rein. If the world only knew on how tight and short a rein we were kept throughout our childhood, the stinginess and meanness with which we were kept, like cattle in a farmyard, that's how we children were kept in Altensam. We were always forced to do things, something was always demanded of us against our will, but even if it was something we wanted to do, it was demanded of us at a time when we didn't want to do it. We were ordered to read, for instance, what we didn't want to read, listen to what we didn't want to hear, visit people we didn't want to visit, wear clothes we didn't want to wear, eat food we didn't want to eat. My brothers, and my sister too, always gave in but I never gave in, they had to punish me to make me give in, I never gave in of my own free will. We had to live by strict rules in Altensam, rules made long ago for other people, for all those generations who'd lived in Altensam before us, rules not made for us at all, but we never had a chance to make and live by our own rules, nor by new rules made for us, so we constantly and on every occasion and non-occasion had to obey rules never made for us, rules that were decades behind their time, as everything in Altensam has from the start been behind its time. Because I understood this early in life I found myself in a situation which was constantly life-threatening to me, because I would not submit to those outdated rules and did not submit except under duress, even though the others always submitted, my siblings have always been submissive creatures, but I balked at everything. To my parents, every-thing about me and inside me had been disturbing, all my life, so I wanted quite early in life to live apart from my parents, and from my siblings as well, because they sided with my parents, which always made life easier for them, and it also made them turn out differently from me. I'm not a submissive man even today, rather I am more and ever more contrary, refractory, a quarrelsome character actually, in many ways more unyielding than necessary, all because of my years of desperation as a child, my long years of living in Altensam as a prison, Altensam always did feel like a childhood dungeon to me, it was never anything else, my good days at Altensam can be counted on the fingers of one hand, I had to spend my entire childhood in the Altensam dungeon like an inmate doing time for no comprehensible reason, for a crime he can't remember committing, a judicial error probably. There I was, in solitary, in almost uninterrupted darkness, and speaking with my father was no different from being interrogated by a magistrate after an arrest. I was threatened with ever harsher punishments though my life was already enough of a harsh punishment. When I asked what I had done to be kept in this punitive fashion in solitary confinement at Altensam, I re-ceived no answer. Possibly I was kept in prison, in my parents' dungeon, Altensam, to atone for their crime, for which I was, after all, so far doing a twelve to thirteen year stretch. The only witnesses to my innocence would of course have been my parents, but then my parents were also my prosecutors, they had conceived and born me directly into that dungeon, "con-ceived and born me" underlined. When, in unflagging despair, we have to regard our parents as nothing but our prison wardens in this vast, terrible dungeon, which is what I must call my parents' house, father as the warden of his dungeon, his house, his property, my parental home, parental property, i.e., Altensam. When we can never hope for a review of our case, because such a review is out of the question, for every reason in the world. We can dream of escape but we can never escape because, once escaped from our parental dungeon, we'd perish in no time. Then we're released, they say prematurely released, "prematurely" underlined, and we've taken up the struggle against the dungeon, against the institution of this dungeon into which we were conceived and born, our lifelong struggle, struggle of despair, "struggle of despair" underlined, which is being held against us, first we're imprisoned and almost wholly destroyed by our parents and now, after being released from our prison, having simply gotten away from it by reaching a certain maturity, we are rebuked for opposing our parents, quite openly opposing them. I never visited my parents, incidentally, I went to Altensam only to discuss Altensam and the problems of running it insofar as I was concerned with these problems, I never again felt the need to see my parents, neither my father nor my mother, when I went there it was only to see my sister, who was as if chained to her parents, to visit my sister, on such occasions I simply accepted the presence of my parents and that of my brothers who always sided with my parents as part of the bargain. They went on living for years, all those years I was already living in Cambridge, by and on my own initiative ("own initiative" underlined, then crossed out, then stetted), until they died, I never saw them again for at least twelve years before their deaths, they both died within a week, my mother immediately after my father, she couldn't survive without my father, Altensam would have crushed her, she'd probably realized this, people die in such cases, as they say, of natural causes, the heart stops, but it's actually a case of suicide. But by that time I'd already built half of the Cone and was engrossed in working up toward the tip and I hadn't allowed my father's sudden death followed immediately by my mother's death to distract me in the least from continuing my work in building the Cone, surely these people who'd just died practically overnight were total strangers to me? is what I thought and felt, too. For the funeral, arranged by my brothers, I drove to Altensam, nothing had ever gone more against my grain than that funeral, actually a double funeral, for the first turned into the second almost without any noticeable transition, father's funeral turned into mother's funeral, so I attended my parents' funeral, two weeks of tragic spectacle at Altensam, "tragic spectacle" underlined. Two such people die and all we feel is hatred for these people. Death changes nothing in our attitude, it comes too late to change our feelings for these people. Even later on, no change for the better, on the contrary, in time these people seem to be more and more responsible for our misfortunes. That I am alive and working today I owe to my having been able to extricate myself from my parents at the crucial moment in my life, had it been up to them my life would have been over years ago, even though they might not have consciously wanted to kill me off, they'd soon have killed me off. And my siblings too continue to exist only because they'd completely given themselves up to my parents. Survival by self-surrender, so Roithamer. We go to a grave where we have buried our parents, buried them in accordance with their expectations, a so-called prominent grave along the church wall, where all their predecessors on Altensam are already interred, but all we feel is hatred, we haven't even a chance, we simply have it no longer or never had a chance of feeling the least sympathy with them. That's why I no longer go to my parents' grave either. Because to go on living with such a lie afterward could have only the most destructive effect on everything else. But of course a man can never really liberate himself from anything, he leaves the prison into which he was propagated and born only at the instant of his death. We enter a world which precedes us but is not prepared for us, and we have to cope with this world, if we can't cope with this world we're done for, but if we survive, for whatever constitutional reason, then we must take care to turn this world, which was a given world but not made for us or ready for us, a world which is all set in any case, because it was made by our predecessors, to attack us and ruin us and finally destroy us, nothing else, we must turn it into a world to suit our own ideas, acting first behind the scenes, inconspicuously, but then with all our might and quite openly, so that we can say after a while that *we're living in our own world, not in some previous world,* one that is always bound to be of no concern to us and intent upon ruining and destroying us. Beginning with our earliest flickers of intelligence we have to explore intently our chances of making this world, that's been put on us like a worn, shabby suit of used clothes much too tight or much too large but in any case a shabby and torn and ragged and stinking outfit handed to us, as it were, off the world's rack, we must explore the whole surface of our world and its subsurface, and keep probing it deeper and deeper, so as to discover our chances of making this world, which is not our world, our own after all, our entire existence is nothing but concentrating on such chances and on how, in what way, we're to change this world which is not ours, ultimately to change it, so Roithamer. And the moment of this change, such a moment is followed by the next andsoforth, must always be the right moment, so Roithamer. So that we can say at last, at the end of our life, that we have lived *at least for a time* in our own world and not in the given world of our parents. But ninety percent of us die without ever having lived in a world of their own, only and always in a world that was ready-made, presented and adapted to them by their parents' generation, never, please note, in no way and never in their own world, they live and work out their lives in their parents' world, not their own. Unless ten percent is too high an estimate for those who live in a world of their own making, not that of their parents? Isn't it actually a much smaller percentage who've had a world of their own to live in? We must, from the first signs of intelligence, make the effort to change the parental world into which we have been conceived and born, into a world of our own, each for himself and each entirely for himself at the very first signs of intelligence, so that this effort that takes years, decades, will bring results, admittedly by overexertion, "overexertion" underlined, so that we can say, at the end of our existence, that we existed in a world of our own, so that we will not have to go to our death in the disgrace of having existed only in the world of our parents, because that would be the worst disgrace of all. We must use our heads from the very first to get away from our parents, birth is not enough, it does just the opposite, we must do it ourselves by our own unyielding effort, always strengthening our willpower, so that we can say, one day, that we have lived in our own world, and not only in the world of our parents. I remember that my mother always used to lock me up, in summer, in the so-called southeast turret room with its total exposure to the sun, when she'd been unable to make me submit to her will on some point or other, no doubt I was hard to handle, just as there's no doubt whatever that my parents never shied away from brutality, so she'd lock me up in the turret room which never was unlocked all summer long except to lock me up in it, it was opened for no other purpose, nor were the windows in the turret room ever opened, the window bolts had been immobilized by rust for decades, so the windows couldn't have been opened, that's where she locked me up where the air, the hot, sunbaked air, had long since been suffocated and thousands, hundreds of thousands of dead flies lay about on the floor and on all the furniture, heaps of dead flies, in this turret room with its terrible smell, with those windows covered from top to bottom with fly shit by all those flies in all those years of their hectic death throes, this room left in an indescribable state of filth was where she locked me up for hours on end until she had me *begging* her through the locked door to let me out, because I was choking to death. I remember how she wanted to hurt me and did hurt me, by telling me again and again that I was the last straw, that I was evil incarnate, at an age when such words can already have the most deadly effect on a child's soul. And father said nothing, he devoted himself to my brothers, not to me, he always treated my brothers as his successors, while punishing me most of the time by always referring to me, from the time I was only three or four years old, as a foreign element in Altensam. Even after their death my parents can't be transformed into an idealized image for me, not even a bearable image, I've nothing to support me in such a falsification, so Roithamer. And father's greatest punishment, or shall I call it his last move in his chess game against me, was to toss Altensam at me in his will, Altensam! though he knew how I felt about Altensam, that it filled me with loathing, nothing but loathing. When he did that, however, he also handed me the means of showing my appreciation, in fact and in full accordance with my character, by selling Altensam, selling it and destroying it and using the proceeds for the purpose I've set my mind on. My parents would turn in their graves (this remark is crossed out). It's like dissolving a dungeon, to dissolve Altensam, so Roithamer. Are my hatred and my aversion, these two weapons still in effect against my parents today, also in effect against my brothers? I ask myself. Yes, but to a much lesser degree, so much less as to be basically insignificant, so Roithamer. While our eye is on our work and on the riskiness and vulnerability of our work, we spend most of our time barely trying to bridge over the next time span just ahead, and we think that getting through the time just ahead is all we need to think about, not our work, let alone the complicated work that claims our entire existence. To get through the time itself, no matter how, is what we think, what we instinctively feel we need. Beginning in childhood. How to get on with it, that's what we keep thinking constantly, and yet most of the time it doesn't matter a damn *how* we get on with it, only *that* we get on with it. Because we have to concentrate all our mental and physical forces on just getting along, without achieving anything beyond that, so Roithamer. Work, to bridge over time, no matter what work, our occupation, whether digging in the garden or pushing on with a concept, it's all the same. Then we're obsessed with an idea though we've barely enough strength left to go on breathing, torment enough in itself. We're obligated to (do) nothing, so Roithamer,"nothing" underlined. When we were children, how they talked us into believing that we had a right to live only if we accomplished some sensible work, how they assured us that we had to do our duty. All of it a case of irresponsible parents, irresponsible so-called authorized educators, irresponsibly plaguing us. Stuffed into the same kind of clothes regardless of our different personalities, our different characters, marched to church, made to eat, made to visit people, so Roithamer. Mother's fixed idea that we brothers must always be dressed alike and appropriately for Altensam, whatever that was, and her equally fixed idea, always, that all three of us should always think the same, act the same, believe the same things, do or refrain from doing the same things, but I always did something else and I always refused to wear the same clothes as the others, which led to daily anticipations of apocalypse. We weren't alike, never, so Roithamer, but neither was I, ever, eccentric, it's not true that I was eccentric, though they never tired of calling me an eccentric, it was their way of slandering me, because I acted in accordance with my nature without concerning myself with the others and their opinions, I was denounced as an eccentric, I, who simply tried to live always in accordance with my own, absolutely not eccentric nature, all I did was simply to be true to my own nature, day after day, but that's how I was turned into an eccentric from earliest childhood on, and they also always called me a troublemaker, rightly, in this case, because I really always did trouble their peace in Altensam, I troubled their so-called

peace all my life, in the end I made it my mission to trouble
their peace in Altensam, so the term troublemaker really suited
me more than anyone. That we were something special because we came from Altensam, that everything having to do
with us and Altensam was something special, is a notion I
always fought off, there was every indication that we, my
parents, my siblings, me, everyone in Altensam, were ultimately something special, of course in the sense that everything in the world is something special, but nothing is more
special than anything else, everything is so equally special that
there's nothing further to be said about it, so Roithamer. The
ideas our parents had of us, and the hopes which our parents
attached to these ideas of us and which were not fulfilled,
ideas are not fulfilled, so Roithamer, not ideas all by themselves, "not all by themselves" underlined. We'd had to learn
to play violin, play the piano, play the flute, partly because
mother insisted and partly because each showed some talent
for one or the other musical instrument, but all four of us
hated these music lessons equally, music began to interest me,
to fascinate me, only after I no longer *had to* practice it, once I
could choose freely I became for a time, in fact for years,
totally absorbed in music, I'd started to think that I must study
music on a higher, on the highest, level, I'd even started on
such a course of study but then gave it up again, because the
formal study of music would have put me off, the formal
study of music did not endear music to me, on the contrary, it
affected me the same way as the compulsory music lessons at
home in Altensam. Disobedience at Altensam had always been
punished by inflicting deadly injuries on the psyche. I'd always lived in fear of that sunny-side turret room, but this
special torture was reserved only for me, neither of my brothers was ever locked up in the turret room. For them, a slap in
the face would be deemed enough, but me they locked in the
turret room, the worst punishment of all, or else they said
things about me that did me in, did me in emotionally and

mentally, the worst possible punishment, of course. We were constantly forced to do things we didn't want to do. But we'd always been told that our parents meant it for our *own good.* Every day, very often, we'd get to hear how much they meant it all for our own good, they never tired of repeating that phrase, it was one of their favorite maxims, time and again, we mean it for your own good (speaking to one or the other of us) until I felt more and more intimidated and humiliated, they could easily bully us, our parents, we were so naïve. Such a beautiful house, so artistic, so cultivated, our visitors always said, what could anyone say to the contrary? Such delightful surroundings, every piece of furniture a work of art, all the interiors they ever got to see the most splendid anywhere, all the vistas from Altensam opening on the loveliest, most far-flung landscapes. How, I often asked myself, how is it possible to see oneself going to ruin in so, to quote my mother's constant phrase, luxurious an atmosphere? To be dying by inches, for no reason any outsider could see. Of course I wasn't wholly a stranger to such concepts as joy, beauty, even the love-of-life, the beauty-of-nature andsoforth, so Roithamer. My eyes were as open in that direction as in the other. A man like me, who finds his greatest happiness in thought, most of all when engaged in thought out in the open, in the free (philosophical) world of nature, is saved by this fact in itself, by such an observation as this in itself, so Roithamer. Happiness can even be found in the so-called acceptance of pain, so Roithamer. One might, for instance, find supreme joy in writing well about supreme misery, so Roithamer. The ability to perceive, the ability to articulate one's perception, can be a supreme joy andsoforth, so Roithamer. A statement in itself, no matter what is being stated, can be a supreme joy, as is ultimately the fact of simply existing, no matter how, so Roithamer. But we mustn't keep thinking such thoughts all the time, keep mulling over everything we're about, otherwise we may suddenly find ourselves deadened by our own persistent, relentless brooding and end up simply dead. I began by playing violin, against my will, so Roithamer, piano, against my will, because forced into it, later on the (voluntary) effort to study music on a higher and the highest level, the history of music andsoforth, so Roithamer, all came to nothing because under duress in the one case, in the other voluntary but formal, in the end serious involvement with music, getting into music of my own free will and without formal backing (university etcetera), Webern, Schönberg, Berg, Dallapiccola andsoforth. Began by reading against my will, read everything against my will, because my parents forced me to read, they'd thought that I was inclined to read, but because they assumed I had such an inclination, respect/inclination etcetera, I refused to read, never read anything but schoolbooks till my twelfth year, then, from about my twenty-fifth year on, I read incessantly, everything of my own accord, whatever I could lay my hands on. Because they demanded order, I chose disorder, because they demanded that we wear hats on our heads, never a hat on my head for decades, aversion to hats etcetera, so Roithamer. Because they always tried to stop me from going down to the various villages from Altensam, for all sorts of reasons which were bound to seem unreasonable to me, I'd always go down to the villages behind their backs, I made myself independent down there below Altensam, timidly at first but later with great firmness, while they believed me to be in my room, I'd actually gone down to the villages at night. And so more and more often behind their backs down to Altensam, so Roithamer, until one day I left Altensam for good and went down, never to come back to Altensam, never again, "never again" underlined. But in these outbreaks I was also alone. My siblings never and in no way followed me. Absolute mutual incomprehension among us children even then. There's nothing more for us to explain to each other, so Roithamer. Typical, mother's fainting spells as a form of blackmail, her constant bouts with nausea, she controlled the household from her so-called nausea chair, I almost never saw mother free from nausea or the signs of nausea, father was the opposite, a robust constitution by nature, but she, my mother, always in her moods, always gloomy, bad moods because of her gloominess, father always in a good mood, she couldn't stand it. Unlike his first wife, who had borne him no children, which was his reason, naturally, for divorcing her, as he always said, so Roithamer, she was the daughter of a Klagenfurt attorney, though all she'd ever had in her head was theaters and amusements, my father regarded everything connected with the theater and music as mere amusements, which is what he quite contemptuously called it, he had married this woman because he'd made her pregnant, but the child was born dead, its mother had been half insane for a long time after this stillbirth, so father said, until he, my father, simply couldn't bear it any longer, because it was obvious that she could never have another child, hence the divorce, but then he overhastily married my mother, who certainly could and did give birth and to living children at that, so father said about my mother, she was never anything more to him than a *good breeder,* my father kept saying and he said it to anybody, even mere acquaintances, even strangers when he was drunk, unlike his first wife, who was always young and fresh, but then was completely ruined by that stillbirth, she's still living, my father kept saying, whenever anyone asked him about her, his first wife, she's still living, in France I think, anyway unlike his first wife, his second, our mother, was always an old woman, even as a young woman she was already old, her sort are old even as children, so my father said, a good observation, as I can attest, such people are born with wizened old faces, it's always frightening how ancient their faces look, the kind of newborn human being my mother apparently was always looks from the first moment as he or she is likely to look at seventy or eighty, but this aged look stays on that face, always, our mother was always the Old Woman, from the beginning,

unlike his first wife, his second, our mother, was also a calculating woman, she was all calculation, she never did anything
without calculation, while my first wife, so my father, so Roithamer, without being at all calculating, suddenly became an
*unhappy creature* as a result of that stillbirth, my second wife
was always calculating, with every fiber of her being, to such
an extent, so my father, so Roithamer, that she'd get into a
terrible state whenever one of her calculations didn't happen
to work out, but basically her calculations always worked out,
this type of woman will get a bee in her bonnet, for instance
something unnecessary she wants to buy, so my father, and
she gets her way, even though by getting her way she weakens
the relationship, which she doesn't notice, but she thinks that
she is strengthening her position. When it comes to trying
things, she always got her way when it came to trips or
innovations at Altensam, and she did it almost always by
using her sick spells with which she ruled Altensam for long
periods of time without a letup, especially in the spring, when
Altensam was ruled entirely by nothing but our mother's
nausea, in the heat of summer, in the sudden chill of autumn.
If she'd failed in getting her wish, those wishes and ideas and
projects of hers that always had so devastating an effect on
Altensam, she resorted to threats, and most of all to the most
terrifying of all threats, so my father, so Roithamer, suicide,
she'd throw herself off the top of the wall one day, see if she
didn't, she'd be smashed to bits, because her life meant nothing to us, even though we all depended on her, she was the
*heart and core of our life,* but basically she wasn't the heart and
core of life in Altensam as she kept telling us, but rather the
heart and core of our creeping death in Altensam, and she
never made her threat good, these people, so Roithamer, never
stop talking of suicide, they threaten suicide every time their
wishes and ideas are balked, and because they have no other
resources except this threat, because they're basically without
resources, absolutely without resources, but they don't kill

themselves, they go on living for years, for decades, with this
threat and by grace of this threat, and then they die a perfectly
natural death, so Roithamer. When she was alone in Altensam,
because my father was away on business, she thought about
how she might torment him when he'd come back home, what
kind of horror she could surprise him with, it had to be a
horror with at least a touch of perversion in it, which would
instantly put him in a frightful mood which would of course
have the most frightful effect on us children and on all of
Altensam, and when father was coming home to Altensam,
she'd sit for hours, always looking at her watch, in her turret
room watching the road from the village by which he had to
come up, watching everything that went on down there, always glancing at her watch, noting who was coming up to
Altensam on what errand, who was leaving Altensam and on
what errand and with what baggage and especially what kind
of tools, because more than anything else mother was mistrustful, she completely mistrusted not only us but everything,
and it was probably this mistrust that had undermined her
health from her earliest years, because even as a child she had
been most noticeably mistrustful, and so of course, what with
her organism weakened by her incessant mistrustfulness, she
was almost always sickly, or pretended to be sickly, you could
never be absolutely sure at any given moment whether she
was sickly or pretending to be sickly, what was interesting
about it was just this, that she was always sickly, but never
really sick, never seriously sick so as actually to arouse real
concern, but only always sickly, this sickliness of our mother's
was one of the main characteristics of the atmosphere at
Altensam as far back as I can remember, with her chronic
sickliness she finally infected all of Altensam so that the entire
atmosphere there was sicklied through, everything there in
addition to herself was always equally sickly, it seemed as
though she was quite consciously using this sickliness of hers
as a means to her ends, meaning that she used it against us,

also against her husband, our father, with this sickliness she
controlled not only the most important aspects of life at Altensam but also all the secondary aspects, even the most insignificant ones, and this sickliness was instantly sensed by everyone
who'd come to Altensam, even those who don't know Altensam that well and those for whom Altensam was something
new, such a newcomer was immediately included in this sickliness which had already seized and taken hold and poisoned
everything at Altensam, he couldn't know what it was that
had brought him into this peculiarly ailing condition when
he'd barely set foot in Altensam, but it was nothing else than
our mother's sickliness, whereas father's first wife was always
fresh and young, so my father always said, so Roithamer, his
second, the one he called the nanny, was always old and
sickly, he always stated this quite openly and he'd often told
my mother to her face that her only weapon apart from her
boundless stupidity, was her sickliness, stupidity and sickliness which she used against him and against everything that
made up Altensam, against everything Altensam had been
until she appeared on the scene, and *it is a stage entrance, my
dear!* I can still hear my father telling her to her face, *a stage
entrance, my dear!* stupidity and sickliness, so Roithamer, were
our mother's chief attributes, father was right in his judgment
of her, we children had always suffered from her stupidity and
her sickliness, because our mother's ill nature was fed as much
by her stupidity as by her sickliness, which most times was a
crafty production of hers, a spectacle she put on for us every
day, in which she played the lead. My father had soon turned
away from this wife, our mother, she had borne him children,
*whelped* them, but even this at a time when he no longer
wanted any children, once they were born he realized that he
didn't really want them at all, and so, since they (we) existed,
willy-nilly, we were treated accordingly, always as creatures to
be considered his own children but whom their progenitor
basically no longer wanted and hadn't wanted for the longest

time. Mother, always unkempt, her appearance invariably neglected, as father said, so Roithamer, sloppily dressed, her
buttons half undone, her stockingless feet in unlaced shoes,
that's how I remember her, on her feet all day long only in the
hope of catching one of us or one of the so-called staff out,
running or limping all the time, another typical trait of hers
was a quick succession of injuries or ulcers, inflammations on
her legs, mostly the calves, so she ran or limped along always
smelling of every kind of medication, bought from so-called
quacks, always bought in large quantities, always disseminat-
ing the smell of such medications throughout Altensam, most
of the time wearing an old bathrobe, a legacy from my grandmother, in this bathrobe, which hadn't even been worn by my
grandmother any longer, she'd only used it to cover the dahlias
against the autumn frosts, but my mother had dragged it out
from the heap of rags in the gardener's shack and put it on and
then worn it for years afterward, my father loathed that bathrobe, we children loathed that bathrobe, but mother was always wearing this bathrobe we all hated, she even appears in
this bathrobe in family photographs, the woman in these
pictures is always a total stranger to me, these pictures convince me more than the reality did that my mother was always
some strange woman, she'd turn up suddenly everywhere and
always unpredictably, as if she had sneaked up on you, to
check up on things, no matter whose room it was, suddenly
there she was checking up, she'd always wanted to know what
was going on in the various rooms, she'd rip the door open like
a bolt of lightning and stand there, demanding an explanation,
because we'd always just done something which, in her view,
we shouldn't have done or hadn't been allowed to do, something improper always, if not strictly forbidden, nevertheless
improper or useless or embarrassing, in any case something
typical of us. In the farm buildings she was generally feared,
she was always checking on everybody's work and accused the
farm workers, who'd stayed at Altensam only on account of

my father, whom they loved, she accused them of getting
nothing done, or not enough, she always criticized all of them
for being too slow or careless, yet not one of them was ever
slower or more careless than that woman, our mother. All day
long she was on her feet in her repulsive state of slovenliness,
toward evening she'd always retreat to her room and put on a
simple black dress, basically even elegant, very expensive too,
but on her it somehow didn't look good, something seemed
wrong with it, it was a collarless dress with a large diamond-
studded gold pin on her chest, this pin had come into her
hands from the estate of my grandmother's sister as a wedding
present, and so she got herself ready to go to the theater. She'd
get one of the stewards to drive her to the Linz Theater, on
principle she never missed a première, and returned toward
midnight, never without a totally adverse opinion on everything she'd happened to see at the Linz Theater, making fun of
everything, it was always the same story, she'd get out of the
car in the courtyard, the steward would drive the car back to
the car barn where all the cars were kept, and from the
moment she'd come in the big front door, even before going to
the downstairs kitchen for the hot coffee that was kept for her
there, she'd unloose a tirade against everything she'd just
experienced at the theater, I have never heard her say anything
positive about the Linz Theater, though I must admit that it's
one of the worst theaters extant, always producing only well-
intentioned plays which invariably turned into some kind of
catastrophe or other, in some repulsive way, too, anyway I
never heard her say anything positive about it. Still she had
never managed even once *to pass up* one of their premières. She
was an addicted theatergoer even though she understood
nothing whatever about the theater, a passionate theatergoer;
that the Linz Theater was absolutely the worst theater in the
world, as she said time and again, was of course no secret to
her, especially since she was repeatedly confirmed in this
judgment by others, so-called theater buffs with whom she'd

chatted during the intermissions, but I happen to know that she only went out to the theater in order to lay in a supply of colognes and face creams at a certain cosmetics shop on the way to the theater, before curtain time, she had hundreds of these face creams and colognes in her bathroom and she made incredibly lavish use of the contents of these hundreds of bottles and tubes, unfortunately all these so-called fragrances, our mother's taste in fragrances is debatable, were always overwhelmed by the stinking salves and concoctions of her quacks, they're called health practitioners in our country, so they were basically always superfluous. The theater is only a pretext, so father said, so Roithamer, for stopping at the cosmetics shop for a supply of all that chemical stuff which is so totally ineffective on that woman (our mother), the grand opera is only a pretext for her crazy perfumes, the comedy or the tragedy in Linz is only a pretext for her ghastly moisturizing delusions. She understood nothing, neither the theater nor music, and cared less, but the theater (in Linz) and the music (in Linz), for she also attended the more important concerts in Linz, provided her with an opportunity and a pretext, not only to pick up supplies of every possible kind of aromatic filth (so my father) at the Linz cosmetics shop, but all this theater- and concert-going had also always served to prove to us her appreciation of art and her cultural requirements, but most of all they served to *humiliate* my father, this uncultured man, as she always said, who hasn't the least regard for great art, all these forays to theaters and concerts, which cost heaps of money, so father said, just to rub it in how cultured she was. But in reality our mother was not at all a cultured woman, not cultured in the least, and our father, who in fact couldn't care less about her kind of culture, the kind of culture she had in her head, she was quite right in this respect, he cared nothing at all about it, but the very fact that he cared nothing at all for her kind of culture makes him a cultured man, so Roithamer. Father had at least read a so-called good book from time to

time, but mother had never, to my personal knowledge, read a
good book, she detested everything that had to do with books,
especially good books, as she herself said, hated them like the
plague, and she'd always done everything in her power to keep
us, my siblings included, away from so-called good books,
away from all books on principle, she'd aborted any possibilities for us to get anywhere near good books or any books, it
was typical that our three- to four-thousand-volume library at
Altensam, dating back to the times of our great-grandparents
and grandparents, was locked up, and that we had to ask
mother, not father, when we wanted to get into the library,
which incidentally was always in a state of terrible neglect, it
was never put in order, never even dusted, for decades on end,
and our mother never approved of our desire to read, she'd
always sidetracked us, when we wanted to read a book in the
library, any book, into the music room instead, that's where
she wanted us to spend our time, not in the library, the library
was off limits to us, but she'd maneuvered us into the music
room, doubtless the less dangerous of the two, even though
our mother, our parents, knew that we, my siblings too, loving
music as we did, nevertheless hated making music, because
we'd been forced to practice. We were locked out of the
library, the others were also less interested in it than I was, so
Roithamer, I had no way to get into the library, because
mother had locked the library keys up in her key safe, books
were meant for grown-ups, they'd go to your head like a
disease, mother always used to say, we could read fairy tales,
but we didn't want to read fairy tales, fairy tales yes, everything else, no. She was afraid that I, in particular, might
discover in the library that the world was bigger than Altensam, that it was basically entirely different from the world I
knew, I am speaking of the time prior to my eighth or ninth
year. In my eighth or ninth year there was a sudden complete
reversal: she, my mother, had persuaded herself that I should
be *devouring* the library, that I should go into the library every

day, but now *I* no longer wanted to go in, I refused to read a single book, she couldn't make me, my mother was of course totally baffled by this, so Roithamer, first I want to go in but I'm not allowed in, then I'm supposed to go in but I no longer want to go in. She'd been of the widespread opinion that children to the age of eight or nine have no business in a so-called adult library, but that at age eight or nine they should be *introduced* to these so-called adult books, and she'd meant to follow these recommendations. But now I was no longer interested in our library. It's such an old library, I thought, after all, I'll find new books once I've left Altensam, why bother with these old books now, they'd certainly have interested me, so Roithamer, but I refused to give in to force. Of new books there were none in Altensam, they were all at least forty or fifty years old, and many much older, without counting my father's books on woods, forestry and hunting, which were always kept up-to-date with the latest information on woods, forestry, both practical and research, and hunting. Attempt at a description of father: we'd always trusted him absolutely, but under the influence of that woman, our mother, he'd become more and more estranged from us, we could feel how with the years and everything that happened in all those years, happenings in Altensam always brought about by his wife, our mother, nothing really but pathological processes resulting from that woman's constitutional predisposition, she was simply a disaster for Altensam, how in time we grew away from our father, just as he grew away from us. That woman also exercised a most harmful influence on our father, but he had soon succumbed, after an initial resistance, to her superior willpower and came to be totally controlled by this willpower of hers, everything in Altensam came to be ruled by that woman's willpower, because of our mother, the daughter of a butcher in Eferding, everything in Altensam was suddenly sickly, ailing, though it had never been ailing before, not even during the period of my father's first wife, whom I often visit,

and who has never forgiven my father, never could forgive
him for more or less ruining her life by seeing her only as a
potential breeder of his children, so that she ceased to mean
anything to him once my father's first child was stillborn,
changing her beyond recognition, which caused my father to
remove this wife entirely from Altensam, under the influence
of my mother whom my father quite openly and even to her
own face called a makeshift solution, because he thought that
he must secure the first available woman, so my father, so
Roithamer, under the influence of that woman as a makeshift,
that makeshift as a woman, so Roithamer, "makeshift as a
woman" underlined, who had no sooner turned up than she
tried to transfer to Altensam her lower-middle-class mentality,
her crudeness, yet pitiableness, her ill-bred and incorrigible
ways, and in this she succeeded, my father immediately fell
completely under this influence, which soon took its devastating, in fact annihilating toll of Altensam and everything connected with Altensam, it was only at the start that he was able
to resist this influence, but afterward, after only a brief period
of life with this Eferding woman, when he was about forty, he
gave up, he gave himself up, first he gave up Altensam under
the influence of this Eferding woman, so my father always
said, so Roithamer, then he gave himself up, he was probably
overcome with indifference toward everything in Altensam, all
at once, from one minute to the next, I had made the crucial
mistake of my life, so my father himself said, so Roithamer, I
should never have married this Eferding woman, this butcher's
daughter with her butcher's physiognomy, so my father always said, so Roithamer, with her butcher's way of life. But it
makes no difference in the end, so my father, so Roithamer.
Before this so-called mistake my father, born and raised in
Altensam, had the usual boarding school experiences, then
went through the necessary secondary and university courses
at Passau and Salzburg and Vienna, and eventually led the life
or the existence which the men of Altensam always led, work-

ing at his forestry and his farming on the one hand, comfort-loving on the other hand, with all the love possible in so fundamentally monotonous a life reserved for hunting, he'd led this quiet life of such activities and inclinations, a life unremarkable even in spurts, up to the point when he realized that he could not possibly go on alone, as he had been since his parents', my grandparents', early death, entirely devoting himself to running Altensam, which left him fully occupied yet not really satisfied, for no matter how much such a splendid and always basically well-functioning, going concern as Altensam, always a healthy, untroubled mix of farming and forestry, including lumbering, brick-making, quarries and cement works, no matter how much so healthy an economic enterprise could keep a man like my father, who had grown up with it and was wholly at home in it, fully occupied, it could not in the long run be enough to satisfy even him. But he had no other source of satisfaction by nature, unless he'd given the whole thing up, which he wasn't the man to do, so he'd begun thinking, by the time he was forty, of saving himself by cutting down on all that, and then suddenly decided, purely out of cold calculation, to have heirs, to bring children into the world, after the failure with his first wife, who probably was better suited to him, with the second, the most impossible mate imaginable for him, as became quickly apparent, though she did bear him the desired children, whom, however, at the very moment they were suddenly present, he simply no longer wanted, as I now know and as I secretly always felt, he had needed the children in order to let himself go, to relax the intensity with which he'd been forced to live, freed by now having children, even when they were still very young, as though the children had already begun to succeed him, to take over from and for him, as far as he was concerned, long before it could actually be possible for them to do so. During this period when he let go, when he gave up, and took to devoting himself wholly to nothing but his inclinations, the period after his fortieth year, the effective influence of his second wife, our mother, had naturally been enabled to spread very rapidly, because he was no longer emitting any energies of his own to counteract it, but, as noted, it was all the same to him, "all the same" underlined, he'd made a mistake and he'd also let go, given (himself) up, and from that point on I never saw my father do anything in particular except go out hunting, alone or with friends, often with my brothers, too, but never with me, hunting never even entered into my thoughts, I never understood it at all, while all my father cared about was the forest as forest, not as an economic reality, but just for the game in it, nothing else, till the day he died, and this indifference of his to everything other than his one single interest, hunting, wholly encompassed us, his children. Once he'd realized the aversion he felt for the Eferding woman, his dislike of her that grew from day to day, as he always said, he ended by resigning himself to the presence of this woman in his life as someone unacceptable, whom he couldn't any longer accept, nor could he get her out of the way, but he could have no relationship with her not conditioned by aversion and hatred. He, our father, was the opposite of that woman in every respect and it had become ever more obvious that theirs was the case of a purely accidental encounter, probably during one of his visits to a friend in Eferding, actually it was only despair over the failure of everything he had hoped for from his first wife, which made him actually, and without a grain of sense, as he put it, take the bait of that Eferding woman, who was an absolute nothing, she was simply old and sloppy, which she simply continued to be at Altensam, only to a greater degree. But to judge the whole case in this biased fashion, putting all the blame on the Eferding woman, is also impossible, "impossible" underlined. The fact is that our father had quite often stopped at the public house in Eferding where our mother came from, to which the butcher shop was attached which is still being run by our mother's brother today, and one day he

stopped there again, and this led to the decline of Altensam, or
rather the decline of what was left of Altensam that could still
decline, because at that time Altensam was actually already in
the process of deteriorating, because my father had already
given up on everything inwardly, all he still wanted was to
make good his decision, once he had taken it, to beget children, regardless with which woman, though deep down he no
longer really cared. And from the moment in which he let go
of things and finally gave up, Altensam, what was left of it,
had been let go and had been basically given up. The appearance of our mother at Altensam was then no more than the
outwardly visible sign of his letting-go and giving-up, by the
time we children were born this process of letting-go and
giving-up had been going on for a long time, and we were
already weakened in advance by this very fact alone. Envel-
oped in this process of letting-go and giving-up, we had
naturally been sensitive to this process from the very start of
our existence and had then fallen increasingly under its influence, we could never escape from it, we were swept along
downward in our father's tendency to let go and give up. By
the time we were born, our father had already turned away
from Altensam, turned his back on it, all we ever experienced
was this condition, more prevalent from one day to the next,
this process of decay hastened on the one hand by my father,
who had already turned away from Altensam, and for all sorts
of easily understandable reasons such as her different background, lower-middle-class milieu, lower-middle-class mentality in general and throughout, Eferding etcetera, it was also
hastened along by my mother in truly despicable fashion. A
son in distress, no matter which son, will naturally go to his
father for advice, but I never went to my father, no matter how
troubled I was, and I never asked my father serious questions,
because I knew that none of my questions would receive an
answer from him, because he had turned away from us even
before we were born, and I also never went to my mother,

because I feared my mother. I had no way of reaching my father, although I longed all my life to reach him, because my father was not interested in me, no more than in my siblings, and mother I feared, we feared her, but I feared her more than my siblings did because I was more hated by my mother than my siblings, on the other hand I did have a somewhat better relationship with my father than my siblings did, who leaned toward my mother rather than my father as their parent. Only my sister was loved by my father like no one else, that was evident always and on every occasion, after his death she was the most defenseless creature in the world. She, my sister, was, like myself but perhaps even more demonstrably, her father's child, akin to him, even more than myself who was akin to father, not to my mother, there was absolutely nothing in me, about me, coming from my mother's, the Eferding woman's, side, everything or almost everything came from my father and all this was true in an even higher degree of my sister, while both my brothers take after the Eferding woman in every respect, even though it expresses itself quite differently than with the Eferding woman, my mother, herself. This is also the reason I could never have a closer relationship with my brothers, because I always saw Eferding in them, everything connected with Eferding and the Eferding woman and her origins, while conversely my brothers always saw in me and in my (and their) sister everything connected with my, with our father, they saw more of it in my sister, but they hated me, my sister they always regarded as *peculiar*, they suspected her of being basically crazy, though it was nothing but my father's nature in her, it was Altensam, but because they couldn't openly hate her, a girl, as they hated me, it was Altensam they hated, unconsciously, as my mother did, she always hated everything unconsciously, anyway everything in her and about her took effect unconsciously, though also in the most calculating way, for people like my mother simply aren't rational beings, they are instinctual beings, and her feelings tend to be, actually, nothing but falsifications, in no matter what direction they move, they're unconscious falsifications of nature into something unconsciously *denatured* like themselves. In reality, however, it was a case of my mother at first always trying to win me over, she had soon realized that I, that everything in me, was against her, which is why she left no stone unturned to draw me closer to herself, in every way and by every means, but when she saw, when she understood, that all she did to gain her ends, to bring me over to her side, which in the nature of things simply wasn't possible, was in vain, a senseless struggle, then she gave her contempt and hatred free rein. I'd not been able to go against my nature and enter into hers, lose myself in hers, as she had probably envisioned. It's always clear from the first, what a newborn child is made of and where it is tending, it is always a tendency backward, a tendency of return, in my case I was simply cut out of my father's cloth and it had to be madness to refuse to see this and want to change it. Quite as in my sister's case, but my mother naturally did not let her feel it in the same harsh manner, not in the case of someone so delicate even from childhood on. Though the child always remained a stranger to her, my mother never treated her roughly, she simply didn't dare, or she'd have come into quite unimaginable conflict with my father. And so my parents had brought children into the world, quite consciously, I know what their motives were, motives of securing the succession on my father's side, and motives of securing a lasting establishment and what this meant for her, our mother, namely to get Altensam into her possession, just the same they'd quite consciously committed a crime, that capital crime against nature, to beget and to procreate children out of sheer calculation, "calculation" underlined, children some of whom sided with the father and some of whom sided with the mother, my brothers siding with mother, what I called taking the part of Eferding, so Roithamer, I and my sister with father, what I called taking the part of Alten-

sam, so Roithamer. In this way my parents had seen to it from
the start that Altensam had to fall apart into two deadly
halves. My father always understood all of this, and the reason
why I later let him too go out of my sight and out of my mind
and even for a long time let him disappear from my memory
was the fact that he, and I suddenly see this again before me as
a very definite image, that from the moment we had come into
being he basically only turned his back on us and left us
behind, that's how I actually see my father, in his gray loden
suit, walking into the woods to hunt or quite simply to escape,
always walking away from us, and always walking away from
us to make his escape, basically depressed by nothing but a
bad conscience over having closed his books and given up his
life. For how many years I had tried to win my father over, but
he always pushed me away, no answers, nothing but walking
away from me, not noticing me. Such years and even decades
of rejection and refusal will end in our dropping such a man
out of our thoughts from one moment to the next, no matter
what we may have felt for him only a minute before, we cease
to think of him and it is as if he had never existed, he may turn
up in our thoughts now and then, but we immediately turn
our minds to something else. Until his fortieth year my father
must have been a fairly happy man, from his fortieth year
onward, however, he was the opposite, so Roithamer. Attempt
at a description of Altensam and everything connected with
Altensam, with special attention to the Cone: to be able to
concentrate entirely in the evenings, on Tuesdays and Fridays,
even beginning with my so-called free afternoons, on my
manuscript about Altensam, my room suddenly the ideal place
for this work, after having seemed for years to be unsuitable,
entirely unsuitable for this purpose, with its view of the stone
wall, lately always wet, of the physics institute, a view favorable to my undertaking in any case, a state such as the one that
always prevails in Hoeller's garret, which was always ideal for
my purposes, Hoeller's garret was the only place where it was

possible for me to construct the Cone, just as it is now possible
for me here, in my room at Cambridge, this room without an
actual view, giving only on the damp, wet wall of the institute,
to think about my work on the Cone now that the Cone has
been finished, now that I'm back here and before I've become
totally absorbed again in my scientific work, before it claims
all of my attention, my chance after my return to devote some
time to this work, a writing job, "writing job" underlined, in
retreat, "retreat" underlined, to clarify everything that has
happened these last six years, since I did need six years to
construct and to build the Cone, for one thing the time factor,
a short time relative to myself, my origins, relative to Altensam, but basically much too long a time which very often and
repeatedly drove me to the edge of madness. The idea and the
realization of the idea, the achievement of the realization of
the idea of the Cone as the tackling and the realization and the
achievement of an aim that has totally dominated me these last
years, the problem of making my intention, which has always
been described as only a crazy and totally hopeless scheme,
clearly understandable not only to myself but to everyone else
who was involved with the realization and completion of the
Cone. Taking under consideration the fact that I was on the
one hand committed to England, to Cambridge, while on the
other hand my energies were after all totally committed to my
intention to build the Cone in the Kobernausser forest, I was
duty-bound to this scene of the site of the Cone, the problem
of being always here, in Cambridge, or in the Kobernausser
forest, at the right moment, of not neglecting the one for the
other, the lowest limit of my responsibility. Actually I should
have spent years in Cambridge so as not to neglect Cambridge,
while at the same time staying in the Kobernausser forest,
meaning in Hoeller's garret, specifically, so as not to neglect
the building of the Cone, now that the Cone is finished and
now that I haven't lost Cambridge, I can see that it was
possible for me to muster the necessary energy to build the

Cone without neglecting Cambridge, that is, neither my teaching nor my own research, because it was possible for me to do the one under the stimulus of the other, not to neglect Cambridge by means of energies generated by my work on the Cone, not to neglect the Cone by means of energies generated at Cambridge, and to do both always in the highest state of concentration upon each objective as required. The assurance I acquired in the course of changing my scene of operations, staying now in Cambridge for a time, then again in Hoeller's garret, in England on the one hand, in Austria on the other, always shifting from one to the other at the proper moment, without being aware of this fact, always doing the right thing as a gift, a form of talent, without consciousness, the change of locale, leaving Cambridge for the Kobernausser forest and vice versa, but also moving from one to the other in thought without any transition, for how often I was in Cambridge (in my thoughts) while being in reality in the Kobernausser forest, and how often, conversely, in the Kobernausser forest (in my thoughts) though in reality I was in Cambridge. That I told myself from time to time, even though I was in Cambridge just now, I'm in the Kobernausser forest now of necessity, conversely, of necessity now in Cambridge, although in reality I'd been in the Kobernausser forest. I could always switch my head from one place to the other, instantly, even as a child I could switch instantly from one thing to another. And the very fact that I could be most effective especially in Cambridge for the Kobernausser forest, most effective in the Kobernausser forest for Cambridge, the fact that my intensity is greater for the one when I'm in the other place, and vice versa, and I could exercise this ability because I had complete control of this mechanism from earliest childhood on, so Roithamer. To build the Cone without teaching and studying in Cambridge, studying as I teach, studying by teaching, and conversely, to have intensified my achievement in Cambridge as I did without the actual building of the Cone is unimaginable. We very often

make headway rapidly and with the greatest assurance in some
(most strenuous) work or occupation or passion andsoforth, so
Roithamer, because we've started or become involved or
planned another, similar work or occupation or passion and
never abandoned it, so Roithamer. The one work or occupation
or passion which very often takes us to the very edge of
despair, often solely because we are in fact involved in another
such strenuous effort simultaneously. I alone could have conceived such an idea, the idea of building such a cone, planning
it and actually building it, everybody said so and they're right.
The need to understand what led to this idea, most likely
everything led to this idea. What led to this idea and the
realization of the idea as the effect of its original cause, so
Roithamer, a matter of consistency, just as the realization of
the idea led to perfecting the idea andsoforth. To build is the
most wonderful thing in the world, it's the supreme gratification, "supreme gratification" underlined. It's what everyone
longs to do, building, but not everyone gets the chance to
build, and everyone who does build gets this gratification out
of it. Especially in building something no one has ever built
before. It's the supreme gratification, "supreme gratification"
underlined, to complete a work of art one has planned and
built oneself. To complete a philosophical work, or a literary
work, even if it's the most epoch-making and most important
work of its kind, can never give us this supreme gratification,
nothing like the gratification that comes with actually accomplishing the erection of an edifice, especially an edifice such as
no one ever has erected before. With this one has achieved all
that is humanly possible. Even if going all the way in perfecting this work is sure to cost one all he has and has, in fact,
destroyed him. The price for such an edifice as a work of art of
one's own, the only one of its kind in the world, cannot be less
than everything, "everything" underlined. At first we shy
away from even conceiving such an idea, we're terrified that it
may in time take possession of us utterly and end by crushing

us altogether, so Roithamer, while on the one hand we rise up against ourselves for the sake of the idea, on the other hand we resist the idea in self-defense, yet in the end it turns out to have been a revolt against ourselves and for the idea. The idea demands fulfillment, it demands realization and never stops demanding to be realized. One always wants to give it up, but one ends by not giving it up because one is by nature disinclined to give it up and in fact one sets about realizing the idea. Suddenly one's head is full of nothing else, one has become the incarnation of one's idea. And now one begins to reap the benefit of all one's suffering, of one's origins and everything connected with one's origins, in my case everything connected with Altensam, everything being primarily and to begin with the story of one's origins, even if it all consists of nothing but martyrdom. It all turns out to be useful, and the worst of the horrors are most useful of all. There's a chance of realizing one's idea, because it is precisely the torments of one's family history and the torments of the present, which is as much of a torment as one's history has been, torment and nothing else, it is precisely these past and familial torments, if they are bad enough, the worst possible, which enable one to realize one's idea to a high and even the highest degree. The greater the idea and the higher our aim by way of that idea, the greater our historical and our familial torments are required to have been. Suddenly I realized what an enormous capital my idea could draw upon, in the accumulated capital of torments I had suffered from my family origins and my personal history and all the history connected with me in any way, and I was able to put all these resources to work, in full possession of my faculties, once I had them suddenly at my disposal. For what was Altensam to me other than family as a torment, history as a torment, the present as a torment, leaving out of account the few bright spots such as the quite extraordinary natural conditions here, the extraordinary rock formations, animals, plants andsoforth, as the only chance of retreat andsoforth, so Roithamer. Human, natural, and art history as torment, as the possibility of reaching my aim, so Roithamer. At the terminal point of the conditions that have always prevailed here. The basis, Altensam, "basis" underlined, on which I have been able to realize my idea, finish the Cone, hence Altensam and everything connected with Altensam was absolutely necessary, because each thing always derives from all the others, so Roithamer. The Cone, as it is, is unthinkable without Altensam, just as everything is unthinkable without everything else andsoforth, so Roithamer. *The terrifying idea,* so Roithamer, which, the more terrifying it is, the closer to realization it is. And so everything at the terminal point of my observations made in my childhood and youth in Altensam has been necessary toward the realization and completion of the Cone, everything about (and in) the Cone, everything else andsoforth, so Roithamer. By studying Altensam and my sister and trying to think Altensam and my sister through and by continuing to extend these efforts on and on until they could be extended no further, I enabled myself to build the Cone and realize and complete it. Because I let myself in for the sheer terror of this undertaking to build the Cone, let myself in for the monstrousness, "the monstrousness" underlined, of my life, so Roithamer. As if I had lived, existed, all along, all those years of development, which were nothing else than my development in the direction of the Cone, the direction of this monstrousness. One is called upon to approach and realize and complete the monstrousness, and everyone has some such enormity in his life, or else to be destroyed by this monstrousness even before one has entered into it. In this way people always tend to waver at a certain point in their lives, and always at the particular crucial point in their lives when they must decide whether to tackle the monstrousness of their life or let themselves be destroyed by it before they have tackled it. Most people prefer to let themselves be destroyed by this monstrousness rather than to tackle it, because they aren't equipped by nature to tackle and realize and fulfill their monstrousness, they're rather inclined, by nature, to let themselves be destroyed by their monstrousness before they have tackled it. The matured idea is enough in itself to destroy most people, so Roithamer. And such an enormity as a work of art, a lifework of art—regardless of what this monstrousness is, everyone has such a possibility in him, because his nature is in itself such a possibility—can only be tackled and realized and fulfilled with the whole of one's being. In so tackling such a monstrousness we have entered into pure defenselessness, into being alone with ourselves within ourselves, alone with our idea as an enormity, and everything is against us. Because we believe that we can't do otherwise we keep wanting to give up, because we can't know that we are by nature quite well equipped for such a monstrousness, which we begin to see only after we've realized and completed this monstrousness as an idea, just as I hadn't known whether I was capable of building the Cone before the Cone was completed. But once we've reached our aim, we no longer know anything about the way to our aim and we keep finding it impossible to believe, for the rest of our lives our doubt keeps increasing and we can't believe that we have reached our aim, the realization and completion of our idea as, for example, a Cone, so Roithamer. At the end, when we have reached our aim, no matter what aim, even if this aim is the building of a so-called work of art, we find ourselves frightened by it. Attempt at a description of Hoeller, of Hoeller's wife and Hoeller's garret: before I tackled the study of statics I went to Hoeller in order to observe Hoeller, first to observe Hoeller and then I studied his house, the house he built out of his own head and with his own hands, the study of one thing always presupposes the study of something else from which the first is derived. Hoeller had most readily taken me into his house and into his family, I'd felt that it wouldn't be enough for me to just visit briefly in Hoeller's house, but that I needed to live in it as long as necessary, free to observe him in person and his building construction and his family, in his house and together with all of them, *as long as necessary,* in the way in which I thought I would have to live there in order to be able to tackle the realization of my idea of building the Cone. For the idea of building the Cone, even Hoeller hadn't been able to imagine a cone as a building, and Hoeller also *had* to consider my idea of building the Cone in the center of the Kobernausser forest as a crazy idea, I'd been able to observe that in him, for the idea to build the Cone could be realized only after I clearly understood Hoeller's house, I'd said to Hoeller, and that it was necessary for me to use Hoeller's garret as my base of operations, for Hoeller's garret had always, from the first moment I saw it, seemed to me to be the ideal place in which to do my thinking. To observe and explore Hoeller's house as well as Hoeller's person was the first thing I had to do before I could tackle the realization of my plan to erect the Cone. I tried to make my intentions clear to Hoeller and he understood me immediately. And then Hoeller informed his family of my reasons for staying in his house, he even told the children for what purpose I would be living and staying with them for weeks at a time, quite on my own, to work on my idea. That I would have to explore the Hoeller house, understand it and explore it thoroughly, in order to begin planning my own building. To this end I needed nothing but perceptiveness and the proper application of my perceptiveness to the object under observation, namely, the Hoeller house. So I had brought nothing with me except the absolutely necessary and the will to be able to understand and explore the Hoeller house, to understand and explore the Hoeller house and also Hoeller himself and his *state of mind* and his family and the garret, which I had entered very early one day in April, because I had left Altensam so early that day in order that no one might see me leave, because I'd wanted to leave Altensam unseen, unnoticed, and I'd succeeded in doing that; when we're about to do something unusual, something extraordinary, something like my idea of building the Cone, so Roithamer, we must proceed with all secrecy, keep all our activities as unknown as possible. And so, having arrived in Altensam from England the previous afternoon I'd gone down to Hoeller's house late *that same evening* to discuss with Hoeller whether it might be possible for me to move into his house the very next morning, Hoeller understood at once, in the downstairs family room where they have their meals, this room too had been constructed and realized by Hoeller in every detail to serve precisely and ideally for the purpose of taking meals there with the whole family, ideally functional like all the rooms in Hoeller's house, and I asked myself where he acquired his mastery of the art of building, which can be seen in every detail of his house, or which can at least be recognized, at least felt, in every detail, anyway; in the downstairs room where they all sat together at supper, I had entered almost at the same moment I knocked on the door, surprised by the silence in the room considering that all the Hoellers were sitting there, that they hadn't spoken a word during the entire mealtime and Hoeller had only signed to me to sit down with them, his wife had immediately risen and brought me something to eat from the kitchen, something other than what they'd been eating, I don't remember what they gave me to eat, all I remember is, it was something else, but without a word spoken the whole time, I'd wanted to say something to the children, but the children made it impossible for me by their silence alone to say anything to them, the same with Hoeller and his wife, so I hadn't been able to bring up the purpose of my visit at any time during supper, no one asked me anything nor did I feel any need to talk, yet I'd only just come from Altensam and this very evening, fresh from an argument with my mother, which ended up as a violent argument of everybody against everybody in Altensam, as soon as I'd arrived a quarrel had broken out over a just completed paint job on the farm building, quite unnecessary in my opinion, which I noticed the minute I arrived at Altensam and which caused me to ask why the farm building, which I'd remembered as being outwardly in rather good condition, had suddenly had to be freshly painted for no reason at all, whether that had been my mother's idea, I avoided calling it this crazy idea, this, characteristically for my mother, crazy and senseless and in my opinion really superfluous idea, but naturally my mother had heard, because she's always lying in wait for it, what I hadn't even said, as she always hears everything that isn't said but is being thought against her, and I've always thought against her, all my life long I've always thought against my mother, though these thoughts were hardly ever spoken aloud, but she always heard it even when it wasn't said aloud, which always led to quarrels at Altensam, I'd hardly set foot in the place and already there was a quarrel, even on this afternoon, I hadn't even taken my traveling bag up to my room yet, but while still down in the hall, I couldn't restrain myself and I asked my mother whose idea it was to put a fresh coat of color on the farm building, I said there was no need for a new color on the farm building, that the somewhat older, but not too old color, a reddish tint I believed, had suited the farm building much better, it had suited the whole character of the farm building on its east side, against the sunrise, it's important to consider the situation of such a building when one has to decide on its color, now I could take no pleasure at all in the sight of the farm building, I'd said to my mother, whereas I'd always taken pleasure in seeing it when it was still that old reddish color, especially in the evening, but now it gave me no pleasure at all, I said, that it could only have been her idea, my mother's idea, to touch up the farm building with this hideous green color and at such a huge needless expense for the paint job too, I'd been accusing my mother only in thought, but she, with her uncanny ear for everything I was thinking, had heard what I was only thinking as if I'd uttered it, although I'd never

have said aloud what I was thinking because I was fully aware
how it would affect her, nor had I meant to start an argument
with my mother the minute I arrived at Altensam, after all I
didn't come to Altensam that often from England, that I could
have afforded to start an argument with my mother, always on
my way to Altensam, the closer I came to Altensam, the more I
determined not to argue with my mother, on any account, to
do all in my power to prevent an argument with my mother,
but I'd hardly set foot in Altensam when, presto, I'd be having
an argument with my mother, most of the time I'd hardly sat
down before I found myself already deep in some argument or
other with my mother, and her reproaches, which came fast
and often very loud, to draw the rest of the family, soon there
was no damming them up, and all that mutual dislike and all
that mutual hatred, barely held back for a moment or for only
a few brief moments, have now again broken out into the
open, darkening the scene. I never feared anything so much in
all my life as these arguments with my mother, but these
arguments inevitably broke out, and they broke out within the
first few moments we met, and there was no damming them
up. On that afternoon, when I'd hoped to rest up in Altensam,
after so many strenuous months, a whole long six months
which seemed even longer in that dreadful English climate and
seemed even more strenuous and really terrible, I'd hoped to
relax in Altensam for longer than usual this time, as I'd
planned to spend some time in Altensam, a place after all more
conducive to relaxation than any other place, though it had
never yet been really at my disposal for such a purpose, but
instead, because of the fact that I'd seen the new color job on
the farm building, that I'd seen it at once on arrival, and seen
instantly what a tasteless color job it was, what a brainless
color job, which had, as I instantly suspected, cost a heap of
money besides, it was after all my money too, so then and
there I had this argument with my mother, we were hurling all
sorts of accusations at each other's heads while at the same

time saying over and over again, now I to her, then again she to me, saying *calm down, will you, why don't you calm down,* we'd keep saying this almost perverse *do calm down, do calm down,* tossed back and forth between us, probably resulting only in our getting deeper and deeper into our argument until, in the end, we'd argued ourselves as always into a state of exhaustion, these arguments always ended with both of us in a state of total exhaustion, it was an effort and took the utmost willpower merely to keep upright after one of those battles, then, when mother invited me, at the utmost point of exhaustion from this argument, to have a bite with her in the kitchen, there was no one in it that day, cook was having her Tuesday off, to have a cup of tea, just a snack she had prepared for us with her own hands, a welcome-home snack as it were, so I followed mother into the kitchen and silently drank a cup of tea with her, naturally I ate nothing, I was simply in no condition to eat. Then, as we sat in the kitchen after our argument, so Roithamer, it was always basically the same thing, I arrive, we have our argument, we go in to drink tea, sitting in silence, totally exhausted, simply no longer capable of hating each other, we simply let go, sitting face to face, we let it go as it comes, as it is, nothing can be changed, suddenly she demands a description of my trip, how was my journey, was the weather in London good or bad, what had I been doing, my friends, my colleagues, she touched all these bases, but even the way she pronounced *Cambridge,* the way she said *London,* instantly aroused my anger against her again, the way she said *Dover,* the way she said *Brussels, Cologne,* all the time with her eyes on me, she'd question me with these cue-words that were always the same cue-words, every time I came home from England, she wanted to know everything, every detail, but I remained closemouthed, I was silence itself, as always. She couldn't get a word out of me. I tried a bite of bread, choking on it, with her eyes on me, taking possession of me, as she thought. As always, my siblings were in their rooms, and I thought they were waiting in their rooms for our inevitable argument to be over, for us to have *calmed down,* as they thought, then they'd come down, to put in an appearance for their brother, who had withdrawn from all of them by going off to England. Without a word, "without a word" underlined, I'd got up and left my mother alone in the kitchen, and I went away from Altensam, down to the Aurach, into Hoeller's house. Away from the argument with my mother, into the silence of the Hoellers. Sitting at the table in Hoeller's family room, having supper with the Hoellers, *eating something different from what they were eating,* underlined, still affected by my argument with my mother and so I was in a debilitated condition as the Hoellers watched me, after I'd previously been watched by my mother, but watched differently by the Hoellers than by my mother, how differently, "how" underlined, that's indescribable, but it was an entirely different kind of look, because it was an entirely different perceptiveness, because the Hoellers are different from the Altensam people, I thought, but it's not a greater simplicity, the so-called simple folk are not really simple, I was on the one hand still affected by the argument with my mother, about the new color job on the farm building, and also affected by the silence between mother and me in the Altensam kitchen, that condition of silence between me and my mother, realizing that again we'd had the argument both of us, I as well as my mother, always dreaded, once I'd announced my homecoming to Altensam, and which had of course broken out again this time, whether it's the new color job on the farm building, or some purchase, or a sale, some real estate speculation on which I or my mother can't agree, or as it might be father, by this time totally withdrawn and hardly noticeable any longer, who serves to trigger it off, then on the other hand the silence in Hoeller's room, under the effect of which I was now condemned to the same speechlessness as the Hoellers sitting at table with me. The whole time not a single word at the Hoellers' table, when supper was over the Hoellers stood up, including Hoeller himself, his wife cleared the table, in silence, they all walked out of the room, in silence, the children following their mother into the kitchen to do the washing up, Hoeller went to the hall, I followed him and it was only then, after I had thanked him for my supper, that I was able to come out with my reason for coming down to the Hoeller house this very evening of my arrival, I told him I wanted to lodge at his house for a while, could he, as a favor, let me *room* in his garret for a while, I found myself able, as I had not expected to be, to explain my wish, which I had simply reeled off to Hoeller, who was totally unprepared to hear it, I said to him that to look at this house, to study it, explore it, as well as yourself and everything connected with you and your house, will be the best preparation for my plan to build the Cone. Hoeller agreed to my proposal, he said I could move in tomorrow morning, I said I'd bring only the barest necessities with me, he told me I could stay in the garret as long as I liked, as long as I needed, it would be a pleasure for him to have my company for a time, the mere idea was a pleasure, so Roithamer. We'd spent only a few minutes in the hall, then Hoeller had to go to his workshop, so I said good-bye, it was a relief to know, even if only briefly, that I no longer had to fear having to stay in Altensam, where I'd hoped to relax and restore myself a little, for quite a while as I'd thought, under these, "these," underlined, terrible *circumstances,* a groundless fear now, and so I took a detour, past a hazel hedge I'd loved as a child, back up to Altensam, and withdrew to my room after showing myself briefly to my brothers, my sister was visiting a friend in town. After a sleepless night, like my nights in England for quite a while now, I'd gone quite early, I think it was five in the morning, to Hoeller's house, Hoeller was already up and at work in his workshop at that hour, in order to study it scientifically from the first moment, I was all set to look and study and explore the Hoeller house most thoroughly and with the greatest pleasure from the first. To begin with I immediately had the chance to make comparisons, looking at Hoeller and looking at his house, studying Hoeller and studying his house, what was characteristic of Hoeller was also characteristic of his house, the house inside was like Hoeller inside, by studying the Hoeller house I had a sudden insight into Hoeller and, conversely, by studying Hoeller, I had insight into the house, one served as a simultaneous illumination of the other. I could have said without hesitation, so Roithamer, Hoeller's inside is the same as the inside of his house. I could have said that the strength (or weakness) of Hoeller's character clearly manifests itself in (and by) his house. And just as Hoeller's wife submits to Hoeller, and the children submit to their father, without ever for a moment giving themselves up, as I thought, they subordinate themselves to the house, without giving themselves up. The Hoeller house corresponds to Hoeller, and he and all its other inhabitants conduct themselves in it, in his house, accordingly. And where, I asked myself, did Hoeller get the idea for this house of his, because I am fully aware that I got my idea, to build the Cone for my sister, from Hoeller and his house at the Aurach gorge. But I haven't asked him to this day where he got the idea for building his house, though he naturally must have gotten the idea from a house that another man built for himself (or for someone else) before, probably a house standing nearby, for Hoeller hasn't gotten around too much. Possibly Hoeller doesn't even know where he got the idea for building his house and for building it as he ended up building it, a house so much in accordance with himself, so visibly in accordance with himself, as I've never seen another. I'll ask him where he got the idea, I thought, and I asked Hoeller where he'd gotten his idea, because I simply had to know, while I looked over and studied and explored his house, it was indispensable to me to know. But Hoeller can't remember where he got the idea to build his house. The chances are that the house that gave Hoeller the idea to build his own house is standing quite close by, I thought, as close as can be to the Hoeller house. Yet there's no other house to compare with it, I thought, so Roithamer. It's also possible that Hoeller never saw the model for his house in reality, for in reality there isn't any model for Hoeller's house in the vicinity, I thought, so Roithamer, it must have come to him in a dream. In that case it's quite likely, I thought, that Hoeller didn't see a model for his house in a dream, but that he dreamed the house itself. All he had to do was trust his dream and accurately copy the house he saw in his dream, so Roithamer. Since he's a master of the craft and in addition drew on all sorts of books, as I know, including the kind of books I myself got hold of for my own purposes, for the rest of building knowledge he needed, it was only a question of willpower and endurance for Hoeller to be able to build his house. That he chose, of all places, the Aurach gorge for the site wasn't a matter of low cost, on the contrary, the costs of the site here at the Aurach gorge were, as I know, exceptionally high, it just happens to be characteristic of Hoeller. Just as it's characteristic of me to build the Cone for my sister in the middle of the Kobernausser forest. The monstrousness of realizing my plan is clear to me, I said to myself, after the monstrousness of Hoeller's plan to build his house had become clear to me, but the actual monstrousness of it then turned out to be much more monstrous than I could ever have imagined. But it's the same monstrousness for me to build and to realize and to complete the Cone as it is for Hoeller to build and realize and complete the Hoeller house, so Roithamer, everything regarding his house, the Hoeller house, I thought, so Roithamer, is as much in accordance with his nature as everything regarding the Cone for my sister is in accordance with mine. And because I always felt at home with Hoeller, I also felt at home with the house he had built (for himself and his family), everything in this house is home to me, I thought, and I went on the one hand from top to bottom in the house, and on the other hand from bottom to top,

closely examining everything in my scientific way and checking out everything, but I could see that the inside of the house
as well as the outside of the house at the Aurach gorge, that, in
short, the entire Hoeller house was already familiar to me, one
hundred percent familiar, I said to myself. And so I thought
that everything in the Cone that was to be built and to be
realized must also be familiar to me, one hundred percent
familiar or at least almost one hundred percent familiar, because my sister, for whom I wanted to build the Cone, *wanted
to* at first, but then most decidedly and most determinedly had
to build for her, "had to" underlined, one hundred percent
familiar. Once I have fully grasped my sister's nature with my
intelligence, on the one hand, and on the other hand with my
emotional awareness, then I can begin building the Cone, so
Roithamer. As for me, I wonder why Hoeller has lodged me in
this garret which, as I now see, really belonged so entirely to
Roithamer, surely not only because I was Roithamer's closest
intimate and because I told Hoeller that I was now going to
work on Roithamer's literary legacy, but only in Hoeller's
garret, probably because it seemed the most natural thing in
the world to him, Hoeller, that I wanted to domicile myself in
Hoeller's garret in order to sift and sort Roithamer's papers
there. I told Hoeller that his garret was so full of Roithamer's
living spirit that there could be no better place for working on
Roithamer's papers than Hoeller's garret which is simply one
hundred percent conducive to working on Roithamer's legacy,
besides which it also afforded me the opportunity to study the
contents of the books and articles Roithamer had accumulated
in Hoeller's garret, primarily for his cone-building project, all
of which had a bearing on Roithamer's legacy, what he had
read must be integrated with what he had ultimately written,
the one must be brought into relationship with the other and
everything put together had to be brought into relationship
with Roithamer, by me. Everything in Hoeller's garret belonging to Roithamer and left by Roithamer for my work on

Roithamer's papers, was in exactly the state in which Roithamer had left it just before his suicide, Hoeller told me, nothing had been touched by anyone else since Roithamer left Hoeller's garret, he, Hoeller, was the only person who ever set foot in the garret, he allowed no one inside, not even his wife or his kids, who were always asking, out of curiosity, to be allowed in Hoeller's garret, which had basically already become Roithamer's garret, but their father, Hoeller, had always forbidden them to enter it. The Cone, I'd said to Hoeller on my arrival, was unique not only in Europe, it was unique in all the world, never before had any man yet built such a cone, in the course of centuries, in the course of the entire history of building, frequent attempts had been made to build a cone as a habitation, a pure conical shape as a live-in object, I'd said to Hoeller, but no one ever succeeded, not in France, not in Russia, as Roithamer wrote, "not in France, not in Russia" underlined. He, Roithamer, had had to move into Hoeller's garret in order to be able to build the Cone, he had made Hoeller's garret his construction studio for building the Cone, "construction studio for building the Cone" underlined, because a splendid thing can come only out of another splendid thing, in this case, the Cone out of Hoeller's house. Basically, "basically" underlined, there had never been any problem for Roithamer and Hoeller in understanding each other. Must try to describe mother, the Eferding woman, so Roithamer, compared with my sister: First, personal characteristics. Actually I tried several times to be with my mother in Altensam, just as she probably tried being with me, but these efforts were always doomed at the outset, they never got beyond being mere useless tries equally destructive to the sanity of either of us, they only turned against us and ended by destroying and finally annihilating everything inside us. Actually she always loathed being with me and vice versa; as far as I was concerned, obsessed as I was with my work and my passion for my work only, nothing else, for in fact everything always was my work, "everything" underlined, mother simply always tried, simply because she is my mother, not that she went out of her way for me, but she did try, just as I didn't exactly go out of my way for her, but I did try, but these efforts were always instantly recognizable as mere damnable efforts for the sake of doing the right thing, "doing the right thing" underlined, because what she instinctively hated was never hateful to me, what pleased her displeased me, what pricked her interest had never pricked mine, where she was sensitive I was never sensitive, andsoforth, so Roithamer, the Eferding woman was instinctively the kind who'd repel me and who was bound to destroy Altensam, or at least she was instinctively the kind who was bound to hasten the process whereby Altensam must be destroyed and annihilated, such persons or characters suddenly turn up, like my mother, that Eferding woman from Eferding, they suddenly spring from their family origins into the world of others to destroy it and to annihilate it, no matter whether they realize this or not, the Eferding woman realized it perfectly. This attempt as a description or this description as an attempt, with all the imperfection, uncertainty, which characterizes all of these attempts or descriptions or descriptive efforts, fragmentary stabs at deviations in Altensam andsoforth, such as I've always made in order to understand Altensam, this particular attempt made only because I've heard about that so-called Mother's Day, that's a cue-word, Mother's Day, started me off on this note. How, from my point of view, she was always bound to fail even in the most trifling of trifles, so-called irrelevancies, the disciplines and arrangements that had always been the disciplines and arrangements at Altensam, anyway she had no access whatsoever to the so-called intellectual sphere, nor did she ever try to understand something she was bound to disdain, to hate, even just something, no matter what, of those things that concerned me and for which I dared to exist all my life, the things that had to be the actual meaning of my life and my existence, she pretended to understand but she understood nothing, though of course I too very often pretended to understand, in conversation with her, her concerns, without feeling in the least inclined to such an understanding or even able to understand, because I didn't even want to have such an inclination to understand her, she understood, she often said, and understood nothing, when she said she did she was putting on an act, just as I was always putting on an act about all of her concerns, if only to endure long stretches of Altensam at all in her presence, for it was extremely hard for me even to exist side by side with the Eferding woman, even if I didn't see her, as long as I knew for a fact she was there, she went so against my grain, all these efforts always because I still went on regarding Altensam as my home, even throughout all my time in England, but home is always and in every case a mistake, so Roithamer, "in every case" underlined. When the Eferding woman said that she understood she was putting on an act and this act was instantly recognizable as such, she was all emotion, and since I never wanted to have anything to do with people who exist and act only on an emotional basis, the so-called world of the emotions had always been suspect and always hateful to me, people like the Eferding woman, my mother, constantly pretended to understand but they only have a certain feeling without intelligence, which is repulsive to the other kind, my kind, of person, and even this unintelligent feeling of theirs is a fake, not a reality, this type of female has only a dim perception of emotion, and not even a dim perception of intelligence, so that actually they have neither intelligence nor feeling, and the act they put on of having feeling and intelligence is nothing more than sexual hypocrisy, "sexual hypocrisy" underlined. Although she tried, in the beginning, to draw me into her emotional world, to push me out of my own world which was in opposition to this emotional world of hers, kept trying to urge me out of my own world into hers, she no longer tried to do that later on, because I gave her no opportunity to try it, but her effort in that direction had lasted a long time, her effort to drive me out of my own world into hers, while my effort to acquaint her with my interests, I don't say familiarize her, that would have been a totally hopeless undertaking, her tricks with which she worked at alienating me from myself and eventually also from my father were so complicated, so cunning, she kept on trying it with every possible and impossible kind of finesse, she thought she could deceive me with her simple, yet common, blunt, Eferding household intelligence which in any case always lapsed into rudeness, and had nothing to do with real intelligence, she thought she could manipulate me to suit her purposes, suggesting that it would be better, smarter for me to obey her, not my father, I'd see that soon enough andsoforth, but she always had to recognize that her efforts had been in vain, so Roithamer. Her vulgarity, in no way differentiated from the vulgarity of all her gender, became in her later years an open disgust with everything connected with me, so Roithamer. It was never in all her life possible for her to change, she simply lacked the will and the instinct and the taste required, and for me to meet her halfway, "her" underlined, would have meant the sacrifice of everything I am, so Roithamer. While in England I'd always expected to recover in Altensam, so during my first hours in Altensam, situated as it is in such peculiar and basically unfavorable climatic conditions, requiring all by themselves the supreme effort of willpower just to survive, in those first hours and days, which should have served for my recovery and relaxation after the long strain in England, I'd usually offered her virtually no resistance, I always started by sucking in Altensam just as it was, exposing myself to it willingly, but my resistance soon became most adamant, because she'd actually been irritating me without respite, after only two or three days I had to admit to myself that I could not recover and relax in Altensam, that I had merely fallen victim once again to the delusion that I could recover and relax in Altensam even though I had fallen victim to this delusion hundreds and thousands of times before, a delusion in which I lived in England, at Cambridge, that I could safely strain myself there to the utmost in my mental labors, because I'd be able to recover and relax in Altensam from these mental labors, so I kept going back to Altensam, probably only from sheer habit by this time, no longer with the least expectation of being understood, only from habit, not in the certainty that Altensam would fulfill my wish and my need, namely, to recover and relax, quite the contrary, my visits in Altensam, those terrible visits-from-habit, were clearly from the first destined not to bring me recovery and relaxation in Altensam, they could only upset me and make me sick and drive me crazy owing to those conditions basically the fault of my mother, the Eferding woman, so that as soon as I got there I was immediately entangled in all these quarrels and so-called power struggles in Altensam, things I basically wanted to have nothing to do with, actually it was always the Eferding woman, my mother, who'd been the cause of that sense of impending complications, as soon as I'd arrived, which immediately turned into intimations of catastrophe, but very often, though in fact this too emanated from her, I myself was, as for instance in the case of the color job on the farm building, the one who instigated or sparked off such quarrels and catastrophic moods, which always and in every case turned out to be pointless. Although for the first few moments, I must say, we were most considerate toward one another, after the first few moments we were again totally ruthless against each other, it was only a matter of time as to when we would separate, how soon I'd leave Altensam where I'd only just arrived, our mutual consideration had always lasted only through the first few minutes, then our real feelings, nothing but real dislike, even hatred, ran free again. Yet our efforts at restraint during those first few moments were interesting even so, because both of us had made them again and again, and so often, despite our awareness that they were doomed to failure in no time at all, even before I'd had a chance to hang up my coat, to take my bag to my room, even before I'd had a look around Altensam, I hadn't even got beyond the outer hall, because it was clear to both of us that we stay the same and have stayed the same between times, that we haven't changed, that she, the Eferding woman, hasn't changed in Altensam nor I in England, and the mere idea or any conceivable attempt based on such an idea that we must try to change for each other's sake was nothing but madness, presumption, megalomania, where change was so impossible there was nothing for us to change, because we simply had no way to do it, neither of us was born with the capacity to change ourselves, on the contrary, when we'd tried to change, despite our full awareness that we couldn't change, and when we'd failed again, as we both felt in our bones we would after the first few minutes, after the first words of greeting had been exchanged, though even those had already been uttered in that tone which indicated that we were losing again, because we'd already lost at the moment we'd come face to face, our effort to change had simply made matters worse. At first we'd always look at each other as if we'd changed, because we thought the interim might have changed us, but the interim all by itself had never changed us, I remained myself, she remained herself, we made believe that the interim had transformed us into people other than those we were before the interim, I'd persuaded myself that I'd turned from an unbearable (to her) man into a bearable (to her) man, just as she'd persuaded herself that in the interim she'd become bearable (to me), though she'd always previously been unbearable (to me), we'd also imagined that we'd made certain efforts to improve, though we could no longer think what efforts, we'd only, as we remembered it, considered making efforts in our minds, but in reality we'd made no efforts at all, we'd never translated our thoughts about efforts into any real efforts, we never could, because if we could have we'd at least have made an acceptable person out of ourselves (for the other one) in the interim, which was, after all, a most eventful interim for the most part, an interim certainly full of the most enormous changes in Altensam (owing to her) as in England (owing to me), but these changes had occurred only outside of ourselves, not within us, we had remained as and what we were prior to each interim, our characters, as we could clearly determine at our very first contact, had not only not changed, they had, on the contrary, only hardened, which made our pretense of mutual understanding only all the more ridiculous. She didn't stand a chance of winning me over, any more than I stood a chance of winning her over, because she was always predisposed against all I *was*, and owing to this predisposition her character had kept pathologically hardening in the mold of her own tendencies, whether we wished it or not, it no longer mattered, we were going to be for the rest of our lives against each other, she against me and I against her, I'd be focused entirely on myself, she entirely on herself, concerned with our own interests and totally monopolized by these interests, we'd just play a polite charade with each other for hours, for days, for weeks, until all our differences, all the barriers between us, had come again quite visibly into the open between us, until Altensam, whatever it had become through the Eferding woman, however this mechanism of destruction came into motion again because of our mutual dislike, repudiation, this mutual hatred of ours, moving always not only to disturb us but to destroy us, so Roithamer, where everything repelled me as far as she was concerned and re-pelled her as far as I was concerned. Nevertheless both of us were always incapable of simply giving up seeing each other ever again, she'd write, inviting me home, to England, and I came from England to Altensam, as if something had changed, each time we'd said good-bye we did it in the expectation of never seeing each other again, of parting forever, because there was simply absolutely nothing uniting us, we had not a scintilla in common, except for disgust and dislike, nothing, yet we were not only unable to stick to our decision never to see one another again, but the intervals between trips from England to Austria, to Altensam, had actually become increasingly shorter in the last few years. And the ordeals to which we subjected each other, once I was back in Altensam, kept getting worse, in fact they were getting to be terrible ordeals because we had reached a high degree of natural ease in the art of tormenting ourselves, our mutual hatred went even deeper than that, and everything indicated the possibility of an even greater deepening of that hatred, our methods became more sophisticated with every one of my visits to Altensam. Still, it's unimaginable, so Roithamer, with what a degree of mindlessness persons like the Eferding woman seem to be capable of existing, with what emotional callousness, considering that emotion and nothing else is all she has, her entire being set against everything, and takes the most antagonistic action every time. At first it was still possible for me to think that a certain shyness with regard to the life of the mind, to what is regarded as, after all, male intellectuality, had turned, in her, to outright disgust with everything intellectual, so Roithamer, but as time went on, and time had indeed accelerated the process once she indubitably had the upper hand in Altensam, her hatred had grown to the point that she had to hate not only paper covered with my script but every piece of paper, every kind of paper, she regarded paper as a foundation for mental activity, instantly aroused her hatred, it was as though her hatred of paper alone was enough to reduce her to total exhaustion every day, I often thought, pencils, pens, aroused an unimaginable hatred in her, not even to mention books, pamphlets, periodicals, she even hated newspapers, because newspapers were also printed papers which made them supremely dangerous and they were above all, as she thought, aimed at her, she'd hated papers all her life and had turned this hatred of papers, of all the papers in the world, into an actually bound-

less hatred of everything around her which was connected
with these papers, and she'd been driven by this hatred all her
life as by a mortal disease, or rather by her own, "her" underlined, mortal disease, on the other hand, as regards myself, I
always had the feeling that I was lying in ambush for her, that
I was setting her a trap, that I'd often given her cause to
remember her hatred as a mortal disease and to show this
hatred openly, that I set her so-called paper traps to catch her
out in her hatred of paper, so that I could watch her open
outburst of hatred, paper hatred, with malicious satisfaction,
because there can be no doubt, so Roithamer, that I did take a
malicious satisfaction in her hatred and all her extreme carry-
ings-on, because her hatred was so extreme, her ways in
general were so extreme, actually I'd let less than a couple of
minutes pass before I started to criticize her, or at least looked
her over critically, in other words, the moment I turned up in
Altensam, and I always turned up abruptly, I'd already set her
a trap, and when she fell into my trap, I criticized her for
falling into my trap, I always lay in ambush to catch her in one
or another of her repulsively feminine ways and then took her
to task, not even two minutes went by after I'd arrived at
Altensam before I'd picked on some trifle to criticize her for,
because basically I disliked everything about her, or rather,
because everything about her was nothing but repugnant to
me, no matter what she basically did or didn't do, whatever it
was, I found it repugnant, no matter what she wore, for
instance, I found it repugnant, whatever she said, whatever she
thought, it was never anything but repugnant, that's the truth,
so Roithamer, to keep such facts to myself wouldn't make
sense, so I won't keep these facts to myself, because these are
facts that certainly characterize the Eferding woman and me,
"certainly the Eferding woman and me" underlined. So I naturally always wondered how it could be possible for two people, who were in addition mother and son, not mother's son
but father's son, leaving this out of account, however, how is it

possible that these two people, who keep on tormenting each other constantly, with a truly unexampled ruthlessness, who feel compelled to torment each other to the very edge of madness, who do it every time and always do it again, and who keep hating each other more deeply and more ruthlessly, nevertheless go on seeing each other again and again? But the chances are that it was precisely these possibilities of mutual tormentings, this mutual hatred, this mutual readiness to be tormented, that kept drawing me again and again from England to Altensam, so Roithamer. Probably, so Roithamer, because I needed everything my mother, the Eferding woman, had in these last years turned into a horrible Altensam. And I did after all leave Altensam again at once each time, and took refuge, as I had every chance to do, in Hoeller's garret, which began by being a books-refuge, a so-called books-and-papers refuge, for I had squirreled away in Hoeller's garret every conceivable book and paper I could lay hands on and that could be of use to me, as well as all the books and papers I could do without, and I'd torn the pages I most valued out of these essential books and papers and tacked them on the walls of Hoeller's garret, pages of Pascal, for instance, again and again, much of Montaigne, very many pages of Pushkin and Schopenhauer, of Novalis and Dostoyevsky, I'd tacked almost all the pages of Valéry's *M. Teste* on the walls before I'd covered the walls of Hoeller's garret with my plans and sketches for building the Cone; to gain perspective I've always pasted or tacked all the papers important to me on my walls, even as a child I'd covered the walls of my room in Altensam with other people's most important (to me) ideas, pasted or tacked on, so I'd first covered the walls of Hoeller's garret with the most important sayings of Pascal and Novalis and Montaigne, before I'd tacked them up and pasted them up with my sketches and anyway all kinds of ideas for building the Cone, and so I always could immediately clear out of Altensam and move into Hoeller's garret and find refuge in Hoeller's garret in those thoughts on the walls of Hoeller's garret, the fact that it is possible for me to go to Hoeller's garret where I always found everything I needed for my thoughts and *re*flections, all those thoughts of other men and through them, also all my own thoughts, every time, made it possible for me to leave Altensam without going to pieces, so Roithamer, the minute I'd arrived in Altensam I thought of nothing else but getting away from Altensam, because being with the Eferding woman was unbearable to me from the first moment, and so I went to Hoeller's garret, quite often taking the detour over Stocket into Hoeller's garret, so Roithamer. Little by little I had stowed away all the books and papers I'd had in Altensam up in Hoeller's garret, where they'd really be safe, for they were no longer safe in Altensam, all these exceptionally useful books and papers, not to say that they were probably indispensable to my life, I lived in constant fear that mother, the Eferding woman, would one day use all these books of mine as firewood, that she would stage a great bonfire of all my papers before all eyes, that is, before the eyes of my father and my brothers and my sister, one day, this was what I'd always feared, after all, but she had never done it, though my fear was justified, or else she hadn't got around to it before I'd moved all my books and papers to safety in Hoeller's garret, there, in Hoeller's garret, I always thought in England, those books and papers are safe, now I needn't worry from one minute to the next that they might be destroyed by my mother, the Eferding woman, Hoeller's garret is where all these books and papers of mine belong, not in Altensam, where the atmosphere is antagonistic to them. And so the thought that I'd carried these books and papers of mine, not many but all the most important of them, to safety in Hoeller's garret from my room in Altensam, while I was in England or wherever I was far away from Altensam, was always a good, reassuring thought. That my mother is capable of burning or otherwise destroying my books and papers, which I'd read and studied and worked through afresh again and again, that she is capable of suddenly destroying them, or of simply withholding them from me, specifically during my absence in England or elsewhere, has always been clear to me. While my mother and I had always tried, so Roithamer, during the first few minutes of my arrival in Altensam, to get along with each other, and had done all we could, even though it went against the grain, to make it work, we soon ended up doing it all only as proof that we simply could not get along with each other, and so we had a chaotic situation, a situation no one could be expected to stand, we simply made existence a torment for each other, perhaps this had simply become a habit because by now we'd been together against our will too often, so the habit of mutual torture came to play the largest role in our encounters, but it was always, as I thought, *she* who took the initiative in tormenting me, even though I was the one who kept coming back to Altensam because I couldn't stand it in England after a while of trying to adjust to it, and so I always showed up at home again, just as if it were somehow possible for me, as it simply no longer was or never had been, to spend any time at all with my mother. As regards any kind of intellectual interests, she could only pretend to them, in which respect she differed in no way from the rest of her sex, in fact I'd say that everything in and about her was nothing but pretense, but then our whole era is anti-intellectual at heart, it only pretends to be interested in intellectual matters, these days the trend is all against intellect and for hypocrisy, it's all an era of hypocritical pretense, hypocrisy everywhere, nothing real left, it's all hypocrisy. She hated my sister, so the Eferding woman hated what she called my doting talk about my sister, in fact I was always instinctively moved to speak of the sister I loved more than anything in the world, it's true that I was almost constantly intent upon studying my sister's personality, while at the same time I kept loving her and having to show my love for her quite openly and in fact I did show it at all times, most of all probably because I hated my mother, the Eferding woman, I compulsively made her witness my love and tender concern for my sister, the studied care which I lavished on her even in my thoughts, especially the care and delicacy with which I made every effort to treat her when we met, without actually having to make an effort because care and timidity came quite naturally to me with regard to my sister, all this was naturally hateful to the Eferding woman, everything I had noticed about my sister in the course of my life that had made her more and more the peculiarly lovable person that my sister always was for me, more and more endeared her to me and ended by making her a sort of second and superior self, in the way I saw her and felt about her, it all acutely distressed the Eferding woman, at first she had always tried to draw me over to her side by means of her so-called pretended sympathy for my sister, whom she knew to be no more her partisan than I was, my sister naturally was of my father's party all her life, and like myself, though most of the time secretly she was happy in her loyalty to him, but the Eferding woman tried to win me over by her so-called hypocritical sympathy for my sister, but precisely because the sympathy she offered, which always turned out to be hypocritical anyway, was repellent to me, her efforts always ended up by repelling me. My sister always had innate good taste, good taste inherited from my father, while my mother, that is to say, her mother and mine, was totally deficient in taste or tact, she had never known how to please people in a friendly and natural way, while my sister always had the gift of pleasing through her friendliness and naturalness, so Roithamer, our mother suffered from this defect and whenever she'd suffered from it for any length of time she'd always go to Eferding, to her father's house, the butcher's house, for sanctuary, but of course she'd only come back, after some days or weeks, back to Altensam, with even less sympathetic understanding for Altensam than before, and even less understanding for us. But my brothers never sensed any of this, since they

were of the same mind as the Eferding woman, who had been
able to endure life in Altensam at all only because her own
children, our brothers that is, I am safe in saying that my sister
and I did not consider ourselves *her* children but only our
father's children, but our brothers were on her side, they felt
deeply akin to her family, our brothers had often gone with
her to Eferding and felt at home there as nowhere else, while
for me Eferding had always been an imposition, mentally and
emotionally, and I'd gone there only a few times, when I was
forced to go, on quite ordinary occasions, weddings of my
mother's relatives, their funerals, or perhaps to stock my
mother's larder with meat out of her father's butcher shop
during the war, but that always involved sending the Altensam cattle down to Eferding, where they'd be butchered in my
maternal grandfather's butcher shop, then dressed, and then
we brought back the meat butchered and dressed in Eferding,
up to Altensam. Our mother hadn't wanted to adapt herself to
Altensam, which would have been the most natural thing, but
she had tried to adapt us to Eferding, "us" underlined, in
which she of course did not succeed, under all the prevailing
conditions at Altensam, the fact being that our father was
always a quite original character, just as Altensam was altogether original by nature, though I must admit that this entire
situation must be considered an extraordinary one. I can only
say that she hated everything as she hated herself, because,
once she was in Altensam, she had to hate everything and
therefore also herself. But it would be overhasty to describe
her only as an unhappy person, "overhasty" underlined. She
hated everything and everyone and in this pathological process
she was as if arrested by an incurable paroxysm against everything, of course she was an unhappy person, she was not alone
in this unhappiness but rather in the company of almost all
human beings who've never for a moment tried to understand
the causes of their unhappiness, who constantly blame particularly the people closest to them for their own unhappiness,

and never once seek a single cause of their unhappiness in themselves, she had never worked on herself, even though she was always full of doubts about herself, but not in a way that would have forced her to dig for causes, she had buried herself steadily deeper into her eventually hopeless life against Altensam, just as my brothers buried themselves in their hopeless life against Altensam, isolated themselves, for undoubtedly my brothers, siding with the Eferding woman, had also isolated themselves, they'd actually in time worked their way entirely out of Altensam, because they'd basically always worked with my mother against Altensam. In Altensam, ever more deeply buried in isolation in Altensam, while at the same time working their way out of Altensam, so Roithamer, "at the same time . . . out of Altensam" underlined. It's a logical consequence that now, after they'd always worked against Altensam, after their mother's death, after the death of the Eferding woman, they will have to leave Altensam; by my selling Altensam this process is rounding itself off, so Roithamer. My brothers were also Eferding people, so Roithamer, and there have always been two parties living against each other and existing ever more intensively because of their mutual opposition while always trying to liquidate this in the opposing party, the Eferding party on the one hand, viz. my mother and my brothers, and on the other hand the Altensam party, that is my father, my sister, and me. Because of her ultimately misanthropic nature and her environment- and self-destructive spirit, which was an Eferding spirit, her face had in time become a misanthropic and self-destructive face and every morning upon awakening she already entered, almost in panic, into her misanthropy and self-destruction as facial destruction, as if into an incurable malignant disease, and with all these malignant, pathologically malignant facial features she encountered us early in the morning over breakfast. Mistrustfully or at least with a most insulting reserve she met each and all of those whom she associated with Altensam, all persons who came to Altensam and had been instantly classified by her as belonging to Altensam; she thought she had a right to hate people because she thought everybody hated her, so Roithamer. Not one, not one single hour of my life have I spent in harmony alone with my mother, "in harmony" underlined, so Roithamer. And so it wasn't easy, either, to go out and meet people with her, because she could meet all these people only with mistrust and rejection, because these people all tended to belong to Altensam, and Eferding was far away, so Roithamer. As a child I'd hardly met people with her, no matter whether in Stocket or in another of the villages below Altensam, when these people, no matter what they were like, were irritated by her, they'd instantly noticed that something was going on here against them, whether they were conscious of this peculiarity or not, they usually took their leave of us at once. She mastered the art of separating me from people I valued, it wasn't long before hardly anyone came up to Altensam to see me, and I soon had very few friends left, so-called playmates, in my childhood, friends from Stocket for instance, once she noticed a spiritual kinship to Altensam in them, she was against them, so Roithamer. Because she had determined to exploit Altensam for her own purposes, such as, for instance, to take possession of me, simply to take possession of Altensam, she naturally always ran into opposition at Altensam, just as my brothers, the Eferdingers, had always run into opposition. Whenever I showed my sister an article that was bound to interest her, so Roithamer, my sister was always most charmingly, "most charmingly" underlined, ready to discuss the contents of that article with me, to try to understand the contents of the article and then the reasons for the article, along with me, precisely what I'd found stimulating in that article was what she'd also found stimulating, I had told her what it was that particularly interested me in that article, what particularly attracted me, for instance, what was true or false in it, and we'd always noted a particularly deep accord in our shared view of the various subjects of whatever kind, my sister was always interested in hearing my opinion, just as she'd always been able to listen, unlike our mother, who could never listen, just as I was always interested in hearing my sister's opinion (on this or that subject). But my (and my sister's) mother had always shown a lack of interest in everything that interested and concerned us, no matter in what sense. All her life she had always reacted to us with a total lack of interest, so Roithamer, "total lack of interest" underlined. Just as my sister always took an interest in my own scientific work, any of my intellectual work, it was more than an interest, actually, in what I was thinking and writing, my inventions and fantasies, so I took more than an interest in all of my sister's artistic inventions, and in everything she thought, but most of all in her miniature painting, in which she quickly achieved great mastery, her miniatures, painted on enamel and porcelain, are the most beautiful imaginable, between me and my sister there's always been the greatest and most loving sympathy, she, my sister, had always entered wholly into anything concerning me, as I always wholly entered into whatever concerned her. For days on end we'd amuse ourselves talking about a book we'd read one after the other, exchanging ideas about this book until we could sum up all these ideas in a single idea which precisely characterized that book, or else a work of art, a painting, for days on end we could discuss and debate a certain formulation we had read somewhere, for the two of us our reading was always the most important subject, without reading neither my sister nor I could have stood life for any length of time, not that we had been brought up to read, quite the opposite was the case, as already described, but in the course of time we had managed to acquire our passion for reading, our delight in books, the pleasures of experience by way of reading, the intellectual discipline connected with reading, while pacing the floor together in my room or in hers, we could talk about every kind of thing we'd read or heard or observed or about every kind of discovery we'd made, each on his own, we talked it all out, quite in contrast to our mother, the Eferding woman, with whom all of that would never have been possible. Undisturbed we spent entire nights together up in the attic, considering and concerning ourselves with books we'd just been reading, studying, without noticing that daylight had broken already, because our discussions had always been full of the greatest intensity, yet also the greatest possible serenity. Our favorite place for these talks, critical reflections, suppositions, andsoforth, was always the attic, though very often, in summer, also the area behind the farm building from which you could see down country all the way to Stocket. Very often, too, we'd walk through the park, quite casually in every way, finding its neglected state more and more of a stimulus to conversation, because the park at Altensam was all the more beautiful for having been left to run wild, overgrown with weeds, and hence all the more conducive to our rambles back and forth. From a certain, no longer exactly identifiable point on, what I most enjoyed was to withdraw into my reading, my scientific, natural science, a kind of reading which my mother most particularly loathed my doing, just as she, the Eferding woman, also secretly hated my sister's work, her miniature painting, though she didn't dare hate it openly, for what and how my sister painted could not but please even my mother, and in contrast to my scribbling it wasn't dangerous, either, but she could not quite suppress her dislike of everything that's Altensam even in this respect. Actually I asked myself over and over again why I didn't break off contact with my mother, simply stopped going to see her, but then I'd have had to stop going to see Altensam and after all I was attached to Altensam, just as I kept on feeling attached to my childhood, be it how it may have been, Altensam was my childhood and childhood is in every case an obstacle to making a final break, "final break" underlined. That woman, I keep thinking, so Roithamer, who hated my sister because I loved her and vice versa and who basically also hated our father because he couldn't hate us, so Roithamer. How those two could keep on living together, I asked myself, my father and mother, I don't know, I can only suppose that they've always lived with *extremest difficulty.* The question is, however, how these two could have joined together, married each other, when they had absolutely nothing in common, never anything in common, the whole thing goes back only to the unlucky circumstance that my father stayed the night in the Eferding hostelry, which happened to be my mother's home, so Roithamer. My father simply must have totally lost his head, "lost his head" underlined. There was absolutely nothing to justify such a union at all. We always wonder, when we see two people together, particularly when they're actually married, how these two people could have arrived at such a decision, such an act, so we tell ourselves that it's a matter of human nature, that it's very often a case of two people going together, getting together, only in order to kill themselves in time, sooner or later to kill themselves, after mutually tormenting each other for years or for decades, only to end up killing themselves *anyway,* people who get together even though they probably clearly perceive their future of shared torment, who join together, get married, in the teeth of all reason, who against all reason commit the natural crime of bringing children into the world who then proceed to be the unhappiest imaginable people, we have evidence of this situation wherever we look, so Roithamer. People who get together and marry even though they can foresee their future together only as a lifelong shared martyrdom, suddenly all these people *qua* human beings, human beings *qua* ordinary people, so Roithamer, enter into a union, into a marriage, into their annihilation, step by step down they go into the most horrible situation imaginable, annihilation by marriage, meaning annihilation mental, emotional, and physical, as we can see all around us, the whole world is full of instances confirming this, so Roithamer, why, I may well ask myself, this senseless sealing of that bargain, we wonder about it because we have an instance of it before us, how did this instance come to be? that this highly intelligent, extraordinary, exceptional man could attract and marry this utterly common and ordinary, even thoroughly vulgar person and could even go on to make children with this person, it's nature, we say, it's always nature, every time, that nature which remains incomprehensible to us and unknowable as long as we live, that nature in which everything is rational and yet reason has nothing whatever to do with it, so Roithamer. At first we hear nothing unusual from all these people, if we do hear something about them, and then we hear only revolting things, only revolting things, so Roithamer, "only revolting things" underlined, just as, in our own case, we see nothing unusual in our parents at first, but later we see only revolting things. Nature is that incomprehensible force that brings people together, forcibly pushes them together, by every means, so that these people will destroy themselves, annihilate, kill, ruin, extinguish themselves, so Roithamer. Then they throw themselves down a rock cleft, or off a bridge railing, or they shoot themselves, like my uncle, or they hang themselves, like my other uncle, or they throw themselves in front of a train, like my third uncle, so Roithamer. We ourselves are the most suicide prone, so Roithamer, "prone" underlined. And didn't our cousin, the only son of our third uncle, kill himself too, after he got married to a doctor's daughter from Kirchdorf on the Krems, a marriage that simply couldn't have worked out, so Roithamer, that handsome man, so Roithamer, "handsome man" underlined, who threw himself into a cleft in the rock in the Tennen Mountains, over a thousand meters down into a dark cleft in the rock. Because I wanted to see how deep that cleft in the rock was, I once made a detour on my way home from England to Altensam to this rock cleft in the Tennen Mountains, I went climbing up those high mountains in a constant and worsening state of vertiginous nausea, putting the utmost strain on my physical resources as I'm not cut out by nature for climbing high mountains, and I actually made it to that cleft in the rock and I looked down into that cleft because I couldn't believe that so deep a cleft in the rock could exist, but that cleft is even much deeper; so it was here, into this very cleft in the rock that my cousin threw himself, I thought, standing at its rim and looking down into its depths and for a moment I was tempted to throw myself into that cleft too, but suddenly, when this idea was at its most compelling, this idea seemed ridiculous to me, and I took myself out of there. I know how much I hate the high mountain country, but my curiosity to see that deep cleft in the rock, of which I'd only heard up to that point and the depth of which I couldn't believe, drove me to climb up all the way to that cleft. But it takes a great sense of life, in fact it takes the greatest will to live and to exist, not to throw oneself down such a cleft when one is actually standing at its rim. But I didn't throw myself down that cleft. He, my cousin, had thrown himself down into it, why into this particular cleft I don't know, I certainly don't, so Roithamer, "I certainly don't" underlined. They'd found his shoes at the rim, his jacket too, six months after they noticed that he was gone, his young wife hadn't missed him until then, from the fact that his shoes and his jacket were found on the rim of that cleft in the rock they deduced that he had thrown himself down the cleft, but there's no real proof, these clues, yes, but no proof at all, because nobody can get down into the bottom of that cleft. Many people had supposed he'd gone abroad, but then some mountain climbers found his shoes and his jacket at the rim of the cleft, so he must have, I suppose, taken off his shoes and his jacket before he threw himself down into that rock cleft, he *didn't want to throw himself into that rock cleft in his jacket and shoes,* so Roithamer. Another of those *lonely men*, underlined, acquiring a wife at the unhappiest time of his life, a wife who brought him to the point where he threw himself down that rock cleft. The inclination to suicide as a character trait as in the character of my cousin who finally threw himself into that rock cleft, a specific kind of suicide, first climbing up those high mountains, just to throw himself into the depths of that rock cleft, so Roithamer. Because he spoke of it so often and with such passion and such scientific precision at the same time, they no longer believed that he would actually commit suicide, for anyone who talks about it as much as our cousin did, as incidentally the others did too, his father for instance always talked about suicide and kept bringing it up and every time in a better organized frame of mind, such a man, they think, won't really commit suicide, on the contrary, such a man keeps clarifying the idea of suicide in his head and as a result he doesn't commit suicide, *having this clarification in his head and being constantly capable of analyzing this clarification, he simply can't commit suicide anymore,* because he has this constant clear understanding of suicide, so Roithamer, to act out in reality something he'd always been talking about and which must basically always be repellent to him, he simply couldn't do it, every possible argument, every possible reason, every possible negation could lead to anything, usually to a mortal disease, but not to suicide, so Roithamer, because ultimately everything inside such a head is against self-destruction, and yet it's remarkable how regularly such a man will talk about suicide and about self-destruction, the subject gave him no peace, it tended to warp his reason, which he then proceeded to restore again, and yet one couldn't help being struck, so Roithamer, by the way our cousin kept talking almost incessantly about suicide after his marriage to the doctor's daughter from Kirchdorf, but nobody took him seriously, so Roithamer, nobody had the slightest apprehension that he would actually commit suicide, because he was constantly talking about suicide as if he were talking about a subject he entirely understood, though it did remain fascinating to him, just as though he were talking about some work of art, with the most scientific detachment. And anyone who talks so scientifically about suicide, as though it were a work of art, talks about it with a clear precision that humbles the rest of us, why, such a person simply doesn't commit suicide. Not until he nevertheless did commit suicide, of course, throwing himself down that fissure in the rock, so Roithamer. But to return to my subject, I was speaking of human unions, of living together, of marriage, so Roithamer. People are forever denying the proven fact, so Roithamer, the simple fact of nature's workings, that the female sex, because it is female, nobody dares to say it in so many words nowadays, that the female sex is anti-intellectual and emotionally predisposed to champion emotion, that it is in fact against intellect in all its possible aspects just as it is emotionally predisposed to emotion in all its possible aspects, so Roithamer. The current fashion is one thing, nature is something else. But then, our times are given over to nonsense and to warping all ideas and all the facts and turning them topsy turvy. I personally know from experience, so Roithamer, that the female human being, "female human being" under-lined, that the female sex is incapable of going beyond the first impulse in the direction of the life of the mind. In our case, that of my mother and me, she was only interested in winning me over even if in the process she had to destroy everything I am, my personality, my character, my mind, she had to try it, again and again, in her perverse determination that it must be possible eventually to turn so stubborn a mind as mine, a mind so crazily intent on its own inventions, from its single-track obsession with itself, *my*self that is, and push it into a crude, Eferding-type domesticity, so Roithamer. She had to cut me down to her own Eferding size, her own existential minimum, and with me she meant to achieve this fully, not only partially as with my father, whom she certainly managed to alienate from himself to at least a high degree, she did alienate my father from himself to a *very high, to an ominous degree*, as she knew, to her lifelong (Eferdingian) satisfaction. To be fascinat-

ed by a man who is different from his observer, viewer,
antagonist, yet pitting everything against this man and against
the fascination he exerts, to be bent on taking from him
everything that makes him fascinating. That woman from
Eferding basically hated everything I did or didn't do and
everything my sister did or didn't do and everything my father
did and didn't do, the victims of her hatred were primarily all
those with whom I had intellectual intercourse, beginning with
all natural scientists, writers, even poets, philosophers named
in my books, in whom she thought she recognized me, and she
thought she recognized me in all the books I had in my room,
in the most widely differing books belonging to me and used
by me all the time. In each one of these books she was *bound* to
recognize me and she hated these books as she hated me, but
she didn't dare to destroy the books, to do away with them,
she didn't have the nerve to do that even though her thoughts
and everything in her tended in that direction. If I merely
think of all the things we came to quarrel about on our so-
called walks, with such regularity and occasional obsessiveness, we'd taken our nature walks only to quarrel, always, we
walked through the woods, and quarreled, over the meadows,
and quarreled, through our gardens, and quarreled, even on
the grassy riverbanks, always outwardly exemplars of the
greatest serenity at the outset, we quarreled and transformed
those grasslands in no time into a noisy, suddenly malignant
landscape, where our attacking voices, shouting nothing but
insults, could be heard, so Roithamer, all up and down the
river. And it always began with trivia, but all these trivia had
soon triggered off enormities against our fellow beings, against
everything. Even in company the Eferding woman was incapable of controlling herself, of restraining herself, and so our
father never took her out socially, after his first efforts along
those lines had failed lamentably. Because the good name of
*all* Altensam was always at stake, he had never taken his wife,
our mother, the Eferding woman, to any social gathering,

though she craved going out socially, but because of my father's adamant refusal to take her out she soon found it possible to go out only to *her* own kind of social gathering, the so-called Eferding social gatherings and no longer to the Altensam social gatherings, but her own kind didn't interest her, what she wanted was to get into Altensam society, which my father, however, denied her; I barred her way, so my father often said, so Roithamer, otherwise she'd have robbed Altensam, which had already lost most of its good name in her time, the Eferding woman's time that is, she'd have robbed Altensam of all that was left of its good name, so my father, so Roithamer, "all that was left" underlined, but the consequence of this, that my father, after those first failed tries, simply no longer took her along into society but left her sitting at home, was that our mother, the Eferding woman, suddenly hated Altensam more than anything in the world, "more than anything in the world" underlined. My father had fallen prey to the error that he could turn a person like the Eferding woman, an Eferding person that is, into an Altensam person, one kind of person can never be made into another kind of person, so Roithamer, "never" underlined, most especially not an Eferding person into an Altensam person, it was probably because of this error that he took her home and married her, because he understood too late that you can never make an Altensam person out of an Eferding person, never change one species into another. Now and then she tried reading a book, it was all a hypocritical pretense, "hypocritical pretense" underlined, a book of which I had a very high opinion, a book about which I might have said something in her presence showing my great esteem for it, but these efforts of hers were from the first a transparent pretense, of course the Eferding woman's *position* in Altensam was always untenable, she should never have come to Altensam in the first place, for if such a person, who isn't an Altensamer, goes to Altensam, so Roithamer, that person will be destroyed, everything will be done to destroy such a person, to remove the person from Altensam because this is a person who doesn't belong in Altensam, because this person is different by nature, "different by nature" underlined, the Eferding woman should never have committed the crime of coming to Altensam, our father should never have brought her to Altensam, *he should have explained to her,* but he brought her up to Altensam out of embarrassment and weakmindedness and exposed her from the first to a situation she simply wasn't equal to handling, even if she never realized it, she, the Eferding woman, simply never had been equal to Altensam, though most of the time she might have thought she was equal to Altensam, even that she dominated Altensam, most of the time, she was not equal to Altensam, though she actually came to dominate Altensam, so Roithamer, as I know, actually did dominate Altensam, but she was never really equal to it, so Roithamer, our father had to pay dearly for the crime of marrying an Eferding woman, so Roithamer, the Eferding woman had to pay for her crime of coming up to Altensam with lifelong unhappiness, for it was by the fact of coming to Altensam that the Eferding woman became an unhappy person, prior to that, in Eferding, in her father's house, as the daughter of a butcher and an innkeeper, she'd never been unhappy, or she wasn't likely, during those years, to be considered an unhappy person, not until she came to Altensam. The photographs I've seen that show her as the butcher's daughter, innkeeper's daughter from Eferding, don't show an unhappy person, they show a young, though already old person, but not an unhappy person, the pictures of her in Altensam that I've seen, and my own experience are of an unhappy and always old person who is constantly ailing. We children naturally showed no consideration whatever toward our mother, "no" and "whatever" underlined, we, my sister and I, so Roithamer, we Altensamers in contrast to the Eferdingers, our brothers. In the early days when I returned from England, for instance, the Eferding woman had often said

she'd like to walk down to Stocket with me, because she knew
that I always liked walking down to Stocket, but once she'd
walked down to Stocket with me, it was soon obvious to me
that she'd really had no desire whatever to walk down to
Stocket with me, because basically she hated this walking-
down-to-Stocket with me and hated Stocket and hated the
people down in Stocket. Or else she affected to be interested in
a scientific article because she knew that I was interested in
this article, but it was all pretense, "pretense" underlined, so
Roithamer. On such occasions I always countered with some
malevolent remark that exposed her utter impudence, and our
mutual hatred was reestablished. But it's not true that we
didn't *want* to be in agreement. But if I happened to say, I hold
so-and-so in contempt, for such-and-such a reason, she always instantly agreed with my verdict and so with my remark,
without thinking, and this was bound to repel me. If I happened to show a liking for a certain play and praised this play,
she felt obliged to praise the play though she hadn't seen it,
not for my sake, as I know, but for her own sake, even though
she didn't know the play, she nevertheless thought she could
praise it too, and I was repelled by that. For instance I'd always
said, time and time again, that I loved Goethe's novel, *Elective
Affinities*, but I knew that she hated *Elective Affinities*, basically there was no book in the world she hated as intensely as she
hated *Elective Affinities*, yet she claimed that she shared my
love for *Elective Affinities*, this was simply bound to repel me,
so Roithamer. Then she claimed to have read Novalis, though
she had never read as much as a line by Novalis, but every
time it wasn't really an effort to come closer to me, to try and
bring about a real accord between her and me, between us, but
rather an attempt to set a trap, but I never went into this trap,
at least not in later years, for at first, in my childhood and
youth, I did indeed and very often walk into her traps, the
Eferding woman had always set traps in Altensam and all of us
had always walked into her traps. *Elective Affinities* as a trap set

for me, so Roithamer. She had often given me to understand
that she was intellectually engaged upon the same subject at
the same time I was, but I'd soon found out that it was nothing
more than one of her pretenses, that again she'd set me a trap
that I was supposed to walk into. All these notes to be utilized
one day for a description of my mother, in comparison with
my sister and in contrast with my father and brothers, so
Roithamer. We must always utilize, work up, everything.
When we're occupied with a so-called intellectual subject, and
this subject is so great that we're totally fascinated by it, we
must be absolutely alone in our room (Hoeller's garret) or
wherever we happen to be, even if we're not (in reality) in
Hoeller's garret, nevertheless in Hoeller's garret, the place
where we happen to find ourselves occupied with such a
subject must become Hoeller's garret for us, we mustn't tolerate the slightest distraction, even if it came from the person
closest to us (sister), we must forestall everything that inter-
feres or could interfere with our concentration on that subject,
and therefore could destroy, annihilate, extinguish this subject, which fascinates us, for such a subject is too easily
destroyed and annihilated and extinguished and it always is
the only subject for us, "only" underlined. This intellectual
subject matter must be held fast, until we have mastered it, so
Roithamer, "mastered" underlined. Attempts to comprehend
Altensam, to understand it, and little by little to comprehend
and understand *everything* connected with Altensam, especially
everything relating to my father, to keep on trying to find the
causes and from these causes arrive at the effects of these
causes, nothing can be fully grasped and explained by means
of mental and emotional acuity on the one hand, nor by
mental and emotional hypocrisy on the other hand, I have to
keep reminding myself that it's all from *my point of view,* not
from the *others' point of view,* always only from my point of
view, from the others' point of view it's something entirely
different, probably the opposite. But the opposite is not *my*

task. I'm getting closer to Altensam, but I'm not getting closer to Altensam in order to solve its mystery; for others to explain it *to myself* is why I am getting closer to Altensam, to *my* Altensam, the one that *I* see. While she lived I never asked my mother, never asked her all these unanswered questions, never once asked her a single crucial question, because I never could formulate such a question, I was afraid I might put such a question wrong somehow, and so I never posed it, and so I got no answer. Now the Eferding woman is dead, I can't ask her, she can't answer. But would it be any different now, if I could ask her, and she could answer? We don't ask those we love, just as we don't ask those we hate, so Roithamer. Actually I'm shocked by everything I've just written, what if it was all quite different, I wonder, but I will not correct *now* what I've written, I'll correct it all when the time for such correction has come and then I'll correct the corrections and correct again the resulting corrections andsoforth, so Roithamer. We're constantly correcting, and correcting ourselves, most rigorously, because we recognize at every moment that we did it all wrong (wrote it, thought it, made it all wrong), acted all wrong, how we acted all wrong, that everything to this point in time is a falsification, so we correct this falsification, and then we again correct the correction of this falsification and we correct the result of the correction of a correction andsoforth, so Roithamer. But *the ultimate correction* is one we keep delaying, the kind others have made without ado from one minute to the next, I think, so Roithamer, the kind they *could* make, by the time they no longer thought about it, because they were afraid even to think about it, but then they did correct themselves, like my cousin, like his father, my uncle, like all the others whom we knew, as we thought, whom we knew so thoroughly, yet we didn't *really* know all these peoples' characters, because their self-correction took us by *surprise,* otherwise we wouldn't have been surprised by their *ultimate existential correction, their suicide.* It's only a thought which keeps turning up,

but we don't take steps to correct ourselves. We sit here for
hours on this chair and think about it, we may even be sitting
here for days on this same chair, or stand at the window (as for
instance in Hoeller's garret), we may pace the floor in our
room, lie on the bed, locked up in Hoeller's garret or in my
room in Altensam, which has always seemed to me my actual
correction cell, "correction cell" underlined, but I kept putting
off my correction, kept delaying it, though I never gave up the
idea of correcting myself, we do it suddenly, quite suddenly
we walk out, go away, break off everything, one step off the
road, away, gone, so Roithamer, because we've lost our mind,
so Roithamer, or because we suddenly are everything extreme,
so Roithamer. We're in a state of extreme concentration, we
don't even permit ourselves to change a piece of clothing, we
permit ourselves nothing beyond this concentration, but we
still don't do it. We're always quite close to correcting ourselves, to correcting everything by killing ourselves, but we
don't do it. Ready to correct our entire existence as a bottom-
less falsification and misrepresentation of our true nature, so
Roithamer, but we don't do it. While this thought keeps
sinking in deeper, we're at its mercy and we yield to it in every
respect because we have become totally concentrated on this
thought, but we don't do it. Then we forget this theme, make
no corrections, go on existing, until we're back with this
thought, addicted to it, so Roithamer. But one day, from one
minute to the next, we'll do what we have to do, and then
there'll be no difference between us and those who've already
made their correction, killed themselves. To write to someone,
for instance, because we can no longer bear our loneliness,
we've borne our solitude to the limit, but we can bear it no
longer, we write in order to be no longer alone but to be two of
us, to my sister for instance, that I'd be glad if she'd come to
England, *soon, now, we write, to the person we love, the one we know
most intimately,* I write and telegraph simultaneously, my most
intense idea now is that my sister must come to me, from

Altensam to England, as quickly as possible, to put an end to
this condition of solitude into which I've *maneuvered myself,* so
Roithamer, she must come if I'm to be saved, I'm thinking,
though I don't write it, but I think she *must* come, to save me,
because I've exhausted all my means of distracting myself, all
my tricks of distracting myself, because I can think only this
one thing, that I must come to an end in my room, unless this
familiar, beloved person comes, I've *no chances left.* For days I
wait for an answer, then my sister suddenly sends a telegram,
she can't come, so then I somehow keep going, I don't put an
end to it. It's back to my work again, total immersion. Suddenly I no longer have any reason to kill myself, to make that
correction. The message that my sister isn't coming because
she can't come is enough to *prevent* me from doing it. But
would I have done it? I ask myself, so Roithamer. Instead of
committing suicide, people go to work. All their lives long, as
long as their existence allows for this constantly recurring
process, so Roithamer. The death of my uncle, so Roithamer,
surprised even Hoeller, for Hoeller, like myself, had always
been of the opinion that a man like my uncle, who kept
coming back to the subject of suicide in conversation, because
of the very fact that he keeps coming back to it and talks of it
almost constantly, will not commit suicide, but he did commit
suicide, the atmosphere in Hoeller's house at the time was
totally conditioned by the surprise of my uncle's suicide, he'd
thrown himself down the cheese-factory's air shaft in Stocket;
the whole Hoeller house, even Hoeller's garret, I think, so
Roithamer, this whole simple house with its complicated conditions, or vice versa, complicated house with its simple conditions, so Roithamer, lay as if under the pall of my uncle's
suicide. The moment I set foot in Hoeller's house, that's to say,
the moment I clapped eyes on the huge black stuffed bird
hanging on the wall of the vestibule, it was clear to me that the
whole Hoeller house was under the pall of my uncle's suicide.
Then I remembered my last meeting with my uncle from

Stocket, so Roithamer, and I asked myself whether there was
anything about the man, on that last encounter, that might
have given me a hint of his subsequent suicide, observing him
first at the forest's edge, with his rubber boots, short, frayed
old jacket, so Roithamer, the hazel walking stick he'd whittled
himself, the black hat on his head, and probably, considering
his immobility, he'd had a wooden leg for years, also in view
of my sudden presence, he was preoccupied with a so-called
philosophical subject, I said to myself as I walked toward him,
time had fashioned him into a so-called *nature man,* because
everything in him and about him was predisposed that way,
not a comic figure such as we see very often, everything about
him said: I can no longer escape from nature; as I walked
toward him, probably he didn't even notice that I was coming
toward him because everything seemed to indicate that he
never noticed me, he was so preoccupied with his philosophical subject, that philosophical subject which had to do with
nature. When he spoke, it was only by indirection, he'd always
been *my philosopher,* it was on his account that I always came
down to Stocket from Altensam, the idea of thinking came to
me in my first hesitant, then determined encounters with this
man who'd always been my highest authority, my philosopher
who had taught me to think, most unobtrusively, at first, but
from the first with a decided firmness that endured. I'm no
philosopher, he'd always said. He had a preference for old
clothes, early rising, and washing in cold water. He placed
Novalis above everything. Nature, not yet polluted by human
beings, hence his early rising. A minimal breakfast, thick socks
his sister had knitted from raw, untreated wool, and one of
Novalis's ideas. Time was to him only a means toward the
constant study of time. Must I be with another person? he
always answered: no, I need be with no other person. This
question and this answer of his do more to explain his character than mine, so Roithamer. We admire a man like my uncle,
who killed himself because he *could no longer endure the unhappi-*

*ness of mankind,* as he wrote on the slip of paper they found in his coat pocket, dated by him on the day he threw himself down the air shaft of the cheese factory, because he's ahead of us in having the capacity to commit suicide, not only to talk about committing suicide but to commit suicide in fact, so Roithamer. It's always those upon whom we'd hung our hopes, so Roithamer, who kill themselves, those whose talent and personality we loved and whose presence was the most pleasing and most familiar to us, so Roithamer. Then: I often woke up in the night and asked myself, how high are the costs of building, actually? what if the costs of building the Cone exceed my means, on the one hand exceeding my financial means, on the other hand exceeding my intellectual means? How often I came unrecognized to Austria and to Altensam and stayed in the Kobernausser forest, in the wooden shack I put up myself on the spot I'd picked out as the site for the Cone, in the precise center of the Kobernausser forest, so Roithamer. And very often I came from England to Altensam, unrecognized, and into the Kobernausser forest and stayed there, at its very center, for days and once even for weeks, totally concentrated on the Cone and then went back just as unrecognized to England, to Cambridge. Several times, "several times" underlined, I started to write a letter to my sister, but I never finished writing those letters because I had to keep the Cone a secret from my sister, of course, and if I did drop a hint to her, and I had in fact dropped a hint several times, she'd think I was crazy, even my beloved sister thought I was crazy, so Roithamer, which is why I had to keep silent always about the Cone, even toward my sister. The edifice that was to bring me deep gratification but to my sister the highest, the supreme happiness, so Roithamer. Such a letter about the Cone would have been sure to have frightened her. What a lot of ideas go into the making of the Cone, all adding up to the idea of the Cone. He, Roithamer, I can see that now, lived in fear that he might go mad deep inside the Kobernausser forest, on precise-

ly the geometrical centerpoint in the middle of the Kobernausser forest he had himself determined, because he had a
bent in that direction, "bent" underlined. Like his sister, he
inclined to sudden madness, from sudden overstrain of his
whole being, he feared that from overstraining his head he'd
suddenly go mad. He'd decided at once on the size of the Cone
and on the character of the interior, but he could no longer
recall the exact point in time, to pinpoint that moment now,
after so many years, "after so many years" underlined, he
found impossible. We must remember the onlookers who note
our moment of weakness, mental weakness, in so enormous an
effort, and use it to kill us, so Roithamer. We must never let up
in intensity. Time is realization, idea, despair, and vice versa,
so Roithamer. But I mustn't act exclusively in accordance with
my plan and a dead geometry, so Roithamer. It's all right to
hesitate, but never out of even the slightest weakness. Everything is equally important, whether it's the idea (as a whole) or
its smallest constituent. Actually always the simultaneous contemplation of the idea, I must contemplate everything at the
same time and train myself in this simultaneity of contemplation in such a way that I come to see everything ever more
clearly, nothing less sharply focused than anything else, so
that the edifice exists (in my head) and then I must move it out
of my head onto the geometric point. The question is, will I
achieve my aim in my own way by talking, or not, or will it
turn out to be only resignation as a fact, so Roithamer. Resignation, weakness, emptiness, the failure to make it real. It's all
a matter of schooling oneself, a school in which I am both the
teacher and the pupil, and in the intensity between the two
there's one's logical consistency, there's the Cone. My lucidity
peaks at night, an exceptional condition of my head, so Roithamer, then in the morning the Cone falls apart in my head.
Always assuming that my idea of the Cone corresponds precisely to my sister's needs, her character, her nature. Novalis:
the Cone is not what she *is* at this point, it is rather everything

about her, corresponding to her eyes and ears, her hearing, feeling, intelligence, alertness, attention. Corresponding. It is the fact itself which dumbfounds and benumbs, not the rest of it, so Roithamer. And so I've never talked with a soul in Altensam (including father) about the Cone, though they all know that I'm building the Cone, they've all heard of it. Such a building changes the man who is building it, by the ways in which he speeds the work along and completes it. I used to be open to everything before I had the idea (of building the Cone), but now I'm nothing but the victim of the man who is building the Cone. If my head had *known*, so Roithamer. It seems that one's head keeps being drawn irresistibly to the most impossible problems, every time, to prove itself, so Roithamer. If we don't, every time, involve ourselves in the most problematic undertakings, we're lost, there's nothing left, so Roithamer. What then follows is the catastrophe of break-down, whatever our idea was about deserts us when we sleep-walkers awaken in the middle of what we were doing, so Roithamer. Once we recognize the process, it's already broken off, nothing's left but a man who's been destroyed, killed. We retreat to an idea, possibly the only idea we know nothing about, so Roithamer. We try to grasp the things we experience mentally. If I don't work hard enough, I'm destructive, if I work too hard, I'm destructive, so Roithamer. The question always arises, whether it's the right moment. We see every-thing ridiculously interrelated, from England, from Altensam, in the middle of the Kobernausser forest. We have an idea, in the end it's nothing, so Roithamer. Once he actually went as far as his sister's door, in order to admit everything about the Cone to her, three o'clock in the morning, so Roithamer, I'll wake her up and explain. But at four o'clock I laughed out loud and went back to my room. And if another man should faithfully follow my notes, my plans, everything I've got in my head, in executing the Cone, it still wouldn't be the same Cone, so Roithamer. But if I had neglected my scientific work, genetic mutations, I'd also have neglected building the Cone, as it is, by not neglecting my scientific teaching and studies, I also did not neglect the building of the Cone. For I was actually (most intensely) occupied with building the Cone in the Kobernausser forest while I was working my hardest on genetic mutations in Cambridge, and vice versa (March 3). The cause of work for and intensification of the one, the cause of work for and intensification of the other, so Roithamer, I never asked myself whether I am neglecting my scientific work by pushing on with building the Cone, and vice versa, it was a question I dared not ask myself, so Roithamer. The time was as favorable to my Cone building as it was for my scientific work, I achieved *all I could,* so Roithamer. Now I've left science and the Cone to nature, so Roithamer. Just as no one will ever set foot inside the Cone again, so no one will enter into my scientific work. That it's possible to consider and act simultaneously upon two (seemingly) contradictory opposites, so Roithamer. To make full use of one's mental state in every case and at every moment and never weaken in that direction, so Roithamer. We may not question our actions, so Roithamer. Juxtapose my lack of sympathy to my mother's, my parents', my brothers' lack of sympathy, so Roithamer. The Cone cost more to build than any other edifice in Austria, as I hear, I've obtained the figures on it, so Roithamer. Total isolation in Cambridge alternated with total isolation in the Kobernausser forest, where I fixed up a room for myself in the builder's work hut, for the times when it's impossible for me to stay in Hoeller's garret, because I have to be at the building site (March 7), so Roithamer. The secrecy with which I pursued building the Cone in Cambridge, the same secrecy in Altensam, the same secrecy at the Hoeller house, so Roithamer. But at night I worked on genetic mutations, in the builder's hut as well as in Hoeller's garret, even though I was wholly occupied with the Cone, so Roithamer, there was no outward indication by which an onlooker could have recognized that I was work-

ing on genetic mutations while overseeing the building of the
Cone in the Kobernausser forest, and on the Cone in Cambridge, while I was teaching and studying, so Roithamer. Every
day one idea connected neither with building the Cone nor
with my natural science, so Roithamer. The highest demands
made of the one discipline applied to the other discipline, so
Roithamer. To build, and realize, and complete such an edifice
means always to hear and see *everything* connected with the
edifice, meaning of course to hear and see everything and to
act on one's experience of all this hearing and seeing, so
Roithamer. What if I'd suddenly *informed* my sister about my
building the Cone? which I didn't do, so saving myself and my
plan. We keep silent about what we know, and make good
progress, so Roithamer. At night he'd always heard the woodworm in Altensam, the voracity of the woodworms would
keep him awake all night, everywhere and naturally most of
all at night, because of his keen hearing and that oversensitive
head of his, he heard the woodworm, the deathwatch beetle, at
work, in the floor planks and under the floor planks, in the
wardrobes and chests, in all the chest drawers most of all, so
Roithamer, in the doors and in the window frames, even in the
clocks and the chairs and overstuffed armchairs, he'd always
been able to distinguish exactly where and in which object,
which piece of furniture, a woodworm was at work, the woodworm had actually already gnawed its way into his own bed,
while lying awake in bed all night long, so Roithamer, he'd
watched the woodworm's progress, had to watch it, with most
concentrated attention, he'd breathed in the sweetish smell of
the fresh wood meal and felt depressed at the thought that
through all the years thousands, possibly tens of thousands,
hundreds of thousands of woodworms had infiltrated into
Altensam in order to devour Altensam, to keep gnawing away
at Altensam and devouring it until it collapsed in one moment,
a moment that would quite possibly not be too long in coming.
There wasn't a single object in Altensam, so Roithamer, with-

out the woodworm in it, and even if it happened to be a new object, something recently acquired, the woodworm would have invaded this new object in no time at all, so Roithamer. When I take a piece of underwear out of a drawer, so Roithamer, I have to shake it out, because it's full of wood meal, overnight my fresh laundry is full of wood meal, so Roithamer, when I take a handkerchief out of the drawer, I have to blow the wood meal off of it, even the dishes in daily use have to be blown and wiped off, so Roithamer, because they're covered with wood meal, and actually everybody in Altensam is always full of wood meal, their faces are covered with wood meal, their heads and bodies covered with wood meal, so Roithamer. They were all constantly afraid they might break through the floor planks, because the floor planks were already ominously giving way here and there, because Altensam was constantly changing under the influence of the woodworm's work (and the dry rot, of course!) they lived in chronic anxiety, because in fact the most noticeable and frightening manifestation in Altensam has been the work of the woodworms, so Roithamer. At first everything was tried against the woodworms, but in the end we had to admit that nothing can be done against woodworms, and we stopped trying. All our lives long in Altensam we were confronted with millions of woodworms, without a chance of defending ourselves against these millions of woodworms. Helpless against the woodworms, so my mother, so Roithamer, we fought the woodworms all our lives, but had to give up the struggle in the end, so my mother, so Roithamer. Each generation in turn, so Roithamer, had pitted itself against the woodworm in Altensam, each feared.*it* would be the one over whose heads Altensam would suddenly collapse, because Altensam is totally riddled by the woodworm, so Roithamer. Once my father sent for a so-called pest control man from Linz, who came up to Altensam and spent weeks there, in vain of course, so Roithamer. And so everyone in Altensam had become accustomed to walking around there in an oddly circumspect manner, because of the woodworms and their centuries-long work of undermining Altensam to the point of having almost worked their way through all of it, everyone adapted his walk most carefully to the floor planks and the wooden ceilings, with an eye to the furniture as well, such an oddly careful manner of walking, simply being considerate of Altensam, and when we had a general conversation, so Roithamer, which happened at most once a year in all these years, then it was the woodworm we talked about. No matter how quiet it is in Altensam, so quiet at times that not a sound seems to be heard, one nevertheless hears the woodworm at Altensam, so Roithamer. The wardrobes, the tables, all stand at a slant, the chests of drawers, the chairs, so Roithamer, the floors are subsiding, the windows no longer fit into their framework, so Roithamer, the struggle against the woodworm had been totally given up (March 9), so Roithamer. Suddenly, after weeks of concentrated mental work, so Roithamer, I went to Marks & Spencer to buy a pullover because my old one, which I've worn incessantly all year long, suddenly looked too shabby to me. Walking down Oxford Street to Marks & Spencer I felt supremely happy, so Roithamer, and back to my room with the new pullover (March 11). He locks himself into his room and tries to start his work on the allopolyploids, an inescapable task, already far advanced, so Roithamer, so that he couldn't shake off his obsession with this task, but after he had made all his preparations for this work, checked the window, checked the door, so Roithamer, checked his chair as well as the door, all these important steps prior to beginning his work taken and checked out, including checking out the precisely geometric arrangement of all objects he had personally placed on his table and around his table, in his working area, everything had its place and the slightest deviation would have made it impossible for him to begin his work, so Roithamer, he always had to spend a not inconsiderable amount of time putting all these objects into the position favorable to the starting off of his work process, his own person being also subjected to this drive for order, this absolute discipline of order, physical condition, clothing, everything; for instance, the top shirt-buttons had to be undone, sleeves rolled up andsoforth, so Roithamer, "rolled up" underlined, but first and foremost, the door to his workroom must be locked, the key turned twice in the lock, this dual turning of the key always was of the utmost importance, for the mere chance of someone suddenly opening the door and walking in, someone who was bound to disturb him, whoever it was, this was totally incapacitating, so it often happened that he'd already begun on his work, he'd be all set mentally and had sat down at his worktable, but had forgotten to lock the door, so he had to jump up again and lock the door, but by then it was too late, this short interruption, when he'd already sat down at the table, jumping up, that is, in order to lock the door, was all it took to make further work impossible for him, or else something was wrong with the curtains and he'd have to jump up and put whatever it was with the curtains in order, or some noise made him jump up and forced him to look out the window, or else it was something fallen to the floor, a piece of paper or a crumb of food or a thread or even a dead fly he'd overlooked and which suddenly constituted an unbearable irritation, in total contrast to Hoeller's garret, so Roithamer, where everything was always simply *ideal* for him, but if he worked anywhere else, as for instance in his room in Cambridge, under the circumstances sketched above, circumstances which were always invariably awful, time-consuming and nerve-wracking, he was always wishing only that he might be in Hoeller's garret instead, whenever he couldn't be there, so Roithamer, even if he was disturbed only by the sudden thought of such a possible form of disorder. It wasn't the actual object itself, all it took was the thought of such an object possibly lying about in disorder, so Roithamer, to make him rise from his desk at once, to find out for certain,

whether his supposition was correct andsoforth, so Roithamer,
he might happen to be deeply absorbed in his work and the
work might be going rather well and then suddenly he'd
discover something out of order in his surroundings, even if it
were only a shadow cast by an object which was itself in order,
but was brought into disorder by its shadow, the kind of
shadow that might be cast on the windowsill or the floor or
even on the desk as a worktable, so Roithamer, which suddenly disturbs everything to the point of destroying everything,
and he'd have to get up from his desk and first straighten out
this particular object, because he couldn't stand the disorder, at
the very least he had to see what exactly the disturbing
element was, so he actually found it impossible, most of the
time, to work (in Cambridge), only every third or fourth day,
because there was always some obstacle or other, or else
because, after he'd begun to work and had possibly become
deeply immersed in work, possibly very deeply immersed,
suddenly some irritant presented itself, an irritating sound or
an irritating object, which he possibly hadn't seen or hadn't
heard before he began his work, he often had to get up or
jump up only because a book on his desk was not positioned at
the correct right angle, or because a so-called bookmark in a
book or pamphlet suddenly annoyed him, one of the many
hundreds of bits of paper he tore off the daily newspaper to
use as bookmarks, which he used to mark his page in all the
books and periodicals lying around all over the place, for when
such strips of newsprint used as bookmarks stick out of the
books beyond the bearable length of six or seven or eight
centimeters, when he'd suddenly noticed it and couldn't stand
it, or else he'd noticed a fingerprint that had escaped him up to
that point, the kind of fingerprints on the books and papers,
on his desk or even on the door, on the window frames
andsoforth, so Roithamer, which other people naturally don't
notice, can't notice, or suppose it's a whole handprint, so
Roithamer, "whole handprint" underlined, even if he only

imagined that there might be such a fingerprint or a whole handprint on the door, he had to jump up and check the door or the windows, and once he was disturbed in his work, no matter how deeply he had already immersed himself in it, at first not to a degree that would interfere with his work, but then suddenly he did turn out to be most ruthlessly disturbed, from an observer's point of view, in his work to a degree that indeed interfered and in fact brought his work to a sudden stop, he'd have to break off his work because he suspected there was a fingerprint (his own or that of another person) on the door or the window frame andsoforth, and he'd get up and rush to the door, "rush" underlined, and examine it, and actually he'd always find what he'd suspected would be there, even if it was the most senseless suspicion, he'd find it confirmed, everything suspected always turned out to be a fact, if for instance he suspected that something wasn't quite in order under his desk, though he couldn't see it, since the tabletop naturally prevented him from seeing beneath it, and if he proceeded to act on his suspicion without regard to the disturbing effect such an interruption would have on the work he had just begun, if his suspicion turned out to be founded in fact, he'd break off his work, crawl under the table, find the disorderly or disturbing object andsoforth, so Roithamer, he *always* found something wrong, something disturbing, once he crawled under the table, such a suspicion had never turned out to be unwarranted, so Roithamer, anyway he found it and straightened it out, though it jeopardized his work, the concentration required for his brain work which he had started but had to break off because of the disorder, but he *had to* straighten out the disorder under his desk or on the window or wherever it might occur in his study, and I tried, so Roithamer, after once more making sure that I really was locked into my room, by turning the key twice in the lock, so Roithamer, I was in control, and having taken control I felt reassured that I was indeed locked into my room, and I tried to make some progress in my work on the allopolyploids (March 17), so Roithamer, "tried" underlined. I recall a little essay on the thorn apple, the so-called *datura stramonium,* that he did after his sister's death, on coming back from Altensam to Cambridge, to regain his peace of mind, while I went to the Tate Gallery, so Roithamer, alone, because I always had to visit this museum alone, it's my favorite museum, the only museum in the world which I not only could endure but could actually love, during this visit to the Tate, so Roithamer, I was able to gain a little peace of mind by working on the thorn apple, the so-called *datura stramonium,* because I was working most intently, while at the Tate Gallery, on this little paper which I believe turned out rather well, I was working on William Blake for one thing, and for the other on the thorn apple, it was good for me in the condition in which I was left by the death of my sister, in that mentally dull, mind-disturbing and mind-*de*stroying condition, so Roithamer, which suddenly inspired me to write something about the thorn apple, for my own distraction, to distract my head from the death of my sister, so Roithamer. My study of the thorn apple, written while totally stunned by the cause of my sister's death: my finishing the Cone, so Roithamer. Taking refuge from one science in another, so Roithamer, an artful device to break off one (tormenting) subject by taking up again another (an old, ancient) subject, so Roithamer (19 March). The thorn apple, because I considered my work on the Cone concluded, so Roithamer. But haunted by the notion that I must work on the Cone, so Roithamer, although the Cone is a closed chapter, the Cone is now exposed and abandoned to nature, so Roithamer. The notion I had from the first moment, regarding the site for the Cone: the middle of the Kobernausser forest, which corresponds with the present site of the Cone. Supreme happiness, so Roithamer, as the instant cause of (my sister's) death, so Roithamer. The notion of turning a calculated center (forty-two kilometers from Mattighofen) into an *actual* center, incessant doubts

(March 21). First the natural history, then statics, or first statics, then natural history, statics as natural history andsoforth, so Roithamer. Nature/man/statics, so Roithamer. To put the men to work like one's own brain and to treat these working people as one treats one's own brain, driving both toward the target to the limit of their capacity (March 23), so Roithamer. Giving it all they've got every minute. Ease, insolence, we see the building developing from our plans, the building plans turning into a reality, *event, fulfillment of the event.* To be in England, while the Cone is being built in the Kobernausser forest, but to remain for all the future in England. What we do secretly, succeeds, so Roithamer. What we publish is destroyed in the instant of publication. When we say what we are doing, it's destroyed. The strain so exacerbated that it must end in the destruction (of the head and the body) of the nature of head and body, so Roithamer. We work on the periphery (England) in the center (Kobernausser forest). In company taciturn, then suddenly, out of this taciturnity, to talk, to talk again and again, to persuade, to despair, to talk and be afraid, over and over, and make them afraid, a constant process of making things known, everything known, they fear this as much as we do, so Roithamer. Until our ability to take it in is exhausted. When one studies statics, he learns to understand nature more and more, so Roithamer. First I let all these hundreds of books into my head, then my loathing for all these books, papers, which I've suddenly given up (April 2). First I bind (chain) everything to my head, then to my body, body and head all at the same time, "all" underlined. The Cone represents the logic of my (my sister's) nature. I built the Cone as a natural scientist, so Roithamer, from England, in Austria, I wouldn't have had the strength to do it from Austria, so Roithamer. First the idea of destroying the Cone (after my sister's death), but I shall leave it to nature, *entirely.* But the edifice as a work of art is finished only after the death of the person for whom it was built and finished, so Roithamer. We think we are building an edifice, a work of art, but what we have built is something else. The doors of the Cone all open toward the inside, so Roithamer, "inside" underlined. At eighteen or nineteen I could *not* have had this idea, at forty-one I could no longer have had it, so Roithamer. The so-called architects, so Roithamer, all thought I was crazy, such an edifice cannot be built, but it is a question of the occasion of mental acuity (April 3). The question was not only, how do I build the Cone, but also, how do I keep the Cone, the building of the Cone a secret, so Roithamer. Half of my energies were concentrated on building the Cone, half of them on keeping the Cone a secret, so Roithamer. When a man plans such an enormity, he must always retain control of everything and keep everything secret, so Roithamer. First based on my reading, then on the basis of reading no longer taken into account, so Roithamer. My own ideas had led with logical consistency to the realization and completion of the Cone, when my sister was frightened to death, the Cone was finished, so Roithamer, *I could not* have taken her into the Kobernausser forest *at any other than the deadly moment,* she had dreaded this moment, when she dreaded it most deeply I took her there and so killed her, at the same time I'd finished the Cone (April 7), so Roithamer. For supreme happiness comes only in death, so Roithamer. Detour by way of the sciences to supreme happiness, death, so Roithamer. The experts, the critics, the destroyers, annihilators, so Roithamer. We always come close to the edge of the abyss and fear the loss of equilibrium, so Roithamer. When a body that has briefly lost its balance instantly resumes its original equipoise, then it has a stable equilibrium, so Roithamer. If, on the other hand, a body appears balanced in any given new position, "new position" underlined, without returning to its original position, then its equilibrium is indifferent. When a body whose equilibrium is briefly disturbed does not return to its original balanced position but seeks a new equilibrium, then its equilibrium is labile, so Roithamer.

The Cone's physical center of gravity rests on its axis, so Roithamer, through the gravitational center of the base and the tip of the body at one-fourth its height a body needs at least three points of support, not in a straight line, to fix its position, so Roithamer had written. When we wake up, we feel ashamed, waking up is the always frightening minimum of existence, so Roithamer (April 9). The situation is always the same, in rational terms: wake up, wash, get dressed, work, see people, don't despair, try not to despair (April 11). We accept (April 11). We answer the letters we receive, no matter whom or where they come from, not because a trap has been set for us in all of these letters (April 13). If I had not become involved with the art of building, it would have been *something else, equally terrible.* One is always suddenly repelled by seeing how common people are, by their viciousness, bad taste, brutality, vulgarity. Understood nature, by understanding myself, nothing. They (friends) come in and sit down and the talk is, as it always has been; about philosophy, building, natural history, travels, natural catastrophes, books, the past, the future, theater andsoforth, it seems to be as always, but it's suddenly deadly (April 17). *Everything* is ultimately the Cone. When I'm listening, I'm struck by the fact that I tend to think everything out beyond what the thinker who is doing the talking does, so Roithamer. The building of the Cone has probably caused her mortal illness to break out, my sister has always had her mortal illness, just as everyone has his mortal illness from the first. One temporizes with a mortal illness, with death, then abruptly death comes, so Roithamer. Pine trunks: gigantic asparagus stalks of death, so Roithamer. The Kobernausser forest the end for her (my sister), for me (April 19). Mozart, Webern, nothing more (April 21). To build an edifice for a person, the most beloved person, as a crazy idea and to destroy, to kill this person with the completion of that edifice, the Cone. At first: many rooms, then: few rooms, then: suitable rooms, rooms suitable for her, so Roithamer. A body is not necessarily tipped over by all the forces acting on it, so Roithamer, insofar as regards the critical tipping edge these forces rather impart a varying impetus for turning the body around, so they partially *counter*act the tipping over (April 23). A body does not tip over when the force holding it upright in place is stronger than the force pushing it over. Lawfulness of the material. There is no backing out so close to the goal, so Roithamer. At the time I had decided to build my sister the Cone, my knowledge of building was not yet sufficient to enable me to start building in confidence, so I'd begun to build in a state of extreme nervous tension, while at the same time beginning an even more comprehensive study of building, at first I'd planned *a year's* study, then *two years,* but I ended up having to study statics and stress analysis and building technique for *three years.* My talks with the experts involved had led to nothing, my reading ultimately led to nothing, it was only my discussions with Hoeller and then my totally independent approach to building that made it possible for me to realize my plan, so Roithamer. The experts had only distracted, deceived and delayed me, the progress I made in my thinking about the Cone I owed to my constant contemplation and study of the Hoeller house. Books, articles, experts had never really been much use in my case anyway, so Roithamer. All those experts thought they were dealing with a madman, so that my talks with them were always setbacks in my plan, so Roithamer. If I'm going to build my sister an edifice suited to her nearly a hundred percent, I had thought, then I must first of all study my sister's personality and in addition the basic principles of statics and stress analysis, so Roithamer. The more openly I spoke of my plan, the crazier I seemed to my listeners, but in the end I didn't care about the opinion of all those people who considered themselves experts, all I cared about was my project, the execution of my plan, the realization of my idea, which kept looking crazier to me, too, the deeper I got into it, but every idea is a crazy idea, so Roithamer. Like all those who pursue an idea, which is *ipso facto* a crazy idea, I had to pursue my crazy idea, and I could not allow myself to be dissuaded from this crazy idea by anything whatever, especially not by myself, for I had the greatest doubts, but the greater my doubts, the more stubbornly I pursued my idea, and in the end nothing could have made me abandon my idea, I wouldn't have let anything make me abandon it, I'd allowed myself to be irritated over it all the time, but not to abandon it, but the chronic irritation by my idea finally resulted in my having the absolute certainty that I would pursue my idea till I reached my goal, its realization and fulfillment in the Cone, so Roithamer. All those irritations effected in me only a greater obstinacy and a greater fascination with my idea, so Roithamer. As my irritation increased, I was forced to think and act with greater precision, so Roithamer. A man who says he is building for his sister a Cone *in which she must live in future,* is bound to seem crazy, so Roithamer. And when he says he is building a Cone for his sister in the middle of the Kobernausser forest, in *its exact geometrical center,* impossible to calculate according to the experts, but I was finally able to prove it, he must seem even crazier, and when he says that he is building for his sister, in the middle of the Kobernausser forest, a Cone *in which his sister must live for the rest of her life and be happy, supremely happy,* he must be regarded as even crazier still, so Roithamer. But we mustn't let ourselves be so irritated that we abandon our intention, so Roithamer, only irritated enough to further our intention, for irritation is also most useful to no matter what intention, even the craziest, so Roithamer. We always think that we're now so irritated that we'll have to abandon our intention, no matter what intention, because the people around us will not tolerate such a plan (like the building of the Cone), but we must not suffer the kind of irritation that will force us to abandon our intention. Wherever we look, we see nothing but abandoned intentions, for the so-called realized and completed edifices we

see everywhere in the world are also nothing but abandoned
intentions, so Roithamer. But I, in contrast to all these hundreds of thousands and millions of so-called realized and
completed, but in reality abandoned (building)-intentions
which are seen standing around all over the surface of the
globe, I fulfilled my intention, I managed to realize and fulfill
it even though I had to do so in a frenzy of irritation, everything tends only to irritate me, so Roithamer. Every idea leads
to extreme irritation, so Roithamer. The head of a planner and
builder, so Roithamer, has to reach and fulfill its aim in a state
of extreme irritation, so Roithamer. First there were the so-
called geologists whom I felt obliged to consult and who
caused me the utmost irritation with their disdain, then I
suffered extreme, utmost irritation and disdain from the so-
called architects, then from the skilled workers, again extreme
irritation and disdain, but all this utmost irritation and disdain
was necessary, so Roithamer, to make me create and perfect
the Cone, I'd never have reached my goal without my irritation and their disdain, I'd simply have been too weak to fulfill
it. They all told me that I lacked all the necessary qualifications to create, much less fulfill my plan, yet now I am in a
position to say that I had *precisely all the necessary qualifications*,
because the Cone is done, perfectly. Even though the effect of
the finished Cone is not as anticipated, so Roithamer, but the
effect of a finished task is always unexpected, it's always the
opposite of what we expected and very often a deadly effect,
so Roithamer. They told me that while I have the talent I do
not have the staying power, but I did have the staying power
and luckily I was also, during the whole time they were
building the Cone, absolutely unyielding against everything,
"everything" underlined. Suddenly I'd realized that the people
around me, whom I'd considered competent because I thought
them more experienced than myself, were totally incompetent,
that the so-called competent people are never and in no way
competent and that it's always only one's own head, and only

that part of one's head which is wholly concentrated on its objective, which can be competent, so Roithamer, but to reach that point I had a long, weary, and painful way to go. A man who says that he is building for his sister an edifice designed especially for her, with the air- and light-conditioning that will be perfect for her, and who even names the site (an impossible site to obtain) and says that he won't let anything get in the way of his plan or the realization of his plan, such a man is seen as a madman by all those to whom he's confided his intention, so Roithamer, and so, while they had to accept me as an established scientist they also had to regard me as an absolute madman. And so the people around me simulate respect and do all they can to destroy my ideas, all ideas, so Roithamer. Wherever we turn in this world, all we see is nothing but destroyed ideas, all there is, as any reasonable person must admit, is nothing but destroyed ideas, just as everything is only a fragment, it's always only an abandoned intention, so Roithamer. But the world has resigned itself to this state of affairs and made itself at home in it, so Roithamer. While they (the so-called architects) regard themselves as competent, as renewers of the earth's surface, as bold, open-minded free planners, they're in fact nothing but chronic deserters of original ideas, they create nothing, build nothing, accomplish nothing, they only produce mere fragments, always, so Roithamer, the earth's surface is cluttered with their fragments. They couldn't and certainly wouldn't understand my idea, anyway they never had accepted it, while all the time masquerading as the most fearless avant-garde building artists in the world, so Roithamer. They hadn't gone along with my ideas at all, never went *with* me for even the shortest distance in my thinking, made too uneasy, probably, by the thought of where I might lead them, so they'd always given up at the outset, when I asked them to join me in my ideas, in my thinking, they held back, but after never even entering into my thinking they decided I was crazy, in the very act of pronouncing the idea I'd given them of my plan *interesting*, they were saying that I was crazy, so Roithamer. They were afraid of choking to death inside my mental processes, so Roithamer. And so I had only Hoeller, in reality and in fact, Hoeller followed me into my mental processes from the first, he'd dared to follow me in my thinking because it was not unfamiliar to him, it resembled his own, so that he had preceded me there, to him it wasn't the dark frightening maze it was to those architects, though he might have felt a bit queasy entering into my much longer (than his) mental processes, so Roithamer, but Hoeller never thought me crazy, never, so Roithamer, because he, Hoeller, was experienced along such lines of thought and had no need to be afraid, "no need to be afraid" underlined, of and inside such lines of thought. One has to be able to get up and walk away from every social gathering that's a waste of one's time, so Roithamer, to leave behind the nothing faces and the often boundlessly stupid heads, and to walk out and down and into the open air and leave everything connected with this worthless society behind, so Roithamer, one must have the strength and the courage and the relentlessness even toward oneself, to leave all these ridiculous, useless, dim-witted people and heads behind and breathe free, breathe out what's been left behind and breathe in something new, one must abandon at top speed these useless social agglomerations, banded together for their inevitable dim-witted purposes, so as not to become part of these dim-witted social groups, to get back to oneself from these social doings and find peace and light in oneself, so Roithamer. One must have the courage and the strength to break away from such company, such entertainment, such verbal violence andsoforth, in which one has become involved against one's will, one must break away under any circumstances, so Roithamer, one must break off every one of these unspeakably stupid conversations, break away and walk away from all these senseless, useless and invariably dangerous subjects, to save oneself, rescue one's own head by escaping at any moment, at any time, from wherever it is, to escape into the open air, so Roithamer. To be honest, almost all the social gatherings we've ever been drawn into, without quite knowing how or why, strike us as useless, they serve no purpose at all, all they do is weaken us. At the right moment we must get up and leave such gatherings, circumstances, conditions, for what naturally becomes a lengthy, lasting, always unending solitude, so Roithamer. Such a rising up and going away is a daily occurrence, always we leave behind a society that repels us, so Roithamer. But as we keep leaving them, they more and more regard us as crazy and hate us, a situation that worsens from day to day, that militates against our head and against our character and against our whole being, so Roithamer. That the people I described in "About Altensam and about everything connected with Altensam, with special attention to the Cone" are not the same as those I knew grew clear to me when I stepped into my train, my second-class compartment, in London, or rather at Victoria Station. Even before the train left, so Roithamer, I'd realized that everything I'd described in my manuscript was not so, that everything is always different from the way it's been described, the actual is always different from the description, Altensam and everything connected with Altensam, it's different. Dover, Brussels, Cologne, I had to recognize that everything in my manuscript was all wrong, the characters are different, the character is another, so Roithamer. As my brothers came forward to meet me in Stocket, I had the evidence that everything I'd described was all wrong. Even before Dover I'd started to make corrections in the manuscript and little by little I'd corrected everything and finally realized that nothing in it expresses the reality as it actually is, the description runs counter to the actuality, but I drew the logical consequences from this insight, so Roithamer, I did not hesitate to correct everything all over again and in the process of correcting everything all over again, so Roithamer, I destroyed everything. That none of them are what they are, that nothing is what it is, so Roithamer, as I realized back at Victoria Station. The fact of my sister's funeral on the one hand, the fact that everything is all wrong on the other, I was preoccupied with these facts while crossing the Channel to the Continent and on through the incessant downpour along the whole plain all the way to Altensam, where my first encounter with my brothers proved to me that everything I feared was indeed true, so Roithamer. I had taken my manuscript out of my traveling bag and I'd seen at once that everything in my manuscript was all wrong, that I'd not only described some things badly, but that I'd described everything all wrong, because the opposite is true, so Roithamer. Yet I suddenly again felt like changing what I had done in years of hard effort into something else, suddenly on the train I was once more in the same state in which I've always been when I believed I was finished with something, at such a moment I know it's all the other way round, and I'm willing to do it over the other way around. Little by little a new manuscript would be the result, as it is now again, an entirely different, new manuscript resulting from the destruction of the old one, but best of all was not to let a new one come into being, to stop making positive corrections, best to destroy it altogether, so Roithamer. When I make corrections, I destroy, when I destroy, I annihilate, so Roithamer. What I used to consider an improvement, formerly, is after all nothing but deterioration, destruction, annihilation. Every correction is destruction, annihilation, so Roithamer. This manuscript too is nothing but a mad aberration, just as perhaps and with certainty, "with certainty" underlined, the erection of the Cone was nothing but a mad aberration, those who always regarded the building of the Cone as a mad aberration, seem to have been proven basically right, so the manuscript was also nothing but a mad aberration, but he'd have to accept responsibility for this mad aberration and take it to its logical conclusion, it was absolute madness, so Roithamer, to build the Cone and to write this manuscript about Altensam, and these two crazy acts, one resulting from the other and both with the utmost ruthlessness, have done me in, "have done me in" underlined. When I said to my sister, *the Cone is yours, it belongs to you, I built it for you, and specifically in the center of the Kobernausser forest,* I saw that the effect of the Cone on my sister was devastating. What followed was sheer horror, so Roithamer, nothing else, slow death, immersion in her sickness unto death, nothing else, from that moment onward everything led to her certain death (May 3). All of them secluded in their rooms waiting for their supper, which has always been an occasion for every kind of mutual recrimination, as though supper were the time to release twenty-two hours of accumulated hatred, aversion, mutual hatred, mutual aversion, so Roithamer. Silence at first (but a different kind of silence from that in Hoeller's house) then recriminations, politeness followed by insinuations, then open hatred in every direction, so Roithamer. The Eferding woman always had more than one complaint to air, insinuations against myself and my sister primarily and against my father who ended up always taking his food in a state of apathy, fixedly staring at the tabletop, he simply withdrew from all that mealtime verbal filth, so Roithamer. The rest all went at it, attacking each other brutally every way they could think of, vulgarly, viciously. With the entrée came the overture, as it were, of accusations, the main course was the outbreak of the verbal storm, so Roithamer. Wounding the heart and the mind, so Roithamer. Crippling souls, wrecking brains, so Roithamer. It was all far beyond anything an outsider could imagine, day after day, the terrifying regularity of it, so Roithamer. When we had guests, we might exercise some self-control for an hour, no longer, then it broke down, we were no longer embarrassed even by the presence of the guests, soon guests became a rarity at Altensam, so Roithamer. Even in earliest childhood I'd preferred being alone, I lived a shut-in solitary life, my childhood

was always lived alongside, but not with, the others. Alongside my parents and siblings, I was always alone, alongside my
schoolmates, I was alone, alongside the others I pursued my
studies, my science, realization, fulfillment, destruction, annihilation. In every case and in every cause this was the sequence, so Roithamer. I could be among (and with) people for
only the briefest periods of time, my tendency was to start
withdrawing, retreating from them, even at the moment of
approaching them, even while drawing closer to them, so
Roithamer. Experience teaches you to keep your distance to
the end of your life, because people only come close and close
in on you to disturb and destroy you, always, so my uncle, so
Roithamer. A man approaches another only to destroy him, so
Roithamer. We go out to meet people because we think it's to
our advantage to do so, always keeping the true (only) reason
for meeting them, society, to ourselves, our so-called selfless-
ness is a false front, so Roithamer. Whenever we see someone
getting along well we soon take a hand, we go to him to
disturb him, to destroy, to annihilate him, if we can. However
we can manage it, so Roithamer. Parents seen as the first
destroyers of their children, annihilators of their children, and
vice versa. Being on our guard against everything, we end up
being for the longest time alone with ourselves, totally, painfully out of touch, so Roithamer. If we make contact, we must
break it off at once, if we're men of character, *still have*
character, so Roithamer. More and more only the briefest
social experiences, so Roithamer. While building the Cone I
met all sorts of people, never before so many, and I worked
with all of these people and was happy with all these people,
but I was never so alone as with and among all these people, so
Roithamer. Completely alone with my idea, so Roithamer. We
are different from the person who is being judged when it is
our own person, our own character, that is being judged, so
Roithamer. Like the landscape, like the natural scene in
(around) us, like whatever we have created, so Roithamer. We

see a landscape and we see a man in that landscape and the landscape and the man are always different, each moment, although we assume that everything always remains the same, and thanks to this false assumption we dare to go on with our existence, so Roithamer. So we're never exactly the person we are, but always already something different, though still just barely ourselves if we're lucky, so Roithamer. We've developed by surrendering something of ourselves, little by little, and so we've remained the same, though changed, so Roithamer. But the schools we've attended have been wholly devastating in their influence on us, they *depressed* me, every school I ever attended, had to attend, has *humiliated* me. At first I listened in every direction and entered into all these directions, then I stopped listening, stopped entering into things, so Roithamer. Soon I'd latched onto one system, then to another system, now I'd be convinced by the one, then again by another, so Roithamer. In the schools it's always the same old stale stuff that's spread before us, it destroys the mind and the spirit of the learner, the student, stage by stage, in the schools we are turned into despairing men, who can never again escape from their despair, so Roithamer, we enter a school only to be destroyed by that school, annihilated by history, so Roithamer, mathematics annihilates us, the unnaturalness of school annihilates us, so Roithamer. We never recover from school once we've left school, any school, we're branded by the school, i.e., we're destroyed, so Roithamer. We always enter a school only to be annihilated, the schools are gigantic institutions for the annihilation of the young, those who come to them for help are annihilated, but the state has its own good reasons for financing the schools, so Roithamer, once we leave school, our slow death has simply reached a more advanced stage, nothing else. Like madmen those who need spiritual help enter a school and leave it as dead men, and no one rebels against this, so Roithamer. The young people, healthy individuals, enter the schools looking for help, they come out de-

stroyed, crippled, debilitated for life, so Roithamer. The destruction of the very young starts in grade school, so
Roithamer, imagine then what goes on in the secondary
schools and the institutions of higher and highest learning.
Institutions for the deformation of human beings, so Roithamer. "About Altensam and everything connected with Altensam, with special attention to the Cone" I had first to bring to
its conclusion before I could realize that everything is different, "everything" underlined. Correction of the correction of
the correction of the correction, so Roithamer. Signs of madness, insomnia, feeling sick of life. More and more of this
soliloquizing, because I haven't got a soul left, apart from
Hoeller not a soul, left alone with myself in Hoeller's garret, I
haven't a chance of ever leaving Hoeller's garret (May 7). A
prison, a prison to soliloquize in (May 9), so Roithamer. We
read a book, we're reading ourselves, so we loathe reading, so
Roithamer, we never open another book, we don't permit
ourselves to read anymore. To hear and see (May 11), so
Roithamer. We can't always exist at the highest pitch of
intensity, so we start to slow down in our thinking and doing
(feeling), so that after a while we can go back to thinking,
doing, feeling with even greater intensity, and in this way we
can eventually reach ever greater degrees of intensity; as long
as we haven't crossed the border, the extreme limits, we're not
crazy, so Roithamer. In contemplation of the yellow paper
rose, nothing else (June 3). We always go too far, so as not to
fall short, we always bring our plans to realization, relentlessly
against all opposition and especially against ourselves, we go
to the extreme, but without breaking through the final barrier,
so Roithamer. We always go on to the absolute limit, we don't
shy away from that, just as we don't shy away from death.
One day, in a single instant, we'll break through the final
barrier, but the moment hasn't come yet. We know how, but
we don't know when. It makes no difference whether I go
back to England from Austria or back to Austria from England,

so Roithamer. We still have a reason not to cross the final barrier. We're tempted to do it, we don't do it, so Roithamer, we keep thinking: do it, don't do it, consistency, *in*consistency, until we cross the final barrier. Science for one thing, my plan, the Cone, for another, supreme happiness/supreme unhappiness, in creating and fulfilling something extraordinary we've arrived at nothing more than what everyone else also arrives at, nothing but solitude, so Roithamer. When a body is acted upon by external forces besides its weight it tips over on one side of the base if the (so-called) weight (vector) acts along a line through the so-called center-of-mass that intersects the supporting surface outside the base of the body; in the case of a stable equilibrium, the weight vector points inside the base, in the case of an unstable equilibrium it points exactly toward the tilting edge of the base, "tilting edge of the base" underlined. We always went too far, so Roithamer, so we were always pushing toward the extreme limit. But we never thrust ourselves beyond it. Once I have thrust myself beyond it, it's all over, so Roithamer, "all" underlined. We're always set toward that predetermined moment, "predetermined moment" underlined. When that moment has come, we don't know that it has come, but it is the right moment. We can exist at the highest degree of intensity as long as we live, so Roithamer (June 7). The end is no process. Clearing.

A Note About the Author

Thomas Bernhard, born in 1931, lives in Ohlsdorf, Upper
Austria. One of the most important and internationally acclaimed
writers in the German language today, he is the author of *Gargoyles*
(1970), *The Lime Works* (1973), and of numerous plays. His three
forthcoming volumes of autobiography are currently being translated.


A Note About the Translator

Sophie Wilkins, who lives in New York City, has translated,
amongst other distinguished works, *The Lime Works* by Thomas
Bernhard, Botho Strauss's *Devotion*, and the revised edition of C. W.
Ceram's *Gods, Graves, and Scholars*.